also by Adam Mars-Jones

LANTERN LECTURE AND OTHER STORIES

Mae West is Dead

ff

MAE WEST
IS DEAD

Recent Lesbian and Gay Fiction

Edited by
Adam
Mars-Jones

faber and faber
LONDON · BOSTON

First published in 1983
by Faber and Faber Limited
3 Queen Square London WC1N 3AU
This edition published in 1987
Printed in Great Britain by
Redwood Burn Ltd Trowbridge Wiltshire
All rights reserved

British Library Cataloguing in Publication Data

Mae West is dead.
1. Short stories, English
I. Mars-Jones, Adam
823'.01'08 [FS]   PR1309.S5

ISBN 0–571–14898–0

Don't you ever tire, Martin says, of all this campery? These are the eighties, darling. Mae West is dead.

Contents

Acknowledgements

Grateful acknowledgement is made to the publishers of books and magazines in which some of the stories in this anthology first appeared:
"How to Engage in Courting Rituals 1950s Butch-Style in the Bar": *Common Lives/Lesbian Lives*, no. 4, 1982; "Some of These Days": *A Day After the Fair*, Note of Hand, New York, 1976; "Idyll": excerpt from *Good Friends, Just*, Chatto & Windus, London, 1983; "Barney": *Company*, October 1979; "Daddy": *Mother, Sister, Daughter, Lover*, Crossing Press, Trumansburg, 1980; "A Perfectly Nice Man" and "The Day I Don't Remember": *Outlander*, Naiad Press, Tallahassee, 1981; "The Cutting Room": *The Notebooks of Leni Clare*, Crossing Press, Trumansburg, 1982; "Two Bartenders, a Butcher and Me" and "Victor": *Human Warmth and Other Stories*, Grey Fox Press, San Francisco, 1981; "Cass, 1959: First Day of a Courtship": *Common Lives/Lesbian Lives*, no. 6, 1982; "The Loveliness of the Long-Distance Runner": *Time Out*, February 1980; "First Communion": *Gay Sunshine Journal*, no. 47, 1982; "The Prisoner of Love": *Couplings*, Grey Fox Press, San Francisco, 1981; "Phantom Limb Pain": *Thin Ice and Other Stories*, Seal Press, Seattle, 1981; "Slim": *Granta*, 1986.
The editor and publishers would also like to thank A. M. Heath and Co. Ltd for their permission to reprint extracts from *The Last Woman in His Life* by Ellery Queen.

Introduction:
Gay Fiction and the Reading Public

Cyril Connolly in 1938 pinpointed the advantages enjoyed by the homosexual writer: combativeness, curiosity, egotism, intuition and adaptability, "equipment", as he put it, "greatly to be envied".

At the same time Connolly assumed that homosexual writers would always, "until we can change society", have to avoid certain subjects and substitute others, just as stammerers learn to avoid the syllables that give them trouble.

This was, for its time, and despite its tacit omission of women, a distinctly enlightened opinion; in practice Connolly was offended when Isherwood implied that his feelings for a lover were comparable to Connolly's own feelings for his wife. But that time is in any case past; for the past fifteen years homosexual men in Britain have been accorded a lavish fraction of civil rights. Homosexuals are, intermittently, freer than ever before.

The result has not been an explosion of unleashed sensibility and the instant integration of the minority (perhaps only Leo Abse, MP, expected these things); it takes people a while to get over the shock of decriminalization. The result has been an assortment of improvised moralities combining in various proportions reaction against, and imitation of, heterosexual precedents. By and large, they resemble the provisional motorized vehicles which appeared before someone realized that a horseless carriage need not look like a carriage without a horse.

America, where social change is chronic as well as epidemic, has played a large part in the shaping of gay attitudes in Britain. Whereas in Britain an urban area needs to have several years of solid gentrification behind it before it becomes possible to buy food there after 6 p.m., in America a neighbourhood (whatever its previous reputation) can be transformed by a single newspaper article in the right place; at the end of a week the streets will reliably bristle with roller-skate-hire firms and exotic-pet shops.

Gay Americans have been quick to exercise their rights in the marketplace; for years now it has been possible for a gay man in America to live entirely in a subculture of bars, baths and gay-owned businesses.

Such concentrations of gay men may or may not have political power, but they certainly have bright green dollars in their faded-denim pockets. So it shouldn't be surprising that Avon Books (a division of the Hearst Corporation), publishers of Bard, Camelot and Discus Books, should have had spectacular success with titles aimed specifically at this market.

Gay women present a less susceptible marketing profile than gay men. Their lower income prevents them (as a group) from affording a high turnover of attitudes and accessories, and if they do mobilize their resources they are as likely as not to move away from a city. Feminism, moreover, gives them a certain immunity to the siren voices of the marketplace.

Gay men's periodicals tend to be weekly, fortnightly or monthly (the *New York Native*, the *Advocate*, *Christopher Street*) and to be based in a traditional gay stronghold. Women's magazines are more likely to be quarterlies put together in provincial cities; *Common Lives/Lesbian Lives* in Iowa City, for instance, *Sinister Wisdom* in Amherst, Massachusetts.

Avon's gay-targeted books are available mainly in gay areas, and are imported into this country only by specialist bookshops; they tend not to be reviewed in newspapers with cultural pretensions. Some, like the novels of Gordon Merrick (*The Lord*

Won't Mind, Perfect Freedom, Now Let's Talk About Music),
dispense frank pulp; others have a certain sophistication.

My plan is to dissect a sophisticated example of Avon's output,
to see what it has to say about the way men and women behave.
This isn't a matter of a highbrow beating hell out of an unliterary
text; it's actually an advantage that Avon Books don't represent
any sort of personal vision. In any case, gay liberation doesn't
need to have literary pretensions to be largely a verbal matter; its
first products, after all, were slogans, and it sets out to construct
a new rhetoric to neutralize the prevailing one. Twenty years
ago, to use an uncontroversial analogy, it was possible to hate
your job, to go through your working days in a trance of boredom
and misery, but it wasn't possible to have a "mid-life crisis"; this
term solves no problems, but by providing a category for
experience it asserts that certain underprivileged emotions are
real. The rhetoric of gay liberation has become very various and
sophisticated, but it is still a set of manoeuvres which responds to
the techniques of literary criticism.

Nahan Aldyne's *Vermilion*, a detective novel set in Boston, was
published by Avon Books, as a paperback original, in October
1980. It was successful enough to spawn a sequel, *Cobalt*, in
1982. It received enthusiastic reviews in magazines that are
either gay (*Alternate Magazine*, the *Advocate*, *Numbers*,
Drummer), Boston-based (the *Boston Phoenix*), or both (*Gay
Community News*).

You are only likely to get a negative review in the *Boston
Phoenix* of a novel set in Boston if you get the bus routes wrong,
and the same general rule applies to the other publications. The
view of gay life in *Vermilion* is either authentic, or plausible
enough for its inaccuracy not to be noticed by experts in the field;
it is true at least on the level of myth.

Vermilion so successfully represents the mainstream of gay
fiction that the reviews of it concentrate on its genre ("a first-rate
mystery", "a classic whodunit", "a wonderful detective novel")
and treat its gay setting as an utterly neutral medium. Is this the
atmosphere that gay men breathe? What is its composition?

A gay detective novel is certainly a variant with possibilities. Homosexuals, after all, have little excuse for being in love with the police, while the police traditionally regard homosexuals, not as an especially vulnerable group, but as trouble-making degenerates. So there are at first sight better reasons for a homosexual to be dissatisfied with conventional criminal enquiries than for a vain little Belgian with an egg-shaped head and luxuriant moustaches to give a little help to his old friend Inspector Japp.

The victim of the murder, moreover, is a young hustler called Billy Golacinsky, whose death the police would normally regard as uninteresting.

The reason for the police's abnormal interest is the location of the corpse; the body was dumped on the lawn of Representative Mario Scarpetti, "an ignorant, loudmouthed, and powerful enemy of Boston's gay community". This is the excuse for the selling line on the book's cover: *The murderer had a weakness for boys . . . and dirty politics.*

Scarpetti wants a scapegoat.

As things turn out, the dumping of the body on Scarpetti's lawn had no significance and was purely a matter of chance; Scarpetti's home was simply a house on a dark street in a quiet suburb. In this respect, *Vermilion* breaks the rules of the classic detective novel, where apparently neutral details can turn out to be unnoticed oddities, but where the reverse never happens; flagrantly unusual events cannot simply be ascribed to chance. Any misleading impression must be due to a human agency; red herrings may very likely clutter the landscape, but they must have been planted by a person with something to gain from every intricate deception.

Thrillers, after all, deal in reassurance as well as fear (both in homoeopathic doses), and people who say they like a good mystery usually mean they like a seamless solution. It isn't only Representative Scarpetti that wants a scapegoat, and a book that fails to tie up loose ends fails to resolve the emotions that it trades in.

The murder of a hustler is likely to trigger two orders of fear in a gay reader: the generalized fear that gay sexuality is by definition destructive, and the more circumstantial fear that a life of urban anonymity, with the sexual instinct hived off from all others and expressed in isolation, brings with it a massive vulnerability. Gay men living in urban ghettos distance themselves still further than other Americans from the privilege enjoyed by more settled communities, of being killed by people they know.

Vermilion can counteract the first fear only if the killer turns out not to be homosexual, so that the murder has no actual connection with gay sexuality. It is in any case unthinkable that a book so accurately targeted on a gay readership would preach damnation to the converted by revealing a homosexual as the murderer.

Things have changed a great deal in ten years. In 1970 Ellery Queen, winner of five Edgars (including the Grand Master award of 1960) and both the silver and gold Gertrudes awarded by Pocket Books, Inc., published a detective novel called *The Last Woman in His Life*.

A millionaire playboy is murdered in his bedroom. Near the body lie an evening gown, a wig, and a pair of long white gloves, belonging (one item each) to the playboy's three ex-wives. And here is an excerpt from the killer's confessional monologue:

From the start of the weekend I felt a kind of crisis in identity that turned physiological with great rapidity. It sapped my usual control. That Friday night, when Audrey, Marcia and Alice came downstairs all dressed up, something happened to me. Audrey's stunning evening gown with the sequins, Marcia's silly "fun" wig, Alice's elbow-length gloves ... all of a sudden I was wildly attracted to them. I had to have them ... put them on ... parade around in them. If we'd been in the city I could have used one of my own drag outfits, but we were in that damned backwoods town ... And there was my beloved Johnny—the unsatisfied passion of my life— practically in my arms ... signaling to me, as I thought, giving me the come-on . . .

I can forgive the murders. I can forgive the lifetime of deceit. But what kind of monster would steal Marcia's fun wig?

It does seem a bit hard, though, not that a homosexual should be revealed as a murderer, nor that a murderer should be revealed to be a homosexual, but that someone should be unveiled all at once as a cross-dressed murdering invert, as if these elements had a natural affinity. Many homicidal transvestites, of course, are heterosexual, and would bitterly resent the imputation of abnormality.

There is no question in the book of analysis in depth; you don't win Edgars and Gertrudes for your sympathetic portrayal of minority groups. Homosexuality in *The Last Woman in His Life* (guess who?) is used purely as a thriller prop. The fact that no one detects the killer as homosexual is not a piece of social comment ("they're not so different from us"), but assimilates homosexuality to the status of an untraceable poison; the crucial point here is simply absence-of-clues.

In the same way, the victim's dying words (on the phone) are carefully contrived:

> "J–J–J . . ."
> "Johnny? Is this Johnny?'
> "Yes. El . . ."
> "Yes, yes, what's wrong?"
> "Dying."
> "You? Wait! I mean, I'll be right over."
> "No . . . time."
> "Hang on—"
> "M–m–m . . . Murder."
> "Who, Johnny? Tell me. Who did it?"
> "Home."
> "I mean, who attacked you? . . . Hold on, Johnny, hold on! Who did it? . . . Try to tell me."
> "Home . . . Home . . . Home."

Johnny refrains from naming his killer, or from describing him explicitly ("It was a queen, Ellery ... a goddamned cross-dressed kleptomaniac homicidal queen"), for no human reason, but because for the purposes of the novel it is necessary that he be misunderstood. Johnny uses (but is unable to finish) the word "homosexual", apparently with a long first syllable, not because it is a neutral term, but because there can be no equivocation with the more likely words "fruit" or "faggot". "Home" as the unsuspected first syllable of "homosexual" admirably obeys the detective-story rule that apparently neutral details may turn out to be unnoticed oddities; but that's about all that can be said for it.

The Last Woman in His Life, remember, appears the year after the Stonewall Riots and the beginnings of gay liberation, and the terms "gay" and "cruising" are used by the killer in his monologue of confession. There is even a wistful plea for understanding ("If only people stopped regarding us as some sort of monsters . . ."), though the fact that these sentiments are voiced by someone who steals Marcia's fun wig and kills people may lessen the impact of his message on society.

The assumption made by *The Last Woman in His Life* is not in any case that homosexuals are not people, but that people in any given group are not homosexual. From Ellery Queen's point of view (or points of view, since "Ellery Queen" is in fact two people who pretend to be one in order to write about violent death) it is about as likely that a homosexual should read detective novels as that a native of Borneo should write a letter of protest to the author of a detective story about his use of untraceable poisons, pointing out that the tribesmen use them only for executions, a method infinitely superior in humane terms to such barbarous devices as the gallows or the guillotine.

Nathan Aldyne is on much firmer ground with the assumption that very few more heterosexuals or women than murderers will read *Vermilion*; the novel's scapegoat will hardly be gay. At an early stage of the book, we are told that the Boston *Globe* would like to see it turn out that Billy Golacinsky was murdered "by a straight couple out for sleazy thrills". By implication this is a reactionary theory, determined solely by Representative Scarpetti's denunciations of a gay conspiracy.

But the *Globe*'s wishful thinking is not so very different from the novel's. Billy was indeed killed by a straight couple out for sleazy thrills, with the extra twist that they were commercial purveyors of sleazy thrills; one of their clients was a policeman ashamed of his sexual nature, and Billy, having witnessed their goings-on, was blackmailing him. The conspiracy, in fact, was between "a straight couple and a Boston cop".

Hidden homosexuality, responsible in *The Last Woman in His Life* for the murder and all its consequences, plays a surprisingly similar role in *Vermilion*, since Lieutenant Searcy's inability to accept his attraction to men sets the plot in motion; but all the stigma has been transferred from the homosexuality to the hiding of it. Don't blame the skeleton, blame the closet that has kept it out of circulation for so long.

A novel whose denouement exonerates healthy homosexuals and incriminates hypocritical self-described heterosexuals might be felt to have done its bit for the peace of mind of gay readers, but *Vermilion* has more reassurance to offer.

Its hero, Daniel Valentine, is presented as the sum of all gay virtues; it would be an understatement to describe him as an idealized role-model. The reader is simply denied any opportunity to question the values he represents.

In the first scene of the novel Daniel Valentine meets Billy Golacinsky, the hustler; it is a bitterly cold first of January, the last night of Billy's life. Billy is trying to pick someone up; he's broke, and was thrown out of his lodgings earlier in the day. Daniel, who is out walking a dog, is described from Billy's point of view:

> The tall slender man appeared well built beneath his black pea coat. Sandy blond hair showing beneath his black knit watch cap matched the color of his well-trimmed beard. His features were not exceptional, but his expression was one of self-confident easeful strength . . .

Billy finds Daniel attractive, but the feeling is apparently not reciprocated. Daniel offers only advice:

"Listen, kid, nobody's out tonight. Nobody's playing. Nobody's buying. Everybody shot his wad last night. Remember? New Year's Eve. John is home with his wife, John is home with his lover, John couldn't get his car started in the cold. John is not going to show up on the Block tonight. Your timing's bad, kid. Go home and get warm."

This sets the pattern for the rest of the book. Daniel is more desired than desiring; and he has an inordinate amount of worldly knowledge. He has never been so poor as to have to sell his body, nor so unattractive as to have to buy someone else's; yet he knows more about hustling than a hustler does.

Daniel goes home, and Billy gets killed; Daniel has no alibi for the murder.

Daniel works as a bartender in a gay bar called Bonaparte's; he is thus placed squarely in the middle of the subculture. There is already an element of exoneration in this; Daniel can spend a great deal of time in a sexually charged atmosphere without choosing to do so. His is a privileged access to sexual attention.

But Daniel has multiple exemptions. We learn that Daniel tends bar as a stopgap, until he can return to his real job. He lost his "real" job, as a prison counsellor, when he exposed corruption in the prison service, by reporting a superior who had used ten thousand dollars of taxpayers' money to buy curtains for his living room. He must now wait for a change of administration before he can be reinstated.

There are three levels of exoneration present in this piece of background information. For a start, it establishes Daniel Valentine as an exile from the dominant culture, making a casual living in the gay subculture through no wish of his own. His values, moreover, are actually superior to those of the dominant culture, since his reward for a public-spirited action is dismissal from his socially useful job; and still he retains his idealism, waiting patiently until he can take a salary cut and resume his career. Then, too, in his capacity as a prison counsellor he spent his working life trying to rescue people from a (criminal) subculture. How many jobs fit this description?

Daniel Valentine, in fact, may have no alibi for Billy Golacinsky's death, but he is given an impressive set of alibis for his own daily life. He may look as if he is leading an entirely subcultural existence, but he is in some important sense somewhere else, doing something quite different.

Daniel's self-confident easeful strength seems to need quite a lot of propping up.

Daniel doesn't actually do anything in the course of the book to distinguish him from stereotypical inhabitants of the subculture, but evidence is constantly being offered of his unfettered access to people of all sorts and conditions.

The bartender Mack, for instance, has only one big speech, which runs as follows:

"I tell you, Lieutenant: twenty-five years ago it was straight men got me in trouble, and ten years ago it was straight men that got me put in jail. It was a *fag* that got me out of jail, and it was a *fag* that made sure I got a decent job. I got *nothing* against 'em. I'm not a fag, but I know what they know ... that straight men are just trouble."

Sixty pages later, we learn from Daniel the identity of his helper: "Mack's one of my success stories."

Another of Daniel's success stories (Silber, breaking and entering, three-to-five, now working as a florist) makes an appearance in Chapter 16 to offer thanks. His only function in the novel is to endorse Daniel's value as a human being, and since Silber is an old man, he might just as well come out and say: "This boy doesn't just care for the young 'uns."

The relationship of Daniel's that we see most of, though, is his friendship with Clarisse Lovelace, Nora Charles to his Nick. Clarisse is a successful estate agent, in spite of her somewhat cavalier attitude to her employers. In Bermuda, at an unspecified date in the past, Clarisse and Daniel had something that was almost an affair:

> "Those happy days when I fell in love with you by the pool, those happy nights in my cabana, and those happy mornings that you spent in bed with the assistant manager—"
>
> "I didn't know quite how to break it to you . . ."
>
> "I thought your impotence was *my* fault—but by the time you got around to me in the evening, you were just worn out. God was I upset when I found out!"
>
> "I would have been impotent *without* the assistant manager," smiled Valentine, consolingly.
>
> "So why did you even try?"
>
> "Because you were in love with me, and I was in love with your tits. I still am."

Notice that in this penultimate sentence a woman who wants to have a sexual relationship with a man is described as being "in love with him", whereas a man who doesn't want a sexual relationship with a woman is described as being "in love with her tits". Even in contemporary Boston, and no matter what anybody actually wants, women are emotional creatures, while men by their nature deal in sexual objectification.

Not that Clarisse is consistently characterized. In a curious way she is called upon to be both a woman and an honorary homosexual.

Clarisse is an honorary homosexual in the sense that she lives a largely subcultural existence; her clients at the estate agent's are predominantly gay, and she spends much of her leisure time in bars like Bonaparte's or Nexus. She has adopted a milieu that doesn't cater to her, and she has also adopted its values.

In this context she is perfectly well able to treat men as sexual objects; when at a late stage of the investigation she spies on an orgy from a balcony, she comments approvingly on the muscular "definition" of one man, and disparagingly on another, who "doesn't work out" and should join a gym. Although as a woman she carries a torch for Daniel Valentine, as an honorary homosexual she rates casual sexual encounters above relationships. She prescribes a week of debauchery in San Francisco to a client whose lover has left him; "Believe me," she says, "after a week ... you won't even remember who George was."

Nowhere in the book does she diverge, in her assessment of a man, from the gay men around her; and they for their part show an astonishing unanimity of taste.

Clarisse has achieved her emancipation from conventional lifestyles without benefit of feminism. She sees no conflict between being a career girl and being a sex object; for her, they are different terms for the same thing. "I rent more flats," she says at one point, "if I don't wear a bra." But then the gay men in the book don't refer to social movements of the sixties either; they may be proud that there are no more "squishy faggots" in Boston, but they show no sign of knowing that gay liberation was started by a riot and not by an article in *Uomo Vogue*.

Although in theory Clarisse is a solitary heterosexual surrounded by gays, in practice she is the character who resorts most readily to camp. Camp, with its brittleness and insistent triviality, is a conversational style that is perceived as compromising, however enjoyable, by contemporary gays; over-indulgence in camp is felt somehow to be letting the side down.

Clarisse, feminine already, has nothing to fear from the stigma of effeminacy. She can get away with the occasional brutally bitchy remark, which would corrode the masculinity of any man who uttered it: "Maybe now you can pass for butch," she says to Daniel when a lover gives him a leather jacket.

Most of the time, though, she is content to embody Hollywood's imagery of women for the benefit of the men around her. "Oh, God, I feel like Joan Crawford in *Rain*," she says at one point; she does dinner-table impersonations of the stars for Daniel's entertainment (notably Ida Lupino in *They Drive by Night*), and even her Afghan hound is called Veronica Lake. She delivers the final line of the book: "In the immortal words of Mildred Pierce, 'let's get stinko!'"

Clarisse has a certain amount to gain from moving in a gay milieu; she has plenty of social life, and some of the social skills rub off on her. When two men renting a flat from her talk about their girlfriends, she knows when they're actually gay.

Her sensitivity to the bush telegraph, though, is less than perfect, since she is, after all, only a hanger-on. She is attracted to Lieutenant Searcy, whom all the bona fide homosexuals in the book spot as a closet case, busily denying his nature. Once and once only does she compete with Daniel for the attention of a man, and then Daniel gets the date.

Clarisse's sex life takes place out of the confines of the book. "Last week", apparently, she went off with an insurance agent she met at the Laundromat; at an unspecified period in the past she had a short affair with a wholesale florist. In Chapter 6 she has coffee with a "cute fireman" and they arrange a date, but it doesn't take place in the timespan of the book.

Clarisse's sex life in fact follows a gay model of casual pick-ups and short liaisons, although she doesn't have to cope with the social disapproval that generated that model in the first place. Are there experiences in her past which determine her behaviour in the present, or is she issued by her author with a standard model of consumerist urban lifestyle, as a matter of routine?

Only in one respect is Clarisse treated differently from the men.

On her first appearance she is described, like Daniel on his, from a stranger's point of view, in this case Lieutenant Searcy:

His gaze went no further than the foyer, trapped by the woman he saw there. She was tall and leggy beneath a mahogany-brown fur coat. The garment was cut in the 1940s style, with padded shoulders and wide cuffs . . . She snatched off her fur skullcap; a great mane of hair cascaded in soft black waves beneath the dull red light of the foyer . . . Her cheeks were flushed with cold. She had strong, even features, large dark blue eyes accented with blue eye shadow, and a full sensual mouth softly tinted with pale coral lipstick . . . The fur fell

open to reveal large breasts beneath a tailored, expensive blue
work shirt, blue jeans tight-belted around a slender waist and
hips. The jeans were tucked into knee-high brown leather
riding-boots . . .

Clarisse is clearly an object of value, just like Daniel, but she is
described much more in terms of her clothes. Daniel wears
"boots". Clarisse wears "knee-high brown leather riding-
boots". If a man was wearing her shirt, it wouldn't be described
as "tailored" or "expensive", however much it cost, however
artfully it was cut.

Clarisse's outfits are described in some detail over the five days
of the book's action. On Wednesday she wears "full-cut black
corduroy slacks and a white silk blouse opened one button too
many". On Friday she wears "a gray silk dress with wide padded
shoulders, black seamed hose and matching gray heels". On
Saturday she wears "new denim jeans and a western shirt with a
flowered yoke".

If a man was wearing those jeans, they would just be "jeans";
their material would be taken for granted, and their newness
tactfully passed over. This doesn't mean, though, that Clarisse's
specifications for jeans are likely to be more stringent than a
man's; rather the reverse. On the streets of a subcultural
America, if you aren't wearing faded Levi's 501s (new if
necessary, but never looking it), you might as well be wearing
bombazine for all the good it will do you. Gay men's dress is
subject to laws of some rigour.

But *Vermilion* presents men as natural, women as artificial.
Men are somehow nouns, and unadorned; women are encrusted
with adjectives.

Take hair, for instance. One evening Clarisse asks Daniel for
advice about her hair; what style would suit her? Would short
hair make her look like Faye Dunaway or Diana Dors, Glenda
Jackson or Marjorie Main? The next day, although in the end she
doesn't have her hair cut, an important scene is laid at her
coiffeur's, Chez Marcel.

Women are composite references to other women; men are originals.

So where does Daniel get his hair cut? The subject isn't raised. As far as hair goes, he resembles that quintessential sixties person, the Tressy Doll (Her Hair Grows). Tressy's hair grew only in the sense that nylon fibres could be pulled through a sort of sieve on her scalp, and winched back by way of a plastic key in her back. Daniel's hair grows just like Tressy's does, when there's no one around.

Part of the point here is presumably to clear gay men of any taint of narcissism, but the end result portrays Clarisse as a consumer on a grand scale (buying 200 dollars' worth of perfume at one point), while Daniel's lifestyle verges on the austere.

Vermilion proposes women as the sum of a series of decorative decisions, men (in the teeth of the evidence) as creatures of a substantial solidity, requiring no explanation.

Daniel changes his clothes very little in the course of the book. After a visit to the International Health Spa on the Thursday he keeps on a red sweatshirt under his coat, but that's about it.

Clarisse seems to do his washing for him. Certainly she goes to the Laundromat, where "last week" she met that insurance man; Daniel complains that she went off with her new friend, and let his underwear melt in the drier.

Only one garment of Daniel's is described in real detail: "a waist-length jacket. It was of shiny dark-brown leather, had zippered pockets, a wide collar, and dark-fur lining." This orgy of description is excused by the fact that the jacket is a present to Daniel, and so doesn't represent any incriminating choice on his part.

Mark, who gives Daniel the jacket, is a lumberjack from New Hampshire who had a two-week affair with him the previous August, and fell in love. In the course of the book he returns to Boston, hoping to continue the relationship.

Daniel has other ideas.

It isn't that Mark is short of attractions. As he puts it: "Mark is hot, Mark has the body of death, Mark is just about the handsomest most rugged man I've ever come across in my life, and he'll make somebody a great wife, but not me!" Nor is it that Mark's personal qualities lag behind his appearance; *Vermilion* doesn't acknowledge the existence of qualities as opposed to attributes, those fractional selves that the men in the book project towards each other.

It's just that Mark's clinging to the outmoded notion that experience is not infinitely interchangeable, that it is possible to prefer one person to another, even in bed, makes him an embarrassment.

He doesn't even have the excuse of isolation; true, he is up there in the wilds of New Hampshire, but he is surrounded by 300 lumberjacks, so his feeling for someone less available can only be perverse.

In the course of the book Mark is led gently from a romantic late-adolescence to a casually exploitative maturity; and though this plot-strand is entirely unconnected with the murder story, it is in many ways much more neatly constructed.

The world of *Vermilion* is threatened, after all, by monogamy or any approach to it, not by hustling; a mutual prostitution (with money changing hands only to remedy a gross disparity in the attractiveness of the partners) is in fact the book's model for sexual encounters.

What would happen if gay men formed relationships? They would stop frequenting Bonaparte's, for one thing, and they might stop renting an apartment from Clarisse. They might move out of the subculture, to the suburbs even.

They must be saved from themselves.

Both Clarisse and Daniel have a vested interest in a system of sexual exchange. A gay bar may be a subcultural meeting-place, but it is first and foremost a commercial establishment, and the sexual possibilities, like the bowls of peanuts so freely offered, are there only to make you drink more.

All the energies of *Vermilion* are devoted to removing sex from the realm of the personal, the emotional, the subjective, and establishing it firmly in the marketplace. At the same time, the book is too canny to make this process explicit; the element of choice in the lives of gay men is downplayed to the point of extinction, since otherwise the marketplace might be called on to justify itself. This might not make pretty reading.

So monogamy is presented as a matter of bad taste, as a gaffe like drinking white wine with steak, rather than an immoral option.

Monogamy is only one form of bad taste, but it is linked with others more obviously pernicious, just as soft drugs are linked with heroin. So when Clarisse and Daniel let themselves into an apartment, using Clarisse's keys, so as to spy on the next building, they are confronted with an appalling vista of flocked wallpaper, plush velvet, veneer, chandeliers and crystal frogs, all in clashing colours.

The lovers who live there have forfeited the privilege of having their interior resemble an illustration from a recent magazine; they no longer listen to the voices which tell them what to buy, and (just as important) what to discard. Consequently their apartment fails to impress those who break and enter in their absence.

Mark's bad taste is much less entrenched; there is hope for him. But he does turn up at Bonaparte's on Thursday bearing "an enormous package, done up in bright red foil paper and wide gold ribbon tied in a grotesquely large bow", which he gives to Daniel. The package contains the leather jacket.

This is the beginning of Mark's redemption from bad taste; the packaging may be tacky, but the choice of gift is astute. Although Clarisse describes the jacket as a wedding ring ("most beautiful wedding ring I've ever seen"), it has none of the disadvantages of one; it doesn't remove Daniel from the sexual marketplace (rather the reverse) and it embodies no private message. Moreover, it immediately declares its value on the open market (Clarisse estimates it at $175), while a wedding ring's worth can only be guessed at by those not in the know.

Mark's emancipation from romance takes great strides later that night; he has agreed to meet Daniel at midnight, for what

Daniel privately terms their "divorce", at a bar called the Eagle.

Daniel is late for the rendezvous, and by the time he arrives Mark is dancing with another man; Boston has wrought in thirty minutes what New Hampshire couldn't manage in five months, and Mark has woken up to reality.

So in the end the dreaded confrontation with Mark is less like a showdown than a Platonic dialogue, with Daniel as Socrates gently prompting a newcomer to logic:

> For a moment, Mark said nothing, thinking hard. Then he smiled. "I know," he said at last. "I guess I expected more, but I'm glad to see you again too. I guess when I was up in New Hampshire, I had some funny ideas. I was thinking about you all the time, I was always thinking about coming down here to see you in Boston . . ."
>
> "You weren't thinking about *me*," said Valentine, "you were just thinking about *men*."
>
> Mark nodded. "I guess so . . ."

So that's all right then.

Mark gets his reward that very night for the progress he's made. His new friend, Joseph, is also from out of town, and they have nowhere to stay. What to do?

Daniel is only too pleased to help; Mark already has the keys to the apartment (he left his luggage there earlier in the day), and Daniel himself will crash at Clarisse's. "Crisco's under the sink," he says, "poppers are in the freezer."

Mark in fact gets every element but one of the fantasy he cherished up there in the wilds of New Hampshire: Daniel's address, Daniel's furniture, Daniel's bed, Daniel's drugs, even Daniel's lubricant. The fact that he isn't sharing these facilities with Daniel is a minor matter; the body of the loved one becomes the most easily substituted element, in this version of gay life, an accessory to all the accessories he owns.

Mark has learned his lesson, although he does show signs of wanting with Joseph the relationship he wanted with Daniel. But perhaps there's nothing better available in the provinces.

Mark has come to realize the limitations of provincial morals. As he asks Daniel despairingly, "Is everybody from New Hampshire as much of a hick as I am?" tactful Daniel makes no answer.

There is a certain selectiveness, though, in this matter of backgrounds. Minor or unappealing characters tend to have their roots exposed; so Lieutenant Searcy, we are told, was brought up on the South Side of Chicago, and Billy Golacinsky comes from Harrisburg, Pa., though he claims (without knowing that San Francisco is north of Los Angeles) to come from California. A pair of lovers is given, crushingly, an origin in Ohio.

None of the other characters comes from anywhere. Daniel has a father (he and Clarisse are the only people to know Daniel's phone number; we are told nothing else), but no other means of arriving on the planet. But if *pretending to come from California* is an embarrassing piece of pretension, what sort of manoeuvre is *not coming from anywhere*?

It may be that the principals are left blank in this respect so that they are easy to identify with; *Vermilion* is certainly anxious that its major figures be liked. But there's another set of reasons.

Vermilion presents an urban life of casual sexual exchange as the only option for a male homosexual; but at the same time it doesn't present this lifestyle as a matter of choice. Consequently the book must exclude all other possibilities.

First to go is any whiff of the counterculture; and so, although Boston is the single American city with the strongest radical tradition, you would be hard put to deduce that from the book. Reference is made to the gay papers *Esplanade* and *Gay Community News*, but Boston as presented in *Vermilion* is essentially a subcultural city, a string of bars and baths where there isn't even a bookshop where you could buy *Vermilion*. Otherwise Boston exists purely for local colour.

Hence too the disappearance of any lingering subjectivity in sexual matters. Only if there is total agreement about the attractiveness of a man, expressed as an absolute and not a relative value, can a system of sexual exchange emerge as an ideal, with any sustained relationship incurring the disapproval reserved for those who hoard a commodity and thus create an artificial shortage. Why would you want to sleep with someone on a regular basis, any more than you would want to read a detective novel more than once? It's a good read, and that's all there is to say about it. Read another one.

Backgrounds are the next to go. If Daniel Valentine has a background he also has a past, in which he quite possibly collected crystal frogs and had a crush on his best friend. No one is born, after all, with a subscription to *Architectural Digest* and a membership card for the Club Bath chain. If *Vermilion* acknowledges any such previous state of affairs, it must also acknowledge the series of choices which have led to the current Daniel. This would run counter to the whole spirit of the book.

Luckily a novel, unlike a repressive government, isn't forced to rewrite the history books; it can simply omit them. So Daniel Valentine has no place of birth, no childhood experience, no existence on the planet prior to his time at university (he was a history major at Tufts, where he shared a room with one of the book's minor characters).

These are trifling omissions; it's not as if sexuality has anything to do with early experience.

Another conspicuous absentee is Christmas. Although the novel's timespan runs from the first of January to the sixth, and there is still a Christmas tree in Valentine's apartment, not to mention a massive blue spruce in Prudential Plaza, Christmas as a family ritual is never mentioned, even to be dismissed. When Daniel says, "I hate Christmas," he means that he abhors the bad taste of disco carols and seasonal tat, not that he resents the continuing tidal pull of a family which can be ignored for most of the year. But perhaps his father phoned, from out there in the void, for a festive chat.

Vermilion's strategy throughout is to associate a certain style of sexuality (any approach towards monogamy) with a sort of civic bad faith, like hanging on to an overdue library book, without ever admitting the existence of a library, which might have dues or restrictions on membership.

It's quite a *tour de force*, to describe a gay urban lifestyle on its own terms, without acknowledging the forces which have created it. On occasions a different tone of voice can't help but creep in, as in this description of the gym that Daniel frequents:

> Though set a little to one side, the bench press was the "center ring" of the place. For the straight men who visited the International Health Spa it was the essential element in foundation building, and they employed it to develop bulky, rounded upper bodies which, according to heterosexual lore, was the universal turn-on to beautiful women. Gay men, on the other hand, flocked to the defining equipment, the barbells and the UGMs, after a short while on the bench press, to carve out their muscles, until, ideally, they resembled a page out of Gray's *Anatomy*.

Here at least is a suggestion that gay men make choices; the existence of "heterosexual lore" at least implies the possibility of a gay equivalent.

Except that *Vermilion* needs to protect Daniel from the appalling possibility of choice. So exercise becomes something that Daniel hates, a duty that he fulfils with resignation rather than eagerness, something that is somehow imposed on him from outside. Once again, he is elsewhere at the time.

He isn't allowed, though, whatever his feelings about exercise, to perform at less than an Olympic level. On the Thursday, although he is a smoker, has let himself slide over the holidays, and wore himself out with exercise only the day before, he manages (in his second hour at the gym, mind) a hundred of those fancy press-ups where you clap your hands in self-applause at the top of each push.

It isn't that he's not allowed to win. It's just that he mustn't be seen competing.

His sex life follows the same pattern. On Wednesday morning he wakes up with the feeling that someone "ought to have been lying on the other half of the bed, although he had no idea who".

Perhaps it was only a dream.

But no, it turns out that last night's man has had to go to work early. Sex in *Vermilion* is a supremely efficient transaction, so he has left no involuntary trace, but he has left a flattering note on the coffee table ("Thanks for a great time. Call me soon.") and signs himself Gary. He leaves his phone number.

It isn't likely that Daniel will phone him, since he can't remember what Gary looks like. Nor can Gary contact him in order to remind him, since only Clarisse and Mr Valentine, Senior, know the phone number. Daniel has taken the precaution of removing the number from the phone itself, in case an early-rising trick gets presumptious. Some people have no taste.

This is, of course, "only a dream" in a different sense, a dream in which you make a much stronger impression on other people than they do on you, in which they endorse your sexual status without your needing to remember their names or faces, and in which the phone doesn't ring only because no one knows the number. There's an army of men out there pining for it. But you have to be firm.

Can you help it if you're an *homme fatal*? Well, yes, actually.

A sexually attractive person isn't a person without needs, simply a person whose needs are appetizing to others. At best, and with a lot of help, a sexually attractive person can dodge the unrewarding task of examining those needs. So what if he's worn quite smooth by the need to be desired?

Daniel doesn't even need to make breakfast, since Clarisse arrives freighted with pastries; she has catered for three, but nothing goes to waste.

Daniel's kitchen window is brightened by three Boston ferns, but these again are gifts from Clarisse (short affair with wholesale florist) rather than tell-tale signs of domestic aesthetics on his part. Daniel in fact resents "the demands put upon him by green plants", and declines to water them. Clarisse sees to their needs behind his back.

This is the life.

The apartment, too, though it has only three rooms, makes demands on Daniel that he resents. Housework depresses him, but he doesn't like to see other people clean up either. So a maid comes in three nights a week, while he's at work.

In Quentin Crisp's philosophy of dust, you resist any temptation to clean up, since after three or four years it doesn't get any worse. In Daniel Valentine's, you have the dust invisibly removed, so that you see neither the dirt nor the cleaner. Gay men living alone seem to theorize about housework, either reconciling themselves to the reality of dirt or denying its existence.

So how does Daniel express his personality, in an apartment full of magically surviving plants, where the ringing of the phone can never announce an unexpected caller, where the build-up of dirt can never announce the passage of time, where the murmuring fridge keeps the stimulants in tip-top condition, and the vegetable shortening waits under the spotless sink for the next successful applicant? He collects playing cards.

Daniel's collecting urge verges on the obsessive; it leads him to break hygienic taboos (picking up a torn and filthy ten of spades from a storm drain) and even infringe property laws (stealing the joker from a Monte Carlo casino pack in a bedside table drawer). He has his choicest examples framed or embedded in a coffee table.

He hates card games, and never plays them.

For a card-player, cards are symbols; for Daniel, they are fetishes. He has removed cards from a realm of play into a realm of repetitive possession, fixated on differences between packs which would make no difference to someone who actually used them.

In a book like *Vermilion*, any single detail may be accidental; but every element is characteristic.

Daniel's relationships with objects and institutions are in fact warmer than his relationships with living things, excepting Clarisse, who combines heterosexual status (when the two of them walk arm in arm they look "like an affianced couple in the

'Living' section of the Sunday *Globe*'') with a blessed immunity to heterosexual lore, who wants him but doesn't blame him for not wanting her.

Since he has no sexual responsibilities towards Clarisse, he can be her friend; and since Veronica Lake is not his dog, he can take her for walkies.

True, when Clarisse embraces Daniel so as to escape detection by someone they are following (Clarisse's obscuring mane of hair coming in handy), Daniel bites at her tongue, just to remind her that this isn't the real thing; and when Searcy beats him up, he prefers to lick his wounds in private rather than go to Clarisse's for comfort. But perhaps someone who was born as a university student doesn't associate physical contact between friends with warmth and consolation. To be physically intimate with a friend would break the rules of *Vermilion* just as profoundly as treating a sexual partner as a friend; these are the little sacrifices that city life demands.

Daniel's relationship with his new jacket, since it was never human and and is no longer alive, is distinctly tender and expressive. Teasingly he fingers its zip. He takes great care to hang it up; even if the phone is ringing when he enters his apartment, the jacket must come first.

The jacket, after all, as he says in his speech of thanks to Mark, will mean an improvement in his love life. The library book has a new cover, and will circulate more smoothly than ever before.

It shouldn't surprise the reader of *Vermilion* that an article of clothing should be perceived as part of a person's attractiveness; the book consistently blurs the distinction between qualities and attributes, essences and labels. Daniel himself once followed Ms Winifred "Boots" Slater, who always wears leather, for three blocks, thinking she was "a hot new man in town".

Apart from this momentary lapse, Daniel is spared the stigma of trouser-chasing. In the course of the book he makes no sexual overtures; he goes to bed with two men (unmemorable Gary and an unnamed taxi-driver), but in neither case does he make the first move. He is given one moment of pathos, when late one night he almost regrets refusing two offers of intimacy, but that is as close as he comes to expressing desire.

This is in a sense oddly passive behaviour, though it accords well with the book's presentation of sex as performance, sex as marketing, sex as status, sex as anything but need.

But how does Daniel actually express himself, with Gary, with the taxi-driver, when at last he takes up the burden of pleasure? Daniel's sexual practices aren't specified, any more than a general level of desire is admitted, although in effect we are told that they are specific (nothing wishy-washy about Daniel): when he lends Mark his apartment keys he detaches them "from his back belt loop", and when Clarisse wants to borrow a bandanna he gives her a blue one "from his back pocket". In the context of an urban subculture, this means he is giving clear sexual signals, but without being told which side he wears these accessories, a gay reader can't work out exactly what they are.

For a gay reader, the hero of a novel can just as easily be a role-model or a pin-up, a subject of identification or an object of desire. But he can be both these things only if his behaviour remains studiedly vague. Someone who is giving clear sexual signals by implication narrows his market, while increasing his chances of success within it; but *Vermilion* is anxious to hang on to every scrap of approval from its audience, and so must leave its hero an all-powerful blank, perfectly full of status, perfectly free of role-playing.

There are other ways of writing about roles than pretending they don't exist. The system of sexuality which *Vermilion* advocates makes demands on those who enter it; it makes some transactions possible and others impossible. But it can't indefinitely pose as natural.

Consider for contrast this passage by the estimable Merril Mushroom, which focuses on the actual moment of entering a subculture:

When Buddy came into my room and announced that these two women we knew who were twenty-one years old would loan us their proof of age so that we could finally go to the bars, I was ready. My first lesbian affair was behind me, and I'd been hanging out with the gay kids for the past year. At seventeen, I was a hot-shot dyke, ripe for the bar scene.

Buddy and I spent the rest of the week preparing for our big debut. We went shopping for men's trousers and shirts. We bought a large bottle of Vitalis "greasy". Buddy decided that she would be a butch. I was not sure if I wanted to be butch or fem—it was important to be one or the other—so I decided to go out butch Friday night and fem Saturday night and see which role I felt most comfortable with.

On Friday evening Buddy and I showered and dressed in our new clothes, then spent an hour doing our hair, slicking it back just so neatly, spreading on more Vitalis and wiping it off, making sure the one casual curl hanging down in front was just casual enough, making doubly certain that the duck's ass in back creased perfectly straight and that it was the only straight thing about us. At last, clutching our borrowed proof of age, bearing phony nicknames to match, we left for the bar . . .

That first butch night out, Buddy and I were the objects of a lot of cruising, since we were new dykes on the scene. Invariably we were asked if we were butch or fem, and I answered that I was butch; and if the woman said something like, "Oh, that's too bad," I'd respond with something like, "Well, I'm coming back tomorrow night fem."

The next night I met Sharon and was smitten. Sharon wasn't sure if she was butch or fem either, but since I was fem that night, she decided that she'd be butch for me. We made a date to honeymoon the following weekend.

("Bar Dyke Sketches: 1959", *Common Lives/Lesbian Lives*, no. 5, 1982)

This passage makes no bones about the artificiality of the system it describes, but once that is confronted it becomes possible for a person to express herself through it. When, a few pages later, one woman is described as a "butchy-looking fem" and another as a "femmy-looking butch", it's hard to feel that the forms are constricting; the system has been transformed, without being denied, by a sense of play and of adventure.

Perhaps women are better able to work this transformation than men, since for them being allowed to choose between roles in itself represents an intoxicating freedom. Men have rather more to lose from acknowledging the artificiality of social arrangements.

Vermilion, though, is solicitous about men and their claims to status. It embodies a scale of values on which men who define themselves by their relationships with other men enjoy a clear superiority over their fellows. Straight women come next in the hierarchy (best of a bad job), then straight men (sad waste) and finally gay women (wilful abandonment of status).

Not that lesbians abound in the world of *Vermilion*. No declared gay woman inhabits these pages, but on the Thursday evening Daniel Valentine practises his powers of observation:

> Valentine watched carefully the dismay of two young women who had stopped in front of the window. *Students*, thought Valentine. *Boston University, School of Applied Music, 700 Commonwealth Avenue, one has a boyfriend who's a trumpet player, the other is a closet lesbian.* They moved on before he could delve any deeper into their obvious lives.

Or before he can find out that they are attached to one of the Boston area's 400 other colleges, if they are students at all.

Gay men in *Vermilion* not only have all the status, they have all the knowledge. Daniel knows something about a woman, at first sight and without benefit of conversation, that she imagines she is hiding even from her intimates.

The tone of this passage is startlingly dismissive, and the overcompensation involved fairly astounding. If a friend whose sight seems to be failing reads a number-plate at the end of the street, you are likely to be reassured. But if he offers to read a number-plate in Tokyo, your doubts will actually increase.

Clarisse lags behind in the intuition stakes until the end of *Vermilion*, when she solves the murder. The ability to do so is entirely at odds with her other characteristics, but she is already such a compound of contradictory elements that the reader may not notice. In the course of the book she has shown herself unable to organize so much as a handbag or a bunch of keys, constantly cutting herself in a lovably feminine manner, losing her contact lenses, getting on the wrong train, but she ends the novel in a blaze of analytical cunning, working out all those ticklish details about the angle of the fatal blow which vain little Belgians dispose of in Chapter 3.

Clarisse's solution doesn't in fact stand up to examination. A handkerchief smeared with vermilion lipstick was found on the body of Billy Golacinsky. In the book's overall structure this clue leads unmistakably to a female impersonator ("Trudy") who works at Bonaparte's as a cabaret artiste and did, as it turns out, pick Billy up on the night of the murder; this is the book's first false solution.

But Clarisse's eventual solution requires Billy to have been given the hanky, or else the lipstick, by a woman whose invariable costume is black leather, and who would hardly have a tube of vermilion lipstick tucked away in a pocket of her motorcycle jacket. The circumstances are never explained.

If Clarisse's solution had incriminated a gay man, it would have had to resist a much closer scrutiny; but readers of *Vermilion* will have no particular objection to the guilt of a straight couple and a Boston cop. The actual mechanics of the solution are of little consequence, as long as the presumed reader's group is cleared of blame.

If, as Confucius suggested, nothing is more obvious than what a man seeks to hide, the most obvious characteristic of the community which produced and consumes *Vermilion* is fear; fear of isolation and fear of dependence.

These are legitimate fears in a community which is constantly being reminded of its provisional status, but they are never expressed directly by the book. They are denied without ever being mentioned, just as Daniel Valentine's dust is cleared away without his having to admit its existence. An artificial state of affairs passes itself off as natural. If this is the atmosphere that gay men breathe, why does it contain no oxygen or nitrogen?

Some less defensible fears, fears of pleasure, fears of responsibility, fear of choice and fear of need, are attemptedly exorcised by *Vermilion*'s propagandist version of gay life in the city. The book's genre, comedy-thriller, makes no promise of realism, but how many casual readers of *Vermilion* appreciate the wildness of its wish-fulfilment? Gay Boston in *Vermilion* is an idealized version of gay life in a subculture, in the same way that levitation is an idealized version of gravity.

My analysis of *Vermilion* is necessarily a jaundiced account of an unexceptional piece of work; but there's a lot to be said for taking the yellow view.

Vermilion contains no more silly lies about human behaviour per hundred words than, say, *Doctor No*, but its position in the marketplace is different. There was not, when Ian Fleming embarked on his literary production, a thriving community of secret agents longing to be told how to treat their women and their enemies, desperate to keep up with the latest styles in Lugers and martinis. The fantasy dispensed by *Doctor No* and by books like it was frankly distant from the daily lives of its readers, and made only a small contribution to the formation of their ideas about sex and power. They could draw their worldly knowledge and their sexual lore from many other sources.

Readers of *Vermilion*, by contrast, are likely to be hungry for roles and codes of conduct, grateful for any image that presents gays as people of importance and interest. *Vermilion* provides them with a good read. It also provides them (in a sort of ideological version of subliminal advertising) with a series of attitudes which they are invited to take for granted. Because the book is a comedy-thriller and innocent of any claims to literary stature, it is assumed by its readers to be telling them nothing new. In this way, and thanks to a generalized air of sophistication, a number of dubious propositions can be sneaked past the reader's peripheral vision, which he might view very differently if he was invited to consider them on their own merits.

How much damage is actually done by what people believe, and how much by what people assume other people believe? If you take a group of people and tell them, "A person under hypnosis (as I'm sure you know) is unable to move his or her dominant hand", your statement will become true of members of that group, if you then hypnotize them. The crucial point is placed in parentheses (I'm telling you nothing new) as if it was unimportant, and manages to trigger uncritical acceptance rather than scrutiny.

The ghetto sets you free. Men are monoliths, women are mosaics. Politics are irrelevant. It's tasteless to mix your sex life and your social life. Nothing is subjective. Gay men and gay women have nothing in common; lesbianism doesn't exist anyway. Only in the city is gayness possible. Sexuality is determined by market forces. Experience is interchangeable. These ideas, though not mentioned in the blurb, are in a real sense what *Vermilion* is about.

Few of these ideas stand up to analysis when their air of self-evidence is taken from them. The book's suggestion, for one, that membership of a subculture involves no separation from the dominant culture, is as good as disproved by the book's own marketing strategy; exquisitely it homes in on urban gays, and receives reviews only from partisan journals. Its sequels are likely to go on reassuring a commercialized ghetto that there is nothing outside it.

People at least have the choice of whether to betray you or not; institutions can't help it.

If Nathan Aldyne's future books stop advocating a system of casual sexual exchange, the 1982 epidemic of panic and sexual fear will probably be responsible. This epidemic has already changed attitudes almost as much as the decade did that separates *Vermilion* from *The Last Woman in His Life*. In time, the level of perceived realism in *Vermilion* is likely to dwindle to nothing.

In the meantime, between one backlash and the next, with the appropriate fears and the appropriate confidence, this collection of lesbian and gay fiction sets itself as much against the expectations of subcultural commerce, as against the studied indifference of the dominant culture.

How to Engage
in Courting Rituals
1950s Butch-Style in the Bar

You are sitting by yourself at the bar in the club you hang out at, legs wide, leaning on your elbow, holding your cigarette deep in the crotch of your fingers. There can be no doubt about the fact that you are a butch. You notice a woman you've never seen before sitting at a table, and you are attracted to her. She has short hair and is wearing a little makeup, but she isn't obviously femmy-looking. You are not sure if she's butch or fem—a critical issue—so you call over the bartender. You say, "Don't be obvious, but see that woman over there? Do you know who she is?"

If the bartender responds, "Yeah," you ask, "Is she butch or fem?" If the woman is a fem, you may proceed with the rituals. If the issue remains uncertain, proceed as though she were a fem. If she is a butch, forget it unless you are still attracted to her. In that case, consult with the bartender as to her opinion on whether you should try "flipping" her.

Ritual # 1
Cruising

You look at the woman, stare at her aggressively, arrogantly, trying to catch her eye. Does she look back at you? Does she look at you and then away? Does she not look at you? Any of these could be a sign of interest. Stare at her for a while. If she does not look back at you at all, and you are getting impatient, proceed to ritual # 2. If she glances at you and then looks away, you may want to try ritual # 3 next. If she looks at you and smiles, proceed immediately to ritual #4, and if she raises one eyebrow, go directly to # 5. If she runs her tongue over her lips, she is most likely on the make. If she looks at you and frowns, forget it.

Ritual # 2
The Buying of the Drink

Call the bartender over. She is well practiced in these rituals and will be ready for your next question, "What is she drinking?" The bartender tells you, and you say, "Send her over one from me." You watch the woman's response as the drink is delivered to her along with the message that it is from you (unless you say to the bartender, "Don't tell her it's from me"). If the woman looks over at you and smiles, proceed immediately to ritual # 4. If she looks at you and frowns, forget it. If she sends the drink back, really forget it. If she does not look at you, try to read her expression. If she seems to be bored, buy her another drink.

Ritual # 3
The Playing of the Jukebox

This is an especially good ritual if you are not ready to approach the woman directly, as it provides indirect contact and also gives her a chance to get a good look at you. Be sure to pass her table on the way to the jukebox, no matter how devious a route you may have to fabricate; but be sure not to look at her yet. Lean on the sides of the jukebox with your arms straight in as butch a position as possible. Experiment at home with jukebox poses, and get a friend to tell you what angle you look best in against the light. Be extra casual and take a long time with your selections. Be very intent on your choices, but try to see out of the corner of your eye if she is watching you. You may, if you want to, look at her significantly before you press the button for a particular selection. When you are finished, straighten up and look directly at her. If she seems bored or annoyed, you may want to forget it. If she looks at you shyly, boldly, or arrogantly, smile at her. If she smiles back, immediately approach her and ask her to dance (ritual # 6). If she does not smile back, proceed to ritual # 4.

Ritual # 4
The Approach

Walk over to where she is sitting. Be sure to be casual and swing your arms as you walk. Remain standing close to her, but be careful not to make her crane her neck into an uncomfortable position to look at you. If there is an extra chair, prop one foot up on it and lean over to talk to her, resting your forearms on your thighs. Look at her intensely, right in the eye. If you are bold and confident, you can say, "Hi, mind if I sit here?" as you are already sliding your butt on to the seat. If you are not quite that aggressive, you can open with something like, "Hi, are you *with* anyone?" or "Hi, I've been looking at you from the bar. Aren't you a friend of (make up any name here) 's?" or "Didn't I see you at the (make up any place here)?" If the light where she's sitting is really dim and you want to get a better look at her, you can invite her to come sit at the bar with you "where the air is a little better" or you can immediately ask her to dance. It's a good idea to hold conversations and even exchange names on the dance floor, because it gives you something else to do while you are really seeing how your bodies fit.

Ritual # 5
The Lighting of the Cigarette

The fem makes a brief motion toward her cigarettes. You immediately grab your own pack from your breast pocket and extend it to her gracefully, snapping the pack so that three cigarettes shoot up a distance of $\frac{3}{4}''$, $\frac{1}{2}''$, and $\frac{1}{4}''$ respectively (this takes a lot of practice), while with your other hand you smoothly slip your zippo lighter out of your hip pocket, flip the lid open so that it rings, and slide the wheel along the leg of your denims so that you can present it to her with flame ready. This also takes practice, and until you become adept, you can use your thumb to flick the wheel. She plucks the tallest cigarette from the pack with the tips of her index and middle fingers, even if it isn't her brand, and deposits it firmly between her lips, perhaps licking her lips slightly before closing her mouth around the filter tip (never offer a fem a cigarette that does not have a filter tip). Although the air in the bar is still, you cup your hand around the flame, touching her fingertips or brushing the back of her hand in the process. She either lowers her eyes or else looks at you intensely as she draws in the smoke deeply, cupping her hand around yours and allowing the tips of her fingers to quiver slightly.

Ritual # 6
The Asking to Dance

This shows interest––butch: wanna dance? fem: sure!

This shows lack of interest—butch: wanna dance? fem: nope.

This sort of exchange should be followed by a return to, and continuation of, ritual # 4.

This shows definite lack of interest, i.e., forget it—butch: wanna dance? fem: fast or slow? butch: slow. fem: no thanks. butch: OK, fast then. fem: no thanks.

If she is sitting with other women, this shows interest—butch: anyone here wanna dance? fem: whaddya mean, "anyone"?

This shows very blatant interest—butch: anyone here wanna dance? fem: whaddya mean, "dance"?

Ritual # 7
The Dancing

This is one of the most important of the rituals and the most blatant form of foreplay. Dancing in the fifties, whatever the style, involved a great deal of body contact. Never forget that a butch *always* leads when a couple dances, a fem *always* follows. If you get as far as the dance floor and the woman insists on trying to lead, forget it.

The Slow Dance was very frequently done in the fifties. Be sure to begin with a general foxtrot-type step and don't hold your partner too close unless she seems receptive. If you don't know many fancy dance steps, you can do a simple two-step. Lead with your right hand behind her back while she holds you around the neck with her left hand. You can begin dancing by holding hands on the other side (your left, her right), but if she is receptive, you can ease your hands closer to your bodies until you manage to move your left hand around her waist. If she moves closer to you, you can begin a slow fish movement, rocking your pelvis, thighs and breasts against hers in time to the music, with perhaps just a bit of syncopation every now and again. If she moves with you, you might want to breathe slightly on her neck. If she holds herself away from you, or if you are too shy to want to dance a slow fish right away, you can converse while you are dancing. This keeps you both safe from having to get too physically close, because you both have to lean your heads back to talk to one another. It also gives you something to pay attention to besides your bodies and how they feel together. If you can do fancy steps and she follows well, you can use whirls and dips as a good excuse to hold her tighter. This is a good way to impress both her and onlookers, but be very careful not to get out of control through showing off and stumble, fall, or—worst of all—drop her.

Fast Dancing was usually some form of the Lindy, Chicken, or Panama City Bop, although there were also line dances like the Madison and the Hully Gully. There is usually not a lot of full body contact unless you do a Dirty Boogie. Fast dancing provides an excellent opportunity to show off. You can do a lot of fancy twirls and twists, and if you are strong enough, you can do lifts and swings. You can exchange names and immediate information while fast dancing, but usually there is no need for further conversation, since most of your energy then goes into keeping your breath. Be sure you don't wear yourself out, so that you have to quit and sit down before the record is finished.

Welcome

The bar closed at two-thirty, by which time the beautiful people had all gone and all that was left was scrag end, and Abel Baker could have some time to himself. Only the truly desperate stayed till three when the lights went up. Abel Baker hated it when the lights went up, and usually stayed in the foyer, chatting with Misha the bouncer, and waiting for Maggie the hat-check-girl, when they did. You couldn't talk to Maggie till well after three. The desperate and the scrag end kept her too busy. Misha the bouncer was more decorative than functional. He was one of McTeague's cast-offs, and looked stunning in black tie. On the one occasion that Abel Baker could remember that there had been a disturbance, a scuffle almost, at reception, Misha had vaulted Maggie's counter and hidden among the coats, leaving Maggie to cope with it. McTeague, as Abel Baker had good cause to know, was generous to his cast-offs. To each according to his level, if not his capacity, which was why Misha was a bouncer and wore black tie, and Abel Baker was a welcomer and had an account at Brown's. At half-past three Misha, Maggie and Abel Baker always went down the street to Oakapple's for breakfast, before each took his separate taxi home. There had been a time when Abel Baker had tried, or hoped, to prevail upon either Misha or Maggie to share his taxi home, but that was before he knew what was what. Loneliness is loneliness after all, and has its rules, and is not to be trespassed upon. It was not impossible anyway to find something at Oakapple's if you really had to. There was an established procedure for it, of which from time to time either Misha, or Maggie, or Abel Baker availed themselves. Once eye-contact had been established, and smiles exchanged, the one concerned stood up and said goodbye to the others, and was henceforth invisible. Any further comment or contact was a great breach of tact. It was understood that at that hour of the morning standards were not high. Of the three it was Misha who was most often invisible. He was the youngest, and his appeal, in Abel Baker's eyes at least, the most obvious. Abel Baker left before the others, except on the nights of Misha's invisibility, when Maggie became silent and sullen and stomped off early. Once, leaving shortly afterwards, Abel Baker had seen her leaning against a parking meter, crying, and had passed by on the other side of the street, thinking: What can we do? We are all of us long past the good Samaritan stage. We all know exactly what we are doing, and could quit tomorrow if we wanted to. It was neither the first nor the last time he had had the thought.

At three-thirty Misha bowed out the last of the scrag end, and closed the door. Maggie came out from behind her counter and joined Misha and Abel Baker in a cigarette.

"A busy night," she said.

"Not bad," Misha said.

"Another glamorous evening," Abel Baker said.

They drew on their cigarettes. From behind Maggie's counter the telephone rang. She answered it, and held out the receiver to Abel Baker.

"CMG," she said.

"Oh God," Abel Baker said.

He took the receiver and covered the mouthpiece with his hand.

"Take a deep breath," Misha said.

Abel Baker raised his eyes to heaven, uncovered the

mouthpiece, and spoke.

"Hi," he said. "Right. Now? OK, I'll be straight down."

He hung up.

"An interview," he said. "An audience. A vocation."

"We'll wait," Misha said.

CMG's office was at the back of the club. Through the restaurant, down the spiral staircase, past the bar, the disco, and the dance floor. So Abel Baker would have to face the turned-up lights after all.

It had been McTeague's idea to keep the disco simple. Let the people provide the colour, he had said. So everything was plain, all cane and stainless steel, and glass and smoked mirrors. White tablecloths, and cool perspex-framed prints clamped on to taut vertical wires. When the lights were down it worked. When the lights were up it looked shabby, the walls stained, the steel and glass finger-marked, the oatmeal carpet drink-splashed and cigarette-burned. Abel Baker crossed the restaurant and went down the staircase with his eyes focused on his feet. The dance floor was being vacuumed, and the noise echoed in Abel Baker's ears, which were already ringing from the night's exposure to relentless disco. His throat was dry too, after hours of shouting above the music, and he cleared it painfully before he knocked on CMG's door.

CMG was, of course, one of McTeague's cast-offs. The initials stood for Call Me God, a nickname that Maggie had started and now had gained universal acceptance, even from CMG, who had initially showed signs of resentment. There were rumours that McTeague himself had laughed when he had heard it, and what McTeague liked, even from as far away as San Francisco, went.

CMG's office was a biscuit-coloured, windowless cube, furnished with steel and leather deckchairs, potted fig-trees, and two square yards of smoked glass, behind which CMG sat night after night, totting up sheets of figures, and writing letters to McTeague. There were two electric fans on the desk, and a centre punkah. CMG liked to be cool. The effect, as Abel Baker came in from the dance floor, was like opening up a fridge.

"Hi," Abel Baker said.

"Hello," CMG said, without looking up. "I'll be with you in a minute."

"You wanted to see me," Abel Baker said.

CMG looked up from his desk.

"Oh, it's you," he said. "Pour yourself a drink. I'll be through here shortly."

"No thanks," Abel Baker said. "I've had enough. It's been a crowded evening."

"Really," CMG said. "It was that I wanted to see you about. I won't be long."

Abel Baker sat in a deckchair. He turned up his jacket collar, and hugged himself, and shivered. CMG tapped his pen on his papers. Abel Baker shifted in his chair, and yawned.

"I was hoping to make a quick getaway," he said. "Like I said, it's been a crowded evening."

"None of us is indispensable," CMG said. "Like I said, I'll be through here in a minute."

So Abel Baker waited. CMG ran his pen down the margin of his paper, tapped the page when he reached the bottom, and turned over to run his pen down the margin of the other side. He let the paper fall on to the desk top, and screwed the top on to his pen. He tapped his pen on the desk top, and looked across at Abel Baker.

"I sometimes wonder", he said, "if you understand the nature of your position here."

Abel Baker tipped an eyebrow.

"I mean," CMG continued, "I am here to run the place. That means I'm in charge. That means what I say goes. You're here to be a welcomer."

"In a menial capacity," Abel Baker said.

"Sort of in between," CMG said. "Neither one thing nor the other. Not floor staff, and not management. Definitely not management."

"Like a governess," Abel Baker said. "Between floors. Neither staff nor family. I get the picture."

"Definitely not management," CMG said. "Which means that what I say goes with you too."

"Not welcome on either level," Abel Baker said. "I get the picture."

"I wonder if you do," CMG said. "Don't confuse yourself with the people you're paid to welcome. They are the stars. You are the employee. No matter how many of them you know. No matter how smart you are. You still have to do as I say."

"I really do get the picture," Abel Baker said.

"I've had complaints," CMG said.

"Oh," said Abel Baker. "Who have I insulted now? It's a week since I spilled a drink over anyone."

"It's a week since you scored more than two bottles of champagne a table," said CMG. "How you meet your clients is your business, just as long as they come back for more. And they're not coming back. Just look at this."

With the tip of his pen he flipped open a large leather padded book, span it round, and pushed it towards Abel Baker, who leant forward in his deckchair to receive it.

"Complaints," he said. "From stateside."

"Stateside," Abel Baker said. "Dear God, what books have you been reading? Who's been getting these complaints, anyway? You or me?"

"Well, strictly speaking, me," CMG said. "I do run the place."

"Credit where it's due," Abel Baker said.

"But I've pinpointed the cause," CMG said. "It's in there. Look at it. Who is Mick Dacres, for God's sake? And Karen Goodhue? That book is for names."

"So," said Abel Baker, "the place is falling off. It's in the nature of things. Mick Dacres is the bass guitarist of a group called Heartthrob. Their record is number thirty-six. Karen Goodhue is a model. She was in last month's *Harper's*."

"Like I said," CMG said. "That book is for names. Not third raters and session men."

"Fashion moves on," Abel Baker said. "That's how clubs

work, in case you hadn't noticed. You begin with stars, and end up with stargazers. We had the stars and they've moved on. There isn't a damn thing you or I can do about it."

"Unfortunately," CMG said, "it's your job to do something about it. And mine to make sure you do. From now on I'm inspecting the Visitor's Book every night. And it's going to look up. Get on the phone. Get your smart friends here. No more Mick Dacres and Karen Goodhue. I want names, and a lot of them. Or you're out."

"Now wait a minute," Abel Baker said. "I'm just welcomer here. Nobody said anything about touting for trade."

"So show me your job description," CMG said.

"I shall call McTeague," Abel Baker said.

"I dare you," CMG said, "I dare you, that's all."

Abel Baker snapped the Visitor's Book shut, and tossed it back across the desk. He extracted himself with difficulty from the deckchair, and stood leaning his hands on the desk.

"You're a fucking liar," he said. "Complaints. You haven't heard a bloody word."

"So you're going to call and find out," CMG said. "I'd make damn sure before I risked that if I were you."

"Bastard," Abel Baker said.

"You're marking the desk top with your hands," CMG said.

"What is it?" Abel Baker said. "What is it that makes you dislike me like this?"

"Call me God," CMG said. "You think you're unassailable, don't you? That you can go around making up names for people. You think you're God, or something? And I'm supposed not to resent it. To smile and take it. Get your hands off my desk."

Abel Baker put his hands in his pockets, straightened his elbows and hunched his shoulders forward as if standing in the rain. He knew it suited him. He had hundreds of photographs of it suiting him, left over from his days as a model, days before McTeague. He only did it when he felt threatened. It made him look insolent. Frowning against an incipient headache, he turned and walked to the door, and turned and walked back again.

"It wasn't me," he said, "who made it up. That wasn't me."

"You make me sick," CMG said. "With your loose tie. Your turned-up collar. And your floppy hair. Get out of here."

The dance floor and the spiral staircase were dark when Abel Baker left CMG's office. He felt his way to the stairs and sat on the broken step with his elbows on his knees and his head in his hands. After a while he bit the back of his left hand hard and clenched his eyes shut. He hated himself in minute particular. The door at the top of the staircase opened and Misha's shadow in a wedge of light flashed on to the wall. Abel Baker unfastened his teeth from his hand.

"Dark," Misha's voice called. "He must be still in the office."

Abel Baker stood up. "I'm just coming," he said.

"Maggie was fretting," Misha said.

Abel Baker ascended the staircase.

"Bad?" Misha said.

"Not good," Abel Baker said. "Not the worst, but not good."

"He's a fink," Misha said. "He's a bastard. Don't let it get you down. He can't help it."

"Misha," Abel Baker said, "I feel sick."

Misha put his arm around Abel Baker's waist, and walked him through the dining room. The lights were still up, and cane chairs inverted over glass-topped tables aired their ravelled bottoms. The last cleaner unplugged the last vacuum. Abel Baker put his arm around Misha's waist.

"Better?" Misha said.

"Well, over anyway," Abel Baker said. "For the moment. Until next time."

"Come on," Misha said. "I'll buy you a drink."

"The next time," Abel Baker said.

Maggie, in the foyer, looked at their linked bodies and said, "Oh dear," and twined her arm round Abel Baker's waist from the other side.

"What we need", she said, "is breakfast. And something frivolous to drink. We'll let Oakapple dream up something special."

Three abreast they negotiated the door. As they left the club, dawn was breaking over Curzon Street. They turned their backs to the rising sun, and walked, still linked round Abel Baker's waist, down the street to Oakapple's.

"Well, hallelujah!" Oakapple said. "See who it ain't. The e-ternal tri-angle."

No one had tried to keep the decor simple at Oakapple's. Oakapple herself would have howled with boredom at the suggestion. What she wanted was vulgarity, and noise, and lots of it. Reggae thumped, lights flashed on corrugated-tin roofs slung over rattan tables, tropical vegetation—as tropical as Mayfair could manage—burgeoned. One whole wall was given over to the representation of a storm at sunset, with wind-dashed palms and heaping waves.

Oakapple, turbanned and wearing what appeared to be some four or five multicoloured bedspreads, presided from a high stool at the bar. She peered at Abel Baker over the top of her bamboo-framed glasses.

"Welcome, honey, welcome, you look like shit. What can I press you to?"

It was a theory of Oakapple's that the best way to express your personality was through your choice of drink. And she liked your personality to be complicated. She liked to mix cocktails, and was never happier than when shaking a Bosom Caresser, or a Sloe Comfortable Screw up against the Wall, or balancing layers of subtle liquors one on top of the other into a Rainbow Sundae. Misha usually humoured her and ordered some towering and deadly confection. Maggie and Abel Baker pleaded their livers and stuck to lager. Lager depressed Oakapple.

"Tonight, Oakapple honey," Maggie said. "We need you. Tonight is the pits. Tonight is the ass. Tonight is the fat end of the wedge."

"Ain't it always, honey," Oakapple said. "Take a look around you, and see what the tide washed up. Nothin' but the mackintosh brigade. Nothin' stronger than a Brandy Alexander in the place. How's tricks your end of the market?"

"Don't ask," Abel Baker said. "Just don't ask. Therein is the root of the trouble."

"We need help," Misha said. "To get through the night. Your help, Oakapple honey. Tonight we are giving you free rein."

"No lagers?" Oakapple asked.

"No lagers," Abel Baker said.

"So-ho!" Oakapple said. "Sit down, honeys, and prepare yourselves. Oakapple's going to fix you something that will blow your head away!"

"I sure hope so," Abel Baker said.

They sat at a table in a corner by the bar, and surveyed the scene.

"I can see what she meant," Misha said. "There's not much here for the heart's hunger. I wonder which is the Brandy Alexander."

"So what did CMG want?" Maggie asked.

"He doesn't like me," Abel Baker said.

"So what's new!" Maggie said. "So who would have guessed? So what can he do about it?"

"He's out to get me," Abel Baker said.

"How?" Maggie said. "Just how can he do that? McTeague's on your side."

"McTeague!" Misha said. "McTeague's on everybody's side."

"Misha honey," Abel Baker said. "Tonight you are showing a wisdom beyond your years."

"I sure wish I could see that Brandy Alexander," Misha said.

"It doesn't mean anything," Maggie said. "Oakapple just bullied him, that's all. He probably doesn't even know what he's drinking."

"Nevertheless," Misha said.

"Nevertheless!" Maggie said. "Neverthebloodyless! You sound like CMG."

Abel Baker leant his head back against the wall, and closed his eyes. Maggie and Misha bickered above the sound of reggae. If, Abel Baker thought, people go on and on behaving in the same way, it must mean they like it, mustn't it? You just don't go on and on doing something if you don't like it, do you?

Oakapple swept up to their table, bearing a tray of three mountainous cocktails, each topped with cream, and cherries, and dusted with coconut.

"The answer to all your prayers," she said. "Peacock-hued sweet oblivion in a glass."

"Better set up the next one," Maggie said. "There's a lot to forget."

"Honey," Oakapple said, "you drink two of these, I'll pay the bill myself!"

"That good, huh?" Abel Baker said.

"Oakapple," Misha said. "Which is the Brandy Alexander?"

"Forget it, honey," Oakapple said. "You're not for him. Oakapple can tell these things. You're too young and stupid. He likes the maturer man."

"All this from a Brandy Alexander?" Abel Baker said.

"Believe me," Oakapple said. "I can tell. He likes the maturer man. With brains."

"Nevertheless," Maggie said.

"Neverthebloodyless," Misha said. "Where is he, Oakapple?"

"Other side of the bar," Oakapple said. "Blue velvet trousers, and one of those Walkman machines. My music ain't for him. Don't say I didn't warn you."

"Show me," Misha said.

"Listen, honey," Oakapple said. "He likes them with brains. I told you. What's he going to think of a guy can't even find him by himself. Now, I've got a bar to tend to."

Back at the bar, she hoisted herself on to a stool, caught Abel Baker's eye and winked, jerking her head in the direction of the other side of the room.

You! she mouthed. You! Go get him.

Abel Baker smiled and sipped his drink, and shook his head.

Misha stood up.

"OK then," he said. "I'll go and check him out."

"See you then," Maggie said.

"Not too soon, I hope," Misha said.

"Good luck," Abel Baker said. "Don't forget your drink."

By the time Misha had disappeared round the edge of the bar, Maggie had downed her drink and was signalling to Oakapple for another. Oakapple shook her head.

"Don't you worry, honey," she shouted. "He'll be back."

Maggie thumped her glass on the table.

"Silly bitch," she said. "What do I care if he comes back or not? I want another drink."

She sniffed, and glared at Abel Baker with tear-bright eyes.

"I want another fucking drink," she said. "Shit! Why do I never get what I want?"

She stood up.

"I'm going for a piss," she said.

Abel Baker finished his drink. After a few minutes Misha came back and sat down.

"Where's Maggie?" he said.

He waved his empty glass at Oakapple and gestured round the table. Oakapple got off her barstool and mixed another round of drinks. Maggie came back as she brought them to the table.

"Oakapple, honey," Maggie said. "You're not a silly bitch really. None of us know what we'd do without you."

"Go home straight after work is what you'd do without me," Oakapple said. "Ain't nowhere else to go. Don't forget now. You drink these, I pay for them."

Abel Baker felt as if the floor was rippling under his chair. Maggie leaned her hand on Misha's shoulders as she sat down.

"I daren't think what this drink is," Abel Baker said. "It tastes like syrup of figs. I think I might go to the lavatory for a while."

On his way there he saw the Brandy Alexander, and they exchanged smiles. Definitely not English, Abel Baker decided. French maybe, or Spanish, judging by the clothes. A nice, shy face. I like the way he looks out from under his eyebrows. In the lavatory he plunged his face into a basinful of cold water, and checked himself in the mirror. He twitched his tie, and ran his fingers through his hair.

Oh well, he said to his reflection. Coming, ready or not.

The Brandy Alexander was sitting with his back to the lavatory door. Abel Baker went up behind him, and touched his hair. The Brandy Alexander turned round. Good eyes, Abel Baker thought. My God, he must be all of nineteen.

"Hi," he said. "What are you listening to?"

The Brandy Alexander took off his headphones.

"*Comment?*" he said. "Sorry. I did not hear."

"I said hello," Abel Baker said. "And what are you listening to?"

"Monteverdi," the Brandy Alexander said. "Hello. Please, sit down and join me."

"I have a better idea," Abel Baker said. "Why don't we both sit down somewhere else? Like in a taxi. Back to my place."

The Brandy Alexander put his headphones round his neck.

"OK," he said.

He reached into his pocket and turned his tape-recorder off.

"I don't need music now," he said. "You are enough."

Maggie and Misha were still sitting at their table as Abel Baker took the Brandy Alexander out. Neither nodded, or smiled, or waved. Misha took up Abel Baker's drink, and swallowed it.

"You like music?" the Brandy Alexander said, in the taxi. "What sort of music do you like?"

"Monteverdi," Abel Baker said.

The Brandy Alexander leaned his head on Abel Baker's shoulder.

"Tired?" Abel Baker said.

"Go on lying to me," the Brandy Alexander said. "I like it."

"I do," Abel Baker said. "I have records at home."

The Brandy Alexander nuzzled Abel Baker's ear. Abel Baker noticed with horror that he was wearing sandals and blue nylon socks.

"Tell me what you do," the Brandy Alexander said.

"I welcome," Abel Baker said. "I am a welcomer. I work in a club, and whenever anyone famous comes in, I rush up and make a fuss of them, and ask them to sign a book. It makes them feel loved."

"Make me feel loved," the Brandy Alexander said.

"Do you mind if I wait till we get home?" Abel Baker said. "I'm not good in taxis."

"Hold me," the Brandy Alexander said.

Abel Baker put his arm round the Brandy Alexander's shoulder. The Brandy Alexander inserted his hand between Abel Baker's thighs. The taxi pulled up outside Abel Baker's flat.

"So," the Brandy Alexander said, as Abel Baker showed him into the sitting room. "Where are all the Monteverdi records?"

"Make yourself at home," Abel Baker said. "Sit down while I put one on."

The Brandy Alexander sat on the sofa, and Abel Baker put on the 1610 Vespers.

"There," he said. "I told you."

He knelt on the floor between the Brandy Alexander's legs. The Brandy Alexander leaned forward to be kissed. His eyes were half closed, and his eyeballs were turned up under his lids, so that all Abel Baker could see of them was two white crescents in the middle of his face. Abel Baker kissed him, and ran an exploratory hand under his T-shirt. The boy's shoulders were rough to the touch, and proved, on closer inspection, to be speckled with innumerable blackheads. Nevertheless, Abel Baker persisted in his embraces.

At half-past one the next afternoon Abel Baker woke to an empty space in the bed beside him. He had had trouble sleeping. The Brandy Alexander had been disposed to be cuddlesome, and none of Abel Baker's devices—twitching legs, falling asleep and waking up with a jerk, even a determined move to the other side of the bed—had been able to dissuade him. He wanted to fall asleep in Abel Baker's arms. He wanted to rest a tousled head on

Abel Baker's chest, and every now and then raise a fuddled face for a kiss. Abel Baker had lain sleepless, cross, and increasingly hot, till eventually the Brandy Alexander had slept, and he could disengage himself. Even so his sleep had been punctuated by mumbled endearments, sleep-furred kisses, and palping hands. Now he surveyed the empty pillow next to him with relief, and would have slept again had not a furtive noise from the sitting room made him sit up and think: Oh God, he's stealing something.

Swiftly Abel Baker enumerated to himself the small movable objects in his sitting room and mentally adjusted himself to their absence. His wallet, he knew, was nearly empty, indeed had cost more than was ever in it, but his cheque book and credit cards were on his desk. He was running over in his head the drill for reporting their loss when the Brandy Alexander, clothed and coated for the street, came back into the bedroom.

"Ah," he said, "you are awake. You slept well?"

"As you see," Abel Baker said. "I slept beautifully."

The Brandy Alexander took Abel Baker's hand and sat on the bed.

"I too," he said. "Very fine. But now I must go."

Abel Baker threw back the sheets.

"No," the Brandy Alexander said. "Stay. Go back to sleep. I must go. I will say goodbye now."

Abel Baker stood up.

"No," the Brandy Alexander said. "Lie down again. I don't want to disturb you. I will let myself out."

He took Abel Baker in his arms.

"You are a good man," he said. "You gave me a good night. Thank you. Now get back into bed."

Abel Baker lay down, and the Brandy Alexander tucked the sheets round him.

"Sleep now," he said, and kissed Abel Baker's eyes closed.

"Goodbye," he said.

Abel Baker waited till he heard the front door close, then got up and went to survey the sitting room. Nothing was missing.

His wallet, cheque book, passport, everything was where it should be. The Monteverdi record had been taken off the turntable and returned to its box, which lay on the coffee table holding down a note, which Abel Baker sat on the sofa to read.

If one day, he read, *you come to Paris remember this fellow you cross the time of a night. He lives in the 18th, and likes Monteverdi. If you have nothing else to do than to remember a night on the sweating catacombs of London, just come to him. Sure he'd be happy to see you again. I give you his address.*

> *His name is: Dominique Chaussure.*
> *And he lives: 8, Passage Daunay*
> *75018 Paris.*

"Chaussure!" Abel Baker said. "Oh God. Dominic Shoe."

He folded the note carefully and put it in his wallet. If ever, he thought, if ever by some remote chance I might be seduced into thinking myself a nice guy, all I shall have to do is take out that note and read it.

He made himself a cup of coffee and went back to bed. He smoked a cigarette and stared at the ceiling. He dozed and woke to cold coffee. He looked at his watch. Three o'clock. Early morning in San Francisco. He reached for the phone and dialled.

"Hello," McTeague's voice said.

Abel Baker covered the mouthpiece with his hand.

"Hello," McTeague said again. "Hello."

Abel Baker lay the phone down on the bed. McTeague's voice went on saying Hello impassively and at intervals, until Abel Baker hung up.

Misha, even more stunning in taut blue denim than in black tie, threw his coat over the counter to Maggie, and blew Abel Baker a kiss.

"Give us a break," Maggie said. "It's your night off."

"Can't help it," Misha said. "Here's where the action is. Can't stay away."

"See you later maybe," Maggie said. "Will you be coming to Oakapple's?"

"I hope not," Misha said. "I sure as hell hope not. I don't know why I keep going to that place."

The club door opened, and Abel Baker poised himself, flashing a welcoming smile, but it was only an early bit of a scrag end, so he relaxed again. Misha passed and tweaked his cheek.

"Have a good night, old love," he said.

Abel Baker went and leaned on Maggie's counter.

"How do you feel?" he said. "She sure as hell mixes a mean cocktail."

"I got home in the end," Maggie said.

"Misha?" Abel Baker said.

"We walked," Maggie said. "We couldn't get a taxi so we walked. If you can call it that. We propped each other up."

"Oh well," Abel Baker said. "And here we all are again."

"Why?" Maggie said. "I wish I knew that. Why the fuck do we go on doing it?"

We are all, Abel Baker thought, caught in a trap with no door. We could leave, walk out, tomorrow. All it takes is a phone call to San Francisco.

This observation, though comforting, though giving him the courage to stay where he was, Abel Baker judged premature, unwelcome even, in Maggie's case, so he kept it to himself. The door was opening anyway, and he sprang forward.

"Mick!" he said. "Karen! Hi! Come in! Welcome!"

Annie

Annie and I are the only women in the bar. She introduces me as her second cousin from Paris and says, "That's how come she cain't talk to y'all. Duddn't know a damn word o' English." This is her way of telling me to stay quiet so we can play one of our games. So I smile a lot and nod and laugh demurely when everyone else is laughing. I look at her with the look she's named my "sweetest lil' thang there ever wuz" face, which all the cowboys read as the ignorance of a foreigner. And Annie "translates" to me in the gibberish that passes for today's exotic language. They're always interested in my dress; do all the young girls in France (Tasmania, Russia, Italy, New Jersey) dress like me? And Annie will surprise me with something new, like, oh no, that I'm an exception where I come from too, a girl on the fringe, a slave princess, an exile, a bohemian, a turkey herder. Or she'll just stick with the old standard, as she does today. "Yup. They're all jest lahk 'er, each 'n' ever' one."

Her clothes are wonderful. They're hanging in the wagon and it's evening. Annie's out fixing us some stew and cornbread. I've just come back from bathing in the stream and, clean again, I drop my towel and squat down to straighten into even rows her pairs of boots and moccasins. I run my fingertips over the skins of lizard, snake, armadillo. Then I stand up and touch her clothes. I love the sturdy softness of the long-worn leather, the limp clean fur that gives to my touch, the heavy white muslin and thin white cottons. I love the thin dust-colored fringe across the back of her fancy jacket. I wrap the sleeves around me and bury my head in the inside where her shoulders fit. I close my eyes and breathe deep the smells of leather, of prairie, of western sky, of Annie. And then her voice breaks in, "Come on now, honey, grub's up!" I slip into my jumpsuit and join her by the fire.

Our forks clink against the thin tin plates. The shape of the cup is clear and simple. Annie's stew is plain and coffee strong. She'd laugh if I tried to tell her about Hamburger Helper or Crazy Salt or beef-stew flavor packets. She'd be in stitches if I told her about Cremora, Coffee-mate, non-dairy coffee cream. When she asks me what I'm smiling about I shake my head and tell her nothing. She wipes her mouth with her forearm and tells me stories about this place when no one had ever been here before. She's anxious that her elbow room is being invaded. She goes on and tells me about when the sky was bigger and the land stretched further. Her voice is even and round and I vow to myself that I will never *ever* breathe a word to her about Los Angeles. She spreads her arm beside her in a smooth arc as far as she can reach, to show me the horizon she remembers.

I wonder what she wonders when I go. I've explained to her as much as I can, or at least as much as I've told myself she can handle. I expect her to be puzzled, torn with curiosity, but she always seems completely satisfied. "Everybody's gotta saddle up and git sometimes," she comforts me. I tell myself that I should be the one to comfort her about the things in me that she can't know about. I remind her that there are places I go and things I do and people I am that she couldn't begin to understand. And sometimes, I must admit, I try to sound mysterious and tragic. But she looks at me clearly, waits for me to finish and tells me, 'Well, a girl can only say what she can when she can, she jest gotta see about th' rest."

I point out to her that the only things she knows about where I

go and what I do when I get there are what I tell her, and
then I ask her why she believes me. She looks hard at me,
squints and wrinkles up her nose as if I were trying to talk to her,
seriously, in gibberish. I try again, "Aren't you afraid one time
I won't come back, that some day I will leave you?" And then
she laughs her big laugh like it's a joke she's just understood.
She winks and tells me, "Well, yew jest tell me whin, 'n' I won't
look for y'."

My mother still has pictures of me like this, in my cowgirl
clothes. Every Christmas until I was eight or nine, I got cowgirl
clothes to replace the ones I'd outgrown. Skirts and vests and
shirts and boots. Boots changed the fastest. I went through black
pairs, brown pairs, beige pairs, even a pair of red ones.
Somewhere early along the line I got a hat that was too big for
me. The Christmas morning I ran down and found it, I put it on
my head and it bumped into my glasses and nose. But I insisted
on wearing it. I walked around that morning with my neck
stretched and my head tilted back, looking down my nose and
out at the world through the slit between my face and the dark
line of my hat. It must have fallen off my head at least thirty
times and stopped itself with the soft black and white string held
together with the knot and wooden bead around my neck. Later
that week my mother padded the inside of the hat to fit me. I
wore it with the pride of a child who believes she has been
mistaken for being older than she is.

Twice a year, in summer and right after Christmas, my family
made the trip north to my grandparents' home in Oklahoma
City. There were a couple of reasons why I didn't like the winter
visit. First of all it meant I left almost all of my new toys and all of
my friends and *their* new toys for a week in that most crucial and
short-lived time when toys are still "brand-new". Plus I always
considered the drive up a waste of precious time that could
otherwise be spent in productive play. The "excitement of
travel" and "gorgeous scenery", which my parents suggested I

try to appreciate, were not my idea, as a pre-school cowgirl, of a good time.

The summer visit, however, was an entirely different matter. I loved it: it was the high point of my year. And though I didn't know the word at the time, it was my pilgrimage. Because on one day of that summer week I was taken to "Westown" and on another to "The Cowboy Hall of Fame".

Westown, I now know, was an amusement park, a tacky little pre-fab money-maker, but I knew something different then; I knew it was a ghost town. But not quite even a ghost town, because somehow, by some miraculous dispensation, this town had stayed alive when all the rest had died. There were saloons with horses tied to posts in front, emporiums and general stores and every kind of Old West shop there could be. You could buy authentic frontier food, beef stew and cornbread, beans and white bread, molasses and grits, hamburgers and hot dogs. You drank sasparilla out of tin cups at the bar and your parents had coffee out of the same. Some people walked around looking like people anywhere, but some of them were dressed like true cowboys and cowgirls and Western gentlemen and ladies. I wore my cowgirl outfit and sometimes I'd pretend to get lost from my parents so I could walk around alone and pretend I lived there, and I was sure some people thought I did live there because they'd always smile at me and say, "Well howdy, pardner." And you could pay money and ride around a ring for ten minutes on Buffalo Bill's horse's grandson and get your picture taken. I did this every year. I remember vaguely wondering about this one year, when the horse was brown and I thought I remembered it being black, but my mother insisted that it was the same horse and I was just confused. Only last year did my mother show me the pictures of all the years together, and only then were my dark suspicions confirmed, when I saw myself on different sizes and shades of horse in the fuzzy black and white photos.

Each day ended with a trip to the Western Store when my father bought me one special thing, anything I wanted. All the stacks on the aisles were tall and I had to look up far. I was always

scrupulous and careful. I weighed the pros and cons of
everything I considered—a bronze belt buckle shaped like a
bucking bronc, a holster or a pair of spurs, a hand-tooled leather
belt that they could write my name on, a special red Westown
bandanna, a cowboy tie, a band of feathers for my hat, a brand
new hat with red silk on the inside with the Westown logo
written on it. The decision overwhelmed me. There was just too
much to look at. And it wasn't just the things you could buy—it
was everything. There were pictures on the walls of famous
cowboys and famous cowboys' horses. There were old rifles and
samples of so many different kinds of barbed wire I couldn't
count them. There were authentic horseshoes from famous
cowboys' horses, Indian blankets and head-dresses. There were
snakeskins hanging on parts of tree limbs and Wanted posters of
famous outlaws under glass. There were wagon wheels and cattle
brands and a life-sized wooden Indian. There was old blue and
silver Indian jewelry and beads and beaded moccasins. And after
a whole day of Westown, this store and this decision were too
much, like trying to decide between pecan and pumpkin and
mincemeat pie or ice cream or sherbert or meringues for dessert,
and all that *after* Thanksgiving dinner.

So I'd pick my choice, my heart trembling as I approached my
father waiting at the counter, thinking *Is this exactly what I want?
Wouldn't the spurs be better?*, knowing that the decision was
ultimate and irrevocable. And when I finally handed my father
whatever I'd decided on and he finally put it on the counter and
then at last he finally paid the money, I was stricken first with
regret—if I'd only waited one second longer maybe the strong,
true, right revelation would have come and I would have *known*
exactly and without a doubt what was the perfect thing to buy;
and then with relief—it was done, what I'd set out to do. I could
check it off a list of things that I'd lived through.

I don't remember most of what I got, but I do remember a
certain hat, though probably more because of what happened
when I got it than for the hat itself. I left the store, heart
pounding, palm sweating as I held my father's hand. My hat felt

sturdy and pretty on my head. My parents and I had just stepped off the wooden sidewalk in front of the store when—Bang!—a shoot-out! Quick as a kid I spun down and took cover behind a big sand-filled oil drum they'd converted into an ash can. I was proud of my cowgirl instincts and the skill I'd learned from sliding into homeplate at sand-lot baseball games. The shooting continued for some minutes complete with loud-mouthed hollers and threats. "Yew cain't git me, yew yella bellied dawg." "This town ain't big enuf fer th' two of us." I tried to stay completely still but I was worried about my parents. I looked around for them and couldn't see them. I squatted down further in my hiding place and prayed to the little Lord Jesus that they'd escape all right. I also told him I was sorry for being proud about my cowgirl instincts.

When the fighting stopped and I heard the last body bite the dust, I stood up and saw three dead cowboys on the street. I looked frantically to find my mother and father and I saw a crowd of people standing in a loose semi-circle on the street. I spotted my parents in the group just as they spotted me. My mother waved to me then put her hand to her head. I put my hand to my head and realized my new hat had fallen off. I picked it up. It was dusty and I started to brush it off but then I didn't because I wanted to keep the dust to remember the shoot-out. I put my dusty cowgirl hat back on and started to run to my mother and father to see if they were OK, then I saw them start to clap. Everyone in the semi-circle was clapping and I stopped to see why. They were all looking down the street so I did too and that's when I saw the three dead cowboys stand and smile and slap the dust from their chaps and hats and take their smart and often practised bows.

Annie's silhouette against the evening sky: she's sitting on top of Cowgirl. She's wearing her fancy jacket and though it's still, the fringe on her sleeves, particularly near her elbows, stands out straight as if a breeze was blowing. Her two limp braids rest on

her shoulders. She's facing the horizon, watching the sun sink in
the west. Behind her the sky is brilliant orange and muted pink
like an August peach. The land is flat except for a slight rise to
her left. And just about the line where earth meets sky, a tiny star
is twinkling. The sun rests, only a semi-circle above the line, like
the half coins in the March of Dimes display. Cowgirl's tail
swishes and she raises her hoof then lowers it with a gentle soft
"thoop" of a stamp. A tiny bit of dust kicks up around this foot,
then settles light as the snow in a dollar-twenty snow-scene in a
bottle. I can just see the line that Annie's leg makes in her fancy
skirt. Her holster rests against her thigh and I can see the curved
line of her boot top and her naked calf below her skirt.

Saying these words is like speaking avocado, warm ripe juicy
mango. "Appaloosa", "stirrup", "bay", "ride the open range".
"Rope the herd", "meet at sundown", "Goodnight-Loving
Trail". "Chaps" and "lassoes", "spurs" and "mares", "the
coyote's cry at night". "Saddle up", "the lonesome trail", "the
big wide open sky". "Rawhide leather", "Westward Ho!",
"sleeping under stars". "Cattle rustler", "Remington", "six
shooter", "riding shotgun". "King Corral", "the fastest gun",
"the sinking sun", "The West".

In my brother's eighth-grade shop class, he made me a leather
holster. He cut the pieces by himself and shaped it to fit the new
toy gun my father gave me on my birthday. My brother tooled
my name on the holster and a picture of a cowgirl hat. I wore the
holster to school, even without the gun. I fastened the belt
around my skirt and carried my pencil bag where the gun
would've fit. I was happy when I sat down and the holster hung
down the side of my desk. I made a point of changing pencils
every five minutes. I quick-drew my pencil bag and in a flash
picked a new pencil to follow vocabulary dictation. After several
pencil changes, my teacher told me I was making too much of a

disturbance and would I be so good as to hang my holster in the cloakroom with the other children's things. So I went back and hung my holster with the lunch pails and sweaters and caps. I did it reluctantly, and made a point to "forget" and leave my pencil bag in the holster, so that when I "accidentally" broke the pencil I was using later that period, I had to go back to my holster and get another.

I wasn't allowed to wear it to school anymore after that, but every day when I got home, as soon as I changed into my play clothes, I put my holster on, complete with gun, and wore it very proudly.

Late that night, we ride into town and tie up Kid and Cowgirl by the Red-Eyed Jack Saloon. We walk in side by side, each of us pushing open one half of the swinging door. The whole saloon is quiet for some moments. Annie looks at me. I nod and she says, "Bring us a bottle of yer best whiskey, Jimbo. And set us up two shots." Jimbo looks at Annie then looks at me, then back at her again. He hesitates, and when he says to her, "Annie?" his voice is slow and tentative, like a kid unwrapping a present too good to be true and asking unbelievingly, "For me?" Annie grins and looks at him, then looks down the entire bar. Everything is silent and still except one cowboy who shifts uncomfortably in his seat. The sound of the creaking leather of his chaps startles him and he holds his breath. Annie scans the whole place, then looks back at me and winks. She slips around on her barstool and faces the whole saloon. She spreads both her arms out wide, pauses, arms in the air, "Now is *this*," she slightly dips her arms, "what ya'll call a proper homecomin'?" And then the whole crowd bursts. Jimbo slaps his forehead, yells, "Shit fahr damnation, Annie!" Cowboys whoop and jump from their chairs and run up to Annie and hug her. "Goddamn yew, Annie", "Sheeeee-ut, Annie's home!" Jimbo declares free drinks for all. Someone finds a harmonica and starts dancing. Cowboys toss their hats in the air and holler. Everyone slaps everyone on the back. When Annie introduces me they shake my hand and take off their hats and tell me, "Pleased t' meetcha," and later in the night they give me bear hugs. They give Annie capsule histories: Wally's with the railroads, Doc got married and Lou left town with some man from Chicago. Lucky ran to Mexico. Sally 'n' Jack got hitched up and took on Old Widow Whitley's place. And Jimmy's got his eye set on the Foster girl but his Momma 'n' Daddy don't know what they think of her. They ask her about Buffalo Bill and the travelling Wild West Show and she tells them everything.

Part of the floor gets cleared and all of us are dancing. The cowboys stamp their boots. Annie takes a turn with Jimbo, and I with some young hand just passing through. Annie's skirt whirls around her and her braids fly. I watch her body spin through Jimbo's arms. The fringe strings on her jacket look alive and bright and I can pick out the sound of her boots clicking in the midst of all the rest. The night goes on forever. Cowboys collapse with happiness and booze. Little by little the cowboys leave, coming up to hug me and Annie again before they go and saying, "Hon, we're so glad t' have y' back. How long y' stayin'?"

When the only ones left standing are Annie and me, we help Jimbo make the passed-out cowboys comfortable, remove their hats and cover them with blankets. When this is done Jimbo puts his arms around us, "Now y'all please stay as long as y' can. I had Jimmy take care o' Kid 'n' Cowgirl for y' 'n' Miz Burnley gotcha'll a room all ready." Then he looks at Annie and squeezes her. "I knew yew'd come back, Annie." The three of us step out on to the boardwalk and Jimbo offers to walk us over to Mrs Burnley's Hotel, but Annie tells him we'll be just fine. When we walk out into the street alone, Annie takes her hat off and leans her head back to look up at the sky. I look at her face in the light of the moon then I look up at the giant sky. I hear her breathe in a big deep breath. Then I hear the sound of the stretch of her sleeve, the flap of the fringe on her jacket, and then a whoosh and she's flung her hat in the sky and I see her hat soar high. I see it climb, the brim all white with moon like a spine.

Every year there was one new statue. You saw the picture of it on the wall when you came in and I was always eager and excited to see it, and part of me wanted to run right to it and find it. I knew exactly where it would be, but part of me told myself to wait and save the best for last. I always wore a dress because it was inside. You went in and the air was cool and it felt very different from the hot heat of the blacktop of the parking lot. My grandmother came because she could, because it was cool and there were places to sit. I wore anklets and the last time I went I carried a little purse. It was a wooden box purse and it had two horses painted on it and they were running on the land.

You were quiet there and you walked slowly, reverently, you spent time poring over the index cards next to the exhibits behind the glass looking for words you knew. And you tried to remember the names they read you or that you could read yourself: Cheyenne, Durango, Cimmaron. There were maps and photos and scale models. There were simulated rooms that looked like schools and barber shops and stores. There were movies for free. In the new part there were black and white photo portraits of rodeo champs, and world-record holders for bronco busting, cattle roping, bull riding. On both walls of a hallway there were pictures of Best All Around Cowboy for every year. There were big cards on the wall that told you history.

My grandmother read me the one about the pioneers and it always took her a long time because she told me about her father who was an Indian doctor. At home she showed me things the Indians gave him. She showed me a leather pouch, a blanket of wool, a pipe, a bag of charms, a round black pot, some arrowheads, a jar of painted sand, a necklace of colored beads.

The last thing in the Cowboy Hall of Fame was this year's statue: and the last year I went there I got upset because this year's cowboy was just a cowboy singer and I wondered if he was really a true cowboy at all.

My first horse was a broom that I named Trigger. At first

Trigger lived in the kitchen pantry where my mother kept her cleaning things, but then when Trigger became Trigger she moved into my bedroom. Sometimes my mother would borrow her, and when Trigger came back she'd have bits of cat hairs and tiny specks of wilted lettuce in her tail. So I'd brush her tail out and pat her neck. My brother attached long stringy reins to the metal hook that was Trigger's mouth. I rode Trigger all round the house. You could always hear me coming from my upstairs room because Trigger's tail always thumped the stairs on the way down. Sometimes I rode her so fast my hat would fall off and thank goodness it caught at the string around my neck. Whenever I needed to stop at the saloon for a snack I'd tie Trigger to the kitchen table. And if no one was there I'd rustle up my own vittles, but if my mother was there she'd ask me, "What'll it be today, pardner, the usual?" and I'd say, "Yup," and then she'd find me cookies or twinkies or a piece of fruit. "How's Trigger today?" she'd ask, and I'd say, "Oh, just fine," and I'd tell her stories about the caves and plains and woods I'd ridden through that day, the Indians and outlaws I had met and saved her from or won over to our side.

The whole day's still. It's hot high noon; the sky's so blue it's white. But now I notice almost none of this. It's only in my memory that I will watch the sky get waved with heat, or see the fine dust film that mutes the color of the cacti, the curled-up snake that's sunning on the rock.

Because Annie and I are riding. We're tearing through the desert on an urgent, crucial errand. I don't know where we're going. We break the stillness. Somehow I feel that this is a violation. The hooves of both our horses pound. They run in rhythm, side by side, and we travel in one huge cloud of dust. I can hear the gentle slap of our night packs on the horses' backs. I turn around from time to time to check and see my bundle's still intact, but Annie's tied it tightly. I grip one hand tight on the reins and clutch the saddle horn with the other. The reins relax in

Annie's hands. She never kicks or slaps at Cowgirl. She can say most anything with a movement of her body or a click of her tongue; she moves forward, left or right, and Cowgirl knows. She grips her horse close with her thighs.

Beside me, Annie leans forward. Her braids stand out behind her. Her jacket billows up. "Annie!" I shout across to her, tightening my grip on the saddle horn, "Annie!", but she can't hear me above the pounding hooves. We move so fast the dry air hits me like a fan. Only it's hot, not cool. And I think I'm beginning to feel burned from the sun. It's a healthy feeling, but I wonder if I've remembered to bring my sunglasses and Coppertone. The sun glints on her stirrup next to me and it flashes at me every time I look at her. I start coughing from the dust. I lift the loose bandanna around my neck and cover my mouth and nose to keep the dust out. The cloth smells dusty and I know that in just seconds I'll be uncomfortable from the moisture of my sweat and breath. I must hear something from her because when I turn she's already looking at me. She says something. I yell that I can't hear her then I point to my ear and shake my head, "no". I can see her laugh and nod. Then she points to her nose and chin, not covered by bandanna, then to me. And then she draws her pistol with a flick of her strong wrist. She stretches her arm into the sky and fires and fires again. She shakes her head with pleasure and points her face up to the sky and shouts a long "Hooooooo-eeeee!" of happiness. Her knees press Cowgirl and she races off ahead of me like I was standing still. She disappears in a cloud of dust. The only thing she leaves me with is the tail end of the whoop of joy behind her.

Annie tries to teach me how to cook above an open flame. She tries to teach me flapjacks, bacon, grits. The bottom half of everything burns and the top half is always raw. I burn my palm trying to grab the hot black handle and dump grease and batter into the fire. She tries to teach me to toast bread on a stick; the bread falls in the flames. I burn the coffee and scorch the beans.

She doesn't even use tin foil. I want to tell her about adjustable-flame gas burners, but I don't want to sound like I'm whining. She mixes things without a book. The only seasoning she'll use is salt. I think of woks and cuisinarts and frozen vegetables. She brushes her teeth with baking soda. I sneak behind the wagon and press mint-flavored Crest on to my toothbrush. She's never tasted mint before. I don't want to confess.

I'm thrilled. We're in a stage coach. I'm wearing gloves and button boots and a long-sleeved dress with lace around the sleeves and high neck collar. I have a hat and veil on. "Now jest who yew tryin' t' keep outta there anyhow, honey?" she asks and laughs out loud, then slaps her ungloved hands against her knees. "Jeee-umpin' Jehosefat!" she nearly shouts and looks out the window beside her. "Looks all little bitty when y' got a winda' 'round it." She leans out the window and shouts at the scout who rides his horse beside us. "How's thangs out there, Willy?"

"Jest fahn, Annie."

"Well, I tell yew," she hollers back, "it shore looks dif'ernt from in here, Willy-boy!"

"Now doncha fret there, Annie, ain't nobody gonna pull nothin' over on y'!"

She smiles back and keeps staring out the window until gradually her lips are straight. She leans her elbow out the window ledge and puts her chin in her hand. I watch her quiet profile against the landscape moving fast and flat behind her. She's always ridden on horseback outside the coach before. The brim of her hat casts a shadow down most of her face. She's wearing her fancy skirt and fancy jacket and a bright pink shirt I bought for her when I bought my dress and boots. On the shelf above her, our two suitcases; her beat-up leather bag with the rounded, well-scratched metal corners, and my ladies' light, sky-blue American Tourister.

I find a lacy handkerchief in the beaded bag beside me and

gently dab at my neck and upper lip and forehead.

Then I pull out my embroidery and try to teach her how to stitch.

Tonight I undo Annie's braids. She sits facing the boudoir mirror in our hotel room, in what is now a ghost town in Nevada. I sit behind her working on her hair. She's tied the bottom of the braids with leather. The braids are tight and smooth and gold with sun. I undo one and then the other, untying them at the bottom and separating the three even groups of hair in each. Then I shake them evenly and brush her hair out straight and all together. Her hair is wavy from the constant braids but I can tell it's naturally straight. I brush firmly, starting at the very top of her part and continuing down in strong hard strokes the whole length of her hair. I brush the sides above her temples and underneath the back of her head. Her hair parts naturally in the middle and back. I expect it to be coarse, but it feels like a baby's.

I brush and brush until her hair is smooth and soft as silk, and shiny. It looks like still gold water. Then I look up at the mirror to catch her eye and ask her what she thinks. But her eyes are closed. She's sitting up straight, asleep. I study her face and notice something missing that I'd come to believe was always there. It's something she can't tell me.

But Annie prefers the open range to hotel life. She likes to sleep in whistling distance of Cowgirl. "Thangs weren't always lahk this now," she tells me. And it's hard for her to break the habits that she made when things weren't tame.

I've stopped telling her to relax, to let other people care for Cowgirl, to cook her meals, and wash her things behind her. I think perhaps her work *is* her true pleasure.

I started riding lessons when I was five. In the family album there's a picture of me, tiny and blonde, my light blue glasses with the pointy frames slipped down to the end of my nose. I'm sitting on a huge brown horse. My feet reach way above the middle of the horse's back. My head doesn't reach as tall as the horse's. I remember my seriousness in posing for this photo. I refused to wave or smile because I didn't want it to look like a game. I wanted it to look like this was something I did every day, quiet and serious.

The horses I rode had these names: Penny, Marshal, Slim, and Little Bit. Blackie, Kit, Friskie, Nick. Old Tom, Old Paint, Old Gray, Brandy. Roger, Ho-boy, Loosa, Beaut, Carson, Big Boy, May.

I'm given priority seating at the Wild West Show. I sit between a railroad tycoon and a meat packer from Chicago. The only other women there are wives or gentlemen's companions. I'm wearing a plastic photo ID on my blouse. I assume that this allows me access, along with the other VIPs and invited guests, to the private quarters and refreshment rooms. But oddly enough, I'm the only one with a tag. And even more oddly, no one seems to notice that I've got one. I watch for Annie through a pair of opera glasses. Of course she is the star. She introduces all the acts and takes care of people before they hit the ring. And I know, though we don't see this, that she also acts as everybody's friend, encouraging, counseling, helping out. The people around me in the box discuss the show with terms like "quaint" and "rugged". I hear myself tittering with them at their urban jokes and holding my teacup with my little finger extended. When Annie races out of the waiting stall and charges into the ring, six-gun firing, I hear the whole crowd gasp and clap and cheer. The people in the booth I'm in clap evenly and nod to one another and say, "charming", "lovely", "marvelous." After the show, when the others in the box tell me of their oil deals in Texas, their railroads in Ohio and their newest warehouse in the city, they ask me, roundaboutly, how I'm with them in the box. I nod and tell them, "I am an acquaintance of Miss Oakley."

This time when I come back, I bring her a present. Annie unwraps the boxes and laughs at the paper with the flapper-girl designs. When she first pulls out her newly laundered fancy skirt and jacket, she doesn't recognize them, then she does. "Well, land o' goshen, honey, what the dad burn'd yew do t' these thangs?"

"I had them dry-cleaned, Annie."

She looks at me and nods with that tentative nod you give when you feel like you should say, "yes", but you don't really know quite why.

"And weather-proofed," I add proudly.

She looks at me and squints.

"Feel that?" I take her hand and rub it over the newly treated leather. "That'll protect it from the rain and keep it stronger."

"Uh-huh," she says, her face still puzzled. She brings the jacket to her face, looks at it closely, sniffs it.

"Never needed it before," she says.

I nod, "I know, but this is better."

Annie takes the skirt and jacket and the three special blouses from the box. She gingerly places them out flat on the table and looks them over again. "Hmmm-mm," she mutters.

The ladies at the dry-cleaner had been impressed. They'd ooh-ed and aah-ed at the leather and fine hand work. I'd told them they'd been in the family for many years and asked them to be extra careful. I'd hoped Annie would be pleased they looked like new. I was.

This night when I wake up it's not a nightmare; it's a storm. When my eyes spring open I see Annie sitting by the bed, polishing her boots in the dim light of the oil lamp. When I sit up, she looks at me and I ask, "What are you doing? Why are you awake?" The canvas cover of the wagon heaves with blowing air. Lightning cracks and thunder interrupts her voice.

"I thought y' might wake up and git afeared, so I thought I'd be here in case y' did."

I look at her and I don't know what to say.

She looks away from me then tries to sound buoyant and matter-of-fact, "Besides, I hadda polish these dang thangs."

I pretend that I accept all this for what it is and think nothing more. I close my eyes as if I were asleep and listen to her breathe, and the swish and buff of her hands at work beneath the sound of rain.

We're out in the open and it's almost fall. I try to read in the changing light of the open fire. The only sounds are the crack of flame and the soft wet sound of Kid and Cowgirl chewing, then the sound of Annie's boots walking back from checking on the horses. Her boots scrape across the rough dry ground.

"Nice night," I say as she returns to the fire and stretches her hands to the warmth.

She nods and looks into the flame, but I don't think she's looking at anything.

"How's Kid and Cowgirl?"

"Oh, fahn . . ." She nods. Her voice is tired. I watch her as she sits down by the light. She stoops, puts her hands on her thighs, then on the ground beside her. She exhales as she finally sits then breathes in loud. She brushes back the hair that's fallen in her face then rubs her eyes. She pulls her hand down over her whole face, stretching her cheeks, then she rubs the back of her neck and twists her head. Her eyes are closed and I can't tell if it's the shadow of flame or if it really is bags under her eyes, and wrinkles at the outer edges. And I tell myself that now I will tell her and I say very softly, "Annie?" But Annie doesn't hear me.

There's a feeling you get when you're away and you think, "If only I was there . . . if only I was with . . . " and you look forward to it and you save up things for when you are. You think,

"If I was there, if I was with . . . then I'd say this and this . . ."
But then you are there, truly and at last, and you think, "This is
what I wanted. This is when I can say those things . . ." but
something happens and you can't or don't say them. Then you
tell yourself that things aren't what you hoped they would be.
You still can't speak and now you wonder if you'd have been
better off never to have learned this other meaning of "alone". If
it would have been better always to have been able to look
forward, or back, and think, "If only . . . when . . ."

But I don't not miss her when I go: I do.

The next time I come back I tell her, "Annie, I want you to
come with me. This time. When I go away."

Annie looks straight at me, smiles, tells me, "OK, pardner."

My favorite show was *Have Gun Will Travel*. The second was
Gunsmoke, then *Bonanza*, and *Batt Masterson*. Next, *The
Rifleman*. You knew what day of the week it was by who you'd
get to watch. And the next day the playground buzzed with
recaps. We talked about everything, debated points of character,
how things could have turned out, "if only . . ." We tried to top
each other by saying how early on we knew just who'd done it
and how it was going to end. We guessed about the fate of future
episodes. We screened our own scenarios and we fantasized a
meeting of all the greats together—all of them—Batt Masterson,
Matt Dillon, Palladin, the entire Cartwright family. I wanted to
be there. I started all these talks.

"Tarnation, honey, I never saw a damn thang lahk it." Annie's
standing on the balcony of my thirty-second floor apartment
suite in Manhattan. She's looking out at the city. I push aside
clothes in my closet to make room for her things.

Annie and I walk the city for weeks. Some parts of it she'll recognize, or tell me what used to be at this address. She reminisces about performing in the Wild West Show with Buffalo Bill at Madison Square Garden. She can't believe how the city's grown, how many cars and lights, the height of buildings, noise and speed of everything. She loves the accents that she hears in delis, clothes stores, on street corners. But her favorite things are movies.

The first Western I take her to see is *High Noon*. We have a great time and start haunting old movie houses and taking in all the Westerns. Pretty soon, that's all we do. We see *Shane, The Great Train Robbery, The Gunfighter, Gunfight at the OK Corral, The Covered Wagon, Man With a Gun*. At first she laughs at them, she can't believe we take them seriously. But after a while she's fascinated. We have to see one every night. Every night when we hit a theater, Annie dresses in her cowgirl best and I in something chic and new. And though sometimes we get glances, this is the city and people don't look twice.

After a while she gets restless during the day. The city is too crowded and fast and loud for her. We buy a video-cassette machine so she can always have a Western on hand.

I start to get concerned. Is she unhappy? I throw a huge party and invite all the nicest and most interesting people I know. This is the first night we don't go see a Western. I hope that she'll be happy. The night goes beautifully. My friends all think she's great and we have fun. Annie tells stories of her growing up, her early career, the nation's adolescence. Everyone's entertained. "Oh, Annie," they say, "you should write a book." And everyone thinks her clothes are just right and ask her where she found them.

Late that night we start a hand of cards. I urge Annie to challenge everyone to poker and she does. While I refill my guests' daiquiris, Bloody Marys and Perrier-and-limes, Annie measures out her own shots of whiskey. They all lose to her and love it. At the end of the night they owe her millions, but Annie says, "Y'all have ardy paid me mor'n enuf in kahndness."

Early that morning when the last guest is gone, and Annie and

I are emptying ashtrays and wiping up spilled booze and dip, I thank her and tell her that this is the best party I've ever given. I say, "I haven't had this much fun since I was a kid." I tell her and she smiles. "They loved you, Annie," I nearly shout.

"Well, yer frinds'r most obligin'."

"Come on, Annie," I insist, "it's *you*. You're the greatest. There's something about you. It's ... everybody loves it ..."

"Yer ver' ver' kahnd."

Annie kneels over a spot in the carpet trying to pick out bits of crushed up macadamia nut. I look at the bottoms of her boots then up at her cowgirl hat. I step over to her, take the hat off her head and put it on mine as I flop down on the couch beside her.

"Hey, Annie, do you like it here?"

She continues what she's doing. "Yup. Enuf—"

"Come on, Annie, what do you really think of this—well, all of this—?" I sweep my arms out wide though she's not watching me.

And when she answers me she's still looking at the floor. "Well, I think ..." she hesitates, "yer here ..." she hesitates even longer, "so I lahk it."

I'm so busy with my train of thought I almost miss her meaning. In fact, part of me tries to miss her meaning, but the part that doesn't imagines itself kneeling down with her and touching her, holding her in its arms. And the other part hastens away from that, pretends that things never mean anything more than they seem to. And this part stays frozen, seated, nervously pats Annie's hat down tighter on my head and tells her:

"Annie, ol' girl, I think you're gonna be a hit."

And when Annie looks up at me from her chore, I put my index finger to my lips, look out the window at the city getting pink with light, and say, before the one part of me tells the other part to change its mind, "Yeah, I think you could be *very, very* big."

I try to explain the finer points to her. But she's never even heard of most of these things. "A self-fulfilling prophecy is when you say something and just the act of saying it is magic; it makes it happen. Foreshadowing and symbols are names you give to things in art, but they happen in life as well. Are you listening, Annie? Sometimes I look at you when we're happiest and that's when they come on me and I wish we weren't happy. Because once you have something, you want it. And you still keep on wanting it when you can't have it." Her face is curious and calm and puzzled. She genuinely doesn't hear me.

I tell her, "Dear Annie, one day we'll wish none of this had happened. There's a price you pay for having what you want. You pay with the wanting that stays on after you stop having. You can want everything, but you can't *have* everything."

I explain these things to her when she's asleep. I tell myself I'm practising and when I finally get it right, then I'll tell her straight, outloud.

Your first lessons you have to ride around a ring. They teach you how to walk and trot and canter. You have to do everything with everyone and that is no adventure. I always wanted to be let out on my own and ride free through the woods that started just fifty yards or so from the lesson corral. I'd never been in there but I saw where the trail went in and then you couldn't see any more. I saw people ride in there sometimes. Older people, people that worked there who always wore boots and hats. I wanted to go into those woods by myself and ride and ride and ride. One lesson I brought a canteen and a sandwich in my brother's boy-scout bag and wore them on my belt because that day, I swore to myself, when the teacher wasn't looking, I would go. I'd gallop to the woods and follow that path as far as it went and then go further. I'd ride and ride and ride. I'd spend the night in the woods and live off nuts and berries. I'd drink water from streams and tie my horse to a tree and sleep by a dying fire. Then I'd meet up with some cowboys and they'd show me how to get to the open plains and I'd go and find a cowtown and then I would visit there, and then go from cowtown to cowtown, meeting people and living like a cowgirl.

Annie's signing autographs at Saks. We've timed it so the release of her authorized biography coincides with the arrival of the special line of new fall fashions—Annie Oakley Western Wear. Annie sits on the ladies' side-saddle which they've rigged up on a chair and chats with customers and buyers. Saks fashion models dressed in cowgirl Western wear scurry in the crowd around her. They smile a lot and offer free champagne and hors-d'oeuvres, and turn to show the catchy lines their outfits cut. They all wear hats and underneath their hats their hair is permed or streaked or blowdried. They make sure each buyer gets the right amount of time to say hello to Annie, joke with her, buy her book, and then they subtly, persuasively, draw people away to buy some Western clothes. Annie laughs and sometimes she does a quick-draw show or spins a tight, fast lasso. The whole crowd loves her, listens rapt to her stories about the range, six shooters, the setting sun. Clearly she is a hit. They laugh at every joke she tells and sigh at every story. When they say things to her they sound sincere and grateful and loving. She is their heroine. They're all in love with her.

I stand apart, sipping my champagne by the escalator. I keep one eye on everything around her, while I pretend to enjoy the chit-chat with the customers. When it gets near time to close the crowd thins out, the "cowgirls" begin to go back to their rooms and change. Annie's pretty much left alone. I duck into the ladies' room and then when I return I see her talking to one of the workers undoing the display. They're laughing with each other and Annie's face is live with animation. I stand still and watch her tell her story for some minutes, then when the story gets too long I walk over and tell her briskly, "You don't have to do this anymore. You've put in your time."

Annie's face falls. The worker snaps back to the job.

That evening in our hotel suite after our bags are packed for our
night flight to L.A. we start to dress for dinner. *High Noon* plays
on the VCR. We aren't watching it but we don't dare turn it off
and listen to the silence. Annie's pulling on her boot and I'm
holding her pair of spurs when I say, "All right, Oakley, spill it."

She stops, her leg outstretched, the boot poised at an angle in
the air. She looks at me and doesn't say anything. I step over to
the tube and turn the volume all the way down.

"Go on," I start into her, "tell me how much you love having
all those good clean folks ooh-ing and aah-ing over you. Tell me
about that precious little janitor sighing up at you. Christ."

And then I clasp my free hand over my heart and say in my
best fake sweet starstruck voice, "She's even more wonderful
than I imagined. Oh gosh, oh gee. She's so—so—good." I stare
up toward the ceiling mocking the romanticism of the people I'd
seen that day. I stand still a second then I fling my hands out like
I'm trying to strike at something. "Jesus Christ, you made me
sick today. I mean it. You're something else. You really are
something goddamn else." I pause. "But hell, what am I being
upset about?" I shrug my shoulders and smile my sweetest smile.
"You're only giving them what they want." Then I raise my
voice in imitation again. "Gosh, were things really like that? Gee,
Annie, you're a dream come true. Boy, Annie. I feel like I can
really talk to you." I catch my breath and clench my free hand
into a fist. I walk to one end of the room then back, tossing the
spurs back and forth from one hand to the other. Then I turn and
face her directly and look at her a second, and I try to make my
voice sound calm and very matter-of-fact but I can't, and I say
with all the spite I can, "You fucking whore."

Annie's eyes widen and her mouth opens slightly with sadness
and surprise. She looks like she's about to cry. I feel horrible and
know I'm wrong and I want to take back everything but I'm too
afraid and proud to change my mind so I raise my voice and spit
out at her, "But what did I expect? You're Annie Fucking
Oakley. Annie Fucking Jesus Oakley. You only give them what
they want—"

Then Annie interrupts me. It's the only time she ever interrupts me in her life when she says, "Yew said yew wanted them to lahk me. Yew said I should be lahk that. Yew said that's why *yew* lahked me."

Then she's quiet and then she says, "I only did this fer yew."

I don't know what to say to her. I look back at the movie and watch Gary Cooper mime a passionate appeal to my patriotism. I walk over to the set and turn the volume up full blast and look at Annie, knowing we won't shout above the movie.

On my way out the door I remember the spurs and spin round and hurl them at the set. I slam the door and hurry away before I can hear anything else.

I leave a message at the desk for them to call for Annie when the limo arrives and to tell her that I'll meet her at the airport.

I walk uptown but I don't go in any bars. I do pass one I stop and glance at. The name of it's "The Dude Ranch". And three blocks further on I see "The Bucking Bronc", but I try to walk past without even giving it a second look. I see a couple in cowboy hats and try to see if they're really from out West or just New Yorkers trying to be chic.

I try to remember how long those bars have been here.

Annie's drinking a strawberry daiquiri in the airport bar when I find her. Just as I walk up to her I hear our flight announced. We're going to Los Angeles. I throw a twenty on the table and help her stand. And then I see she's crying. "There, there," I say as I help her up, pretending it's just the departure that's made her cry.

In the first-class compartment Annie orders daiquiri after daiquiri. She experiments with different flavors—banana, peach, lime. I don't know whether to pray that they do show a

Western, or to pray that they don't. We're on our way to Hollywood to negotiate the rights to her biography. She's never been drunk before.

"I'z afraid yew wudn't be comin' back." It's the first word she's said to me since I found her in the bar.

"I told the clerk I'd meet you at the airport."

"But I didn't know if yew meant it. All the stuff y' always used t' tell me 'bout leavin'. I wuz jest tryin' t' figure it out."

I close my eyes and remember, with shame, things I'd tried to tell her, but I can't remember anything clearly, just vague words and unconnected thoughts—something about self-fulfilling prophecy, trying to sound mysterious and tragic, foreshadowing, the seed of doubt. I flinch when I think of what I've cooked up and fed to her.

Her eyes are closed beneath her hat which tips awkwardly over her face. I take her hat off and put it in the cabinet above us. Then I smooth her hair down and hold her hands and look at them. I wipe her face and hold the tissue as she blows her nose. I feed her her lime daiquiri.

"Annie?" I whisper, "Annie? Annie?" I don't know what else to say.

She's mumbling things I can barely make out. I wave away the stewardess who offers us the movie earphones. Then I think that I hear Annie say, "I don't belong . . . I miss the gang . . . cain't we go back? . . . please, cain't we go back? . . ." I wipe the moisture off her face then hold both her hands in mine. Annie sleeps. I don't think of anything and then the lights go dim and the cabin screen gets light and I see the camera pan across the great vast open plains, a classic Western sunset. Just as the cowboys start across the screen, I close my eyes and thank God that I can't hear the sound track. The cabin air feels cold and dry. I can hear the chilled air coming in. And then I know that I will send her back. And I'll awake alone in California.

But I don't know when in the night she'll go. So I don't know if this is a dream I have or something I see that happens when she goes back:

Annie's riding Cowgirl. They're tearing through the desert with a leather pouch for the Pony Express. Her just-cleaned jacket gets blown with dust. Annie's getting winded. The sun is hurting her eyes. Her hand that grips the saddle horn lets up and she pats all her pockets, searching for what I can only guess must be her sunglasses. Her body jerks up and down on Cowgirl. There's nothing smooth or graceful between them.

And though I know she can't remember me, I wonder if she does because the look on her face is a mixture that's strange—a thing poised taut between a type of fear, and boredom, and something not at all unlike nostalgia.

Some of These Days

What my landlord's friends said about me was in a way the gospel truth, that is he was good to me, and I was mean and ungrateful to him. All the two years I was in jail, nonetheless, I thought only of him, and I was filled with regret for the things I had done against him. I wanted him back. I didn't exactly wish to go back to live with him now, mind you, I had been too mean to him for that, but I wanted him for a friend again. After I got out of jail I would need friendship, for I didn't need to hold up even one hand to count my friends on, the only one I could even name was him. I didn't want anything to do with him physically again, I had kind of grown out of that somehow even more while in jail, and wished to try to make it with women again, but I did require my landlord's love and affection, for love was, as everybody was always saying, his special gift and talent.

He was at the time I lived with him a rather well-known singer, and he also composed songs, but even when I got into my bad trouble, he was beginning to go downhill, and not to be so in fashion. We often quarrelled over his not succeeding way back then. Once I hit him when he told me how much he loved me, and knocked out one of his front teeth. But that was only after he had also criticized me for not keeping the apartment tidy and clean and doing the dishes, and I threatened him with an old gun I kept. Of course I felt awful about his losing this front tooth when he needed good teeth for singing. I asked his forgiveness. We made up and I let him kiss me and hold me tight just for this one time.

I remember his white face and sad eyes at my trial for breaking and entering and possession of a dangerous weapon, and at last his tears when the judge sentenced me. My landlord could cry and not be ashamed of crying, and so you didn't mind him shedding tears somehow. At first, then, he wrote me, for as the only person who could list himself as nearest of kin or closest tie, he was allowed by the authorities to communicate with me, and I also received little gifts from him from time to time. And then all upon a sudden the presents stopped, and shortly after that, the letters too, and then there was no word of any kind, just nothing. I realized then that I had this strong feeling for him which I had never had for anybody before, for my people had been dead from the time almost I was a toddler, and so they are shadowy and dim, whilst he is bright and clear. That is, you see, I had to admit to myself in jail (and I choked on my admission), but I had hit bottom, and could say a lot of things now to myself, I guess I was in love with him. I had really only loved women I had always told myself, and I did not love this man so much physically, in fact he sort of made me sick to my stomach to think of him that way, though he was a good-looker with his neat black straight hair, and his robin's-egg blue eyes, and cheery smile . . . And so there in my cell I had to confess what did I have for him if it was not love, and yet I had treated him meaner than anybody I had ever knowed in my life, and once come close to killing him. Thinking about him all the time now, for who else was there to think about, I found I got to talking to myself more and more like an old geezer of advanced years, and in place of calling on anyone else or any higher power, since he was the only one I had ever met in my twenty years of life who said he cared, I would find myself saying like in church, *My landlord*, though that term for him was just a joke for the both of us, for all he had was this one-room flat with two beds, and my bed was the little one, no more than a cot, and I never made enough to pay him no rent for it, he just said he would trust me. So there in my cell, especially at night, I would say *My landlord*, and finally, for my chest began to trouble me about this time and I was short of breath often, I would just manage to get out *My lord*. That's what I would call him for short. When I got out, the first thing I made up my mind to do was find him, and I was going to put all my efforts behind the search.

And when there was no mail now at all, I would think over all the kind and good things he done for me, and the thought would come to me which was blacker than any punishment they had given me here in the big house that I had not paid him back for his good deeds. When I got out I would make it up to him. He had took me in off the street, as people say, and had tried to make a man of me, or at least a somebody out of me, and I had paid him back all in bad coin, first by threatening to kill him, and then by going bad and getting sent to jail . . . But when I get out, I said, I will find him if I have to walk from one ocean shore to the other.

And so it did come about that way, for once out, that is all I did or found it in my heart to do, find the one who had tried to set me straight, find the one who had done for me, and shared and all.

One night after I got out of jail, I had got dead drunk and stopped a guy on Twelfth Street, and spoke, *Have you seen my lord?* This man motioned me to follow him into a dark little theater, which later I was to know all too well as one of the porno theaters, he paid for me, and brought me to a dim corner in the back, and then the same old thing started up again, he beginning to undo my clothes, and lower his head, and I jumped up and pushed him and ran out of the movie, but then stopped and looked back and waited there as it begin to give me an idea.

Now a terrible thing had happened to me in jail. I was beat on the head by another prisoner, and I lost some of the use of my right eye, so that I am always straining by pushing my neck around as if to try to see better, and when the convict hit me that day and I was unconscious for several weeks and they despaired of my life, later on when I came to myself at last, I could remember everything that had ever happened in my whole twenty years of life except my landlord's name, and I couldn't think of it if I was to be alive. That is why I have been in the kind of difficulty I have been in. It is the hardest thing in the world to hunt for somebody if you don't know his name.

I finally though got the idea to go back to the big building where he and I had lived together, but the building seemed to be under new management, with new super, new tenants, new everybody. Nobody anyhow remembered any singer, they said, nor any composer, and then after a time, it must have been though six months from the day I returned to New York, I realized that I had gone maybe to a building that just looked like the old building my landlord and I have lived in, and so I tore like a blue streak straightaway to this "correct" building to find out if any such person as him was living there, but as I walked around through the halls looking, I become somewhat confused all over again if this was the place either, for I had wanted so bad to find the old building where he and I had lived, I had maybe been overconfident of this one also being the correct place, and so as I walked the halls looking and peering about I became puzzled and unsure all over again, and after a few more turns, I give up and left.

That was a awesome fall, and then winter coming on and all, and no word from him, no trace, and then I remembered a thing from the day that man had beckoned me to come follow him into that theater, and I remembered something, I remembered that on account of my landlord being a gay or queer man, one of his few pleasures when he got an extra dollar was going to the porno movies in Third Avenue. My remembering this was like a light from heaven, if you can think of heaven throwing light on such a thing, for suddenly I knowed for sure that if I went to the porno movie I would find him.

The only drawback for me was these movies was somewhat expensive by now, for since I been in jail prices have surely marched upwards, and I have very little even to keep me in necessities. This was the beginning of me seriously begging, and sometimes I would be holding out my hand on the street for three-fourths of a day before I got me enough to pay my way into the porno theater. I would put down my three bucks, and enter the turnstile, and then inside wait until my eyes got used to the dark, which because of my prison illness took nearly all of ten minutes, and then I would go up to each aisle looking for my landlord. There was not a face I didn't examine carefully. My interest in the spectators earned me several bawlings-out from the manager of the theater, who took me for somebody out to proposition the customers, but I paid him no mind ... But his fussing with me gave me an idea, too, for I am attractive to men, both young and old, me being not yet twenty-one, and so I began what was to become regular practice, letting the audience take any liberty they was in a mind to with me in the hopes that through this contact they would divulge the whereabouts of my landlord.

But here again my problem would surface, for I could not recall the very name of the person who was most dear to me, yes that was the real sore spot. But as the men in the movie theater took their liberties with me, which after a time I got sort of almost to enjoy, even though I could barely see their faces, only see enough to know they was not my landlord, I would then, I say, describe him in full to them, and I will give them this much credit, they kind of listened to me as they went about getting their kicks from me, they would bend an ear to my asking for this information, but in the end they never heard of him nor any other singer, and never knowed a man who wrote down notes for a living.

But strange as it might seem to anybody who will ever see these sheets of paper, this came to be my only connection with the world, my only life—sitting in the porno theater. Since my only purpose was to find him and from him find my own way back, this was the only thoroughfare there was open for me to reach him. And yet I did not like it, though at the same time even disliking it as much as I did, it give me some little feeling of a resemblance to warmth and kindness as the unknown men touched me with their invisible faces and extracted from me all I had to offer, such as it was. And then when they had finished me, I would ask them if they knew my landlord (or as I whispered to myself, my lord). But none ever did.

Winter had come in earnest, was raw in the air. The last of the leaves in the park had long blown out to sea, and yet it was not to be thought of giving up the search and going to a warmer place. I would go on here until I had found him or I would know the reason why, yes, I must find him, and not give up. (I tried to keep the phrase *My lord* only for myself, for once or twice when it had slipped out to a stranger, it give him a start, and so I watched what I said from there on out.)

And then I was getting down to the last of the little money I had come out of jail with, and oh the porno theaters was so dear, the admission was hiked another dollar just out of the blue, and the leads I got in that old dark hole was so few and far between. Toward the end one man sort of perked up when I mentioned my landlord the singer, and said he thought he might have known such a fellow, but with no name to go on, he too soon give up, and said he guessed he didn't know after all.

And so I was stumped. Was I to go on patronizing the porno theater, I would have to give up food, for my panhandling did not bring in enough for both grub and movies, and yet there was something about bein' in that house, getting the warmth and attention from the stray men that meant more to me than food and drink. So I began to go without eating in earnest so as to keep up my regular attendance at the films. That was maybe, looking back on it now, a bad mistake, but what is one bad mistake in a lifetime of them.

As I did not eat now but only give my favors to the men in the porno, I grew pretty unsteady on my feet. After a while I could barely drag to the theater. Yet it was the only place I wanted to be, especially in view of its now being full winter. But my worst fears was now realized, for I could not longer afford even the cheap lodging place I had been staying at, and all I had in the world was what was on my back, and the little in my pockets, so I had come at last to this, yet I did not think about my plight so much as about him, for as I got weaker and weaker he seemed to stand over me as large as the figures of the film actors that raced across the screen, and at which I almost never looked, come to think of it. No, I never watched what went on on the screen itself. I watched the audience, for it was the living that would be able to give me the word.

"Oh come to me, come back and set me right!" I would whisper hoping someone out of the audience might rise and tell me they knew where he was.

Then at last, but of course slow gradual-like, I no longer left the theater. I was too weak to go out, anyhow had no lodging now to call mine, knew if I got as far as a step beyond the entrance door of the theater, I would never get back inside to its warmth, and me still dressed in my summer clothes.

Then after a long drowsy time—days, weeks, who knows? —my worse than worst fears was realized, for one, shall I say day?—for where I was now there was no day or night, and the theater never closed its doors—one time, then, I say, they *come* for me, they had been studying my condition, they told me later and they come to take me away. I begged them with all the strength I had left not to do so, that I could still walk, that I would be gone and never bother nobody again.

When did you last sit down to a bite to eat? A man spoke this direct into my ear, a man by whose kind of voice I knew did not belong to the porno world, but come from some outside authority.

I have lost all tract of time, I replied, closing my eyes.

All right buddy, the man kept saying, and *Now, bud*, and then as I fought and kicked, they held me and put the strait-jacket on me, though didn't they see I was too weak and dispirited to hurt one cruddy man jack of them.

Then as they were taking me finally away, for the first time in months, I raised my voice, as if to the whole city, and called, and shouted, and explained: "*Tell him if he comes, how long I have waited and searched, that I have been hunting for him, and I cannot remember his name. I was hit in prison by another convict and the injury was small, but it destroyed my one needed memory, which is his name. That is all that is wrong with me. If you would cure me of this one little defect, I will never bother any of you again, never bother society again. I will go back to work and make a man of myself, but I have first to thank this former landlord for all he done for me."*

He is hovering between life and death.

I repeated aloud the word *hovering* after the man who had pronounced this sentence somewhere in the vicinity of where I was lying in a bed that smelled strong of carbolic acid.

And as I said the word *hovering*, I knew his name. I raised up. Yes, my landlord's name had come back to me . . . It had come back after all the wreck and ruin of these weeks and years.

But then one sorrow would follow upon another, as I believe my mother used to say, though that is so long ago I can't believe I had a mother, for when they saw that I was conscious and in my right mind, they come to me and begun asking questions, especially *What was my name.* I stared at them with the greatest puzzlement and sadness, for though I had fished up his name from so far down, I could no more remember my own name now when they asked me for it than I could have got out of my strait-jacket and run a race, and I was holding on to the just-found landlord's name, with the greatest difficulty, for it, too, was beginning to slip from my tongue and go disappear where it had been lost before.

As I hesitated, they begun to persecute me with their kindness, telling me how they would help me in my plight, but first of all they must have my name, and since they needed a name so bad, and was so insistent, and I could see their kindness beginning to go, and the cruelty I had known in jail coming fresh to mind, I said, "I am Sidney Fuller," giving them you see my landlord's name.

"And your age, Sidney?"

"Twenty, come next June."

"And how did you earn your living."

"I have been without work now for some months."

"What kind of work do you do?"

"Hard labor."

"When were you last employed?"

"In prison."

There was a silence, and the papers was moved about, then: "Do you have a church or faith?"

I waited quite a while, repeating his name, and remembering I could not remember my own, and then said, "I am of the same faith as my landlord."

There was an even longer silence then, like the questioner had been cut down by his own enquiry, anyhow they did not interrogate me any more after that, they went away, and left me by myself.

After a long time, certainly days, maybe weeks, they announced the doctor was coming.

He sat down on a sort of ice-cream chair beside me, and took off his glasses and wiped them. I barely saw his face.

"Sidney," he began after it sounded like he had started to say something else first, and then changed his mind. "Sidney, I have some very serious news to impart to you, and I want you to try to be brave. It is hard for me to say what I am going to say. I will tell you what we have discovered. I want you, though, first, to swallow this tablet, and we will wait together for a few minutes, and then I will tell you."

I had swallowed the tablet it seemed a long time ago, and then all of a sudden I looked down at myself, and I saw I was not in the strait-jacket, my arms was free.

"Was I bad, doctor?" I said, and he seemed to be glad I had broke the ice, I guess.

"I believe, Sidney, that you know in part what I am going to say to you," he started up again. He was a dark man, I saw now, with thick eyebrows, and strange, I thought, that for a doctor he seemed to have no wrinkles, his face was smooth as a sheet.

"We have done all we could to save you, you must believe us," he was going on as I struggled to hear his words through the growing drowsiness given me by the tablet. "You have a sickness, Sidney, for which unfortunately there is today no cure . . ."

He said more, but I do not remember what, and was glad when he left, no, amend that, I was sad I guess when he left. Still, it didn't matter one way or another if anybody stayed or lit out.

But after a while, when I was a little less drowsy, a new man come in, with some white papers under his arm.

"You told us earlier when you were first admitted," he was saying, "that your immediate family is all dead . . . Is there nobody to whom you wish to leave any word at all . . .? If there is such a person, we would appreciate your writing the name and address on each of these four sheets of paper, and add any instructions which you care to detail."

At that moment, I remembered my own name, as easily as if it had written on the paper before me, and the sounds of it placed in my mouth and on my tongue, and since I could not give my landlord's name again and as the someone to whom I could bequeath my all, I give the enquirer with the paper my own real name:

James De Salles

"And his address?" the enquirer said.

I shook my head.

"Very well, then, Sidney," he said, rising from the same chair the doctor had sat in. He looked at me some time, then kind of sighed, and folded the sheaf of papers.

"Wait," I said to him then, "just a minute . . . Could you get me writing paper, and fountain pen and ink to boot . . ."

"Paper, yes . . . We have only ball-point pens, though . . ."

So then he brought the paper and the ball-point, and I have written this down, asking another patient here from time to time how to say this, or spell that, but not showing him what I am about, and it is queer indeed isn't it, that I can only bequeath these papers to myself, for God only knows who would read them later, and it has come to me very clear in my sleep that my landlord is dead also, so there is no point in my telling my attendants that I have lied to them, that I am really James De Salles, and that my lord is or was Sidney Fuller.

But after I done wrote it all down, I was quiet in my mind and heart, and so with some effort I wrote my own name on the only thing I have to leave, and which they took from me a few moments ago with great puzzlement, for neither the person was known to them, and the address of course could not be given, and they only received it from me, I suppose, to make me feel I was being tended to.

Idyll

Georgina came out of the bathroom in her slip and bra. Maddy was lying stretched out on the bed with her eyes closed. She opened them and looked at Georgina.

"The water's hot and there's lots of it, if you want a bath," Georgina said.

"I've wondered all day what you'd say to me when we were finally alone," Maddy said.

"Oh shut up."

Maddy laughed.

"This *mélange* . . ." Georgina began.

"Malaise," Maddy said. "Malaise."

Georgina thought about it. "You're probably right," she said.

She got her skirt out of the suitcase and shook the wrinkles out and put it on. She wriggled into a sweater.

"Let's go and have some tea. I need comforting."

Maddy rolled over to the side of the bed and sat up. "Your trouble is, you're always looking for comfort," she said. "What about the rest?"

"What rest?" Georgina said. She put on her lipstick without a mirror.

"Are you going to leave your hair down like that?" Maddy said.

"No. I'm going to put it up. Why?"

"It softens you, down. You look like a mermaid. Like the Lorelei. If you were to sing a little song, I'd probably be lured into shipwreck."

Georgina stopped brushing her hair and looked at Maddy. "Would you like that?" she said.

Maddy shrugged. "Shipwreck is a positive thing."

Georgina picked a few long hairs out of her brush. "What do you think about Gunzel?" she said.

Maddy laughed.

"What's funny?" Georgina said.

"You are," Maddy said. "What do you care what I think about Gunzel?"

"I don't *care*. I don't really *care*. I'm just curious, that's all," Georgina said.

Georgina came over and sat down on the end of Maddy's bed. She smiled at Maddy, her face making its familiar arabesque.

"Stop being disingenuous," Maddy said. "It doesn't suit you."

Georgina shrugged and ran the brush through her long hair. Maddy made a little sketch with her finger on Georgina's cheek. Georgina stopped brushing and stared at the floor. Then she kissed the inside of Maddy's wrist, which was near her mouth. Maddy took Georgina's hand and kissed the palm. Georgina was very still, looking at the top of Maddy's head. Then she withdrew her hand.

"My nervous virgin," Maddy said.

"I'm not nervous."

"You are. Do you feel like you're on stage?"

"A little," Georgina said. "You're always watching me."

"Oh no I'm not," Maddy said. "It's just that you always *feel* watched. The Eye of God perhaps."

"Oh for Jesus' sake," Georgina said.

She got up and put her brush down on the bureau. "I don't know why I came," she said to Maddy.

"Shall I tell you?"

"Get dressed, for God's sake. I'm dying for some tea."

Maddy got up very slowly and stretching and yawning went into the bathroom and turned on the water in the hand basin.

Georgina sat down on her bed and tapped her fingers in a tattoo on her knee. She listened to the water running in the bathroom and then she listened to the random splashing about which followed. She stared into Maddy's suitcase, which was lying open on the floor near the bed. She picked a stocking out of the suitcase and looked at it as though it were a very long condom she'd found in the Ladies' Room.

While they waited for tea in the dining room of the Hotel Anadolu Palas, a beggar woman stuck a child with crusted eyes and black feet through the window next to their table. The small cankerous feet dangled just above the white tea cloth like a macabre decoration. At the same moment the woman struck up her money chant: it was a single rhythm and very quick, so that rejection could not be pushed into any gaps between the words.

"Have you ever seen anything so dirty?" Georgina said. "Look at those feet! I thought I'd seen some poor people in Michigan."

"So now you know you haven't seen any poor people," Maddy said. She dropped a lira coin into the woman's outstretched hand. "It's like the rest of your experience: a little ersatz."

"Why are you bent on insulting me?" Georgina said. "That's an interesting question." She watched the small black feet disappear through the window again.

"It's not an interesting question to anybody but you," Maddy said.

"Why ... that's what I want to know. Gratuitously insulting."

"Nothing gratuitous about it," Maddy said. "You've earned every insult."

The waiter brought the tea in a silver pot. Maddy peered into the pot. "No flies. No foreign matter visible. A lucky day again."

"If you dislike me so, why do you want me?" Georgina said. "That's interesting."

Maddy poured the tea and dropped in the sugar. "I'm maddened by your flesh," she said. "Your body drives me to the brink. And then those Hebraic eyes."

Georgina sipped her tea and looked out the window towards the corniche. "What's the time?" she said.

"It's remarkable," Georgina said. "It's really remarkable, the women in this country. Think of our own mothers behaving like that . . ."

"If you want to think of your own mother, that's your business," Maddy said.

They were on the balcony, surrounded by house plants, taking the evening air. Georgina stroked the leaves of a rubber plant. "Where's Melek?" she said.

"In the kitchen, with Mama. And Gunzel's in the john, weeping I think."

"Christ," Georgina said. "It's not as though anything happened. It was a lovely dinner."

"A mother who won't eat with infidels and who's practically in purdah can be very upsetting to an emancipated woman like Gunzel," Maddy said.

Georgina meditated. "Do you think we should go?"

Maddy studied her over the rubber plant. "A long evening alone in the Anadolu Palas," she said. "Think of that."

"I'm not afraid of you," Georgina said. "If that's what you mean."

"You're not?"

"No," Georgina said. "Not at all. Maybe in the beginning, but now now."

"In the beginning of what?" Maddy said.

"In the beginning," Georgina said. "When we first met."

"Oh," Maddy said.

"Girls! Are you out there?" Gunzel shouted from inside.

They came in. Gunzel had a blotchy face and was red in the eye. Her scented handkerchief leaked from her fist. She looked at them speechlessly, shaking her head from side to side and making guppy shapes with her mouth. Georgina walked over and embraced her efficiently. "Don't give the whole thing a second thought," she said. She lit a cigarette and looked across at Maddy. "We certainly don't take any offense."

"Girls, I can't tell you how she embarrasses me, I can't tell you," Gunzel said. "Mohammed was the worst thing that ever happened to her."

"If she's happy with him . . ." Maddy said.

Gunzel clutched Maddy's sleeve and leaned her head against Maddy's shoulder. "I wish there was something I could say! I never thought . . . with my good friends!"

Georgina exhaled a column of smoke through her nostrils and came over and patted Gunzel on the shoulder. "We don't think any the worse of you for it," she said. "Now really, Gunzel, we must be going. Early start tomorrow, you know."

Gunzel looked at Georgina, stricken. "You are angry!" she said. "I can see that you are angry with me. Oh God, what shall I do! It's all spoiled, spoiled!"

"No, Gunzel not at all. Gunzel, not . . ."

"All this whole lovely trip, spoiled!" Gunzel clutched Maddy's arm even tighter. She stared into Maddy's face desperately, her nose a few inches away. "Tell me you forgive me, Maddy. Tell me that," she said.

"I forgive you, Gunzel," Maddy said. "I forgive you, although there's nothing to forgive."

Gunzel wept, clinging to Maddy's arm. Georgina crossed the room and put her cigarette out. She came back and stood in front of Maddy with the corners of her mouth pulled down and her eyebrows even nearer her hairline than usual. "We really must be going," she said to Maddy. "Mustn't we?"

Maddy disengaged herself from Gunzel. "We must," she said. "Truly, we must." She patted Gunzel's arm. "Really, there's nothing to be upset about, Gunzel. Nothing at all. You can't really expect your mother to change her religion for dinner guests. We'll see you tomorrow."

"Say goodbye to Melek for us, will you?" Georgina said. She picked her coat off the hook in the entrance hall.

Downstairs she looked at Maddy and said: "Jesus, that's really disgusting."

"What's disgusting?" Maddy said. "Do you have any idea what you're referring to?"

"The whole thing. The whole thing's disgusting."

"You mean", Maddy said, "a feeling of disgust in the air? Or do you want to be more specific?"

Georgina glared at her. "You make me sick," she said.

"Me? What have I done?"

"You . . ."

"Yes?"

"Oh never mind!"

Maddy laughed.

Georgina brooded. "You never discourage her," she said.

"Discourage her from what?" Maddy said.

"From pawing you, clutching at you and all that."

"I should discourage a human being in need?" Maddy said. "How do I know that clutching isn't salvation?"

"You're a sophist," Georgina said.

"And what are you?"

Georgina stopped walking. "I'm tired, that's what I am. Let's take a taxi, for God's sake."

"And you didn't have to stare at me like that all the way to the hotel," Georgina said. "You didn't have to do that. The driver noticed."

"Of course he did," Maddy said. "He always notices the subtlest changes in facial expression of his passengers. He makes it his business to. It's part of his examination for a license."

"Well, anyway . . ." Georgina said.

Maddy threw her skirt across a chair and went into the bathroom. She ran the water and came out again rubbing cream into her hands. She looked at Georgina. "You are a ridiculous woman," she said. "It's humiliating to me that the sight of you unhinges me completely. Our relationship is concrete proof that Love is Blind." She sat down on the bed and took her shoes off. "You're a brainwashed little ninny."

"Brainwashed!"

"Brainwashed," Maddy said. "You've been conditioned to salivate at the sound of men."

"Listen, you smart bitch . . ."

"What you'd really like to do is play around with me for a couple of winters and marry a rising young Jewish lawyer in the spring. Only you can't figure out how to keep me around all that time without letting me into your precious bed, your Holy of Holies. And that idea makes you break out in a cold sweat, what with the eye of Yahweh and all. Yahweh in this case having become totally socialized."

"Jeeesus . . .!" Georgina said. She threw her blouse across the room. It fell languidly on to the floor near her suitcase. "You are the most insulting bitch . . ."

"It's only fair to tell you", Maddy said, "that I am not a faint Platonic type. Adoring from a distance I gave up when I was sixteen. I've never looked back."

Georgina stared at Maddy. She made small grunting sounds as though her words were running in several directions at once, like little wild panting pigs. Then she sat down on her bed and tears began falling down her cheeks in abundance.

"On the other hand," Maddy said, "you'd really like to go to bed with me, if you could only be somewhere else at the time."

Maddy finished her third piece of brown bread and honey, wiped her fingers on the linen napkin and lit a cigarette. She settled back comfortably in her chair and stared over Georgina's head at the bunting hanging across the face of the Iz Bank on the other side of the street. Georgina poured another cup of tea from the silver pot.

"We'll never get a place we can see from in this mob," Georgina said. "We should have got up in the middle of the night."

"In the middle of the night, you were in no condition," Maddy said. "We're going to watch the parade from the roof of the hotel. I've already spoken to the manager."

"From the roof . . .?" Georgina said.

"He said there's a lovely view from the roof. I thought you'd like a lovely view. All those lovely men in uniform. They even have boys in uniform, all very strong limbed and doughty. You'll like that."

"You're insufferable," Georgina said.

"You've got that wrong," Maddy said. "You're insufferable. I'm suffering. But gracefully, so you'd hardly notice."

"When does it start?" Georgina said.

"At noon," Maddy said. She looked at her watch. "Anytime you're ready, we can go up to the roof. There'll be others up there too. It's common practice, it seems, for the privileged residents of the hotel and other worldly people in the city to view parades and such things from the roof of the Anadolu Palas. Maybe you'll meet someone interesting up there, you never can tell. Just because you didn't get on very well with Osman Bey . . ."

"Get off Osman Bey," Georgina said.

"I just didn't want you to feel defeated or discouraged because Osman Bey didn't work out," Maddy said.

"I wasn't interested in Osman Bey, for God's sake!"

"You weren't?" Maddy said. "I'm delighted to hear that. I thought for a while you were interested in Osman Bey. Oh well, that's a different thing altogether then, isn't it?"

Georgina swallowed her cold tea and stood up. "One of these days, Maddy," she said, "you're going to go too far."

"I've already been too far," Maddy said. "And you're too short to threaten tall women."

Maddy hung over the railing to watch a khaki tank crawl by. There was another Bauhaus man projecting out of the open trap. Several columns of uniformed men followed, chests billowing out like flags in the wind. Two soldiers in front bore aloft a six-foot banner of Atatürk, shrewd eyes three feet across.

Gunzel spindled her way through the crowd, smiling nervously. She grasped Maddy's arm. "You're not angry about last night?" she said.

"Not at all, not a particle," Maddy said.

"I couldn't bear it," Gunzel said.

Maddy touched her shoulder and smiled reassuringly. "Absolutely nothing to worry about," she said. "Just forget about it."

Gunzel smiled tremulously. "You're very understanding." she said.

"Very," Maddy said.

"Are you having a good time?" Gunzel said. She cast quick glances around the roof.

"It couldn't be a nicer day for a parade," Maddy said. "It's like a parody of a parade day."

Gunzel fidgeted, plucking at her collar and shifting from one high-heeled crocodile shoe to the other. "Where's Georgina?" she said.

Maddy motioned to her left. Gunzel swivelled to see Georgina standing a bit further down the roof talking to a very tall eagle-beaked Turk. One of her hips was pushed languidly forward and she was gesticulating prettily with her cigarette. Gunzel stared at her for a moment and then turned back to Maddy. "Have you made any plans for this evening?" she said.

Maddy shrugged. "We are improvising at the moment."

"Perhaps you'd like to go out to the Park. It's a lovely park. There's a lake there, with swans."

"It sounds nice," Maddy said. "But I'll have to ask Georgina what she's got in mind. She may have something else in mind."

"We wouldn't have to stay all evening in the Park," Gunzel said. "We could go to a club, if you wanted to. My brother would be pleased to take us."

Maddy nodded and smiled. She watched Georgina lean forward towards the eagle-beaked Turk, laughing, her breasts shaking under her sweater. She looked at Gunzel. "Would it be all right if I rang you up later and let you know about the Park?" she said.

"Oh fine," Gunzel said. "That would be fine."

In the middle of a sweep with her cigarette Georgina noticed Gunzel. The oblique eyes went Mongolian. She pushed through the crowd, holding her cigarette in front of her like a beacon.

"Hello there!" Georgina said. "I never dreamt you still watched parades, Gunzel. I mean, you must have seen so many of these . . ."

Tall young Eagle-Beak was just behind her, wearing a slightly abstract smile which was not directed to anyone but could be used in an emergency.

Georgina made a little hiatus in the circle of three and gestured at Eagle-Beak over her shoulder. "This is Haluk Ersan," she said. "Madelaine Tilson and Gunzel Vedin."

Haluk Bey lowered his heavy eyelids and the smile became briefly definite and directed. Gunzel stared at him coldly. He ignored her.

"I must be off now, girls," Gunzel said. "Have a good time. Ring me later. You've got my number."

"You bet," Georgina said. She watched Gunzel go. She waved at her when she reached the door leading off the roof. She looked at Maddy for a moment silently. "I suppose you've made plans for us which include Gunzel," she said.

"Not necessarily," Maddy said. "That will depend."

"On what?"

Haluk Bey was staring across the rooftops of the city with a preoccupied air.

"Haluk has invited us to the casino this evening," Georgina said.

"Has he?" Maddy said. She leaned back against the railing and looked up at the bottom of Haluk Bey's chin.

"He's expecting a friend of his any moment," Georgina said. "He assures me this friend is an especially nice person." She smiled archly up at Haluk Bey. "Isn't that what you said. Haluk?"

"That's right," he said. "Hasan is a very nice person. He has traveled, he is a man of the world." A whisper of sarcasm in his voice made Maddy desert Georgina's face. Haluk Bey continued to survey the rooftops in front of him.

"That's very important of course," Maddy said. "Being a man of the world is of the very first importance, like white teeth."

Georgina looked uncomfortable. "Do you want to go, or not?" she said.

"How do I know until I've met this very nice man of the world?" Maddy said. "He could have two heads and still travel."

Haluk Bey laughed. "She's a very sensible lady," he said to Georgina. "Like all American ladies I've met." He had a very languorous voice, as though he were rich and it had never been necessary to hurry.

Georgina smiled at him and took out a cigarette, which he lit for her in an offhand way without the usual Turkish flourish. "Undoubtedly, you smoke too much," he said. "You will ruin your pretty self."

Hasan Bey appeared on the roof. He was shorter than Eagle-Beak. His hair was beginning to recede and his jowls to thicken. His heavy eyelids drooped over his eyes but not enough to conceal the avidity. He smiled intimately at the world. He came over, holding his hand out for Haluk Bey, while he looked over the females. He bowed. He cupped his hand immediately around Maddy's elbow. "French?" he said. "You look very French. No? But you must have some French blood in your family . . ."

"I don't think it bears looking into," Maddy said.

"Let's have a drink somewhere," Haluk Bey said. "The sun makes thirst."

"What do you think of Hasan?" Georgina said.

Maddy was stretched out in a crucifix position on the bed. She stared at the ceiling. "He's rudimentary," she said. "Perhaps inchoate is the word I want."

Georgina stopped filing her thumbnail. "What's wrong with him?" she said.

"I just told you," Maddy said. "God, I'm tired. Brandy and rudimentary people make a fatiguing combination. Only the brandy goes to your head." She sat up and looked at Georgina. "I gather you and Haluk Bey hit it off superbly. He even forgot to be bitter now and again."

"He had an unfortunate affair with an American girl when he was over there studying," Georgina said. "They were engaged and she jilted him at the last moment."

"Really," Maddy said. "So now we've all got to convince him we're OK, harmless and sweet-intentioned."

"You're hard-hearted," Georgina said.

"Does he feel he's got a license to be rude to us all because his heart was broken by a fellow-national?"

Georgina looked at her and then walked into the bathroom. She began running a bath.

"He's just rude enough to appeal to a potentially servile female like you," Maddy yelled over the running water. "I wonder how both of us could have been belched out by the same Y-chromosome."

Georgina came back into the room in her bathrobe. She lit a cigarette and sat down on her bed.

"Do you know", Maddy said, "that Hasan Bey has got an album of photographs of the women in his life? Women in his life in this case meaning anybody he could hold still long enough for the flash-bulb to go off. He told me about his collection. He said how he was looking forward to adding me to his album. Tonight at the casino."

Georgina was silent, smoking.

"He's going to show me the album sometime before we leave," Maddy said. "He insists. It's as though he's not really a lady-killer unless I see the ladies he's killed."

Georgina got up and put her cigarette out. "It's not as though you're going to marry him," she said. "It's just one night at the casino."

Maddy stretched her arms up towards the ceiling and yawned. "One night with Hasan Bey may be the equivalent of a lobotomy. Don't be all night in the bathtub."

When they got to the Lake Casino the Italian band, all members in snow-white suits and fuzzy-skinned white shoes, was just in the middle of a brassy version of "Volare". Hasan Bey smiled happily, snapped his fingers and did a couple of twirls around Maddy as they stood in the foyer.

"One of my favorite numbers," he said. "Let us dance."

"I'd like to check my coat first," Maddy said. "I never like to dance with my coat on. It inhibits me."

He stared at her a moment. Then he said: "You have a very marvelous sense of humor."

They followed the waiter to their table, which was near the ice-cream orchestra all jumping up and down on their spongy soles. The whole band seemed to be moving in random patterns around the bandstand.

Georgina and Haluk Bey trailed along behind. Haluk Bey seemed dispirited and wore his sardonic smile. He kept directing this smile at Georgina, who ignored it. She swept ahead to their table with her face fixed in its most impervious mask and her eyebrows tirelessly at her hairline. She was wearing a red serape from Mexico and when she sat down one end of it dropped on to the floor, where Haluk trod it underfoot. She dragged it up and glared at him icily.

"I beg your pardon," Haluk Bey said and smiled his bitter smile at her. Before she could forgive him, he turned to the wine steward.

"Now that you've got rid of your coat, let us dance," Hasan Bey said to Maddy, snapping his fingers happily. He leaned over towards her confidentially. "I think you must be a very wonderful dancer."

Maddy rose and accompanied Hasan Bey to the floor. While "Volare" pumped through her skull like a nail, she sniffed Hasan Bey's aromatic ear and watched—when she was turned in the right direction—Georgina and Haluk Bey. Georgina was talking animatedly, smoke pouring out of her nostrils. Haluk Bey appeared receptive to the animation. At one point he even dropped his arm across the back of her chair. On the next whirl around they were both silent. Georgina was watching the trumpet soloist with a bored expression. Haluk Bey was emptying a glass.

"You are a very marvelous dancer, so light on your feet," Hasan Bey said. He held her chair for her. He lit a cigarette and passed it to her, his eyes moist with seduction. "I shall always remember our first dance together," he said.

"It was memorable," Maddy said. Haluk Bey laughed.

"What's funny?" Georgina said to him.

"Nothing," he said. "Do you want to dance?"

"How could I resist an invitation like that?" Georgina said. Haluk Bey stood up. "Exactly," he said. They proceeded to the floor.

Hasan Bey poured Maddy a glass of champagne and filled his own glass. His eyes darted around the room like a ferret sniffing out a rabbit. He's looking for the photographer, Maddy thought. God. I am being collected. Who will see me in the future, lying prone in Hasan Bey's album?

"We shall eat now," Hasan Bey said. "A very nice antipasto to begin."

"That's a good idea," Maddy said. She drank her champagne and watched Haluk Bey spin Georgina around the floor. He kept looking over his shoulder at the band and smiling at the saxophonist, whom he apparently knew. Georgina's face was frozen. Maddy looked at her watch. They had not yet been in the casino for an hour.

"And then", Hasan Bey said, "I worked for NATO for a

while, a year or two. I made many American friends during this period."

He waved frantically at the wandering photographer who had just finished blowing off his flashbulb in the face of a nearby couple. "I have many American friends," he repeated. "Next to the French girls, I like best the American girls."

"Really?" Maddy said. She refilled her glass. She looked at Georgina standing rigidly in the middle of the dance floor while the band deliberated cacophonously on the next number. Haluk Bey had gone over to have a chat with the saxophonist.

"Smile." Hasan Bey whispered in her ear, putting his arm around her shoulders and beaming up at the photographer on the other side of the champagne bottle standing in its ice. Maddy arranged her face to resemble as nearly as possible the face of a captive woman in the arms of an amorous SS man and stared at the camera. The bulb exploded and she felt Hasan Bey go limp next to her as though he had been shot or just released from an iron maiden. "Ah," he said. He jumped up to order his prints from the photographer. He smiled at him, embraced him slightly, patted his shoulder and offered him a drink. When the interlude was over, he returned to the table and refilled the glasses.

"What about that very nice antipasto to begin?" Maddy said.

"Ah," Hasan Bey said again. He ordered a menu, which he studied conscientiously. The band had decided on a rhumba but Haluk Bey appeared to be foxtrotting to it. Georgina's face was stony. On the last note she dropped her arms and walked stiffly back to the table without looking around or speaking to Haluk Bey. She sat down across from Maddy.

"I need some of that," she said, pushing her glass towards Maddy.

"Allow me," Hasan Bey said, putting the menu down for a moment.

"We're on the point of eating some very nice antipasto to begin," Maddy said.

Georgina grimaced. "Do you need to go to the powder-room?"

"It just so happens," Maddy said, getting up. Haluk Bey had stopped to say something to a young man two tables away. Maddy and Georgina threaded their way to the powder-room.

Once inside, Georgina looked at Maddy desperately and slumped down on to a little velveteen-covered stool in front of a mirror. "For chrissakes, I can't go through with this," she said. "Such a boor, I can't tell you. Such a . . . such a . . ." She staggered into unintelligibility and a few tears dribbled down her cheeks. "You wouldn't believe some of the things he's said to me."

"Don't worry," Maddy said. "I'll get you out. Now listen, as soon as we finish the antipasto, I'll say that I have a splitting headache and want to go back to the hotel. You will say that you must accompany me, since you know how bad these migraine things get and I mustn't be left alone. Then we'll go. And if the Beys don't feel like taking us back, we'll get a taxi. Finished. How's that?"

"Great," Georgina said, wiping her eyes. She pressed some powder on to her shiny cheeks. "Jesus . . . that Haluk Bey."

They returned to the table, faces inscrutable, secure in their foreknowledge of events. Haluk Bey was sprawled in his chair glowering at the tablecloth. Hasan Bey twirled the gold ring on his left hand and stared vacuously into the thick half-light of the casino. Hasan Bey stood up and waved Maddy through to her seat. Haluk Bey remained sprawled in his chair. He looked up at Georgina with melancholy eyes.

"We are having a wonderful Circassian chicken," Hasan Bey said. "The antipasto comes at any moment."

Georgina folded her hands prayerfully under her chin and leaned forward on her elbows, her eyes as closed away as a conch in its shell. Haluk Bey straightened up and looked at her profile with intense, though saddened concentration. Then he leaned over and encircled her wrists with one of his hands. Georgina turned and looked at him as though he were a pursesnatcher. He looked back at her meltingly, a small rueful smile on his lips. He got up and very gently led Georgina to the dance floor. The ice-cream men were being very restrained and playing a ballad. Haluk Bey pressed Georgina's cheek against his breast, embraced her tightly and moved her liquidly across the floor. Georgina was astonished but her face had no way left to reflect this condition, considering the usual position of her eyebrows and the customary brightness of her oblique green eyes.

Maddy ate an olive off the antipasto tray and watched Haluk Bey smiling mournfully into Georgina's face.

"Christ," she said.

"Is there anything wrong with your olive?" Hasan Bey said.

"I was meditating on the place of vanity in captivity."

"Pardon?" Hasan Bey said. His mouth was full of salami.

"Forget it." she said. "Be good enough to pass me an anchovy."

Georgina returned to the table smiling beatifically like a Perugino Virgin, as though enclosing a precious secret. Haluk Bey was all tender solicitude. He arranged a selection of antipasto and set it delicately before her. Georgina picked at it as though in a dream, talking to Haluk in small murmurs between mouthfuls.

"Let's dance," Maddy said to Hasan Bey. "Swallow all that stuff in your mouth and let's dance."

Hasan Bey looked at her astonished and then wiped his fingers and smiled. "You have a wonderful, very wonderful sense of humor," he said.

By the time they got back to the table after a vigorous samba, Georgina was stony faced again, her lips squeezed tightly together as though she were suppressing tears. Haluk Bey was slumped down in his chair, pressing circles into the tablecloth with his champagne glass.

"I've got a terrible headache," Maddy said loudly. "I must go back to the hotel. Immediately."

Hasan Bey looked at her incredulously. "Headache?" he said. "But on the dance floor—"

"I have a wonderful way of concealing my pain," she said. "But the mask is slipping away from me. I really do have to go, before the attack becomes any worse." She paused.

"It could become a great deal worse. It could render me incapable."

"Oh . . ." Hasan Bey said.

Georgina looked at Maddy with her lips pressed together tightly and said nothing.

"If it gets too bad, I'll have to call a doctor," Maddy said. "Isn't that right, Georgina?"

"What?" she said.

"I said: I may have to call a doctor. For the migraine."

"Oh," Georgina said. She wedged a sip of champagne between her pressed lips. She brandished a tissue vaguely around her eyes.

"I am very sad to hear that," Hasan Bey said. "I will take you to my apartment and give you some medication for headaches which I have. It is very wonderful medication."

"I want to go back to the hotel," Maddy said. "Immediately."

"I will take you," Hasan Bay said, standing up. "You will excuse us?" he said to Georgina and Haluk Bey. Haluk Bey looked up and nodded, preoccupied. Georgina kept her glazed eyes fixed on the antipasto tray.

Finding Out

They had not yet decided to live together, though clearly it would be common sense to do so, since the circumstances of each complemented the other's, Robert being of middle years, Peter young, Robert almost rich, Peter positively poor, Robert's flat with ample room for two, Peter's bedsitter uncomfortable for one, Robert a natural teacher, Peter with so much to learn, both alone. The range of Peter's sexual experience had not been so wide as to promote discrimination: Robert, rightly or wrongly, did not believe that the opportunities available to a man of his age were so numerous as to permit any width of choice. In the matter of companionship, of both physical and mental congress, each was able to provide something of what the other needed. Nevertheless, two people cannot know whether they are able to live together until they have actually done so, and Peter and Robert, though they had known each other now for five months, had not yet spent a full twenty-four hours in each other's company. This holiday was to be a way of finding out.

Peter lay in one of those elaborate deckchairs with a footrest and canopy. Robert sat on a towel at his feet, reading science fiction. A trickle of sweat ran from between Peter's balls down the inside of his left leg. Living mostly inside one's head works very well if what is outside in the everyday world remains everyday, but how do you control your fantasies when you're living one?

The sun was unbearably hot, the whole situation unreal. Peter's thighs were white. He looked down at them, and wondered if he should change position. They had bought him some hideously patterned bathing trunks on their way to the beach, the only ones they could find. The trunks were too large, and he had tucked them up, making them as brief as possible.

Close by, a middle-aged couple settled down to an early picnic lunch. Peter watched them from behind the safety of his sunglasses. They talked to each other without making any noise, and without ever looking at each other, the husband always answering a question before his wife had finished asking it. Their dislike of each other had given them a purpose, which was to make themselves unattractive—to other people if that could not be helped, but certainly to each other.

Robert lifted his eyes from the book. "I shouldn't have too much sun the first day if I were you."

"No. Should I get dressed, do you think, or just sit under the canopy?"

"It's a bit warm to get dressed. Why don't you put on a shirt, and have a walk along the beach? See what you can see."

"Yes. All right."

"Find some ice cream, if it won't spoil your lunch. Got some money?"

"Yes. I've got what you gave me last night."

"Oh!" Robert returned to the book.

"I won't be long."

By now the beach was beginning to be crowded. Young Swedes, each with a tyre of fat above his hip-bone, shielded their eyes to examine Peter as he passed. He wished he had not undertaken this walk. He remembered that his trunks were still tucked up at the bottom, and started to untuck them, first to give him more cover, second (and more important) to give him something to do with his hands, for he had begun to feel like a finalist in a Beauty Contest, walking up and down a cat-walk, and

since he had no place, he knew, in such a contest, lacked the
confidence to take his movement natural.

There was no ice cream that he could see, but he did not wish
to return to Robert too soon, so he found a place on the sand to
sit. Soon they would go back to the hotel for lunch and a short
rest, and then the afternoon would be spent in sightseeing.
Robert had suggested that this might be the best way of dividing
their days, and so it had been agreed.

A boy of about seventeen suddenly appeared, as if from
nowhere. Smiling, he stretched himself out on the hot sand no
more than three feet away from Peter. He was dark with the
suntan of one who is at home in the sun. He was also clearly at
home in smiling at strangers. Lying on his belly and pressing his
toes into sand, he hummed quietly and swayed from side to side.

Peter turned, and looked out to sea, where heads bobbed up
and down, being, both up and under, always on the lookout for
other heads, and a motorboat whined its way round and between
them. The boy slid along the sand, pulling himself closer, always
smiling, always with his eyes fixed on Peter, who undid the
buttons of his shirt for something to do. The boy had closed the
gap between them, and was now lying very close, staring
blatantly into Peter's eyes. Peter closed them, and tried to
concentrate on a suntan, hoping that this would show a lack of
interest. The boy's humming was a sensual, caressing sort of
noise. Suddenly it came to an end, with a loud flourish. Peter
opened his eyes, and the boy rolled over on his back, still
smiling, to reveal the most enormous erection.

Peter stood and buttoned his shirt, all in one movement.

"Don't go, Johnny." the smiling boy said.

"I think my friend is waiting."

And he was.

"What are your feelings towards fish?"

"I like them."

"For lunch?"

"Good idea."

"I thought we might give ourselves a treat, since it's our first day. We won't eat in the hotel."

The waiter rolled up a sleeve, dipped his arm into the tank, and pulled out a lobster. The lobster struggled, and splashed, and clamped its claws together.

"It's a bit small." Robert said, as he studied the depths of the tank with a critical eye. The waiter dropped the relieved lobster back into the water, where it scurried away to a corner, kicking up sand and artificial coral. "How about that one?" A very large lobster, having courteously given up its corner to the escaper, had crawled to the front of the tank to inspect the enemy. The waiter scrooped it up without any struggle.

"That one's older. It knows its purpose in life. Now it's your turn, Peter. Which one would you like?"

The waiter was watching him. Peter looked into the tank. The sand had settled.

"I don't mind really. Any." Why was it necessary to point to one's victim? When one eats chicken, one never hears the clucking, or sees the ludicrous strutting round the yard. And a plaice, once settled beside chips, entirely loses its identity.

"Perhaps you'd rather have something else? Trout? A sole? Or prawns perhaps?"

They were waiting for him, and the large lobster, still held securely between the waiter's thumb and forefinger, was beginning to have second thoughts and flap its claws for freedom.

He pointed at the tank. "That one." He never even saw it. It was just a blur of dark green. The waiter pulled something which Peter refused to consider as lobster, and which was in any case considerably smaller than Robert's, out of the tank, and they moved back to their table.

"I think we can drink a whole bottle, don't you?"

"Yes, I'm thirsty." Peter's thighs and shoulders were already beginning to burn from the sun.

"Your nose is red, Peter."

The wine arrived.

"A bit too cold, but that's a fault on the right side, and we're very thirsty." The waiter poured two glasses, placed the bottle on the table, and removed the ice-bucket. "Now, we mustn't gulp this. It's far too good."

The lobsters, which had been greeny black in the tank, were put before them, pink and shining.

"They've changed colour."

"Yes, that's what happens when you cook them. Help yourself to the melted butter. Take lots. What did you see on your walk along the beach?"

Peter watched Robert pouring melted butter liberally from a silver dish over the grilled lobster, before scooping the white meat from the crusty articulated shell, and copied him.

"I saw a lot of Swedish-looking men. They all seem to have a roll of fat just here. Have you noticed?"

"It's all the cream and pastries they eat." Robert asked the waiter for more melted butter. "It's all carbohydrates and cholesterol in the Scandinavian countries. Long nights, I suppose."

The wine was very good, and Peter drank it too fast. Robert showed him how to draw the meat out of the thin claws with a long silver fork.

"What would you like to do this afternoon? I think it'd be wrong for you to have any more sun."

"Yes, so do I."

"What do you fancy doing?"

"I don't know. What do you think?" He was safe in assuming that Robert had thought, and had worked it all out in advance, but the questions had to be asked.

"Well, it depends what one feels like. I don't suppose we want to be too energetic. On the other hand, we don't want to waste the afternoon. What we could do is take a bus up into the mountains, and have a look at one of the old villages. Or" (an alternative would have been worked out also), "if you'd like to go shopping, there are some good shops in the centre."

"No, I'd like to see a village."

"Good." Robert produced some maps from his pocket. "There's one about six miles inland with a very old church. Well, half a very old church; the other half was razed to the ground by Moors."

"Funny."

"Yes?"

"Raised to the ground."

Robert paused for a moment, and then agreed.

After an inspection of the church which included its history, related to them by a young girl who polished the pews in the hope of becoming a nun, they climbed higher up the mountain above the village.

The view was excellent value, and they made the most of it, moving slowly so as not to tire themselves. The ground was rocky with occasional clumps of withered grass. Peter wondered what the sheep and goats who inhabited the mountain found to sustain them. Nothing moved quickly here, except that now and then, as if frightened by its own imagination, a goat would tear off at speed along a narrow ledge, or gallop at what seemed like a thirty-degree angle up to some higher lonelier place.

"Twenty minutes' sit-down on a rock near the summit, and then down the other side for tea." The top of the mountain itself looked far too steep and unsafe to attempt. There wouldn't, of course, *be* tea.

On the way down, Robert hung back, overcome by modesty, searching for somewhere private to piss. Peter moved on downwards, carried on by the force of gravity, and found a stone wall with a track beside it, both seeming to curl their way round the mountain.

He stood there, and waited; it was not wise to get too far ahead. Robert had discovered, by asking three different people all of whom were in agreement, that at five o'clock a bus would take them from the village back to town, and, indeed, past their hotel.

"Hello."

Peter turned. There was nobody there. Was Robert playing a joke? Would he, at any moment, jump from behind the wall?

"Hello."

The boy—or was he a small man?—was standing on the other side of a tiny gate. The colour of his skin and clothing matched the brown gate so well that Peter had looked at him without seeing him.

The man-boy opened the gate, and stepped through it, but not until Peter had answered his Hello. He pointed at Peter and then up the mountain. "You?" Peter nodded and smiled.

The man-boy placed the fingers of his right hand horizontally above his eyebrows, and spun round on his heels. Peter at once knew that this meant that one could see a long way. So he smiled and nodded in agreement.

Now the man-boy puffed and blew, and made piston movements with his arms. Then he wiped imaginary sweat from his brow, and pointed again to the top of the mountain. He plumped himself down on the ground as though he had reached the top, then again used his fingers to shield his eyes, and surveyed the view. Peter nodded and smiled.

But the man-boy had not finished. He stood up again, and began running on the spot, leaning backwards. He looked exactly as Peter had done on his way down the mountain.

"Hello. Found a friend?"

The man-boy turned to Robert, and stood motionless for a moment before smiling and saying "Hello". Then he did something he had not done for Peter, which was to wipe his hand down the front of his goat-stained jacket and offer it for shaking.

Peter turned to continue their walk, but Robert had sat down on the ground, and was signing to the man-boy to sit beside him. "Are you a shepherd?" The man-boy looked puzzled. Robert pointed to him, and said, "Baa!" The man-boy grinned and nodded. His teeth were almost entirely rotten, which was a pity, because his face was small and delicate, and so were his hands.

"How many sheep have you got?" Robert continued to ask his questions in English, but followed them immediately with signs and noises. The man-boy owned (or looked after; it was not clear) seven sheep and five goats.

Miming an enormous beard and pretending to be an old man, Robert asked the man-boy how old he was. It seemed to Peter that at this point there was some manifestation of unease from the man-boy, but this might have been merely due to the fact that Peter himself had wandered away a little to worry about the bus. Although Robert had mimed the old man very well, no age was given.

Peter rewound his watch. The time was four twenty-five. The bus left at five, and they still had a long way to descend.

He moved, and stood by the wall. Neither Robert nor the man-boy seemed to be any longer aware of him. He didn't exist. It was Peter who had discovered the man-boy, but Robert had taken him over. Both were clearly enjoying themselves, laughing and making signs. They had discovered more about each other in the few minutes they had been sitting on the ground, Peter felt, than he and Robert had done in the five months they had known each other.

"It's five minutes to five. I don't think we'll catch that bus."

"Never mind. We'll hire a car."

He could have called out the time at twenty to five, or even a quarter to, when there would still have been a chance of catching the bus. Why had he waited until it was too late?

The man-boy was now so excited that he couldn't keep still. Jumping up and down and flinging his arms above his head, he described to Robert what had happened the last time a violent storm had struck the village. Odd words of English came spilling out as he remembered them, each starting him off on a new tale. With every word his excitement grew, as though each was a step towards some grand prize in a competition, each a score-draw in his perm and soon he would have sixteen. When he was lost for words, he made noises. Sound-effects of the sea. A ship being wrecked. Lightning tearing open the sky, and the people of the village running, their hands over their ears.

Robert laughed as the man-boy danced about.

It was twenty minutes past five.

"Boom! Boom! Boom! Crash! Boom! Boom!" Houses breaking apart, sheep and goats in panic flight.

Five thirty-five.

"English." The man-boy mimed tourists, locking all the doors and hiding under their beds. Robert almost choked with laughter.

Five forty-five.

"Rocks." The man-boy mimed rocks, breaking away from the mountain and chasing a man downhill.

Three minutes to six.

"Trees." The man-boy made the sound of wood ripping, and then performed an almost perfect prat-fall.

Robert stood, and brushed down his trousers. "We have to go now. Goodbye."

It seemed to Peter that the man-boy's heart had stopped. He could not believe that they were leaving. "No." It was a feeble "No," almost inaudible, but Robert heard it.

"We must, I'm afraid. It's been lovely chatting to you." Robert moved away, and Peter stood for a moment between them, watching the man-boy. Although he expected the man-boy to cry, he could not prevent himself from staring. Sooner or later, the large brown eyes would have to move from Robert, and look at him. He waited. But they never did. He didn't exist. Peter became aware of wanting to touch the man-boy, so he ran.

Barney

They had been high at the time. They had been floating. They had been high on substances. Well, just the one substance, actually; cannabis resin, hash, given to Susan by a large New Zealander with a brown moustache. He had been to see the play (at least, they supposed he had), and had come round backstage afterwards and he had stood in the girls' dressing room, his moustache all bristly with simple enthusiasm. "Great!" he had said. "Great! Terrific! I really mean that." Then he had thrust a tiny cube wrapped in what appeared to be part of a lettuce leaf into Susan's hand, saying, "I want you to have this. I really do," and had turned quickly on his heel, and had left the dressing room with the long loping stride of one used to open spaces.

The New Zealander's gift had not been altogether generous. Later, Susan and Peter had watched him being thoroughly felt all over outside the stage door by two of those peculiarly solid and humourless policemen only to be found in Barrow-in-Furness. "Man! You two are really into body contact," they had heard the New Zealander exclaim, and then the two policemen had thumped him, judiciously and without malice, and bundled him into their car, and driven away, never to be seen again by Susan and Peter, who, believing that it would be safest to dispose of the substance as soon as possible, had shared it that night with Spanish burgundy and slices of black pudding.

Nothing that had happened had been intentional. The substance certainly hadn't. Hash wasn't the sort of goody an actress on £65 a week on a tour of *Hedda Gabler* to the culturally deprived areas of the north-west (subsidized by the Arts Council) could afford; even an ordinary low-tar ciggie could get to seem like something of a luxury by Saturday night. And the fact that Susan hadn't been on the Pill—well, you couldn't call that intentional. First, she'd run out, and then she'd been putting on weight, and she did get these headaches, and anyway she'd quite gone off men. She'd had men, more than she wanted, had enough of them, enough of one anyway. More than enough.

There had been two years, in fact, of one particular man, and he had been married, and he was so fair, had divided his time and his body so fairly between his wife and Susan that she had reached a stage when she was sick of men, sick right up to here. Quentin! How could you love somebody with a name like Quentin, or any of the "-ins", come to that—Quentin, or Justin, or Crispin—how could you love someone who, on the evening he's spending with *you*, tries to teach you how to make apple crumble by his wife's recipe? She had taken the dish of raw crumble, and she had smacked it hard against his face, and rubbed, and then run out of the room, out of the flat and had to spend the night with a girlfriend. Anyway, if she'd gone back, Quentin would only have been *fair*. Narcissistic, selfish prig! She'd gone right off men. There was no point in keeping on the Pill, when it was making her fat.

Luckily the tour had come up shortly afterwards, and there was nobody in the company she fancied. She and Peter were great mates, shared digs, all that, but Peter was gay and made no secret of it, so there were no problems of any sexual sort. It was such a relief to be in the company of a man, and not have to spend half her time fending off passes and the other half enduring the sulks of someone whose pass has been fended off. Susan enjoyed male company. It was just the sex that she'd had enough of for a while.

It had really been a substance of the top quality from

Afghanistan, that little lettuce-wrapped cube. It had helped
them to appreciate the blackness of the black pudding, the
Spanishness of the burgundy. It had expanded their
consciousness. Somewhere on the other side of the wall a
member of the culturally deprived north-west had been playing a
very old Cliff Richard LP, and the substance had taken those
simple sounds, created so long ago by Cliff (it may have been
Cliff; it may have been Cilla; these distinctions are meaningless
to the expanded consciousness), and it had unwound them like
strands of silk, each separate strand of the shining skein which
was the voice of Cliff (or Cilla) so pure, so innocent, that Susan
and Peter had wept tears of joy, and when the LP had come to its
appointed end, lay in each other's arms and listened to the after-
sound, the echoing silence which was even more beautiful.

And Peter had said, "Thank you, Cliff," and Susan, "Thank
you, Cilla."

As for what happened thereafter, it had seemed natural and
proper at the time. It was sensation. It was discovery. It was
contact. It was communion. It was amazingly enjoyable.

Quite unlike the no-longer lamented Quentin, Peter had been
gentle and co-operative, perhaps because he was gay, and
accustomed to the idea that both the people making love ought to
find pleasure in it, or perhaps it was partly the effect of the
substance, which slowed down every action, heightened every
feeling, encouraging them to explore with lips, and tongue and
the tips of fingers even places that one would have ordinarily
thought not particularly sexy, like the insides of thighs, ankles
and armpits.

Perhaps two lovers ought not to lie giggling helplessly in each
other's arms after that supreme moment when time stops and all
sensations fuse together, but Peter and Susan had, and had fallen
asleep, and wakened after a while, with their senses still
heightened by black pudding and substances, and made love
again. And in the morning, no longer with any of that special
heightening given to the senses by hash from Afghanistan, and
both of them with mouths like the nests of insanitary owls, they

had made love yet again, just to assure themselves that it could still be accomplished without the use of artificial aids, and it had been.

And now she was pregnant. The tour was over. The culturally deprived areas of the north-west had decided that being deprived of *Hedda Gabler* was a deprivation they could very easily endure; they had stayed away from Susan's performance in large numbers. Well, you win some, you lose some. There was no doubt about the pregnancy; the test had been positive. She'd have to get rid of it, she supposed.

She lay late in bed (which, being out of work, she could afford to do), and thought about it. Ought she to tell Peter?

Traditionally one did tell the father, because traditionally he ought to help with the cost of the abortion, perhaps bear it entirely. The tradition was that he had put her in the club, and must pay. Except that Peter couldn't have known she wasn't on the Pill. That was one of the unfortunate consequences about the Pill; the responsibility for contraception passed on to the woman. Anyway, Peter had no more money than she, usually rather less, being even less often employed than she was and rather happy-go-lucky with the pennies.

She didn't see Peter very often now. They'd had a good thing going during the tour, but the tour was over. Peter lived in Hendon, she in Barons Court. They were good friends, of course they were, and always would be, but the paths of Hendoners and Barons Courters do not often cross, and anyway Peter had fallen rather heavily for a young merchant banker, whom he had quite literally bumped into one night at Bang's Disco, and having bumped, had remained attached.

Merchant bankers had money. Would it be considered odd if Peter were to ask his boyfriend for a contribution towards an abortion for Susan?

She went to Camden Passage in Islington, where Peter helped out, selling antiques when he wasn't in work. But the antique trade was brisk that day, and although they did go for a coffee during the quarter of an hour Peter was able to take off, it wasn't the right time to talk, not seriously, anyway. Susan came away, having bought a small, enamel brooch at a large discount, but with the larger question still unresolved.

There was always her mother. Susan's mother lived in Tunbridge Wells, where she was lonely. Susan had been the daughter of her parents' middle age, an only child born when they had given up hope of having one. She had grown up, been doted on, left home; her parents still had each other. They would have qualified for the Darby and Joan Club; they were never out of each other's pockets. Now Susan's father was dead, and there was only the one pocket left. He had owned his own shop, which had sold exceedingly well-made bicycles. A building society had bought the site. Susan hated to go down to Tunbridge Wells, knowing that her mother was lonely.

"You're putting on weight, dear," said Susan's mother.

"I've given up smoking."

The question was, how long would it continue to be safe? If she were going to have an abortion, the earlier the better. She had read about a new method, some kind of suction. It had been in the Sunday papers; she couldn't remember when, and somehow lacked the energy to go through the back issues which lay stacked in a corner of her kitchen in Barons Court, waiting for her to tie them together and leave them for the dustmen. The egg, no bigger than a pin's head, was just sucked out. But at three months—well, say three and a half—what was inside Susan must be considerably larger than a pin's head.

She couldn't understand why she had waited so long. She could have gone straight away, the moment she knew, to Patrick, her doctor, and said, "Look, love, I'm in the club. I need an abortion," and he would have helped. He mightn't have been able to manage it on the National Health, but he'd have managed.

She had wasted so much time, mooning, lying late in bed, not really thinking about the problem at all, day-dreaming. Why give up smoking, when she had no intention of actually having the baby?

"I suppose you're pregnant."

Susan dropped a plate.

"Yes," she said, "I am, as a matter of fact. And what's more, I'm going to have it."

Susan discovered that she was shaking, and went quickly to get a dustpan and brush. As she swept the bits of broken plate into the dustpan, forcing her shaking hands to accept the task and feeling her ears burn and her eyes fill with tears, she heard her mother say, "Well, of course you are. Nobody who really knows you could ever have expected anything else, Sukey. You'll have to stay down here for a while with me, however much you hate it. You can't very well have a baby in Barons Court."

Susan said, "I've got nothing against abortion. It's the most practical thing to do. I didn't know myself what I was going to do until just now. I don't see how you could have known."

"You've always wanted a baby of your own, ever since you were a little girl."

And Susan's mother, who had never been known to cry, began to cry. And Susan, who had never been known (at least for many years) to hug her mother, left the dustpan on the floor and stood up and hugged her. And the two women stood there, in a bright kitchen in the better part of Tunbridge Wells, crying and hugging each other, and feeling very much the better for that rare experience.

"Anyway," Susan said, lying, "I don't hate it here. I just can't get down very often."

The baby was a boy. She called him Barney. She had a lot to learn. Her mother willingly taught her.

After a while it came to Susan that, if she and Barney stayed much longer in Tunbridge Wells, they might never leave. She watched her mother lose ten years, and was appalled. She looked at herself in the bathroom mirror, and discovered that at least six of those ten years had found a home on her own face. It was time for her to move on.

Should she leave Barney with her mother? She tried to sort
matters out in her own mind. If she herself left, she would
deprive her mother of what she most lacked, company and
conversation. The ten years would come back; maybe more with
them. But it could be done in a kind way, simply by Susan's
finding a job. Only then there would be the question of Barney.
If she left him behind, he would supply a point to her mother's
pointless life. It would be the decent, common-sense thing to do,
and Susan discovered that she just didn't want to do it.

"Simply!" God, what a word to use, even in the privacy of her
own thoughts. Finding a job was never simple.

She went to see her agent, who was out at lunch. The lunch
hours of agents last, as a general rule, from eleven-thirty to three-
thirty, and do not fit in easily with the times of the trains from
Tunbridge Wells, if one wants to avoid the rush hours. Susan
said to Janice, her agent's secretary, "How would you manage to
do a job if you had to look after a baby less than a year old?"

"With great difficulty," said Janice.

She went to talk to Gingerbread, the one-parent family people,
to ask advice.

"Social security," said Gingerbread.

"But I'm an actress. If I don't work, I don't get work. People
forget."

Gingerbread shrugged sympathetically. Susan said she'd keep
in touch.

In the end she operated a compromise, as people usually do
when two strong but conflicting wants must both be satisfied.

She returned to Barons Court, taking Barney with her. A small
part in a television play, when she wasn't needed to rehearse
either every day or all of every day, meant that during rehearsals
and the two studio days, Barney would spend time with her
girlfriend Vivienne in Pembroke Square. (Odd how a girl's
girlfriend is just a friend, whereas a boy's boyfriend is a lover.)
But when Susan went for a while to the Tyne and Wear
Company, and learned to walk a not-very-high-wire and eat fire
in one of the lesser-known plays of Bertolt Brecht, Barney was

not required to share in these hazardous goings-on, but lived quietly in Tunbridge Wells.

And when Susan was out of work, she would spend hours happily, just looking at Barney. Changing him, feeding him, hushing him, taking him for walks in the pram, to be cooed at by total strangers. But mostly just looking, and thinking of nothing at all.

One afternoon, she came back from the recreation gardens, with Barney in his pram, to find Peter waiting in the street. He said, "Been keeping a secret from me, Sukey, haven't you?"

"No."

"Yes." He looked at Barney. "Why didn't you tell me?"

"I suppose you'd better come in."

Peter helped to get the carry-cot up the stairs. The rest of the pram lived down in the hall. "That'll be nicked," Peter said.

"It never has been."

She made instant coffee for them both. A pot of tea, she felt, would encourage him to stay. Peter was looking older. A bit tatty, his hair thinner at the crown. Well, it must be well over a year since she'd seen him, the paths of Barons Courters and Hendoners being as separate as they were. She said, "You've been to Ludlow, as I hear?"

"That's right."

"You had good notices."

"Only in the *Stage*."

"How was Kate?"

Peter said, "I didn't come here to talk about Kate."

"Love, you are being pompous."

"Why the hell didn't you tell me?"

"It wasn't your business."

He looked at her. She was surprised to see that his eyes were wet. She said, "Look, love, I'm sorry. Please don't get choked up. All right, I should have told you. I did think about it but, you know, I thought you might feel responsible, and want to pay for an abortion and all that. Think you had to; you know how it is. I didn't want you to think that."

"I wouldn't have."

"Wouldn't have what?"

"Wanted you to have an abortion." He looked at Barney. "He's beautiful. I'd have wanted you to have him."

Susan felt that the conversation was beginning to go beyond her. "Well, I have," she said. "So that's all right."

"I'd have wanted to share him."

A silence. Peter's nose had gone pink. He gulped at his instant coffee, and dribbled a little. Susan said, "Trevor all right?"

"Yes."

"You're still. . . ?"

"Yes."

"Well, you couldn't marry me, love."

"You never asked."

"You were spoken for. By a merchant bank."

"You never gave me the choice."

Susan said, "Oh dear!"

"I'd have married you, if you wanted that. Or we could just have shared looking after him. We still could. I mean, when you're working, I could, and when I'm working, which isn't all that often anyway . . ."

Susan said, "Oh dear, oh dear!"

"You never bloody thought of that, did you, not that possibility? It never crossed your mind."

"Well, no," Susan said. "No, it didn't. I'm awfully sorry, love. I know it was your seed, and all that. And it was wonderful at the time; it really was; I still remember it. But seed's just seed, Peter. You've nothing to do with Barney. I made the decision to have him; that's when *he* began. You were nothing to do with that. I mean, I do like you, love," said Susan, opening the door, "but I don't want to live with you, or share you with Trevor, or share Barney with you, or anything like that. I'm very old-fashioned, really. I don't know whether Barney ever will have a father; I shouldn't think so. But if he does, it'll be someone I've fallen in love with first in a really quite old-fashioned way."

She took the coffee mug out of Peter's hand, and set it down on the table. "Every story's got a beginning, a middle and an end," she said. "You were in at the beginning of Barney's, and as far as you're concerned this is the end." She led him to the door, closed it after him, and after a short while heard him start to walk downstairs. Then she went back to Barney.

The idea!

Daddy

I like my Daddy's best. It has more rooms. Mommy just has an apartment and you have to go upstairs. The bathroom is in my room. Daddy has two bathrooms. He owns the whole house. Mommy used to live there when I was a little baby. Before they got divorced. That means not married anymore. You get married when you love each other.

Mommy loves me. Daddy says I'm his favorite girl in the whole world, sugar. He always calls me sugar. We like to go to a restaurant for breakfast. Sometimes we go there for dinner if he has to work in the city. I went to his office lots of times. He has books there. You go way up in the elevator. Sometimes I feel like I'm going to throw up. But I don't. Then you see the river. There's no one there except Daddy and me. Sometimes Ellen comes.

My Mommy works. She goes to meetings. First I have to go to school and then daycare. You can make noise at daycare. At school you have to be quiet or you get punished. But I didn't ever get punished. Mommy helps me with my homework. Sometimes we read a book together. Daddy asks me add and take away. He says sugar you're so smart you can be anything you want to be when you grow up. A doctor or a lawyer or a professor or anything. My Daddy's a lawyer. I don't know if I'll get married.

Daddy said maybe next year I can go to a different school

where they have lots of things to play with. You can paint and go on trips and they have nice books. The kids make so much noise in my class. Some of them talk Spanish and the boys are bad. I got a star for doing my homework right.

My Daddy takes me on Sunday. Sometimes I sleep there if Mommy goes away. I have to be good. Daddy says he'll get me something when we go shopping if I behave. I have to take a bath before I go and brush my hair. Daddy says he likes little girls that smell nice and clean. Sometimes Ellen lets me try her perfume. Once she let me put some powder on my face and some blue stuff on my eyes. That's eye shadow. But I had to wash my face before I went home. Mommy doesn't wear makeup. Or Carolyn. They said it looks silly.

Once in the summer I stayed at my Daddy's for a whole week. Ellen was there. She helped take care of me. You're so helpless David she said. She laughed. We all laughed. I had fun. We went to Coney Island. During the week I just call my Daddy two times because he works hard. Sometimes if he goes on a trip he can't see me. Daddy and Ellen went on a trip to Florida. They had to fly in an airplane. They sent me a postcard every day. You could go swimming in the winter there. Mommy and me went to the country but the car broke.

Sometimes Carolyn stays overnight. We only have two beds. She has to sleep in the same bed with Mommy. When I wake up I get in bed with them. We all hug each other. Carolyn and Mommy kiss each other all the time. But they aren't married. Only a man and a woman can get married. When they want to have a baby the man's penis gets bigger and he puts it in the woman's vagina. It feels good to touch your vagina. Me and Veronica did it in the bathtub. When the baby comes out the doctor has to cut the Mommy's vagina with some scissors. Mommy showed me a picture in her book.

I saw Daddy's penis before. Mommy has hair on her vagina. She has hair on her legs and Carolyn has lots of hair on her legs like a man. Ellen doesn't. Mommy said maybe Ellen does have hair on her legs but she shaves it. Sometimes I forget and call

Carolyn Ellen. She gets mad. Sometimes I forget and call
Mommy Daddy. I have a cat called Meatball at Mommy's but
sometimes I forget and call Meatball Max instead. That's
Daddy's dog.

Daddy is all Jewish. So is Ellen. Mommy is only part Jewish.
But Daddy said I could be Jewish if I want. You can't have
Christmas if you're Jewish. Mommy and me had a little
Christmas tree. Carolyn came. We made cookies. I had
Chanukah at my Daddy's. He gave me a doll named Samantha
that talks and a skateboard and green pants and a yellow top. He
says when I learn to tell time he'll get me a watch.

I wish Mommy would get me a TV. I just have a little one.
Sometimes it gets broken. Daddy has a color TV at his house. It
has a thing with buttons you push to change the program.
Mommy says I watch too much TV. I said if you get me a new TV
I promise I'll only watch two programs every day. Mommy said
we're not going to just throw things away and get a new one every
year. I told her Andrea has a color TV in her house and Veronica
has a nice big TV in her room that you can see good. Mommy
said I'm not getting a TV and that's all. Mommy made me
feel bad. I started crying. Mommy said go to your room
you're spoiling my dinner. I said *asshole* to Mommy. That's
a curse. Sometimes my Mommy says a curse to me. I cried
and cried.

Mommy said get in your room. She spanked me and said now
get in your room. I ran in my room and closed the door. Mommy
hurts my feelings. She won't let me watch TV. She always goes to
a meeting and I have to stay with the babysitter. I don't say a
curse to my Daddy. My Daddy isn't mean to me. I screamed and
screamed for my Daddy and Mrs Taylor next door got mad and
banged on the wall.

Mommy said go in the other room and call him then. Daddy
said you sound like you've been crying. What's the matter,
sugar. Nothing I said. Daddy doesn't like me to cry. He says
crying is for little babies. I can't stand to see a woman cry, sugar,
he says. Then I laugh and he tells me blow my nose. What are we

going to do on Sunday I said. Oh that's a surprise Daddy said. Is it going somewhere I said. Yes we're going somewhere but that's not the real surprise Daddy said. Is it a present I said. Daddy said just wait and see, what did you do in school today. Daddy always asks what did I do in school. I told him the teacher had to punish Carlos. Daddy said listen isn't it about your bedtime. I have work to do. Ellen says hi. Blow me a goodnight kiss.

I hugged my Mommy. She hugged me back. She said she was sorry she got mad. But don't beg for things. A new TV is expensive. We don't need it. Mommy always says it's too expensive. I said I wish you were married to the President. Then we could live in the White House. I saw a picture in school. You could have anything you want. They don't have cockroaches.

The President is a good man. He helps people. George Washington was the President. Veronica gave me a doll of his wife at my birthday. It has a long dress. Mommy said he was mean to Indians and black people. But we studied about him in school and he wasn't. They had voting once. You could vote for Ford or Carter. My Daddy voted for Carter. I'm glad my Daddy voted for who won. My Mommy didn't vote.

Mommy doesn't like things. She doesn't like the President and she doesn't like Mary Hartman like my Daddy. I told her to get Charmin toilet paper like they have on TV because it's soft to squeeze. She said that's a rip-off. She only takes me to McDonald's once every month. I got a Ronald McDonald cup to drink my milk. She said that's a gimmick. I like milk. Milk is a natural. I told Mommy that and she got mad. I said you don't like anything Mommy. She said I like lots of things. I like plants. I like to play basketball. I like sleeping late on Sunday mornings. I like to eat. I like books. I like women. I like you.

Do you like men I said. I don't like most men very much Mommy said. Some men are OK. My Daddy likes women I said. Does he Mommy said.

I asked my Daddy does he like women. He said extremely. Some of my favorite people are women he said. Like you. And Ellen. Why do you ask. I said I don't know. Daddy said do you

like men. I love you Daddy I said. I bet she gets that you know
where Ellen said.

On Sunday we had breakfast at my Daddy's house. We had
pancakes. Daddy makes them. He puts on his cook's hat. Then
we went shopping. Then we went to a movie of Cinderella. Ellen
came too. Then we went to a restaurant. I had ice cream with
chocolate. Ellen and Daddy held each other's hand. Daddy said
now I'm going to tell you the surprise. Ellen and I are getting
married. How does that sound sugar. Ellen said for God's sake
David give her a little time to react.

Daddy said I can be in the wedding. He said Ellen will wear a
pretty dress and he will break a glass. He did that when he and
Mommy got married too. Then Ellen will have the same name as
Mommy and Daddy and me and I can call her Mommy too if I
want. I won't have to see my Daddy just on Sunday because
Ellen will be there to help take care of me. She only works in the
morning. It will be like a real family with a Mommy and a Daddy
and a kid. But I can't say that part because Daddy said it's
supposed to still be a secret.

I didn't feel good when Daddy brought me home. I felt like I
had to throw up. Mommy held my hand. I lay down on the bed
and she brought Meatball to play with me. She asked what did I
do with Daddy today. She always asks me that. I told her we saw
Cinderella. It was OK. She rode in a pumpkin. Some parts were
boring. The Prince loved her. Daddy and Ellen are going to get
married.

I started crying. I cried hard. Then I had to throw up. It got on
the rug.

Mommy got the washcloth. She brought my pajamas. She
hugged me. She said I love you. She said it won't be so
different when Daddy and Ellen are married. You like Ellen
don't you.

I love you, Mommy, I love you, I love you I said. Why don't
you like my Daddy. I love my Daddy.

I don't dislike your father Mommy said. We don't have much
in common that's all. I'm happy living here just with you. You're

special to me and you're special to your Daddy. You see him every week.

I cried and cried. I love you Mommy. I love you and Daddy both the same. And I love Ellen because she's going to be my Mommy too. I'll miss you. I'll miss you so much when I live there. I'll cry. I'm going to have a big sunny room and Daddy said he'll paint it and I can pick a color. I'm going to have a new kitty so I won't miss Meatball. Next year I can go to that nice school and Ellen might have a baby. It would be a brother or a sister. Daddy's going to get me a bicycle. I can take anything there I want. I'll just leave a few toys here for when I come to visit you on Sunday.

A Perfectly Nice Man

"I'm sorry I'm late, darling," Virginia said, having to pick up and embrace three-year-old Clarissa before she could kiss Katherine hello. "My last patient needed not only a new crown but some stitches for a broken heart. Why do people persist in marriage?"

"Your coat's cold," Clarissa observed soberly.

"So's my nose," Virginia said, burying it in the child's neck. "It's past your bath time and your story time, and I've probably ruined dinner."

"No," Katherine said. "We're not eating until seven-thirty. We're having a guest."

"Who?"

"Daddy's new friend," Clarissa said. "And I get to stay up until she comes."

"Really?"

"She said she needed to talk with us," Katherine explained. "She sounded all right on the phone. Well, a little nervous but not at all hostile. I thought, perhaps we owe her that much?"

"Or him?" Virginia wondered.

"Oh, if him, I suppose I should have said no," Katherine decided. "People who don't even want to marry him think this is odd enough."

"Odd about him?"

"Even he thinks it's odd about him," Katherine said.

"Men have an exaggerated sense of responsibility in the most peculiar directions," Virginia said. "We can tell her he's a perfectly nice man, can't we?" She was now addressing the child.

"Daddy said I didn't know who was my Mommy," Clarissa said.

"Oh?"

"I have two Mommies. Will Elizabeth be my Mommy, too?"

"She just might," Virginia said. "What a lucky kid that would make you."

"Would she come to live with us then?" Clarissa asked.

"Sounds to me as if she wants to live with Daddy," Virginia said.

"So did you, at first," Clarissa observed. Both women laughed.

"Your bath!" Virginia ordered and carried the child upstairs while Katherine returned to the kitchen to attend to dinner.

Clarissa was on the couch in her pyjamas, working a pop-up book of *Alice in Wonderland* with Virginia, when the doorbell rang.

"I'll get that," Katherine called from the kitchen.

Elizabeth, in a fur-collared coat, stood in the doorway, offering freesias.

"Did he tell you to bring them?" Katherine asked, smiling.

"He said we all three liked them," Elizabeth answered. "But don't most women?"

"I'm Katherine," Katherine said, "wife number one."

"And I'm Virginia, wife number two," Virginia said, standing in the hall.

"And I'm Elizabeth, as yet unnumbered," Elizabeth said. "And you're Clarissa."

Clarissa nodded, using one of Virginia's legs as a prop for leaning against or perhaps hiding behind.

Elizabeth was dressed, as the other two were, in very well-cut trousers and an expensive blouse, modestly provocative. And she was about their age, thirty. The three did not so much look alike as share a type, all about the same height, five feet seven inches or so (he said he was six feet tall but was, in fact, five feet ten and a half), slightly but well proportioned, with silky, well-cut hair and intelligent faces. They were all competent, assured women who intimidated only unconsciously.

Virginia poured three drinks and a small glass of milk for Clarissa, who was allowed to pass the nuts and have one or two before Katherine took her off to bed.

"She looks like her father," Elizabeth observed.

"Yes, she has his lovely eyes," Virginia agreed.

"He doesn't know I'm here," Elizabeth confessed. "Oh, I intend to tell him. I just didn't want it to be a question, you see?"

"He did think it a mistake that Katherine and I ever met. We didn't, of course, until after I'd married him. I didn't know he was married until quite a while after he and I met."

"He was a patient of yours?" Elizabeth asked.

"Yes."

"He's been quite open with me about both of you from the beginning, but we met in therapy, of course, and that does make such a difference."

"Does it?" Virginia asked, surprised. "I've never been in therapy."

"Haven't you?" Elizabeth asked, surprised. "I would have thought both of you might have considered it."

"He and I?"

"No, you and Katherine."

"We felt very uncomplicated about it", Virginia said, "once it happened. It was such an obvious solution."

"For him?"

"Well, no, not for him, of course. Thereapy was a thing for him to consider."

Katherine came back into the room. "Well, now we can be grown-ups."

"She looks like her father," Elizabeth observed again.

"She has his lovely eyes," it was Katherine's turn to reply.

"I don't suppose a meeting like this could have happened before the women's movement," Elizabeth said.

"Probably not," Katherine agreed. "I'm not sure Virginia and I could have happened before the women's movement. We might not have known what to do."

"He tries not to be antagonistic about feminism," Elizabeth said.

"Oh, he's always been quite good about the politics. He didn't resent my career," Virginia offered.

"He was quite proud of marrying a dentist," Katherine said. "I think he used to think I wasn't liberated enough."

"He doesn't think that now," Elizabeth said.

"I suppose not," Katherine agreed.

"The hardest thing for him has been facing ... the sexual implications. He has felt ... unmanned."

"He's put it more strongly than that in the past," Virginia said.

"Men's sexuality is so much more fragile than ours," Elizabeth said.

"Shall we have dinner?" Katherine suggested.

"He said you were a very good cook," Elizabeth said to Katherine.

"Most of this dinner is Virginia's. I got it out of the freezer," Katherine explained. "I've gone back to school, and I don't have that much time."

"I cook in binges," Virginia said, pouring the wine.

"At first he said he thought the whole thing was some kind of crazy revenge," Elizabeth said.

"At first there might have been that element in it," Virginia admitted. "Katherine was six months pregnant when he left her, and she felt horribly deserted. I didn't know he was going to be a father until after Clarissa was born. Then I felt I'd betrayed her, too, though I hadn't known anything about it."

"He said he should have told you," Elizabeth said, "but he was very much in love and was afraid of losing you. He said there was never any question of his not supporting Katherine and Clarissa."

"No, I make perfectly good money," Virginia said. "There's

no question of him supporting them now, if that's a problem. He doesn't."

"He says he'd rather he did," Elizabeth said.

"He sees Clarissa whenever he likes," Katherine explained. "He's very good with her. One of the reasons I wanted a baby was knowing he'd be a good sort of father."

"Did you have any reservations about marrying him?" Elizabeth asked Virginia.

"At the time? Only that I so very much wanted to," Virginia said. "There aren't that many marrying men around for women dentists, unless they're sponges, of course. It's flattering when someone is so afraid of losing you he's willing to do something legal about it. It oughtn't to be, but it is."

"But you had other reservations later," Elizabeth said.

"Certainly, his wife and his child."

"Why did he leave you, Katherine?"

"Because he was afraid of losing her. I suppose he thought he'd have what he needed of me anyway, since I was having his child."

"Were you still in love with him?" Elizabeth asked.

"I must have been," Katherine said, "or I couldn't have been quite so unhappy, so desperate. I was desperate."

"He's not difficult to fall in love with, after all," Virginia said. "He's a very attractive man."

"He asked me if I was a lesbian," Elizabeth said. "I told him I certainly didn't think so. After all, I was in love with him. He said so had two other women been, in love enough to marry him, but they were both lesbians. And maybe he only attracted lesbians even if they didn't know it themselves. He even suggested I should maybe try making love with another woman before I made up my mind."

There was a pause which neither Katherine nor Virginia attempted to break.

"Did either of you know ... before?"

Katherine and Virginia looked at each other. Then they said, "No."

"He's even afraid he may turn women into lesbians," Elizabeth said.

Both Virginia and Katherine laughed, but not unkindly.

"Is that possible?" Elizabeth asked.

"Is that one of *your* reservations?" Katherine asked.

"It seemed crazy," Elizabeth said, "but . . ."

Again the two hostesses waited.

"I know this probably sounds very unliberated and old-fashioned and maybe even prejudiced, but I don't think I could stand being a lesbian, finding out I'm a lesbian; and if there's something in him that makes a woman . . . How can either of you stand to be together instead of with him?"

"But you don't know you're a lesbian until you fall in love," Katherine said, "and then it's quite natural to want to be together with the person you love."

"What's happening to me is so peculiar. The more sure I am I'm in love with him, the more obsessively I read everything I can about what it is to be a lesbian. It's almost as if I *had* fallen in love with a woman, and that's absurd."

"I don't really think there's anything peculiar about him," Katherine said.

"One is just so naturally drawn to, so able to identify with, another woman," Virginia said. "When I finally met Katherine, what he needed and wanted just seemed too ridiculous."

"But it was you he wanted," Elizabeth protested.

"At Katherine's and Clarissa's expense, and what was I, after all, but just another woman."

"A liberated woman," Katherine said.

"Not then, I wasn't," Virginia said.

"I didn't feel naturally drawn to either of you," Elizabeth protested. "I wasn't even curious at first. But he's so obsessed with you still, so afraid of being betrayed again, and I thought, I've got to help him somehow, reassure him, understand enough to let him know, as you say, that there's nothing peculiar about him . . . or me."

"I'm sure there isn't," Katherine said reassuringly and reached out to take Elizabeth's hand.

Virginia got up to clear the table.

"Mom!" came the imperious and sleepy voice of Clarissa.

"I'll go," Virginia said.

"But I don't think you mean what I want you to mean," Elizabeth said.

"Perhaps not," Katherine admitted.

"He said he never should have left you. It was absolutely wrong; and if he ever did marry again, it was because he wanted to make that commitment, but what if his next wife found out she didn't want him, the way Virginia did?"

"I guess anyone takes that risk," Katherine said.

"Do you think I should marry him?" Elizabeth asked.

Katherine kept Elizabeth's hand, and her eyes met Elizabeth's beseeching, but she didn't answer.

"You *do* think there's something wrong with him."

"No, I honestly don't. He's a perfectly nice man. It's just that I sometimes think that isn't good enough, not now when there are other options."

"What other options?"

"You have a job, don't you?"

"I teach at the university, as he does."

"Then you can support yourself."

"That's not always as glamorous as it sounds."

"Neither is marriage," Katherine said.

"Is this?" Elizabeth asked, looking around her, just as Virginia came back into the room.

"It's not nearly as hard as some people try to make it sound."

"Clarissa wanted to know if her new mother was still here."

"Oh my," Elizabeth said.

"Before you came, she wanted to know, if you married her father, would you be another mother and move in here."

Elizabeth laughed and then said, "Oh, God, that's just what he wants to know!"

They took their coffees back into the living room.

"It must be marvelous to be a dentist. At least during the day you can keep people from telling you all their troubles," Elizabeth said.

"That's not as easy as it looks," Virginia said.

"He says you're the best dentist he ever went to. He hates his dentist now."

"I used to be so glad he wasn't like so many men who fell in love with their students," Katherine said.

"Maybe he'd be better off," said Elizabeth in mock gloom. "He says he isn't threatened by my having published more than he has. He had two wives and a baby while I was simply getting on with it; but does he mean it? Does he really know?"

"We're all reading new lines, aren't we?" Virginia asked.

"But if finally none of us marries them, what will they do?" Elizabeth asked.

"I can hardly imagine that," Katherine said.

"You can't imagine what they'll do?"

"No, women saying 'no', all of them. We can simply consider ourselves, for instance," Katherine said.

"Briefly anyway," Virginia said. "Did you come partly to see if you were at all like us?"

"I suppose so," Elizabeth said.

"Are you?"

"Well, I'm not surprised by you . . . and very surprised not to be."

"Are you sorry to have married him?" Virginia asked Katherine.

"I could hardly be. There's Clarissa, after all, and you. Are you?" she asked in return.

"Not now," Virginia said, "having been able to repair the damage."

"And everyone knows," Elizabeth said, "that you did have the choice."

"Yes," Virginia agreed, "there's that."

"But I felt I didn't have any choice," Katherine said. "That part of it humiliated me."

"Elizabeth is making a distinction," Virginia said, "between what everyone knows and what each of us knows. I shared your private humiliation, of course. All women must."

"Why?" Elizabeth demanded.

"Not to believe sufficiently in one's own value," Virginia explained.

"But he doesn't believe sufficiently in his own value either," Elizabeth said. "He doesn't even quite believe he's a man."

"I never doubted I was a woman," Katherine said.

"That's smug," Elizabeth said, "because you have a child."

"So does he," Katherine replied.

"But he was too immature to deal with it; he says so himself. Don't you feel at all sorry for him?"

"Yes," said Katherine.

"Of course," Virginia agreed.

"He's been terribly hurt. He's been damaged," Elizabeth said.

"Does that make him more or less attractive, do you think?" Virginia asked.

"Well, damn it, less, of course," Elizabeth shouted. "And whose fault is that?"

Neither of the other two women answered.

"He's not just second, he's third-hand goods," Elizabeth said.

"Are women going to begin to care about men's virginity?" Katherine asked. "How extraordinary!"

"Why did you go into therapy?" Virginia asked.

"I hardly remember," Elizabeth said. "I've been so caught up with his problems since the beginning. The very first night of the group, he said I somehow reminded him of his wives . . ."

"Perhaps that is why you went," Katherine suggested.

"You think I'd be crazy to marry him, don't you?" Elizabeth demanded.

"Why should we?" Virginia asked. "We both did."

"That's not a reassuring point," Elizabeth said.

"You find us unsatisfactory," Katherine said, in apology.

"Exactly not," Elizabeth said sadly. "I want someone to advise me . . . to make a mistake. Why should you?"

"Why indeed?" Virginia asked.

They embraced warmly before Elizabeth left.

"Perhaps I might come again?" she asked at the door.

"Of course," Katherine said.

After the door closed, Katherine and Virginia embraced.

"He'd be so much happier, for a while anyway, if he married again," Katherine said.

"Of course he would," Virginia agreed, with some sympathy in her voice. "But we couldn't encourage a perfectly nice woman like Elizabeth . . ."

"That's the problem, isn't it?" Katherine said. "That's just it."

"She'll marry him anyway," Virginia predicted, "briefly."

"And have a child?" Katherine asked.

"And fall in love with his next wife," Virginia went on.

"There really isn't anything peculiar about him," Katherine said.

"I'm sorry he doesn't like his dentist."

"He should never have married you."

"No, he shouldn't," Virginia agreed. "Then at least I could still be taking care of his teeth."

Barring that, they went up together to look on his richly mothered child, sleeping soundly, before they went to their own welcoming bed.

Floral Street

1

We are standing at the junction of Pembridge Road and the Bayswater Road, outside Notting Hill Gate Underground station, looking north. It is early morning. And winter. A man is walking towards us. He is tall, well built almost to the point of caricature, and exactly thirty-six years old. Today is his birthday. He is wearing a tattersall shirt, a yellow tweed tie, loose-cut green drill trousers, a maroon pullover, and brown brogues. Over this a fur-lined brown tweed overcoat, its fur collar turned up to frame his face, flaps open as he walks. His hands are in the overcoat pockets. From his right shoulder hangs a canvas fishing bag. An umbrella is crooked into his left pocket, and flaps with the coat. Under his trousers, for a variety of reasons not all of them sexual, he wears a cockring. He walks with a loose-limbed stride. Just before his face comes into focus he stops to look at the advertisement board outside the newsagent's. From the way he stands you might think he had trained as a dancer. Then again you might think his feet hurt.

That is our opening image. The scene, as it were, before the titles. Our story begins an hour earlier, and a couple of hundred yards away, in the bedroom of a largely white maisonette in Chepstow Villas. The room is beginning to lighten. Two figures, male and female, are intertwined under the duvet. Until a week ago, Martin Conrad, known to his friends as Bear, would drowse through the shipping forecast, only disentangling himself from encircling arms and forcing himself into full wakefulness to listen to the news. Lately, however, he has discontinued this practice. He finds the news depressing, and has advanced his clock radio seven minutes in order to miss it, and begin his day untrammelled by material considerations. He regards this as a great step forward. This morning, then, he is roused by Patricia Hughes's husky Good Morning Campers, and lies listening to Soler's Fandango, which he finds too interesting to clean his teeth to. When the piece is over, he pushes aside his partner's arms, pushes back the duvet, and slips out from under a pinioning thigh. His partner does not wake. He turns off the radio, and goes to the bathroom, where he inspects himself closely in the mirror, showers, cleans his teeth, moisturizes his face, and decides not to shave. He shakes his wet head, pats his hair into the most becoming tangle of curls, shakes his head again but more gently, and puts on his dressing gown. On his way from the bathroom to the stairs he pauses outside his bedroom door, lifts his hand as if to rap with his knuckles, hesitates, and puts both hands in his pockets. He says Happy birthday darling, and starts for the stairs. At the top of the stairs he draws the cockring from his pocket, and stops to put it on, frowning slightly with concentration. This done, he puts his hands back in his pockets and descends the stairs. As he descends, his belt unties and his dressing gown flaps open. He neglects to close it, and proceeds to the kitchen, where his son sits at the breakfast bar over coffee and muesli. His son inserts a spoonful of muesli into his mouth, and smiles. Martin notices that fragments of chewed grain fleck his son's teeth.

His son says, Hi dad.

Martin says, Hi kid.

His son says, Coffee's ready.

Martin pours himself a black coffee, tastes it, and grimaces.

Four years, he says. Four years since I gave up sugar, and I still hate it. They all said I'd get used to it, but I hate it.

His son stands up and walks round the breakfast bar. He hugs his father, and plants a muesli-scented kiss on his cheek.

Happy birthday Bear, he says.

Martin returns his son's hug.

Thanks kid, he says.

They sit opposite each other at the breakfast bar. Martin fills a bowl with muesli, sprinkles bran on it, adds milk, and eats.

How old are you anyway? his son says.

What have you bought me? Martin says.

I haven't bought anything, his son says, but I have got you something. Got something for you.

Martin looks down. He studies his naked feet.

I hate new shoes, he says. Just look at that blister. Don't tell me you've made something. Not another pot. I couldn't bear it. Don't they teach you anything else?

His son says, Not another pot. At the moment I don't have time. O-levels. In case you've forgotten.

Martin says, I haven't forgotten. Resits. The shame of it. So when am I going to get it, this gift?

His son says, Tonight. After school. Jane has dinner planned. For nine, I think. So there's plenty of time.

Martin says, That blazer is none too clean.

His son says, Your dressing gown has seen better days. More coffee?

Martin closes his dressing gown, and belts it.

Sorry, he says.

No need, his son says. I've seen it all before. I'll get the coffee.

How old are you, Fred? Martin says. Sorry to ask.

I have no sense of time either, Fred says. I'm fifteen. And a half. How old are you?

A yell, muffled by distance and closed doors, is heard.

Martin says, She wakes.

Fred says, Saved by the bell. I can always ask her, you know.

What makes you think, Martin says, that I told her the truth?

They smile.

Oh well, Fred says. It was worth a try.

I was twenty when you were born, Martin says. Where's your calculator?

This conversation, Fred says, is getting a bit father-and-son. Not to say schoolmasterly. You'd better get back to Jane.

Martin says, Where are the cats?

That reminds me, Fred says. Jane asked me to remind you to check and see if they've put our ad up yet.

I suppose I'd better, Martin says. I shall miss their miasmal presence. Where have they puked this morning? Not on the records again?

There is another yell from upstairs. This time it is more distinct. The monosyllable Fred! is audible.

I couldn't find any, Fred says. I suppose they do have to go?

It's either them or Jane, Martin says. We can't have her crying all the time. But a new home. Not put down, I promise.

Bags under the eyes, Fred says. Oh well. Fair exchange, I suppose. I like her.

We hear the sound of an upstairs door opening and closing, and the sound of a voice from the head of the stairs.

Fred, you bastard, the voice says. I asked you to wake me. It's Martin's birthday.

Dulcet tones, Fred says.

Martin stands up.

Change your blazer, he says. There's a dear.

OK, Fred says.

Martin goes to the kitchen door and shouts, Go back to bed. I'm still here. He turns back into the kitchen.

Time for her coffee, he says.

Fred pours coffee into Martin's cup and hands it over the bar.

Was it fun? he says. The cockring.

OK, Martin says. I'll see you tonight.

I hope so, Fred says.

Martin takes the coffee cup, and goes back upstairs. He pushes open the bedroom door with his foot, crinkles his nose against the smell of sleep, and enters. What, for lack of a better word, we will call his girlfriend sits propped by pillows.

Happy birthday darling, she says.

Martin says, Bleary and beautiful, puts the coffee on the floor by the bed, and leans down to kiss her. She encircles his neck with her arms, and pulls herself into a kneeling position. She kisses him explosively on the ear.

Don't kiss my ear, he says. I don't like having my goddamn ear kissed. It hurts. It echoes.

Jane says, Crabby and beautiful. I love you.

She hugs him. He kisses her. First on the lips, then on each breast.

Time to get dressed, he says.

Not yet, she says, and leans over to fish under the bed. Martin takes this opportunity to kiss her buttocks. She pulls an enormous parcel out from under the bed. With expressions of rapture Martin unwraps the parcel to reveal the brown fur-lined overcoat already mentioned.

Holy mackerel! Martin says. Wherever did you get it? It's stunning.

He takes off his dressing gown and puts the overcoat on.

I'm going to be unbelievably late, he says. How do I look?

Stunning, Jane says. Why not let's be very late?

Sorry, Martin says. Tonight.

He takes off the overcoat.

OK, Jane says. Dinner at nine.

She stands by the bed and opens her arms. Jane and Martin embrace. Shortly they release each other, and Jane gets back into bed. Martin goes to the wardrobe and speedily dresses. Jane sniffs and wipes her eyes.

Cats, Martin says. I'll check the ad today. Bye.

Bye, Jane says. What is it tonight? Fashion or fucking?

Fucking, Martin says. But I won't be late.

I love you, Jane says.

Good, Martin says.

Yes, Jane says. Very good.

You're beautiful, Martin says.

I know, Jane says.

2

The journey from Notting Hill Gate, where we saw him first, to Embankment has been accomplished. Martin has spent most of it with a disregarded letterpad, of which more later, open on his knees. The pad was disregarded because Martin is worried by his vision. Recently, he cannot say exactly when, he has become conscious of a flaw in his right eye—the eye, incidentally, which is not short sighted. He attributes this flaw to some sort of fleck on his pupil which causes a minute but irritating dot to dance between him and the world. He tends to concentrate on this dot, and has succeeded in training his eyes, and the dot with them, into immobility. He is not unaware of the look of pleasant abstraction that this immobility lends his features. An interesting side effect of this condition is that he now feels unable to pass his journey in the oblivion of reading or writing, and, although he still carries a book or a letterpad, he rarely uses them. Rather to his surprise, as he has always considered himself the sort of person that dreads an unfilled moment, he finds he welcomes the opportunity for increased contemplation that this lack of occupation affords him. This morning's journey was spent rehearsing certain words of advice and consolation he intends to write to one of his friends who is on the brink of separation from his wife. Hence the letterpad. He repeats to himself choice words and phrases as he walks from Embankment to Charing Cross mainline station. He does this in an effort to commit them to memory, although experience has taught him that, when confronted with a white sheet of paper, his mind will prove as blank as the paper. He would, in fact, give his eye teeth, or maybe something less conspicuous, such as his little toe, for the ability to transfer his thoughts to paper with felicity. This is a greater sacrifice than would at first appear, as he is excited by feet in general, and his own in particular.

At the station bookshop he buys a *Times Literary Supplement*, a *Times Educational Supplement*, a copy of *Quarto*, the December

edition of *Gramophone*, for the critics' choice and an article on
early music, an *Uomo Vogue*, and a *Films Illustrated*. He flips
through, but rejects, *Private Eye*, a Wodehouse omnibus,
Harper's Bazaar, and a newly published paperback biography of
Trotsky. He is an avid buyer of printed matter, and can rarely
pass a newsagent's without an effort of will. He will be late for an
appointment this evening, for instance, because he will spend
half an hour browsing through the French section of Grant and
Cutler. This morning, however, because of his rejection of the
mentioned works, he congratulates himself on a comparatively
cheap escape.

He is successful in his search for a single compartment to
himself on the train, and settles down, not without some conflict,
in the left-hand seat facing forwards, to await its departure. His
choice of seat is a recurring problem. He can never decide
whether he prefers the east or the west view from Hungerford
Bridge, and as he regards either of these views as among the most
rewarding in London, the question is of some importance to
him. Certainly he finds the effect of taking off into the air that is
caused by the train's leaving the station inspiriting enough to
make him forgo his usual preference for sitting with his back to
the engine.

The river crossing past, he turns his attention to the letterpad.

Damn, he writes, I've forgotten to take my kelp pills. I shall
be grouchy all day. And my face will go blotchy if I'm not careful, which will be a bore as I have an engagement this evening.
Still, I won't dwell on it because I know you disapprove of all
that.

I know you want me to advise you, but I am unbelievably
reluctant to do it. One thing that being a teacher has taught me is
that one should never, never, give advice. People don't need it,
or really want it. And if you haven't already made up your mind,
it would be an impertinence anyway. The only thing I can, or am
going to, say is: Do what you want. Unblinkered. When you've
decided what it is you want, do it. And take what follows. It is
rent. What you must pay for following what you desire. But it is

very important that you do so in the full knowledge of what you
will suffer in either event. Whatever happens you will be
miserably lonely, or miserable in company, And believe me,
however it may appear in your present state, living alone is
difficult. The grass is not greener. The important things—
feeling hellish in the mornings, wintry afternoon trees, waiting
for buses—are so much less important if you can't share them.
And yet, if the orange is squeezed dry remember that Christ did
not blast the barren fig tree for nothing. And, whatever you do,
do not confuse your love for one person with your love for
another. That's why it is always a mistake to have children in an
attempt to keep a marriage together. All right, keep your shirt
on. I'm not suggesting that that's what you did. But you do have
a child, my dear, and to stay with Steph because you love him is
an insult to both of them, and to you. I know, I know. I'm lucky.
I had it both ways. But I paid my rent. Fred is with me because
Katy died, so I guess you could say that she paid her rent too. He
sends his love, by the way. Fred does. Jane too. And if you think
this display of family solidarity is just rubbing salt in your
wounds, remember that Steph is my friend too. And I would
give, probably shall give, her the same lack of advice that I give
you. Ultimately one has only one loyalty, to honesty, and if this
test has arrived, if you have to give up your wife, or your son, or
both, then you should be glad. Yes glad. Because it wouldn't be
honest to keep them, or rather because keeping them is what you
would be doing, rather than freely sharing with them. And I
think that that is probably enough in-depth emotion for one
morning. Remember, remember dear, that I love you, and so
does Fred, and we love Steph too. You are the base from which
we wander. And you are not to hurt each other, especially not in
the name of anything, and if separation is the way forward, take
it. Separate. And now, as I seem to be close to giving what I said I
wouldn't, I'm going to stop.

Martin sits and rests his eyes. The train slows down, and he
closes the letter pad and puts it in the fishing bag. The train pulls
up at a station which, in Martin's words, shall remain nameless,

out of respect for the dead. With a well but not perfectly concealed anxiety he first taps, then investigates, his pockets for keys, season ticket, wallet, chequebook. He is a compulsive checker of the almost certain, and has been known to get up in the middle of the night to verify that the television is unplugged, the bathroom window open, or the front door properly locked. This done, he recrooks the umbrella into his pocket, slings the fishing bag over his shoulder, and alights.

Hi, he says to the ticket collector.

Morning, the ticket collector says. Funny old colour.

Martin looks around and becomes conscious of two things in quick succession. First, that it is a beautiful morning, the light a clear brumous yellow. Second, and not for the first time, that he is the sort of person who doesn't notice that sort of thing until it is pointed out to him.

Yes, he says. Lovely isn't it?

Disco Annie, who is waiting for him outside the station, winds down the car window and says, My God, what have you got on? You look like a fashion plate.

I am a fashion plate, Martin says. More often than not.

Don't tell me, Disco Annie says. You stole it from Wardrobe.

It's a present, Martin says, getting into the car. From Jane. Though if she stole it from Wardrobe I wouldn't be surprised.

Disco Annie starts the car and moves into the traffic.

Sorry, she says. I forgot.

Don't worry, Martin says. I'm too old to care.

I'll buy you a drink at lunch, Disco Annie says. If there's time.

Why not? Martin says.

Actually, Disco Annie says. There probably won't be. I'm having trouble.

She stops the car at a red light.

Boy trouble, she says. Paul d'Acosta.

Again, Martin says.

Still, Disco Annie says. We saw the educational psychiatrist yesterday. Not much help. We are to make no educational allowances. Whatever that may mean.

The light changes to green. Disco Annie winds down the window.

Come on, she shouts to the car in front. It's not going to get any greener.

He can't stop, she says, once they are moving again. He doesn't know why he does it. It will be jail this time, I expect. They found over two thousand quid's worth of electrical goods under his bed. God knows where he got them from. He won't say. The police are being nice but firm. I was wondering if you'd speak to him.

What the hell can I say? Martin says.

I don't know, Disco Annie says. I've tried everything. He doesn't handle women well, the shrink says.

I'm not surprised, Martin says. She's a ten-valium-a-day mother, you know. Before breakfast.

Yes, Disco Annie says. And I remind him of her. Would you believe? Which makes me worse than useless. Such nonsense. Will you? Speak to him. Please, Bear.

OK, Martin says. But I can't imagine what good it will do.

Lunchtime? Disco Annie says.

Half-past twelve, Martin says. After physical jerks.

Happy birthday Bear, Disco Annie says.

Thanks, Martin says. Thanks a million.

I'll buy you a drink sometime, Disco Annie says.

3

Martin lies on his back on the horse and lifts weights into the air.

Thirty-nine, he says.

It is midday.

Forty, he says. Forty-one. Forty-two.

Shut up and pump, Grace Poole says.

Forty-three, Martin says. Forty-four. Of course I was not always as you see me now. Forty-eight.

Forty-seven, Grace Poole says.

Forty-eight, Martin says. For. Ty. Nine.

Get it up, Grace Poole says. Push, you stuck-up cocky bastard. Push.

Martin holds the weight at full extension.

Grace, he says. Please. There are children present.

Shut up and pump, Grace Poole says. Ten more.

Shit, Martin says. I'll never do it. Fifty-one. Fifty-two. Fifty-three.

Come on, sir, a voice says.

Fifty-four. Fifty-five. Fifty-six, Martin says.

Push, sir, another voice says, and another voice, more daring, Get it up.

Fifty-seven. Fifty-eight. Fifty-nine, Martin says. Christ, I'll never do it.

Get your finger out and shove, Grace Poole says.

Six. Ty! Martin says. Someone take the goddamn thing. Quick.

Schoolboy hands divest him of the weight. He lies, eyes closed, panting.

Not bad, Grace Poole says. If you cared as much for your body as you do for the cut of your tracksuit you'd be OK. Wallbars next. Thirty.

Bitch, Martin says.

Please, a boy's voice says. There are children present.

Martin goes to the wallbars. He climbs and hangs, facing outward. He lifts his knees to his chin.

Christ, a voice to his left says, and the thief.

Martin turns to see Paul d'Acosta similarly positioned. They lift their knees to their chins.

Hi kid, Martin says. Half-past, right? My place. Miss Maitland tell you?

Yes, the boy says. She informed me.

They lift their knees again.

I'm off, Paul d'Acosta says.

He drops from the wallbars.

See you in the showers, Martin says.

Not if I see you first, Paul d'Acosta says.

Martin looks after the retreating boy, then continues his exercise.

Spring jumps next, Grace Poole says. Then back to the weights.

Grace, I have only one life, Martin says. I have an interview.

You'll be late, Grace Poole says. Get a move on.

I'm going to be sick, Martin says.

Not in my gym you're not, Grace Poole says. Get on with it.

Yes matron. Yes nurse, Martin says. Yes Grace Poole.

He gets on with it.

Twenty minutes later, comfortably tired, his hair still wet from the shower, he enters his classroom. Paul d'Acosta stands by his desk, looking out of the window. He does not move when Martin enters, or redirect his gaze.

Hi kid, Martin says.

Name's Paolo, Paul d'Acosta says.

Sorry, Martin says. Force of habit. I'm nice to everybody.

He sits at his desk.

Do you want to sit down? he says. Or would you rather look out of the window?

Paul d'Acosta turns into the room and sits, with apparent unconcern, on the edge of Martin's desk, Martin opens the desk drawer and takes out cigarettes, matches and an ashtray.

Smoke? he says.

Paul d'Acosta shrugs, then takes the proffered cigarette. Martin takes one for himself and lights both.

Thanks, he says.

Sorry, Paul d'Acosta says. Thanks. Sir.

Well, Martin says. I guess you know what this is all about.

You're not, Paul d'Acosta says. Nice to everyone. You treat everyone in the same way. That's not the same thing. Not with everyone. That means you don't care. You don't care enough to be not nice. Even when it's deserved.

And who decides, Martin says, what is deserved?

You use your niceness like a weapon, Paul d'Acosta says. That's not nice.

What purpose would it serve, Martin says, if I were nasty? Would it make you feel better? A satisfying scene, is that what you want? Tears and slamming of doors. Grand opera stuff, Paolo?

Very clever, Paul d'Acosta says.

Well is it? Martin says. A punishment. Is that what you want?

So I'm a masochist, Paul d'Acosta says. That makes it easier. OK. I guess in a way. But it's got to come from someone who cares.

Martin inhales cigarette smoke, and gently exhales.

I mean, Paul d'Acosta says, it's not as if I'm not. Punished. Five times in court. God knows how many good thrashings. My Mum cries, and takes pills, and says she's going to kill herself.

You sound, Martin says, almost proud of it all.

But doesn't mean anything, Paul d'Acosta says. They don't care. It's their morality that's outraged. Their lives that are ruined.

So no one else, Martin says, is allowed any scenes?

They can do what they like, Paul d'Acosta says. They don't fool me. They don't care about me.

And Miss Maitland? Martin says. What about her?

She gets paid, Paul d'Acosta says. And she shoves it off to you anyway.

And I'm supposed to care, Martin says. Is that it?

I don't know, Paul d'Acosta says. That's what we're here to find out, isn't it?

I can't see anything to care about, Martin says. Who do you care about after all?

No bargains, Paul d'Acosta says. I can look after myself.

Right into jail, Martin says.

I can look after myself, Paul d'Acosta says.

Then I don't see what I can do, Martin says. You don't want any help.

I didn't say that, Paul d'Acosta says. Just because I can look after myself doesn't mean I want to have to. I want to decide who I want to help me.

Martin stubs out his cigarette. Paul d'Acosta pinches off the end of his and puts the butt into his pocket.

And how, Martin says, do I prove myself? Always assuming that I want to. No bargains, my ass. You're treating me to a pretty hefty slice of blackmail here.

Yes, Paul d'Acosta says. I am, aren't I?'

Smug bastard, Martin says.

Smug bastard shit, Paul d'Acosta says. I've got a lot to lose here.

And you're also laying a whole lot more on me, Martin says, than you have right to. What makes you think I'm interested in why, or even if, you steal? What makes you think I could give a damn whether you go to jail or not?

Well you're here, aren't you? Paul d'Acosta says.

At Miss Maitland's request, Martin says. I'm doing the job I'm paid to. Like her.

Yes, Paul d'Acosta says. Just like her. That's why she's having lunch and you're here. With me.

You're reading too much into things, Martin says. I care just about as much as she does. Which is just about midway between how much you care, and how much you'll allow us to care. All we are is teachers, you know. Though we do know enough about amateur psychiatry to recognize a standard manoeuvre when we see one. You're pushing us to rejection point so that you can have a couple more people to blame. Poor Paolo. Sure I'm here with you. And you are fighting damned hard to ensure that I'm wasting my time.

Valuable time, Paul d'Acosta says. I'm sorry to be so ordinary.

What's the point of being sorry? Martin says. Any fool can admit his mistake. There's no virtue in the admission if you make no effort to change. You're making me sound like a teacher, Paolo, you're forcing me into your mould. And I resent it. And I'm not letting you get away with it. All right. No bargains. You want to be a loser, be a loser. Sod off then, and leave me out of it.

Kiss me, Paul d'Acosta says. You're beautiful when you're angry.

He stands up laughing, and moves round the desk. Martin stands up and faces him, also laughing.

You don't fool me, Paul d'Acosta says.

Martin stops laughing.

I'm sorry, he says, let's call it a good joke, and leave it at that.

Paul d'Acosta stops laughing.

I'm not blind, he says, and I'm not a fool.

OK, Paolo, Martin says. You can go now. This isn't getting us anywhere.

Kiss me, Paul d'Acosta says. I mean it. Joke over. Please Bear.

Shit, Martin says. Go away. Go read a good book or something.

Magazines, Paul d'Acosta says. I read magazines.

He steps closer to Martin and closes his eyes. Martin doesn't move. After a while the boy opens his eyes and grabs Martin round the waist.

I want you to fuck me, he says. I want to suck your cock.

Martin concentrates his gaze on the wall behind Paul d'Acosta's head. The boy moves his hands from Martin's waist to the back of his head. He grasps Martin's hair and kisses him. The kiss lands on the corner of Martin's mouth. Martin does not move, continues staring at the wall. The boy releases him and walks to the door. Martin sits down at his desk. At the door Paul d'Acosta turns back, opens his mouth to speak, but is prevented.

See you around kid, Martin says.

Not if I see you first, Paul d'Acosta says.

After the boy has gone, Martin continues sitting for some time. Then he opens his desk drawer, looking for his cigarettes. They are neither in the drawer nor on the desk nor anywhere to be seen. He takes a deep breath. Disco Annie enters.

I'm sorry, she says.

How much of that did you catch? Martin says.

Enough to know it didn't work, Disco Annie says.

The little bastard stole my cigarettes, Martin says.

An impossible child, Disco Annie says. Have one of mine.

Never again, Martin says.

Until the next time, Disco Annie says.

A hundred and one things a boy can do, Martin says. Where's that cigarette? I need a bath.

And a drink, Disco Annie says, lighting their cigarettes. I owe you one, don't forget.

4

Five and a half hours later Martin, half an hour in Grant and Cutler behind him, rings the bell of a house in Floral Street. It is snowing. An aria by Verdi floats from an open upper window. Martin stamps his feet as he waits, and spins his umbrella to dislodge snowflakes. The entryphone says hello, and Martin gives his name and pushes the door open. He is immediately enveloped in heat. Tia Juana likes people to sweat.

Come up darling, an upstairs voice calls above the Verdi. You're late.

Martin removes his outer layer.

Sorry, he says. Trains. Isn't this the most sod awful weather. I'm taking my shoes off.

Tia Juana has come to the head of the stairs.

Why not darling? he says. It all comes off in the end. Your umbrella is dripping on my carpet.

I am dripping on your carpet, you *House and Garden* queen, Martin says.

Tia Juana meditates.

Peevish, he says, and makes for his sitting room.

Martin follows him, shaking his head.

And I'm speckling your wallpaper with my sodden curls, he says.

Verdi climaxes as he enters Tia Juana's sitting room.

Perfect timing, Tia Juana says. As usual. That's why I like you.

Amore Vincera, Martin says. Appropriate, do you think?

Allow an actress her illusions, Tia Juana says. Sherry?

La Fanciulla del West End, Martin says.

It's on the cabinet, Tia Juana says. Sweet and sticky. Just for you.

Treacle, Martin says, pouring golden oloroso. Yum yum!

Now, dear Bear, Tia Juana says. Business.

Juana, Martin says. Curb your impatience. I'm tired.

You're looking, Tia Juana says, not the better for wear. You must be careful. We can't afford it.

We can afford, Martin says, damn near anything we want. I'm a gold mine, and don't forget it.

Bills, Tia Juana says, bills.

You could turn the heating down, Martin says.

Not that sort of bill, Tia Juana says. Naive child.

Naif, Martin says. I'm older than you are.

And a teacher too, Tia Juana says. Such a skilful girl.

Don't you ever tire, Martin says, of all this campery? These are the eighties, darling. Mae West is dead.

We are all liberated, Tia Juana says. What an unbuttoned sisterhood we are. Now get that sherry down you, girl, and let's get to it.

Martin carries his full sherry glass across the room, and sits next to Tia Juana on the sofa.

Could we turn it down? he says. Or off preferably.

Tia Juana rises from the sofa, turns down Verdi, and takes an envelope from his desk.

Contact sheets, he says. Last Friday and Monday.

Friday I recall was not a success, Martin says. I told you he was wrong. The story line was pretty tacky too. I don't make a good trucker.

Art, Tia Juana says, is long. And he was long.

He hands the contact sheets to Martin, and reseats himself, Martin sips sherry, and studies the sheets.

He looks at his own cock too much, he says. He gives the game away.

Your lack of interest, Tia Juana says, is not apparent.

Art, Martin says. Well let's see what can be salvaged.

He extracts a pen from a pocket, circles and crosses the sheet.

Not much, he says. It'll do as illustrations. It won't stand up on its own. Let's have a look at Monday.

Monday, Tia Juana says, is good.

Yes, Martin says. I remember. But not comfortable. I never want to kneel on a billiard table again. I got flat knees.

The facial expression, Tia Juana says, is marvellous.

Art, Martin says. The trick is to mix pain and pleasure in just the right proportion, and just a dash of surprise.

He inspects the sheet closely.

Art in this case, he says, was helped considerably by nature. I see it brought tears to the eyes. They'll do. Except for this one. I look drunk. Or doped. Or both. What can I have been doing?

Struggling for air by the look of it, Tia Juana says.

Well, Martin says. What have you got for me tonight?

Tia Juana places his fingertips together.

Tonight, he says, is special. He says he's nineteen. I would guess sixteen.

Boys, Martin says, are rarely clean. I hope you've soaped him.

He's with Pearl now, Tia Juana says.

What's his cock like? Martin says. Clean? Circumcised?

Both, Tia Juana says. He's tall, curly hair, skinny. What are you going to do?

Martin meditates.

The best part, he says, of a boy's body is where the thigh joins the trunk. The lines, you know. And the backsweep to the buttocks.

Yes, Tia Juana says. What are you going to do?

The thing is, Martin says, you must reverse expectation. I shall fuck him, of course. My public expects it. Then he can fuck me. That drives them wild. Bitch fucks butch. And whatever takes my fancy over and above. Depending on how pretty he is.

Not my type, Tia Juana says. I prefer the older type. Pearl, by the way, has a new assistant. Not a pretty sight. But a wizard with lights.

Martin drains his glass.

OK, he says. Time to go upstairs. What's the story line? No

shower work please. All that soap. Scoutmaster stuff, I guess, considering the age.

Play it by ear, Tia Juana says. Not scoutmaster stuff, I think. Bearing in mind the disappointed expectation.

Missionary stuff, Martin says. About an hour? I have to get home.

As long as you like, Tia Juana says. See Pearl. But make it good.

Don't I always, Martin says. When have I ever let you down?

Or him, Tia Juana says. When have you ever let him down?

You're getting sentimental in your middle age, Martin says.

I'm younger than you, Tia Juana says.

Tia Juana's bathroom, to which Martin now repairs, is a spacious venetian-blinded room painted canary yellow, plentifully supplied with tropical plants, of which not a few hang in macramé-slung pottery bowls from the ceiling, and a variety of specialized washing fitments. Martin makes for the mirror, a full-length bamboo-surrounded cheval-glass, before which he undresses. For as long as he can remember he has had an aversion, which he considers pathological, to lavatories. He therefore habitually urinates into the sink. On this occasion he is interrupted in mid-pee by Pearl Fisher's entry.

Sorry, Pearl, he says.

Don't worry about it, Pearl Fisher says. Stranger things happen in this room.

Martin finishes his pee, and adjusts his cockring, under Pearl Fisher's appraising eye.

I shall give myself a callous, he says, at this rate. Will I do?

A bit of sponge work, Pearl Fisher says. Come and stand in the light.

Martin stands in the light. Pearl Fisher expertly handles sponges and brushes.

There, she says. Everything's ready. When you are.

In a minute, Martin says. I must gather my resources.

Pearl Fisher gustily sighs. You and me both, she says. It's been a long day. You are the third since lunch.

She sits on the edge of the bath. Martin returns his attention to the mirror.

You're a genius, Pearl, he says.

He's a nice kid, Pearl Fisher says.

Jesus, Martin says. What is this? Have you and Juana got some sort of conspiracy going here? I shouldn't worry. He's probably been through it all before. We don't get many virgins through here, whatever Juana's handouts may say.

Do you enjoy your work? Pearl Fisher says.

Pearl, Martin says. This is one hell of a time for that sort of question. How many years have you been doing this?

I've known you four, Pearl Fisher says. We've never spoken. Not so's you'd notice. You know that? In all that time we've never talked. Nothing but work. People get hurt you know.

I know, Pearl, Martin says. You've got a heart of gold. Your heart is with the Baptist ladies' sewing guild, even as your hand creates schoolboy bedrooms, log cabins, haystacks, and changing rooms. And I'm a bastard. What is it today by the way?

Just straight bedroom stuff, Pearl Fisher says. A few Navajo rugs. Very tasteful. I cannot say, Martin Conrad, that I like you very much.

Do you have to? Martin says. I just pay your bills. I just keep you in Gucci, Pucci, and Fiorucci. I and a few others, like three since lunch. Like your precious kid in there.

You're running, Pearl Fisher says. Come here.

Again she piles brushes and sponge. Downstairs, filtered by doors, Verdi gives way to Wagner.

Sorry, Pearl, Martin says.

Never mind, Pearl Fisher says. Temperament. By the way you're not to kiss his ear. He says he hates to have his goddamn ear kissed.

Shit, Martin says.

Funny that, Pearl Fisher says.

She gets up from the edge of the bath.

Ready when you are, she says.

Give me a bit, Martin says.

Wash the sink, Pearl Fisher says over her shoulder as she leaves.

Alone in the bathroom Martin takes a deep breath and counts to twenty. Then he walks next door into Tia Juana's enormous studio bedroom where, through banks of cameras and lights, over Pearl Fisher's dimpled shoulder, he sees, supine atop snowy linen and Navajo rugs, Fred's unclothed figure. He walks to the bed.

Hi dad, Fred says.

Hi kid, Martin says.

Martin contemplates with decreasing detachment his son's glabrous nakedness. To his surprise, and here we must bear in mind his previous remarks on the adolescent physique, it is the sight of Fred's coltish knees that he finds particularly arresting. Fred stands up and moves to face his father. He hugs him, and plants a sherry-fragrant kiss on his cheek.

Happy birthday Bear, he says.

Martin returns his son's hug.

Thanks kid, he says.

5

Un vendredi pas comme les autres, Fred says. Taxi? We're running a bit short on time.

Martin closes Tia Juana's door behind them and peers through the snow.

Taxi, he says. If we can get one. How long do we have?

Fred takes his father's hand and holds it.

About half an hour I think, he says. Come on. We'll pick one up in Charing Cross Road.

Hand in hand they stumble over the impacted snow. In St. Martin's Lane Fred slips and falls, almost pulling Martin over with him. They laugh, right themselves, and walk on. At Cambridge Circus Martin disengages his hand from his son's and puts it in his pocket.

Numb, he says.

There's a taxi, Fred says, and runs forward waving.

Martin quickly bunches a snowball and throws it at Fred's back. Fred stops the taxi and gives directions. As they settle into the cab Martin hands Fred an envelope. Fred inspects the contents and hands them back to Martin.

Very nice, he says.

Martin puts the polaroids back into the envelope.

We look as if we enjoyed ourselves, he says. That's the main thing.

We did, didn't we? Fred says. I'm tired.

He lies back and closes his eyes. After a while Martin does the same. The taxi makes slow snowbound progress. It is impossible to say whether they sleep or not, but let us assume that they do. At Chepstow Villas the driver rouses them. They pay him and get out into the snow. As Martin is turning into his pathway a snowball hits him on the back of his head. For several minutes Fred and Martin pelt each other with snowballs, laughing and gasping with cold. Then, wet-haired and, let us suppose, happy, they enter their house. They stamp their feet in the hall. Martin calls, Jane we're back. Jane comes out into the hall.

Hi kids, she says.

Martin and Jane embrace. Fred and Jane kiss. They enter the sitting room. A champagne cork pops. A roomful of people sings Happy Birthday.

Surprise surprise! everybody says.

Passing

His name was Marc. I called him Porc. He didn't mind.

If his name had ended with a "k", it would never have happened. I mean I would never have done it.

"What is it you've done, exactly?" asked my old friend Rose, with a sniff. "Rediscovered heterosexuality." Her voice sagged at the end. It did sound pretty dismal.

"I haven't rediscovered it," I said haughtily. "I've reinvented it."

That brought a smile to her lips. A sceptical smile. She was right. Heterosexuality, at least my heterosexuality, has certain rules, imprinted so long ago they've taken root. Maybe you sip them with your titmilk, maybe you draw them up through the long silky straw of the umbilicus. Maybe they're braided into your DNA. I don't know. We called it "conditioning" in our long-ago Consciousness-Raising sessions, minimizing and maximizing it at the same time, so that it became responsible for all our ills and was simultaneously external to us, like an archaic article of lingerie, tight as a second skin but always possible to remove, could you but find the hooks and eyes; but it was actually something far more stubborn, piecemeal and subtle.

I didn't know that, though it was beginning to dawn on me by the time I got round to telling Rose about Porc. Up till then, I'd Passed.

I was good at Passing. It was a skill I'd learned through fifteen years of marriage. The Janus game. You had a passable face and another face, a face that would wilfully fail to pass. A face of conformity and a face of rebellion, and never, or seldom, the twain would meet.

All I did was reverse them, when I separated and simultaneously met Porc. Now the het face was the rebellious one. The one that passed was the face of the free-wheeling sexual outlaw, the lesbian face.

Who set up the opposition? The conflict was in me, obviously; the two sides failed to knit. They were both too absolute. I had a bad time with absolutes. They warred in me, left me no room to breathe. I'd thought the war would end, once I got myself de-married. I'd thought the het face would crumble away like the mask it must, must be. It had set hard enough. But the clay held. Once again I was a person without integrity, a sexual double agent, a half-caste.

But I had Porc! It was all right to call him that because he *wasn't* a pig. The only resemblance between him and a pig was in the long, tassel-like fringes of his eyelashes, indecent, suggestive, downright fetishistic, especially as what they fringed was a pair of ink-blue eyes. I'd never gone for blue eyes before. At least, I consoled myself, that was a departure from the norm.

No, he wasn't a pig. He was more a deer of some rare, esoteric sort, a deer people prized for its chamois or cashmere. A deer whose horns weren't stunted, not at all, but rather curled back playfully on his brow like question marks. That's what his horns were, not weapons but question marks. He had that in common with pigs as well, the question mark they wear on their rumps. He wore his at his temples, it curled at the end of his name.

Blue and brown he was, my favourite colour combination, shades of the earth-and-sky sandwich I longed to taste. That was the conflict, of course, all along, the old Western split. I cased it in contemporary clothes and called it a gay–straight debate, but it was the old mind–body split, the old Greek division, and there was nothing new under the sun.

He didn't even know he was beautiful. How could he not know? If he knew, what did he do with the knowledge? He was a musician, a trumpet player, and they are not a verbal breed. He didn't talk about music, he made it; the same with love.

His music was jazz, and he loved as he played, with his mouth; I had not known a man who loved first with his mouth and only secondarily with his loins. I had not known such men existed.

His English wasn't too good, which kept our relationship painlessly simple. We couldn't analyse it; we didn't share the vocabulary. I had been involved with a woman for three years, and we had taken our love apart so regularly, so exhaustively, that there was no way it could possibly keep time again. We were much more interested in the dismantling of it than in anything else, and when the time came to junk it I had to scramble around in my mind looking for the bits to discard. They had lodged everywhere. The language gap, with Porc, was a blessed relief, and, of course, his French accent was the *pièce de résistance*.

It was all pretty classic. I watched myself, astonished, as tapes rolled in my mind, tapes of old films I didn't know I still stocked in my archives. They tickled me, those films. Not always, I hasten to add, in my funnybone. Oh, no. I could hear *Lohengrin* and watch white (well, ivory) tulle pour down some anonymous aisle. What could the building possibly be? A church specially created for the occasion and then immediately destroyed? Which would conjure up a great banquet of tradition, of atmosphere, for one great orgiastic feast of feasts, wedding of weddings, from which I would emerge righteous and whole?

I climbed out the window instead, like Greta Garbo at her wedding, only my window was figurative. I found a small loophole. Or so Porc claimed. He screeched at me, finding the hateful words with a facility he'd not had before, not needed before. He'll speak better English without me, I thought.

"You meant to weasel out of it all along," he sobbed. "You plaything!"

I never knew whether to put that down to language or Freud. Oh, how I longed to lick the tears from his lashes! But he wouldn't let me near him. I listened to the stream of abuse and accusation, fearful and angry in turn. Fearful that it was true, that I was hard—"'ard and ruth*less*".

You're either ruthless or toothless, said Anger. That's your choice, with a man.

In the end, I foundered on the Mother Rock. Porc was twenty-nine, I was thirty-five. Ideal. I had two kids, he had none. Nor, he insisted, did he necessarily want any.

"So, I may 'ave some regrets," he said, rolling the "r", Piaf-like. "I expect not to die wifout regrets."

Ah, but that particular regret, that particular sacrifice, would bind me to him with hoops of steel. Was it the binding I minded, or the steel? If he made that sacrifice for me, what would I have to sacrifice in turn?

The virtuous face of it said I couldn't deprive him of the option of children. The other face said I couldn't bind myself to him by that deprivation. The under-underside said I just couldn't give myself the way you were supposed to.

Maybe I was frightened of the temptation of motherhood. I was still vulnerable to it. That vulnerability was in my handbook of Rules for Heterosexual Life. It was another tape, along with the ivory tulle and the candles, the face of my daughter. I have two sons. I have escaped something as well as missed something in not reproducing *myself*, escaped some essential dilution, as Larkin would have it. I can still be daughter as well as mother.

It ended badly, with screams and snarls. In the aftermath I discovered a whole closed-off section of myself all ready to be moved into, like a room. I hadn't landed on my feet, and yet there was someone waiting to carry me over the threshold. So maybe the image of marriage had been an interior thing, after all. Maybe the replay had hitched up my two faces. I looked different to myself. Not bridal; that had gone. But somehow solidified, in motley, like the harlequin I had always identified with from afar. You can't be a clown and a bride. The two figures are in antithesis. I guess I chose, at last.

The Cutting Room

A glistening, rose-colored pear balances on the marble block. Dr Barakian holds it firmly, lifts the knife, cuts through.

"The uterus is opened laterally to reveal . . ."

He picks up a tiny metal ruler and places it against the cut surface.

". . . to reveal a velvety two-millimeter endometrial surface."

As the doctor speaks into the dictaphone above the laboratory where he works, Kelly, who stands near him, goes on separating number tags and placing them on the tops of the plastic containers arranged in a row before her. In the jars are suspended shreds of red tissue from D & Cs, little nubbins of warts, delicate milky cataracts floating like anemone, the yellowish pinkish bag of a gall bladder with its stones lying on the bottom of the jar.

The dictaphone belt turns as Dr Barakian cuts and talks. He dumps the fragments of the uterus back in the jar of formalin and reaches for the ovary.

". . . consists of two small fragments of white fibrous tissue grossly consistent with ovarian stroma . . ."

Kelly thinks how her daughter would appreciate those words. On hearing them, Kim would envision a space taxi streaking toward the Ovarian Stroma in the far depths of the universe. Kelly needs these fantasies, in the cutting room.

She goes out the swinging door and down the hall to the

transcription room, where her two sister-workers are attached to their dictaphones, typewriters clacking away. As the newest person she has been given the task of receiving the specimens when they are brought up from surgery each morning and afternoon, assigning them numbers, writing the pertinent identifying details in a large black book, and taking the specimens into the cutting room where the pathologist cuts them open and describes them. When he hired her, Dr Rook had explained, "Everything that is taken out in surgery comes up here to us. We do a gross report—that is, what can be seen with the naked eye—and then samples of the tissue are made into microscope slides by the cytologist, and we look at them and do a microscopic report."

Kelly reaches for one of the tapes on the desk near her and slaps it into her dictaphone. She attaches the earpiece, then stops to light a cigarette.

Across from her, Brenda begins to mutter furiously.

Kelly glances up to watch Brenda open the top of the yellow pathology-report form, unscrew her little bottle of liquid paper, and begin correcting the mistake on each of the five carbons. The thick waves of auburn hair bob on Brenda's head as she gives the bottle a vicious shake and pulls out the brush to jab at the paper. Her motions are speeded up by the coffee and cigarettes she uses just to stay awake for her ambitious schedule, in which, besides this job, she moonlights at another hospital on weekends and attends night classes at State College.

Kelly experiences periodic mild amazement at Brenda's lifestyle. A placid person herself, who enjoys moving slowly, she keeps up with Brenda in one area only—the consuming of cigarettes. By 9.30 a.m. the two of them have filled the small windowless room with clouds of gray smoke.

"Gross report," Kelly types, and adds to herself, "I'll say!"

"Goddamit, I want a raise!" It is Brenda's voice, grumbling away as she dabs on the liquid paper. "It takes everything I fucking know to do this job, and I know plenty. I'm overqualified for this joint. If I was a *man*, you know

I'd be managing this place and pulling down a decent salary."

Her angry eyes look up to meet Kelly's and Kelly answers, "That's right, you *should* be the boss. You're just the type to push people around."

Brenda blinks, and then grins slowly, and finally breaks into loose laughter.

"Fuck it anyway," she adds.

At the third side of the triangular white desk, Josie sits with lowered eyes. She is younger than the other women, one of many daughters in a large Filipino-American family. Her breasts are pushed up by a tortuous bra inside her tight clothes. She is anxious to be voluptuous for her husband, a handsome student who likes to tell her how the young women at the college pursue him.

It was probably Josie who started it, but Kelly didn't hear the first part because the orderly had just brought her two small unmarked containers of D & C, and had given her the two slips that went with them. She was occupied in looking at these when she heard Josie's voice talking softly across the desk to Brenda.

"You know that Gerald, that black guy that's a lab tech and always wears those beautiful clothes? Yesterday, Bill from surgery told me he's a *faggot*! Can you *believe* it?!"

There comes a slight catch in Kelly's breathing, just a little pause between breaths. She glances up to see Brenda squinting disdainfully at Josie through a cloud of smoke.

"Well, you *can't always tell*, you know," Brenda instructs Josie.

Kelly shuffles the lab slips, moves the containers of reddish liquid.

"I mean, how about Betty in the lab?" Brenda adds.

"Which Betty?"

"You know. Sometimes she comes in here to ask about the autopsies."

"You mean that really cute girl?"

"Yeah."

"Well, what *about* her?"

"She's one."

"No!" Josie's smooth face puckers.

Kelly's stomach begins to shake as if the nerves jangling on the surface of her body sent tremors in to a point under her belly button.

"Yeah, she's a lesbian," Brenda continues. "She's lovers with Donna. They *live* together."

"But she has *long hair*!" A squeal of dismay from Josie.

If either of the other women were to look at Kelly, she thinks, they would surely see her discomfort. But they are absorbed in their conversation.

Lighting a cigarette, pulling in the harsh smoke, she asks herself, Should I tell them? A part of her answers, Yes, just say it and put a stop to this. Another part of her argues, what business is it of theirs? Why should I explain myself to them?

When she looked in the mirror this morning she saw a round-faced woman with blond smooth medium-length hair, large earnest brown eyes. That was definitely a lesbian looking back at her from the mirror. But apparently when Brenda and Josie look at her they see a heterosexual woman like themselves, or they would not be talking this way in her presence.

"That Donna is one, no mistake," Josie says. "I mean, she's so *mannish*."

Kelly strains every nerve to pay attention to the lab slips on the desk. She stubs out her cigarette and reaches for the big black log book to write in the information. When she has transcribed the women's names, surgical numbers, and surgical procedure in the book, she looks up at the two containers. There they sit, next to each other, identical, and without markings.

Panic comes thumping up in her. My God, I don't know which is which!

Brenda and Josie have gone back to typing, the clatter of their machines loud in the room. Kelly sits beneath this noise, her face burning, and stares with stricken eyes at the two jars. In paying so much attention to that conversation, in getting upset about it, she has forgotten to keep the slips with the respective bottles, a rule strictly followed to avoid mix-up. Now she has the two slips, one for Mrs Romerio, one for Mrs Sanchez, and there sit the two bottles with their pinkish shreds floating in clear liquid. Kelly knows that both Mrs Sanchez and Mrs Romerio went to their gynecologists, lay on the table with their knees up, allowed the doctor to put his hand in their vaginas, open their cervices and insert a knife; allowed him to scrape the linings of their uteri and put the scrapings in these two bottles. The pathologist looking through his or her microscope will discover the condition of the cells, and the doctor will know how to proceed. Hysterectomy? Removal of the cervix? With these thoughts Kelly rejects the temptation to cover her mistake by simply putting one lab slip with each jar and sending it on. She sits holding the jars, feeling ill.

Finally Brenda looks up from her work to take a drag of her cigarette.

"What's the *matter*, Kelly?" she asks in alarm.

Kelly swallows, and hears her voice tremble slightly as she talks. "Brenda, help me. I don't know which of these D & Cs goes with which slip."

"Oh." A short, flat sound like breath being knocked out. Brenda stares into Kelly's eyes for a moment, then down at the glass jars, then up again. Her mouth stays part-way open.

"Is there any way I can find out which is which before I have to take them to Dr Rook?"

Josie is listening now, too. Both she and Brenda look as if they are witnessing an auto accident.

"I don't know . . . how you would . . ." Brenda begins.

"Ask one of the pathologists," Josie suggests.

Brenda brightens. "Yeah, ask Dr Wong!"

When they have a problem, they go to the one woman pathologist. It is always easier to talk to Dr Wong because she pays attention to what they say and then she talks with them about what can be done. The male pathologists treat them like children, or seem strangely embarrassed by their presence, or sit staring at their legs as they talk.

Walking down the hall to Dr Wong's office, Kelly struggles with the emotions dislodged and running rampant in her like a river in flood.

"All is not lost," Dr Wong says when Kelly has finished talking. "The specimens can be distinguished from each other when the tissue is looked at through a microscope."

Kelly breathes a little more easily.

"But you'll have to take them in to Dr Rook and explain what's happened so that when the slides arrive he'll be able to recognize them."

Dr Wong's broad gentle face creases in sympathy. Everyone in the lab is afraid of Dr Rook; even the other pathologists stay out of his way.

"I'm sorry, but it's *his* day to do the micros. You'll have to let him know."

It was just this encounter that Kelly had wanted to avoid. Leaving Dr Wong's office, she walks very slowly up the corridor. Rook is the head pathologist, a brilliant and imperious man who flies into a rage if everything is not done exactly as he wishes.

The paper of the surgery slips has begun to wrinkle in Kelly's sweaty grip. She holds tightly to the jars. Dropping them now would be the final disaster. Against all her instincts, she forces herself to approach Dr Rook's door. When she arrives there, she carefully shifts papers and jars to one hand, takes a deep breath, and knocks. Not loud.

"Come in," says a sharp male voice.

Kelly's afternoon is nightmarish. Her mind spins wildly as she works to maintain her composure and do her job. I don't know how to manage this, she thinks, looking across the white desk at Brenda and Josie, who seem now to be separated from her by a chasm. In all her previous jobs—at the Buick dealership, at the insurance office, in the other hospitals where she worked—in all those offices she had been a married lady. A nice heterosexual woman with a child. There was nothing to explain, nothing to reveal. But in the year since she left her last job she has become a lesbian, and that choice has magically transported her into another state of mind. She was so extremely uncomfortable as they talked of faggots and lesbians this morning. She wanted to explain.

Now she stares across at Josie's young face. I know something about her life, she thinks. I know what it's like to work to put your husband through school. I know what it's like to live for a man, caring for him, seeing no future for yourself separate from him. I know something of Josie's life. But what would Josie think of *me* if she knew? Kelly had been straight long enough to know the opinions most heterosexuals hold about homosexuals. She herself had considered "queers" to be sick, sad, partial or undeveloped people; until she became one and found that she was still herself.

Bill from surgery arrives with the tray of specimens.

"How's your love life?" he asks, grinning at each of the three women as he sets the tray of containers before Kelly.

"Better than yours, I'd be willin' to bet!" snaps Brenda.

"Well, now..." Bill straightens up, inflates his chest. "Maybe you'd like to find out for yourself..."

Kelly lifts the jars off the tray and begins checking them against the surgery slips, ignoring Bill.

A laugh of exaggerated scorn comes from Brenda.

Hearing Josie's giggle, Kelly glances up to see a red flush appearing on Bill's bull neck. His eyes are locked on Brenda's face as she goes on typing, and Kelly sees in them a look of dull hatred. But he shifts his weight, rolls his eyes, and gestures with his thumb at Brenda.

"Get *her*!" he says, and mumbles, "Who'd want it anyway?" as he shoulders his way out the door, walking tough.

Now that his urgent pay-attention-to-*me* energy is gone, Kelly concentrates on the jars. At first it had been difficult to accept the specimens. Especially the first mastectomy. But she forced herself to take the top off the jar and look. The liquid formalin was pinkish with blood. The breast floated nipple down. She saw the spongy whitish tissue of the inside, clumped together like massed blossoms; she saw the severed skin. Looking into the jar, Kelly thought of the woman in bed on some other floor of the hospital. She felt as if it were herself. Trembling, she put the lid on the jar and sat looking nowhere. She had read about unnecessary surgery on women, the doctors who make fortunes removing uteri and ovaries and breasts. Was this horror one of those operations just for the doctor's gain? Finally she picked up the surgery slip to read the diagnosis. Carcinogenic tumor. She was reassured. She decided to believe that this was necessary. They removed it so the woman can go on living, she told herself. Awful as it is, you can live and walk and do everything without a breast.

During the first few days on the job, Kelly had existed in a state of semi-nausea and shock. Here in the pathology department it was impossible to avoid the knowledge that human beings are flesh. Chunks of meat can be cut from them and put in a jar, quickly turning grayish in the formaldehyde solution. Pickled meat. Kelly had worked in hospitals before, but she had worked with living, complaining patients. Here in the pathology department, the only intact human beings who arrived for the doctor's attentions were corpses. Everything else had been dismantled. For days Kelly would suffer visual flashes of the specimens while she was eating dinner, would dream that she was dissecting a body in a basement room, sweating in panic because she didn't know how.

Now she looks at the large jar before her on the desk, inside which a being is curled. One tiny hand rests against the wall of the jar; the hand is almost transparent, with perfect little fingers slightly flexed.

The lab sheet tells Kelly that the young woman came bleeding to the emergency room. Hemorrhage—what a dark, swollen word it is. Kelly looks at the fetus, so still and somehow peaceful in its bath of formalin.

"Jesus, that Bill is a jerk!" Brenda comments. "Can you

imagine what his wife had to put up with before she divorced him?"

Kelly places the specimens on the tray and carries them out of the transcription room down the hall and through the swinging doors into the laboratory. Long black tables with sinks in them cross the room. In the air hangs the sweetish smell of formalin.

Through a window is the morgue. Kelly sees Dr Rook at work, his small neat head thrust forward over the corpse, the lenses of his glasses glittering in the bright light. The body is an old man, his skin yellowish, his genitals lying sideways on his stringy thigh. Dr Rook is lifting out the internal organs from the gaping red chest cavity, and once again Kelly is surprised at the bright colors, the yellow fat, the blue veins, the purplish or scarlet or pink tissue of the organs.

But she hurries past the window, hoping Dr Rook will not see her. The visit to his office had been so embarrassing that she wishes she might never see him again. It had been extremely difficult to open his door and step inside, clutching her slips of paper, her two little jars. It had felt like the end of the world. And then to find there were three other doctors crammed into the small office with Dr Rook. Everyone stopped talking. They stared at her as if she were one of the specimens. "I've made a mistake, Dr Rook." (How hard it was to say those words under the eyes of four men.) "I don't know which slip goes with which jar. Dr Wong said you . . ."

Rook's eyebrows shot up.

"*That*," he bellowed, "is not *allowed*!"

One of the men smiled.

Kelly stared into Rook's bright challenging eyes. She waited for a few moments. "Dr Wong said you could tell the difference under a microscope . . ."

Rook stared at her. "She did, did she?"

Again Kelly waited, confused. The one thing she hadn't expected was to be played with.

"Yes. She said if I let you know now, when it came to the micro report you could tell them apart."

"Yes, yes." Now he was impatient. "Give them here."

He snatched the bottles and papers from her and dropped them on a desk piled high with books and magazines and lab reports.

Kelly turned to go quickly out the door. She hurried down the hall to the coffee room, which was deserted at that hour, and stood inside the door biting hard on the knuckles of her fist to stop the trembling and the need to cry.

Brenda is putting on her coat with its thick imitation-fur collar, snapping shut her purse.

"I've got exactly eighteen minutes to get out to State for my special studies seminar," she grumbles to Kelly.

Josie waves to Kelly from the doorway. "Take care. See you tomorrow."

When they are gone, Kelly sees that Brenda has left her last cigarette burning in the ashtray. The smoke drifts up, silent and serene.

How wrong it feels to find herself so alienated from Brenda and Josie now. The three of them in this little room have developed a loyalty; they stick together, defend each other against the doctors when they can, help each other out when one of them gets behind. She felt accepted by them from her first day on the job.

Kelly rips a report from her typewriter and begins reading it over.

For Brenda and Josie, nothing has changed, she thinks. Somehow the madness of this whole thing is that only *I* know that anything has happened. They didn't notice any reaction from me when they were talking. Probably they'd never catch on if I were to pretend, if I just laughed at the jokes, went along with the speculation on who is queer and who isn't. But she knows how alone she has felt during this whole long dreadful day, how filled with a discomfort that had some of the sticky quality of shame. That alarmed her, for it reminded her of the many contradictory feelings she had experienced during the period in which she recognized her love for women and began to act on it. Delight would give way suddenly to terror. Will everyone hate me now that I'm queer? she would wonder, and her own hatred of self would come crashing in. Then she would feel strong again, in possession of herself, launched on a new life. A day later she would be tentative and frightened, ready to flee back into the supposed safety of heterosexuality. It had taken many months, and the help of a number of lesbian women besides her lover, for her to be secure in her new identity.

Now here I am, she thinks, having to go through this again! Her desire is desperate—to escape the building, to break free and walk, mulling over today's incident in her mind, away from the scene. Perhaps she will see it differently. Is it way out of proportion?

She peers at the report form in her hands, reading, "There is no nuclear dyskaryosis and no demonstrable mitotic activity in these areas . . ."

How drained and frayed she feels. And crazy. Yes, absolutely nuts.

Dr Barakian, large in his rumpled suit, comes through the door and drops a stack of dictaphone tapes on the desk. He blinks at her from behind thick glasses. "These can wait till tomorrow."

Kelly nods, watching him turn to leave.

Ten minutes to go. As the newest transcriptionist, she has to stay until five thirty, but usually she is glad for this last hour of relative quiet. Today each minute of it is torture. Brenda and Josie's conversation keeps replaying in her head. Kelly lights a cigarette, one of too many she has smoked today, and draws the bitter smoke into her stale-tasting mouth. Exhaling, she wonders, at which point could she have said something? Said *what*? What could she have done differently so that the mistake with the D & Cs wouldn't have happened?

She spreads her arms on the desk, staring up at the clock. I never want to live through another day like this, she knows, and there comes the realization that there is an endless succession of such days ahead of her, of situations in which she will suffer this anxious interior drama. Already she has experienced it, for in the preceding weeks she had often thought of telling Brenda and Josie about her life. They talked of husband and boyfriend, and she talked about her daughter and her "roommate". She had felt a liar.

Mechanically, she puffs on her cigarette, watching the smoke coil out into the room, and she knows her decision is made. Tomorrow I'm going to eat lunch with Brenda in the cafeteria, she thinks, and I'm going to tell her I'm a lesbian. She imagines Brenda's response: she'll probably pretend she knows all about lesbians. Maybe she took a course on us at State. Kelly does not like the bitterness of that thought. She attempts to continue quite practically. The next day I'll ask Josie to go to lunch with me and I'll tell *her* I'm a lesbian. That will be harder, because she'll probably feel guilty for all the remarks she's made about faggots. And her curiosity about lesbian sex might get aroused. Oh, I hope not. And anyone else they may tell can react however they will!

Easily said, but she does not like to imagine what Bill may do with the information. Or the doctors, if it should get to them.

With deliberate slowness, Kelly puts aside the finished report and unfolds the typewriter cover to put on her machine. She sits holding it, forgetting her purpose, as a phrase repeats in her mind. The specimen is opened to reveal . . . (why should I have to? she objects in anger) . . . is opened to reveal. . . .

But today's experience has been like suffocating.

Shaking herself, she pulls the cover down roughly over the typewriter and gets up to put on her coat. In the little mirror that Brenda has hung on the wall behind her desk, Kelly sees limp blond hair, round face, the expression not so different from this morning except that the eyes look out surprised and chastened. This is definitely a lesbian looking back at her from the glass.

She shuts the door on the room with its three-sided desk, its typewriters and dictaphones, and goes past the cutting room to the elevator that will take her down to the street, to what feels like freedom for the night, until the morning brings her back here for whatever will transpire.

Two Bartenders,
a Butcher and Me

I'd just got over a bad case of meningitis, complicated by my diabetes, and my doctor had told me the day before that I was probably getting kidney stones too. (Nobody knows what pain is until he has had kidney stones, believe me.) So when the guy from San Francisco stared at me in the bar and then came over and asked if I wanted to join in an orgy, you can understand why I felt good. I realized I must look a bit puny with my thin shoulders and thinner arms, my fat lips and dwindling hair (though I'd cut it flat to make it look less obvious). But the guy from San Francisco was making the overture, saying he and his lover, Gil, were arranging an orgy. They'd already asked the bartender if he wanted to have a four-way, and the bartender had said he did. I guess they liked my face. It turned out that Gil was a bartender too—up in San Francisco, not here in Fresno—and for a minute all four of us sort of eyed each other, seeing how we felt about getting together.

To be honest, the Fresno bartender, Rory, didn't turn me on very much. He was cute and growing a nice beard, but somehow he seemed a little silly. (I'd seen him running around the bar lots of times before, but we'd never spoken.) Gil was pretty good-looking. Far better than me in fact, with elegant gestures and a deep voice. The best of the lot was the guy from San Francisco, a butcher, who was slim and solid and lots of fun. Up close, he looked a little dissipated, because of the dark marks under his eyes. That night he'd had about six White Russians and had been smoking grass and even sniffed some amyl out on the dance floor, so I wondered if I would be getting in over my head by getting into an orgy with those guys. But the guy from San Francisco, Bill, was really full of life and having a great time running back and forth between the three of us, finding out who liked to do what.

I began to get sleepy before the bar closed and thought of leaving, since I had to get up and go to work at the Welfare Department in the morning at eight. But somehow or other I hung in there. I was going to lose my job anyway in a couple of months, because the budget had been cut, but I didn't want to lose it for coming in worn-out from an all-night orgy. Still, I kept asking myself how many offers for an orgy at the Fresno Holiday Inn did I get in a year, anyway.

So I waited around while the two guys from San Francisco danced and the bartender closed up. I was getting a little worried because I don't have a very big dick and Bill talked about cock a lot, as though size was very important to him. I didn't want him to be disappointed when I pulled my pants off. (I know it's not supposed to matter if you have a little dick, but it does, it sure does.) I tried looking over at Rory, but he didn't catch my eye, and I figured he wasn't attracted to me any more than I was to him. But I also figured a three-and-a-half-way was better than a no-way, so I hung in there.

Somehow some Italian guy got involved. He was supposed to make up a fifth in the orgy, but when we left the bar I found out, in the parking lot, that Rory had lost interest in the Italian and didn't want him to follow us in our cars out to the Holiday Inn. I felt sorry for the Italian because he didn't catch the hint and followed us all anyway, and then, at the motel, Rory had to lie and say that all of us were acting "so weird" that he didn't plan to stay. So the Italian guy was left out in the cold. I guess he went on home.

The other four of us went into the motel room and took our

clothes off. There was a big tray of dirty dishes and half-eaten food on one of the double beds, and the beds were unmade and clothes were thrown everywhere. It was all a little messy, but I suppose you wouldn't want an orgy to be middle class and super-clean anyway, right?

I didn't know exactly what I was supposed to do, but the butcher gave me a sniff of amyl and asked me to fuck him while Rory was fucking him too. It was pretty wild, I guess. It was the first time I'd ever seen a guy get fucked with two cocks at the same time—and I was one of the guys doing it! I kept thinking about the Italian who'd been invited and then not invited, wondering if he was still in the parking lot, sitting in his car by himself. Of course, I hadn't said anything to the others about asking the Italian to join us, so I guess I made him feel not wanted, too.

So we all fucked each other in various combinations, though Rory and I didn't touch very much, just a little bit near the end. And nobody said anything about my little dick, though I think Bill was maybe a little disappointed. But if I have to defend myself, he couldn't have been fucked by me and somebody else at the same time if we'd both had big ones.

When I got off, I was sitting on Gil's dick, and the other two were watching from the other bed, even encouraging me to come. I suppose if anybody had been watching from a peephole it would've seemed nasty or depraved or something, but it didn't seem like that from my angle. We even joked around a lot and hugged and told each other we were good sex. We got so loud that Bill shushed us and said we'd wake up his mother. I thought he was kidding, but it turned out he wasn't. His mother really *was* in the next room. She was traveling with them, and she knew about him and Gil and took it all with a grain of salt, though she wouldn't talk about it.

The moment I remember most is when Rory, who was really quite a good fucker, was giving it to Bill, who had his legs up in the air and was grunting. Gil and I were resting on the rug and Gil says to me, quietly, "I really love him. I love him so much."

He meant it, too, and I thought that was sort of nice. Here he was watching some bartender from Fresno fucking his lover in the ass and he was glad because it gave his lover pleasure.

About four-thirty I slipped out and left the other three sleeping. Didn't get a chance to say goodbye. I got to work on time (still have a month to go in my job and I can get unemployment for a while after that).

For some reason that evening didn't seem funny or depraved or anything. All I know is that when I was sucking dick and getting fucked and fucking that night, I didn't feel like I was a skinny thirty-eight-year-old with a little dick that nobody wanted. Of course I knew that nobody there in the Holiday Inn "loved" me, but for a while I felt that life wasn't passing me by, and I guess I'm kind of wishing some guy from San Francisco would come on through Fresno some other night, maybe soon. It wasn't perfect, no, but it was *something*. Maybe it was even sort of sad if you think about it too much, but then, aren't most things in life sad?

Cass, 1959: First Day
of a Courtship

"Take each day, and gather the rosebuds in it . . ." sings Cass. I don't know her yet. She's a new woman on the beach. She is decorating the air around her with this wonderful music, her bulk a dark mountain in the middle of the blanket on the sand. She is surrounded by thin, pretty gay boys like flowers clustered about her, all adoring her, as she sings and plays her guitar.

She is beautiful. She sings like an angel. I listen to her, stare at her, feeling desire rise thick in my chest. Her hair is long and dark, hanging in ocean-wet twisted ropes over her shoulders and down her back. One strand sticks in the salt on the skin of her neck. Her eyes are large and brown, cheeks and nose sunburned red, and a roll of soft flesh rests beneath her chin, extending from ear to ear. She is wearing black bermuda shorts and a black short-sleeved blouse, tight on her huge body, fabric shining slick and wet from her swim. She resembles a large seal or a whale, curled on the blanket singing, voice as sweet as anything I've ever heard before, face as sweet as anything I've seen. She strokes the strings of the guitar gracefully, expertly, with thick sausage fingers, and she moves her lips and tongue sensually around the words as she sings. She is lovely.

I am interested. I drift closer and closer to the blanket, listening to her, "cruising" her in traditional 1950s' style—watching her face and trying to catch her gaze. She looks back at

me and smiles through her song, ". . . every day that comes once
in a lifetime . . ." then looks down.

I carefully cover the lurch my stomach gives by drawing
myself up extremely butch. I come closer to the blanket, cruise
harder. Then I move in suddenly and sit on the edge of the
blanket, relieved that the gay boys pull up their feet to make
room for me. When she finishes her song and puts down the
guitar, I speak: "That was very nice. I really enjoyed listening."
I am very cool, very butch.

"Thanks." She is casual. She leans back on to her hands, her
upper arms rippling where they squeeze out of her sleeves. I try
not to look at her body in a crass stare, but I do manage to get a
panorama out of the corner of my eye of average-sized breasts,
big belly with lots of rolls, and fat thighs.

"My name's Moe." I stick out my hand, look directly into her
soft eyes and want to throw myself in head first.

"I'm Cass." She sits up, takes my hand, firm-grips it,
squeezes, then releases it.

"New in town?" I don't want to let go of her hand.

"She's a singer," one of the boys breaks in, sibilant esses
sounding in my ear like a horde of gnats. "She's trying to get a
gig here. So am I." I am not particularly interested in what he is
doing, except that then he stands up and pulls her by the arm.
"*C'mon*, Cass," he whines possessively, "we have to *go*, y'know.
You *said* after this song . . ."

Cass heaves herself to her knees. "We have to practice for an
audition," she sighs. She looks at me regretfully, imploring, long
eyelashes framing the plea: "We'll be rehearsing before hours in
the lounge at the Sea Isle. It opens at four. Maybe you could meet
me there at three?"

I smile, butterflies threatening to riot in my belly. "I'll be
there," I promise.

I go right home to shower and change from my swimsuit
into white ducks and a madras shirt. I want to look nice for her,
want to impress her as a "clean-cut butch"—one of my several
images. I dab on a touch of Canoe, want to smell good in case

we get close, want her to remember me by my scent.

Skin feeling tight from the sun, salt, and shower, I park my big old Buick in the back lot, then walk down the narrow steps behind the Sea Isle. I stride, swing my arms too vigorously, brush against stucco walls which leave a smear of whitewash powdering the skin on my forearm and wrist. Impatiently I brush away the stuff, not wanting to appear clumsy and uncool with whitewash on me. Butterflies in my belly have grown huge, threaten to fly away and carry me with them. My mouth feels hot, dry, and I hold my hand up and blow against it to see if my breath smells bad. Just to be sure, I pop a peppermint lifesaver.

As I near the door to the lounge, I begin to anticipate the relief of air-conditioning, am ready for the aromas of beer and tobacco. I push the door. It swings open. I step through and in, and I am temporarily blinded by the dark. My pupils fight to dilate, win, and the shadows take on more definition. The little hairs on my arms press themselves partly erect against the movement of cool air over their surfaces, transmitting to the rest of my body the sensations of being inside any beer joint or cocktail lounge in every low-priced oceanfront hotel along the South Miami Beach shoreline.

"Hi." Cass comes through the door opposite where I am standing and suddenly I am so excited that I can scarcely breathe. She is wearing a peasant-style dress and sandals. Her feet are fat. Her hair, dried and curled, falls heavily over her shoulders. Her chins lie in splendor down her neck and upon her chest. Her breasts press against the front of the dress, her belly swelling beneath, my memory of her thick legs in bermuda shorts filling in what I am not able to see beneath her long skirt. The blond boy is with her. I am not thrilled about that, pretend not to notice him.

The blond boy goes over to the piano, strikes a few chords, does a scale run. Cass looks at me. "I'm glad you came," she says.

The blond boy makes a sour face, begins a swing progression on the piano. Cass goes to the microphone, speaks into it. It is on.

She belts into a rendition of "St James Infirmary", goes into "House of the Rising Sun", and continues with "Wild Women". She is fantastic.

"Let's try that last one again," the blond boy lisps.

Cass moves her body in a slight rhythm as she sings, swinging her arms, snapping her fingers occasionally in time to the music. Every now and again she looks over at me, and when she does I am glad that the light is dim enough to hide the very un-butch flush which I feel creep into my face. I sit hunched over, elbows resting on my thighs, listening to her, watching her. I smoke one cigarette after another, cruising her. She has full lips and white teeth. She has red lips and brown eyes with long lashes. She has big lips and a small mouth. She is soft and beautiful and sensual, and I want to kiss her.

The bartender arrives, steps behind the bar, drums fingers in time to the music. Cass comes away from the mike, and the blond boy leaves his seat at the piano. "Want a beer?" Cass asks me.

I look around. The time is four o'clock. The bar is open. I feel a sudden hot embarrassment close in on me. I live at home with my mother, father, sister, brothers. I am a teenager. I am underage. Even though I carry fake proof of age so that I can get into the bars, I have to sneak around to do this. My mother is strict. I have to answer to her. I have to be home in time for dinner at five o'clock or I will get into trouble—there is no excuse in my house for being late to supper—and I wouldn't dare even dream of going home with beer on my breath.

"I have to go," I mutter. I can't tell her why; not yet. Cass starts forward, disappointment showing on her face. The blond boy glares at her. I glare at him. "I'd really like to see you again," I say to her. I am brusque, abrupt, very butch. "Here," I scrawl my telephone number on a soggy napkin I have found on the bar. I thrust it at her. "Call me tomorrow morning." I am mortified, do not want her to think I am a baby, a child; do not want her to suspect that I have to leave because my mother expects me home on time. I cover up by being extra tough, super aloof.

I stride out of the bar, pushing the door hard so that it will swing back and forth behind me. I don't look back, but I want to. In my mind's eye, I see Cass snapping her fingers as she sings, her breasts moving beneath her dress, and I know that she will call me in the morning.

Victor

Were those voices? Were they his students? Why didn't they come in then? Were they arguing or conspiring or something? Had one of them sneaked a look through the window? He waited, uncomfortable, his "office" hour after class about up.

Victor was Jewish on his father's side, and embarrassed; he was also gay, and afraid; he looked like Porky Pig besides. Sometimes he told himself that his little arms and legs didn't matter, nor did his porkchop coloring. At other times he told himself that his arched nostrils and slanting eyes made him look sexy, like a Mongolian, an almost blond Mongolian. He'd strike a warrior pose like a member of Genghis Khan's hordes and believe for a few moments that he was a Tartar, as ruthless and savage as the ancestor who'd probably raped one of his great-great-great grandmothers. Then the moment would pass and he'd say to himself that he looked more like tartare sauce. Didn't tartare sauce go with porkchops? No? Well, it went with fish.

It was time to leave. Nobody seemed to be coming to talk with him after twenty minutes, although somebody was still outside the classroom. He removed his flowery tie and stuffed it into his briefcase sitting on the desk. Then he went over and straightened one of the desks a student had jostled in his hurry to leave when class had ended. Victor bent down and picked up a scrap of paper, for there'd been a nasty warning from the high-school principal, who allowed Victor's extension university to use the rooms at night. Some students had left Coke bottles and cigarette stubs in the classroom next door, and Dr Monasch, the director of the program, had issued a notice to all the instructors that classes might be cancelled unless the violations ceased.

He gave the classroom a final check, preparing to douse the lights and go out into the sultry Okinawan evening. He thought about taking off his suit jacket, as he had his tie, but he was afraid someone from the local Education Office might report him to Dr Monasch. Rules were strict about wearing a coat and tie when teaching. Under both arms there was oily sweat, and he supposed his jacket smelled bad—but he needed this job, needed it desperately, and so he left the jacket on. Indeed he was scrupulous about all the regulations, the forms he was required to fill out, careful not to say anything in class about religion or politics or sex—certainly not his own kind of sex—or about the military itself; he even spent extra time with his worst students, tutoring them about fundamentals like what a verb was. He didn't mind the extra time involved, even though it was shocking how awful so many of his students were. Supposedly they were taking college English, and yet some of them could barely read, could barely write a sentence. Some couldn't do that! They were far worse than the students he'd had back in Oregon. When he coached them privately—though they became more human—he discovered that they talked exactly the way they wrote. Still, he told himself, he was uplifting them. He hoped he'd "saved" any number from Ds and Fs because of the extra help he'd given them. As it was, he felt terrible about having to give so many low grades. Sometimes he agonized over a D for several hours, changing the grade in his gradebook back and forth ten or twelve times. *But this is a university!* he would say, if he finally decided to give the student the lower grade. *What does a "university" mean? I'm giving this sergeant a C-minus when he can't even understand what our essays are saying!*

Victor stood with his thumb over the light switch, not wanting to leave. It would be hotter in his own room; he didn't have an

air-conditioner, and even though the one in the classroom
tonight had been defective, its hum seeming to make the
students drowsier than usual, it was still cooler in the classroom
than in the room where he lived.

He thought about Alaska. Maybe he should go to Alaska! He'd
gotten as far as Okinawa, after being let go when his small college
in Oregon had reduced its staff. If he could just get some cash
together—it would be cool there, perhaps even cold, no Dr
Monasches issuing demands and forms, no hot little rooms off
base, no large classes of freshman composition. If only he could
get away from Okinawa, from this extension course he was
teaching! Four more weeks before the term ended, then one
more term after that! He calculated the number of class
meetings, the number of compositions he'd have to mark before
summer school. Of course he knew that he'd really have to teach
summer school as well, to get a few dollars ahead.

He wondered if he should go back and finish his Ph.D. But the
idea filled him with lassitude. He was forty-one now, too old to
go back to school. And even the Ph.D.s were having difficulty.
Dr Monasch had told Victor he was lucky to be getting courses,
since the university had turned down the applications of six
Ph.D.s in one month. Victor had nodded, holding his part-
timer's contract in his hands carefully. The $675 for the eight
weeks would come in handy. More than handy—absolutely
necessary. He remembered Dr Monasch's unattractive eyes
perusing the grade sheet, then the man saying, "No As this term,
Mr Kepko? And only three Bs?" He hadn't said any more than
that. Just an unsubtle hint that Victor was too hard a grader. "I
always like to think that our students are under a special
hardship, being in the military and working long hours and all."
Dr Monasch had smiled, a grim smile that told Victor he'd better
watch himself.

If I could only get away! If only I had some money! he
whispered aloud, flipping out the light and standing in the
darkness. He opened the classroom door and stared at a few
students who were standing outside, smoking. He couldn't see

their faces very well in the dark, but he thought they were black. Victor snapped the lock on the door.

"You got a minute, Mr Kepko?" a voice said.

Victor waited, as one of the group approached. It was Miss Washington, the black WAC in his course. She was holding the theme he'd passed back to her that evening. He'd given it an F. "Why, yes, Miss Washington," he said.

She flicked her cigarette away into the grass. She was wearing fatigues—jungle fatigues, he thought they were called—with a camouflage pattern on them. She was short and bulky and unfeminine. He wondered if she might be a lesbian. She always wore fatigues to class.

"I wants to talk with you about my theme, but I've been waiting to see," she explained.

"Certainly." He looked over at the three other forms in the darkness, two of them male. Were they waiting for her? "Do you want to go back in the classroom?"

"Yeah." Miss Washington turned to the others. "Wait here for me, all right?" They muttered something that Victor couldn't understand.

Suddenly Victor remembered. "Oh, I'm sorry. I don't have a key." He tried the lock again just to be sure. "Can it wait till next time?"

"I'd like to talk to you tonight—if you don't mind." There was more demand than request in her tone. The WAC had crumpled the theme, Victor could tell, and then smoothed it out.

He tried to see the other three persons. "Are they in our class too?" he pointed. "Do they wish to discuss their themes?"

"No, they's just friends of mine. They's not in your class."

Victor felt vaguely alarmed. All through the class period Miss Washington had refused to look at him after he'd passed back the themes and they'd discussed them.

"We could go down nearer the parking lot, if you like," he suggested. "There's more light there."

"Sure." She followed him along the sidewalk until they got to the high school's main parking lot.

He spotted a wooden bench with many initials carved into it and sat down and gestured for the girl to be seated too. "Now, what seems to be the problem?"

Miss Washington didn't sit. Instead she flapped the paper back and forth like a fan, but she wasn't fanning herself. "This here's the *third* one you put a flag on!" she said belligerently. In the light he could see her short, tufted hair, the broad nose, the lip she was gnawing. There was an air of street-wisdom about the girl.

"Is it the third?" Victor said politely. "You didn't turn in the second paper," he added, hinting that she might have four Fs now if she had.

"I was sick," she said immediately.

"You should have mentioned it to me, don't you think?" He'd read her themes with pain because Miss Washington was so obviously a failure. He bent over backwards for black students, feeling that they'd encountered special difficulties in their homes, in their schooling. He was giving Mr Rodgers in the same class a C-minus even though he didn't deserve it. But with Miss Washington's themes there was nothing else Victor could do but fail them.

"You got something *personal* against me?" she asked, putting her foot up on the bench, not far from his knee.

"Personal?" He felt his throat catch. "What do you mean by that?"

"Something personal!" She waved the corrected theme toward him, and he could see his red marks like bloodstains on the paper.

"Why in the world would I have anything personal against you, Miss Washington? I don't even know *whose* essays I'm reading until after I put the grade on them. That's why I have you put your name on the back."

"You sure put this flag here real easy-like." She made some sort of deprecating sound with her lips.

"I have nothing personal against you!" he answered, with a bit more volume. "I grade each paper in light of the assignment and in light of standards of college composition."

"It couldn't be because I'm black maybe, could it?" She knew she was pushing him and didn't meet his eye.

"How dare you," he said clearly, looking over toward the girl's friends who were waiting for her in the shadows. "Are you accusing me of prejudice?"

"I didn't say nothing 'bout that. All I says is that you flunk my papers real easy."

He knew his voice was rising in pitch. "Perhaps you overestimate your abilities." He'd heard his voice once on a tape-recorder; it seemed high and breathy.

She snorted. "Who says? You? I showed this paper to a *professor*, and he say it was good!"

He wanted to stand up so they'd be on eye level, but he forced himself to remain on the bench, quieting his voice as well. "What professor?"

"A professor I knows!" She was airy with contempt now, having made her move. "A professor of English and Math!"

He paused, then said, "A unique combination for a professor."

"Well, *he* like it, even if you didn't!"

Victor placed his hand on his briefcase, for something to touch. "Did he? Did he help you write it?"

"No, he didn't! I wrote it myself!" She was so insistent Victor suspected she had had help from somebody. Her last theme *had* been somewhat improved, if still hopeless wth errors, with confused thinking. It was in her hand now, being shaken in his direction.

"Did you revise the theme before you turned it in?" he asked.

"I worked on it a long, long time!" She was picking at the wood of the bench, splintering it.

Suddenly Victor felt weary, useless. He looked up at the girl standing above him, then past her at the stars. They were trivial and far away. He could feel the weight of the weather and he had to sit forward on the vandalized bench so that his feet would touch the ground. What was the use of everything? he wondered.

What was the use of anything! Miss Washington with her absurd theme! Teaching bored and boring remedial students in Okinawa on a US military base, ekeing out a living on a minimal salary! Here he was talking to Miss Washington about whether she'd revised her theme once or twice. It would be a waste no matter how many times she rewrote it. He felt desperately sorry for her. She had overly thick lips and spoke ghettoese and didn't have two brains in her head, and he felt guilty about failing her. She was a slave, a descendant of slaves, but still a slave, a tough, stupid girl from Chicago or someplace, in the Army now and struggling for the American Dream, encouraged because she was black, because she was a woman. Opportunities were opening up for her now, and he was going to fail her, and burn her dream, because she was stupid and illiterate. It made him sick. And it was so *damned* hot, a dense tropical heat that infiltrated the body like a disease! So hot he could see the sweat on Miss Washington's upper lip as she flipped open the theme to the second page.

"What's you mean by this?" She tapped at some comment he'd made.

He stood up to examine the paper with her, looking where she pointed. The sentence she'd written was: "With the changeing fact of America and in the midst of all dierties, todays women is taking her neutral place in her new life style." He closed his eyes, wondering what to say to her. "My comment is that 'neutral' is not the word you mean here. Maybe you mean 'natural'." He didn't feel he could tell her more, going over the dozens of corrections in the semidarkness.

"I think it sound good!" Miss Washington argued.

"And the singular of 'women' is 'woman'. Or else the verb should be 'are'. That's 8A in our text, remember? We discussed it last Thursday."

"Yeah," she conceded.

What was the use of it all! He ached inside. He could stand there all night long and not change the girl. It was too late, too late! He had eight weeks in a term to eradicate the patterns of a lifetime—not reading, not writing, not studying. It was absurd! It was 8A in the text! He might as well be telling an Eskimo. It was sad and pathetic and horrible, but he wasn't responsible for racial prejudice; it wasn't his fault that Miss Washington's ancestors had been auctioned off on blocks at slave markets, not his fault! And yet here he was stuck with the burden of guilt and responsibility. It wasn't his fault, but he couldn't pass her, no, no, he couldn't pass this girl and hold his head up that he was teaching university courses! Yet it would be so much easier if he simply passed her through—then *she* would like him; so would the Education Center, because then Miss Washington and the others like her would enroll on base next term; the Education Center would get its merit points from PACAF, from the number enrolled. And even Dr Monasch would be happier with Victor; the funds would keep flowing into the university's treasury; the whole process of "education", complete with pious commencement addresses by brigadier generals about our "hard-working students" and all the other crap, would go on unabated! Why didn't Victor just play along, do what they wanted, what was necessary! It would be so much easier, so much, much easier.

"I had a hard life," Miss Washington snapped.

"Am I expected to give you a good grade because you had a hard life?"

"I didn't have no white folks to teach me before!" she said spitefully.

"What do you mean by that?"

"I didn't have no white folks to teach me in high school!" She said more loudly. "Why they got no black men teaching over here?"

He deflected her challenge, feeling them both too intense. "Perhaps you ought to withdraw from the course and wait until a black teacher becomes available, Miss Washington."

"I cain't!" Her eyes were wide and her mouth pouting. "There ain't nobody else on this godforsaken island. That's why I took your course!"

Victor

"Well, you aren't writing on a college level. Perhaps you ought to seek remedial help. There's a PREP program here, I believe, mainly for those who want to complete high school—"

"I done did high school!" she said indignantly. "I had a rough life!" she said.

"Many of us have rough lives, Miss Washington, but we don't use them as an excuse to get special treatment."

"I'll just *bet* you had a rough life!" she said.

He could feel her hatred as ponderous as the heavy night air. He was getting a headache. "Well, there must be some other program you can enroll in."

"I wants to stay in this class! *This* one! I paid for college!"

"I know! But you obviously aren't going to pass, are you? Wouldn't it be better to try another one?"

"I'm gonna stay in this class and you're gonna read my themes, 'cause *that's* what you get paid for!"

He stepped back from her, surprised at her vehemence. "Now just a minute! You aren't acting very smart, Miss Washington!"

"Don't you call me dumb! I'm not dumb! I can do college!" She was sullen and threatening, her body hunched.

"You're not being very smart psychologically—that's what I meant."

"I'm not dumb!" She sounded almost desperate, and Victor felt pity squeeze inside his chest.

"I'm not saying you're dumb; I'm only saying the way to get what you want is *not* to try to intimidate your teacher! It really isn't!" He wished he could take her in his arms and hug her, let her sob on his shoulder, let them both cry, let them weep fat, racking tears until both were exhausted. Let it clear the air between them, between the races, the way it did in television programs. A half-hour of disagreement resolved at the end by an embrace, a handshake, a trustful nod, the way it was on the television programs he sometimes watched in the Recreational Center on base.

"You're sure it's not something personal?" she repeated, tucking the theme into her back pocket, rolled, to let him know that she didn't care about the theme, about him; he was merely an obstacle in her way.

"I resent what you're saying very much, Miss Washington. I want you to know that!"

"I had a sick mother!"

"I'm sorry! I'm truly sorry about your sick mother, about the place where you grew up. But I can't help it! I can't help it, that's all!"

"Maybe the Equal Opportunities Commission would like to know about you!" It was her trump card, and she dealt it rapidly.

He could feel his face scorch. "I think you'd better go, Miss Washington. And take your friends with you!" He gestured at the group loitering over by the classroom. "If you think you can threaten me and get away with it, you've got another think coming!"

"Yeah, they might be interested to know they got a *bigot* on their all-white faculty!"

"You're the bigot, my dear woman! You're the bigot!" He knew he sounded prissy, but he couldn't control himself. "You most certainly had better withdraw from the class now!"

"I'm *not* gonna withdraw, 'cause you's gonna grade my themes fair!" She strode off, then stopped. "Or else I'm gonna kick your ass, you goddamn queer!"

Dr Monasch had asked him to stop in to see him when he turned his final grades into the main office. Victor sat crookedly, waiting, watching Dr Monasch's energetic secretaries typing. In a few minutes a handsome colonel in uniform came out of Dr Monasch's office. The Director and the colonel shook hands cordially.

Then Dr Monasch looked up before turning back into his office. "Oh, Mr Kepko! There you are!"

Victor got up and followed the tall, younger man into the office, which was panelled in teakwood. It was almost cold, because the air-conditioning was turned up so high.

"Sit—sit down."

Victor sat, in one of the wooly white chairs that looked like polar bears, sinking into the cushion. "How have you been, Dr Monasch?" he enquired politely.

"Can't complain. Can't complain at all!" The Director patted his tummy. He was a slimy man, with slushy blue eyes, a colorless complexion, but tall and straight and poised. "Say, what's this I heard about some student complaining about you?" Dr Monasch sat behind his large desk and placed his slush-laden eyes on Victor's face.

"It was simply a misunderstanding." Victor stopped himself. A "sir" had almost slipped out.

"Didn't some black girl accuse you of unfair grading?"

Victor looked down at his grade sheet, which he would turn in before he left. Instructors had to turn in their grade in person before they got their paychecks. "The girl was mistaken, but everything's cleared up now, fortunately."

Dr Monasch should have smiled, but didn't. "Not too good to hear stories like this, Mr Kepko. Gives the university a bad reputation."

Victor felt that he was being swallowed up in the white polar-bear cushions. "It's all over and done with, Dr Monasch."

But the Director wasn't about to be put off—obviously he'd set aside a few minutes that morning to "discuss the matter" with Victor. "I understand your student was black."

"That's right."

"We have some mighty upstanding black students in our program. Wonderful reports on progress." He lifted a fistful of official-looking documents from his desk.

"I'm glad to hear that," Victor said faintly.

"Mighty fine students, mighty fine reports of progress." He waited for Victor to agree with him.

Victor glanced out the window at the Okinawan greenery. Dr Monasch had a splendid view—of a small gorge, a couple of small hills. It didn't even look so hot outside from in here. "Yes," Victor mumbled.

"Speak up, Mr Kepko. I hope you speak up more loudly than that in your classroom. How will the students ever *hear* you?" The Director tidied the stack of progress reports.

"I'm sorry."

"By the way, there isn't anything in your background that would bias you against some students, is there, Mr Kepko? Are you from the South?"

Victor bowed his head. "No, there's nothing in my background. No, I'm not from the South."

Dr Monasch spotted the speck of opposition in Victor. "I mean, we have no room in our academic program for prejudice or bias—we never have and we never will!" He pinned Victor to the wooly chair with a look.

"It was all a misunderstanding. It's all straightened out now."

"Well, splendid! We wouldn't want anything to interfere with your teaching assignment for next term. It's just splendid!" he grinned as he spoke, a combination of slime and intimidation. Victor felt as if someone's rotting hand were doing something obscene to his body; the secretaries typed away enthusiastically outside the office.

"Is that all, Dr Monasch?" Victor asked wearily.

The Director stood up behind his large desk. "I had a call from the Equal Opportunities people. Not a nice call, not a nice call whatsoever!"

"I'm sorry."

"It could do the university no good, *no* good at all if word got around that we've got bigots on our staff. Bigots about whom there have also been unsavory sexual rumours." The Director looked sternly at Victor. "Do I make myself perfectly clear, Mr Kepko?"

"Perfectly."

There was a silence, while only the clack of typewriters and the throb of the air-conditioner filled the spacious office.

"Well, I guess I'd better be going," Victor said.

"Is that your grade sheet with you?"

Victor nodded.

"Do you mind if I see it?" Monasch held out his hand, and after a minuscule hesitation, Victor got up and gave it to him, then sat back down. The man's eyes scanned the names and grades appraisingly. "Yes, yes, yes!" Then he looked at the comment on the bottom that Victor had written in the area provided. "Some of the students in this class were satisfactory. Some needed remedial help." Dr Monasch wrinkled his lean face. "Why, Mr Kepko, this sounds dissatisfied!" He smiled. "Are you dissatisfied with our educational program over here?"

"No, I'm not dissatisfied."

"Well, I'm so glad to hear that. Because, after all, Mr Kepko, there're any number of instructors who just love it over here, just love teaching in Asia! That's why *they* remain. And we always prefer to have people who *enjoy* teaching in our classrooms. Wouldn't you feel the same if you were in my place?"

"Perhaps I would, yes."

"Of course you would! We've been mighty pleased with you so far this year. And I, for one, surely hope you'll continue to want to work with us and the military!"

Victor had to look down. If he could just get out of the office, out of the huge white chair, if he just didn't say anything more, then Dr Monasch would let him teach for at least one more term, maybe two, if he just didn't say anything more.

"What was the name of that black student again?" Dr Monasch was skimming the grade sheet once more.

"Miss Washington." Victor thought he might be catching a cold from the air-conditioning.

Dr Monasch found the name. "There she is!" He laid his finger beside the computer-typed name. "Oh, I see that she earned a C in your course."

Victor stared down at the rug. "That's correct. She improved a lot in the second half."

The Loveliness of
the Long-Distance Runner

I sit at my desk and make a list of all the things I am not going to think about for the next four and half hours. Although it is still early the day is conducive to laziness—hot and golden. I am determined that I will not be lazy. The list reads:

1. My lover is running in an organized marathon race. I hate it.
2. Pheidippides, the Greek who ran the first marathon, dropped dead at the end of it. And his marathon was 4 miles shorter than hers is going to be. There is also heat stroke, torn Achilles tendons, shin splints and cramp. Any and all of which, including the first option, will serve her right. And will also break my heart.
3. The women who are going to support her, love her, pour water down her back and drinks down her throat are not me. I am jealous of them.
4. Marathon running is a goddam competitive, sexist, lousy thing to do.
5. My lover has the most beautiful body in the world. Because she runs. I fell in love with her because she had the most beautiful body I had ever seen. What, when it comes down to it, is the difference between my devouring of her as a sex object and her competitive running? Anyway she says she does not run

competitively. Anyway I say that I do not any longer love her just because she has the most beautiful body.

Now she will be doing her warm-up exercises. I know these well, as she does them every day. She was doing them the first time I saw her. I had gone to the country to stay the weekend with her sister, who's a lawyer colleague of mine and a good friend. We were doing some work together. We were sitting in her living room and she was feeding her baby and Jane came in, in running shorts, T-shirt and yards and yards of leg. Katy had often joked about her sister who was a games mistress in an all-girls school, and I assumed that this was she. Standing by the front door, with the sun on her hair, she started these amazing exercises. She stretched herself from the waist and put her hands flat on the floor; she took her slender foot in her hand and bent over backwards. The blue shorts strained slightly; there was nothing spare on her, just miles and miles of tight, hard, thin muscle. And as she exhibited all this peerless flesh she chatted casually of this and that—how's the baby, and where she was going to run. She disappeared through the door. I said to Katy,
"Does she know I'm gay?"
Katy grinned and said, "Oh, yes."
"I feel set-up."
"That's what they're called—setting-up exercises."
I felt very angry. Katy laughed and said, "She is too."
"Is what?" I asked.
"Gay." I melted into a pool of desire.

It's better to have started. The pre-race excitement makes me feel a little sick. Tension. But also ... people punching the air and shouting "Let's go, let's go." Psyching themselves up. Casing each other out. Who's better than who? Don't like it. Don't want to do it. Wish I hadn't worn this T-shirt. It has "I am a feminist jogger" on it. Beth and Emma gave it to me. Turns people on though. Men. Not on to me but on to beating me. I won't care. There's a high on starting though, crossing the line. Good to be going, good to have got here. Doesn't feel different because someone has called it a marathon, rather than a good long run. Keep it that way. But I would like to break three and a half hours. Step by step. Feel good. Fitter than I've ever been in my life, and I like it. Don't care what Sally says. Mad to despise body when she loves it so. Dualist. I like running. Like me running. Space and good feeling. Want to run clear of this crowd— too many people, too many paces. Want to find someone to run my own pace with. Have to wait. Pace; endurance; deferment of pleasure; patience; power. Sally ought to like it—likes the benefits alright. Bloke nearby wearing a T-shirt that reads "Runners make the best lovers." He grins at me. Bastard. I'll show him: run for the Women's Movement. A trick. Keep the rules. My number one rule is "run for yourself". But I bet I can run faster than him.

Hurt myself running once, because of that. Ran a 10-mile race, years ago, with Annie, meant to be a fun-run and no sweat. There was this jock; a real pig; he kept passing us, dawdling, letting us pass him, passing again. And every time these remarks—the vaseline stains from our nipples, or women getting him too turned on to run. Stuff like that; and finally he runs off, all sprightly and tough, patronizing. We ran on. Came into the last mile or so and there he was in front of us, tiring. I could see he was tired. "Shall we?" I said to Annie, but she was tired too. "Go on then," she was laughing at me, and I did. Hitched up a gear or two, felt great, zoomed down the hill after him, cruised alongside, made it look easy, said, "Hello, sweetheart, you look tired," and sailed on. Grinned back over my shoulder, he had to know who it was, and pulled a muscle in my neck. Didn't care—he was really pissed off. Glided over the finishing line and felt great for twenty minutes. Then I felt bad; should have known better—my neck hurt like hell, my legs cramped from over-running. But it wasn't just physical. Felt bad mentally. Playing those games.

Not today. Just run and feel good. Run into your own body and feel it. Feel road meeting foot, one by one, a good feeling. Wish Sally knew why I do it. Pray she'll come and see me finish. She won't. Stubborn bitch. Won't think about that. Just check leg muscles and pace and watch your ankles. Run.

If she likes to run that much of course I don't mind. It's nice some evenings when she goes out, and comes back and lies in the bath. A good salty woman. A flavour that I like. But I can't accept this marathon business: who wants to run 26 miles and 385 yards, in a competitive race? Jane does. For the last three months at least our lives have been taken over by those 26 miles, what we eat, what we do, where we go, and I have learned to hate every one of them. I've tried, "Why?" I've asked over and over again; but she just says things like, "Because it's there, the ultimate." Or "Just once Sally, I'll never do it again." I *bet*, I think viciously. Sometimes she rationalizes: women have to do it. Or, it's important to the girls she teaches. Or, it has to be a race because nowhere else is set up for it: you need the other runners, the solidarity, the motivation. "Call it sisterhood. You can't do it alone. You need . . ." And I interrupt and say, "You need the competition; you need people to beat. Can't you see?" And she says, "You're wrong. You're also talking about something you know nothing about. So shut up. You'll just have to believe me: you need the other runners and mostly they need you and want you to finish. And the crowd wants you to finish, they say. I want to experience that solidarity, of other people wanting you to do what you want to do." Which is a slap in the face for me, because I don't want her to do what she wants to do.

And yet—I love the leanness of her, which is a gift to me from marathon training. I love what her body is and what it can do, and go on doing and not be tired by doing. She has the most beautiful legs, hard, stripped down, with no wastage, and her achilles tendons are like flexible rock. Running does that for her. And then I think, damn, damn, damn. I will not love her for those reasons; but I will love her because she is tough and enduring and wryly ironic. Because she is clear about what she wants and prepared to go through great pain to get it; and because her mind is clear, careful and still open to complexity. She wants to stop being a Phys. Ed. teacher because now that women are getting as much money for athletic programmes the authorities suddenly demand that they should get into competition, winning trips. Whereas when she started it was for fun and for women being together as women, doing the things they had been laughed at for as children.

She says I'm a dualist and laughs at me. She says I want to separate body and soul while she runs them together. When she runs she thinks: not ABC like I think with my tidy well trained mind, but in flashes—she'll trot out with some problem and run 12 or 15 miles and come home with the kinks smoothed out. She says that after 8 or 10 miles she hits a euphoric high—grows free—like meditation or something, but better. She tells me that I get steamed up through a combination of tension and inactivity. She can run out that stress and be perfectly relaxed while perfectly active. She comes clean. Ten or 12 miles at about eight minutes per mile: about where she'll be getting to now.

I have spent another half-hour thinking about the things I was not going to think about. Tension and inactivity. I cannot concentrate the mind.

When I bend my head foreward and Emma squeezes the sponge on to my neck, I can feel each separate drop of water flow down my back or over my shoulders and down between my breasts. I listen to my heart beat and it seems strong and sturdy. As I turn Emma's wrist to see her watch her blue veins seem translucent and fine. Mine seem like strong wires conducting energy. I don't feel I want to drink and have it lying there in my stomach, but I know I should. Obedient, giving over to Emma, I suck the bottle. Tell myself I owe it to her. Her parents did not want her to spend a hot Saturday afternoon nursing her games teacher. When I'm back in rhythm I feel the benefits of the drink. Emma is a good kid. Her parents' unnamed suspicions are correct. I was in love with a games teacher once. She was a big strong woman, full of energy. I pretended to share what the others thought and mocked her. We called her Tarzan and how I loved her. In secret dreams I wanted to be with her. "You Tarzan, me Jane," I would mutter, contemplating her badly shaved underarms, and would fly

*with her through green trees, swing on lianas of delight. She was my
first love; she helped make me a strong woman. The beauty, the
immensity of her. When we swam she would hover over the side of the
pool and as I looked up through the broken sparkly waters there she
would be hauling me through with her strength.*

*Like Sally hauls me through bad dreams, looming over me in the
night as I breathe up through the broken darkness. She hauls me
through muddle with her sparkly mind. Her mind floats, green with
sequinned points of fire. Sally's mind. Lovely. My mind wears Nike
running shoes with the neat white flash curling back on itself. It fits
well and leaves room for my toes to flex. If I weren't a games teacher I
could be a feminist chiropodist—or a midwife. Teach other women
the contours of their own bodies—show them the new places where
their bodies can take them. Sally doesn't want to be taken—only in
the head. Sex of course is hardly in her head. In the heart? My heart
beats nearly twenty pulses a minute slower than hers: we test them
together lying in the darkness, together. "You'll die, you shit," I want
to yell at her. "You'll die and leave me. Your heart isn't strong
enough." I never say it. Nice if your hearts matched. The Zulu
warrior women could run 50 miles a day and fight at the end of it.
Fifty miles together, perfectly in step, so the veldt drummed with it.
Did their hearts beat as one? My heart can beat with theirs, slow and
strong and efficient—pumping energy.*

*Jane de Chantal, after whom I was named, must have been a
jogger. She first saw the Sacred Heart—how else could she have
known that slow, rich stroke which is at the heart of everything?
Especially back then when the idea of heart meant only emotions. But
she was right. The body, the heart at the heart of it all: no brain, no
clitoris without that strong slow heart. Thesis: was eighteenth-century
nun the first jogger? Come on; this is rubbish. Think about footstrike
and stride length. Not this garbage. Only one Swedish garbage
collector, in the whole history of Swedish municipal rubbish
collection, has ever worked through to retirement age—what
perseverance, endurance. What a man. Person. Say garbage person.
Sally says so. Love her. Damn her. She is my princess. I'm the
younger son (say person) in the fairy story. But running is my wise*

*animal. If I'm nice to my running it will give me good advice on how
to win the princess. Float with it. Love it. Love her. There has to be a
clue.*

*Emma is here again. Car? Bicycle? She can't have run it. She and
Beth come out and give me another drink, wipe my face. Lovely
hands. I come down and look around. After 20 miles they say there
are two sorts of smiles among runners—the smiles of those who are
suffering and the smiles of those who aren't. "You're running too
fast," says Beth, "You're too high. Pace yourself, you silly twit.
You're going to hurt." "No," I say, "I'm feeling good." But I know
she's right. Discipline counts. Self-discipline, but Beth will help with
that. "We need you to finish," says Emma. "Of course she'll finish,"
says Beth. I love them and I run away from them, my mouth feeling
good with orange juice and soda water. Ought to have been Sally
though. Source of sweetness. How could she do this to me? How could
she leave me? Desert me in the desert. Make a desert. This is my
quest—my princess should be here. Princess: she'd hate that. I hate
that. Running is disgusting; makes you think those thoughts. I hurt. I
hurt and I am tired. They have lots of advice for this point in a
marathon. They say, think of all the months that are wasted if you
stop now. But not wasted because I enjoyed them. They say, whoever
wanted it to be easy? I did. They say, think of that man who runs
marathons with only one leg. And that's meant to be inspirational?
He's mad. We're all mad. There's no reason but pride. Well, pride
then. Pride and the thought of Sally suppressing her gloating if I go
home and say it hurt too much. I need a good reason to run into and
through this tiredness.*

*Something stabs at my eyes. Nothing really hurt before and now it
hurts. Takes me all of three paces to locate the hurt: cramp in the
upper thighs. Sally's fault; I think of her and tense up. Ridiculous.
But I'll be damned if I quit now. Run into the pain; I know it will go
away and I don't believe it. Keep breathing steadily. It hurts. I know
it hurts, shut up, shut up, shut up. Who cares if it hurts? I do. Don't
do this. Seek out a shirt in front of you and look at the number. Keep
looking at the number. 297. Do some sums with that. Can't think of
any. Not divisible by 2, or 3, or 5. Nor 7. 9. 9 into 29 goes 3. 3 and*

carry 2. 9 into 27. Always works. If you can divide by something the cramp goes away. Is that where women go in childbirth—into the place of charms? All gay women should run marathons—gives them solidarity with their labouring sisters. I feel sick instead. I look ahead and there is nothing but the long hill. Heartbreaking. I cannot.

Shirt 297 belongs to a woman, a little older than me perhaps. I run beside her, she is tired too. I feel better and we run together. We exchange a smile. Ignore the fact that catching up with her gives me a lift. We exchange another smile. She is slowing. She grins and deliberately reduces her pace so that I can go ahead without feeling bad. That's love. I love her. I want to turn round, jog back and say, "I will leave my lover for you." "Dear Sally," I will write, "I am leaving you for a lady who" (and Sally's mental red pencil will correct to "whom") "I met during the marathon and unlike you was nice and generous to me." Alternative letter, "Dear Sally, I have quit because long-distance running brings you up against difficulties and cramps and I cannot take the pain." Perseverance, endurance, patience and accepting love are part of running a marathon. She won't see it. Damn her.

Must be getting near now because there's a crowd watching. They'll laugh at me. "Use the crowd," say those who've been here before. "They want you to finish. Use that." Lies. Sally doesn't want me to finish. What sort of princess doesn't want the quest finished? Wants things cool and easy? Well, pardon me, your Royal Highness. Royal Highness: the marathon is 26 miles and 385 yards long because some princess wanted to see the start of the 1908 Olympic Marathon from Windsor Palace and the finish from her box in the White City Stadium. Two miles longer than before. Now standardized. By appointment. Damn the Royal Princess. Damn Sally.

Finally I accept that I'm not going to do any work today. It takes me several more minutes to accept what that means—that I'm involved in that bloody race. People tend, I notice, to equate accepting with liking—but it's not that simple. I don't like it. But, accepting, I get the car out and drive to the shops and buy the most expensive bath oil I can find. It's so expensive that the box is perfectly modest—no advertising, no half-naked women. I like half-naked women as a matter of fact, but there are such things as principles. Impulsively I also buy some matching lotion, thinking that I will rub it on her feet tonight. Jane's long slender feet are one part of her body that owe nothing to running. This fact alone is enough to turn me into a foot fetishist.

After I have bought the stuff, I slaver a bit over the thought of rubbing it into her poor battered feet. I worked it out once. Each foot hits the ground about 800 times per mile. The force of the impact is three times her weight. 122 pounds times 800 times 26 miles. It does not bear thinking about. I realize the implications of rubbing sweet ointment into the tired feet of the beloved person. At first I am embarrassed and then I think, well, Mary Magdalene is one way through the sex object/true love dichotomy. Endurance, perseverance, love. She must have thought the crucifixion a bit mad too. Having got this far in acceptance I think that I might as well go down to the finish and make her happy. We've come a long way together. So I get back into the car and do just that.

It is true, actually. In the last few miles the crowd holds you together. This is not the noble hero alone against the world. Did I want that? But this is better. A little kid ducked under the rope and gave me a half-eaten ice-lolly—raspberry flavour. Didn't want it. Couldn't refuse such an act of love. Took it. Felt fine. Smiled. She smiled back. It was a joy. Thank you sister. The people roar for you, hold you through the sweat and the tears. They have no faces. The finishing line just is. Is there. You are meant to raise your arms and shout, "Rejoice, we conquer" as you cross it. Like Pheidippides did when he entered Athens and history. And death. But all I think is, "Christ, I've let my anti-gravity muscles get tight." They hurt. Sally is here. I don't believe it. Beth drapes a towel over my shoulders without making me stop moving. Emma appears, squeaking, "Three hours, 26 and a half. That's great, that's bloody great." I don't care.

Sally has cool soft arms. I look for them. They hold me. "This is a sentimental ending," I try to say. I'm dry. Beth gives me a beer. I cannot pour it properly. It flows over my chin, soft and gold, blissfully cold. I manage a grin and it spreads all over me. I feel great. I lean against Sally again. I say, "Never, never again." She grins back and, not without irony, says, "Rejoice, we conquer."

Cupiditas

Another Valentine's Day. Again on the High Hetero Holiday, I hurry towards a woman. I am a woman.

The train passes the Cunard Hotel, where I first slept with Lilian. On Valentine's Day. What is it, with me?

Madeleine's angry. I'm late. Why wasn't I here the moment her husband was gone? Because I was busy pacifying my own. Husband, that is.

This was meant to be a practical solution: two married women together. A sharing of problems and conflicts turned out to be a multiplying of problems and conflicts. An end to oppression? Mutual oppression.

There's a *Guardian* on their sofa, of course, to match the one in my bag. Full of flabby liberal valentines. Not that they'd read them.

"They"? Do I think of Madeleine as part of a couple? Yes. She *is* part of a couple. I begin to think I will never be that. In some moods it's a brave, uplifting thought. In others, it's not. A handicap, something missing. My glue doesn't hold, my stitches pull apart, and in the process I fall apart. I can't do the Noble Loneliness bit either.

Noble Loneliness. It was Richard Nixon who used that phrase, to sanctify his paranoia, I remember as we neck on the *Guardian*. Maybe it's just as well I don't buy it.

Sometimes I don't want to couple up. Sometimes I want to too much. It never seems to level out, and levelling out seems to be what coupling up is all about.

Madeleine and I will never be a couple. We don't fit. We break ourselves trying, but it doesn't work. Even the sex doesn't work. We have a meeting of minds and that's it. Intellectual companionship. A Boston Marriage. But *Guardian*-reading women of our generation, the ones with intellectual curiosity, don't leave it at that.

There's adventure and warmth, if not ultimate intimacy, and how often do you get that? But I'm stopped, stuck, frozen out of even our makeshift camp on the borders of coupledom.

"What's the matter, Andrea?"

I can't say: I miss Lilian. I can't say: This is a mistake, a nice mistake but—

I can't say: It's me, I'm what's the matter. I open my mouth to try, and at that moment there's a soft thump as the front door is slammed shut, thus informing us it has first been pushed open. By someone with a key. By Paul, who is collusively ignorant.

"Oh, shit," Madeleine bolts out of bed, locks the door, pulls on her clothes in a split-second as if she's been practising for this moment all her life. Perhaps she has. Oh ignoble loneliness, oh Nixonian paranoia! I feel puppetized there on the bed. She holds some strings, he holds others.

She bombs out the door, motioning for me to stay where I am. This is the moment I will retrace my steps to, in hot humiliation. I will correct it a thousand times. I will leap out of their conjugal couch, armour myself, and march out, leaving them to their marital mess, my head held so high it will leave a mark on their immaculate ceiling.

I lie there, listening while Mommie and Daddy buzz, buzz in their adult undertones. I can't make out what they're saying, but I know it's about me. And not about me, not at all, not a bit. That's why I hate them with a confused childish hatred.

That's why they're both so guiltily nice to me afterwards, when the staticky buzzing goes away. Because I'm a patsy, a pawn in their game. Their game is grown-up but not serious. All the serious games are about children.

I lie there. If I'd been a thumb-sucker in childhood I'd suck my thumb now, but I wasn't. I did bite my nails, but I don't find them appetizing any more. I once bit the nail on my left index finger down to the quick, and it became infected. It hurt like hell. I lay in bed and cried, till a girl called Allenah Lorenz came to visit me and taught me how to make roses out of Kleenex with hairpins for stems, and paint them with nail varnish. I wasn't in the least artsy-craftsy, and I was inordinately proud of those roses. There was magic in the way you pulled the thin skirts of Kleenex round the hairpin to produce your rose. Allenah Lorenz was working on her Girl Scout Good Samaritan badge or something. She sat on my bed and stopped me from crying, and when she left the bed was covered with roses, all smelling of nail varnish.

It's all her fault. She corrupted me, that Girl Scout. That's why I'm here. Shall I make Kleenex roses for you, dearest Madeleine? You could stick them in your ass, by the hairpins.

She comes back relieved, reprieved. "I said, 'Andrea's got her period. She's in bed.' He said 'I thought you both were.'"

She smiles. Now I'm confidante, best friend, co-conspirator. Intimacy of a sort, at last. Now, perversely, I want her.

"Want me to cut myself and bleed on the sheet?"

She wrinkles up her nose, offended. "Ugh. Bad taste."

"You, too? Funny, I have a bad taste in my mouth as well."

She averts her eyes as I dress.

He sits behind his desk like an embarrassed headmaster. I am cast as an embarrassed schoolgirl. I'll be what they like, I'm too tired to care. He's still at the stage when he wants to be deceived. This, too, shall pass. I, Tiresias, have foreseen all, enacted on this same divan or bed. I, Tiresias, feel my age as we walk through the park to the underground, or perhaps it's the double scotch she's bought me.

I'm doing penance, perhaps, for having done to other women what she's done to me. I never disowned them, though, or disowned myself in that way. Perhaps in another way? I don't know. I take the train back past the Cunard, dry-eyed, dry-thighed.

The Day I Don't Remember

"You invent your mother to suit your own guilt!" I shouted. "She's *unreal*."

Jean, her back to me, knelt by the living room bookcase packing up *Rubyfruit Jungle*, *Lesbian/Woman*, Adrienne Rich's essays. Beside her was a box already full of copies of *Lesbian Tide*, the *Body Politic*, *Conditions*. And this was only the beginning. It was the third visit in so many years her mother and much younger sister had made to the coast, the third time Jean had packed up all the incriminating evidence of our life together. The first time I helped not only with the books and records but with the pictures, and we rearranged our clothes in the closets. I even put our toothbrushes as far from each other as possible in the holder. Orphaned at ten, I was without experience in tending the sensibilities of a mother, and I was, anyway, newly in love and awed by the experience. The second time I got sick, and Jean had to sleep with me whether anyone liked it or not. This time I was being resolutely combative.

"Do you hear me?" I demanded, sounding like somebody's mother myself.

"You like my mother; my mother likes you. Kinky's only fourteen..." Jean began, still going on with the witch-hunt through the shelves.

"Fourteen is old enough for the facts of life." If I hadn't

known how offended Jean was by details of my boarding school initiation, I would have used my own experience. Instead I tried a trade-off. "I slept alone in a room full of crucifixes when we visited her house, and she's not even Catholic."

"But she had to raise us Catholic."

"She said she didn't mind that you didn't go anymore. She said she'd kept her promise."

"Karin, it would *kill* Mother."

"I don't believe it!" I shouted. "I believe you think it would kill you to admit I matter to you."

"That's not fair," Jean said, giving me her full attention and judgement at the same time.

"Is this?" I asked with a gesture toward the boxes. "We're not even illegal. We're consenting adults."

"For two weeks I also have to be my mother's child."

People deprived early of their mothers are supposed to keep looking for substitutes, but I am frankly embarrassed by any attempt to mother me. That didn't stop me from feeling jealous of Jean, yea, and jealous of her mother, too. Though I was arguing for honesty, loyalty was the real issue. It was time Jean chose me above everyone else, particularly her mother.

"Well, I'm not your mother's child, and I'm not going to lie to her anymore."

I hadn't expected Jean to finally give in. Never having had to come out to a mother myself. I couldn't really imagine how Jean would do it. I just needed to rage around enough for her to know how I felt. Her suggestion that I leave took me totally by surprise. The line went over and over again in my head every day: "Then maybe you'd better find some place to stay . . ."

What if I'd gone on arguing as if what she had said were no worse than her packing up her books? Or what if I'd admitted I was pushing her too hard and actually right then apologized? I was so taken aback I simply asked, "Do you mean that?" And she said, "Yes."

I didn't pack much. Actually, as I looked around, there wasn't much in the place that belonged to me. Jean's the one to buy things; I'm more apt to spend money on dinners out, weekends away. We'd been here three years, and I was only now not noticing that it didn't look like our place at all. It was Jean's, and she was ordering me out of it, just a week before Christmas.

I should have quit my job and left town, gone somewhere I didn't know anybody or taken one of those cruises gay travel agents are always advertising. Only strangers would have patience for my load of anger and self-pity. But I didn't. I slept on one friend's couch until *her* mother arrived. I drank myself out of welcome at another's. On Christmas Eve I put myself up for grabs at the Crossroads and got the kind of sexual punishment I was probably looking for. I don't remember Christmas Day.

I don't even know what day after that it was—Sunday, I guess, because I wasn't at work. I spent hours walking along the beach. Though Jean's mother was the only argument we've ever had that I had lost, I knew the ten days behind me were strewn with similar defeats once Jean had an opportunity to discover and label them. As one of my erstwhile friends had crudely pointed out, I had been shitting in my own front yard.

"Let her try being holier-than-thou!" I shouted.

"Are you going back then?" the same friend asked.

I didn't know what to answer. I hadn't thought. Trying to, I wasn't sure I had that option now. Once I was suspended from school and behaved with so little repentance that I went back to find myself expelled. Why hadn't *I* told *Jean* to leave? She had a house full of crucifixes, a mother and a sister to go home to. My ex-guardian was an uncle who sent me a perpetual subscription to the *New Yorker* and let the bank deal with the rest. Maybe I should have spent Christmas in the vault.

I should have got Jean Tee Corinne's *Cunt Coloring Book* to open on Christmas morning, and let her figure out how to be her mother's child after that! They weren't even my books and records she was hiding. They were her own. That was the sort of stupid hypocrite she was, and I was at least going to go back and tell her so.

Jean's mother and Kinky always left the morning of New Year's Eve. The first year, after we drove them to the airport, we spent the rest of the day in bed and didn't make it to the party we had planned to go to. The second year I was already in bed, and Jean spent the day cleaning and putting everything back in place, the evening playing Olivia records and saying she was sorry. We both were. This year I turned up around three in the afternoon. I left my suitcase in the car. I rang the bell.

"Have you lost your key?" she asked when she opened the door.

"No," I said.

I was going to go on to say I didn't feel as if I lived here anymore, but it all looked so familiar, books and magazines in place, so ordinary and real, that I asked instead, "When did they leave?"

"The day after they got here," Jean said.

"What?"

"I told them," Jean said.

"Why? Why did you do a crazy thing like that?"

"It's what you wanted me to do."

"But not without me, not without figuring out how so—you know—they wouldn't mind."

"I guess I didn't care by then whether they minded or not," she said, sounding not angry so much as resigned.

"What did she say? What did your mother say?"

"Nothing much. That Kinky was still her responsibility. In Dad's memory, she couldn't accept or condone . . . that sort of thing. Just what you'd expect."

"Why didn't you let me know? Why didn't you call me at work?"

"I don't know," Jean said.

"What did you do for Christmas?"

"Nothing."

"Why?"

"I knew what you were doing."

"I can't remember the day at all," I said, and it couldn't have sounded like an alibi.

"Well," Jean said, "here's all your mail."

I started to open it, not knowing what else to do. Christmas cards seemed horribly beside the point. It could have been March or April. Then I came to the most recent *New Yorker* cover, a reindeer with birds in its antlers.

"Christ!" I said, and I could feel Jean, the ex-Catholic, flinch. "As out-of-key with season as I am."

She didn't laugh. I felt more inappropriate than ever. "What do you need me to say?"

After a moment, she said, "It's what I need unsaid."

"Why did you do it?"

"Because you were right."

I was surprised into a hope that I might be allowed to be self-righteous all over again, but something about the way Jean held her shoulders warned me not to capitalize on it.

"I could have been more tactful," I said.

"Why did you leave?"

"You said you meant it."

"Maybe I did. But I was very sorry—too sorry. I more or less threw Mother and Kinky out, too."

I was sorry, too, but I hadn't been here to live through it with her. Anything I did or said would make it worse rather than better. What if I said, "You know, I wasn't being honest; I was being jealous"? Jean would just be sorrier than ever.

"Why do you always believe me?" I asked.

"I don't know. I really don't know. Tell your next lover not to believe a word you say."

"You, too," I said. "And tell her . . ."

But I had no advice, even angry. If there had been less room for me when Mom (I did call her "Mom") and Kinky were around, their absence left no room for me at all. Crowding in instead were these two new lovers between whom the reconciliations would have to take place. Jean and I had got past forgiving or skipped it, maybe on that Christmas Day she sat alone refusing to phone, the day I don't remember.

First Communion

The other dream I walked into this bar looking for you as usual, Robert. But instead I found Superman. Honest I did! I could hardly believe it! I thought maybe I was drunk or something, except I hadn't drunk anything yet. I hadn't even ordered. I just walked in and there he was: leaning against the wall and sipping a beer. I knew it was him because he was wearing blue leotards and a red swimming suit and a cape. And he had this little spit curl right in the middle of his forehead like he always does. And he had the letter S on his chest which was pretty big. In fact it was HUGE! Muscles like you wouldn't believe! And every time he finished a beer he would take the bottle and smash it against his invulnerable head. That's so everybody would know he was really Superman and not in drag. That's why everybody was looking at him. Even the bartender. Because he was so beautiful. So PERFECT. Even the smoke seemed to freeze in mid-air. Every eye in that place was on him. Watching him. Watching every movement. Desiring him. But nobody moved. Nobody walked over to him, or smiled at him, or asked him where he got that neat outfit. They were afraid of him. They were afraid of being rejected by him. They couldn't stand the idea of everybody knowing they had been turned away because they weren't good enough, or beautiful enough. Don't you see, Robert? They have never been beautiful before. They must be beautiful here.

We must all be beautiful. Somewhere.

That's why I was the only one who walked over to him. Because I wasn't afraid. I simply lit a cigarette and walked over and leaned against the wall he was leaning against. And then I looked at him. I looked at him for a LONG time—at his deep dark eyes, at his curly blue hair, at that dent in his chin! HOW COULD I BE AFRAID OF HIM? After ALL those letters I wrote him as a kid? After *all* that love I sent him? He's the one person who would never reject me, or hurt me. I just knew it! All he wants to do is help people. Save people. Not condemn them to Hell. He wants to be touched, not adored. He wants people to be happy without hurting other people. And without being a criminal. That's all. He doesn't want to hurt anybody, or punish anybody eternally. He's never been weak enough to get hurt, so he's never been strong enough to inflict pain. THAT'S why I looked at him. Loved him. Wanted him. Wanted to be like him. That's why I finally said:

"Wanna cigarette?"

Well let me tell you, Robert, when I lit that cigarette, my hand was trembling like you wouldn't believe! EVERYBODY was looking at us. At ME. (It's so hard to approach a beautiful man because everyone's always watching him, watching to see if you'll succeed with him.) I looked up and tried to smile at that Super face, and he smiled back. "What's your name?" he asked, squeezing the flame of my match with his invulnerable fingertips, putting it out, then extending his hand. "You do have a name don't you, kid?" I reached for his hand.

"Y-y-yes," I said, "m-my name is Jerry. Jerry Chariot."

GOSH, Robert, you should have felt what I felt when I first felt him! When I first touched that invulnerable hand! Held it! Shook it! It was like something I could never describe. It was like giving birth to a baby. That's something I could never describe because I'm not a woman. I'm a man. I'm a man shaking hands with a Superman. After all this time. After all those letters. After all these years of being alone. At last I've found him. I've REALLY found him. The REAL Superman! In a bar.

In a dream.

"Jerry Chariot?" he said. And then he said, "Hmmm-mmmmm, it seems like I've heard that name before?"

He rubbed the dent in his chin. He scratched his blue hair. He broke another beer bottle over his indestructible head. He was thinking. He was trying to remember.

"Hmmmmmmmmm," he said again.

I held my breath. I didn't want to interrupt. Gosh, would he REALLY remember? It was only a moment, but it seemed like forever. His hand was still in mine. Or was mine in his? Who dealt the hand? How did I get here? Why are all these people watching us? Staring at us? Why am I telling you all this, Robert?

"Sayyyyyyyy!" he said at last, snapping his fingers and accidentally breaking my beer bottle. There was white foam all over me and his leotards. "Sayyyyyyyy, you're not THE KRYPTONITE KID, are you?"

I blushed ferociously.

"Well I'll be GODDAMNED!" he said, before I had a chance to answer. He slapped me on the back and squeezed my shoulder, as if we were old friends. He wiped the beer off my face with his indestructible cape. "WELL I'LL BE GODDAMNED!" he said again.

And then he looked me right in the eyes. And then he smiled wide, like a kid, and two dimples suddenly appeared, like commas, and then he said:

"I really liked your letters, kid. I really did. Looked forward to them, as a matter of fact. I even took them to the office and showed them to Perry White. God how we laughed! You know, you weren't too bright as a kid, kid. You never fought back hard enough, not until the end. And then it was too late for anything—even your First Holy Communion. But Perry still liked them. He even wanted to run them in a column, but then he thought there might be a libel suit. And besides, who would believe them? You know, I should have answered your letters, kid. I meant to. Trouble was I was so damn busy! You know how it is when you're trying to save people all the time. I figure I must have stopped at least two dozen automobile accidents a day. Not to mention earthquakes, tidal waves, invasions from Outer Space, floods and Mr Mxyzptlk! He was a real pain in the ass. He kept tricking me, trying to make me miserable. I hated that Fifth-Dimensional faggot!

"And then there was Lois Lane. God, every time I turned around she was falling out a window, or trying to figure out who I really was, and how I really felt. It was bad enough trying to hold down two jobs at the same time—but that bitch really made it hard, so to speak. Believe me, kid, it isn't easy trying to make people think you're something you're not. Especially Lois. Do you know what she did one time? We were working late at the Planet, grinding out a weekend wrapup, when she put the make on me. Right there in the office! It was pretty late and no one else was around, so she figured if she got my clothes off then she could see if I was wearing my Supercostume underneath. Pretty clever. But not clever enough for SUPERMAN. When she started kissing me and groping me, I knew what was bound to come. So I slipped away at Superspeed, took off my outfit, put my regular clothes back on, then returned in a fraction of a second. It took less time than a fart, and it was a lot less noticeable. She never even realized I'd been gone. And then I plowed the shit out of her. Right there on my desk. I mean Clark's desk. God, she loved it! The next day she slipped me a note. It said I should meet her in the stockroom after our five o'clock deadline. So I did. Just about every day. She was a nymphomaniac, if you ask me. Her name should be Lois Lain.

"But I got tired of hiding my costume all the time—of pretending I wasn't somebody I was. I'm through with all that. From now on I'm gonna be myself. And if people don't like it, well that's the way the Kryptonite crumbles. And that's exactly what I told her. Boy, you should have seen the expression on her

face! She looked horrified! She couldn't believe it! WHY ARE YOU
TELLING ME NOW? she asked. BECAUSE I'M TIRED OF SNEAKING
INTO THAT GODDAMNED CLOSET ALL THE TIME! I said. IF IT ISN'T A
CLOSET, IT'S A PHONE BOOTH! I'M SICK OF LIVING THAT WAY!

"And I WAS sick, Jerry. That's why I left Metropolis. That's
why I came here, now, and found you. That's why we're talking
together, kid. At last we're ready for each other. At last you can
touch me. Here, go ahead. Put your hand on my arm. C'mon,
touch me, kid. Hold me. Fly with me. Isn't that what you've
always wanted? Isn't that why you wrote me all those letters?
Please do it, kid. PLEASE."

I reached out slowly, carefully, afraid he might dissolve like a
dream into morning. Everyone was watching, even those way in
the back. People could see through people to see me. Everybody
was invisible except ME, Robert. Me and him.

"Don't be afraid," he said, "I WANT you to touch me! That's
what I've always wanted. I may look tough, but I'm not. Not
really. Please touch me, kid. I can't help it if I'm Super—if
everyone looks up to me, thinks I'm strong. That's THEIR image,
so I have to break beer bottles over my head. I can't do anything
about it. But I'm NOT strong. Not really. I'm weak. I need help. I
need love. I need YOU, kid. Because somewhere beneath this
invulnerable skin, inside this indestructible chest, somewhere
deep inside is a speck of Kryptonite—glowing, warm. And
hurting—"

Everyone watched as my hand touched his hand, slipped
up his arm, brushed his cheek. Everyone stared as I touched
him, pulled him toward me, put both my arms around him,
gently.

Everyone saw it.

"Harder!" he said. "Hold me *harder*! Squeeze me! Let me
FEEL you!"

He was yelling now, and wrapping his legs around mine, and
pressing his body into my body. In front of everybody.

"C'mon, kid, let me FEEL you!" he said. "Let me feel that HOT tongue!"

He opened his mouth and attacked my lips and licked them, chewed them, bit them, then sucked them—drawing out my tongue, letting it slide down his deep, moist, invulnerable throat.

It was REALLY embarrassing, Robert.

I mean, you just don't do those things in a bar. Not with people watching.

I think he sensed my uneasiness because after a while he stopped. He tucked his shirt back into his leotards. He smoothed his cape. Ordered another beer. Then said:

"You used to have a friend, didn't you? What was his name? . . . Ronald? . . . Or Robin, or . . ."

"Robert," I said. "His name was . . ."

"ROBERT! Of course, now I remember. Had freckles, didn't he?"

"Yes, he . . ."

"I've always hated freckles myself. Kept telling Jimmy Olsen he should get them removed. Even offered to pay for it. Said I'd get a piece of coal and squeeze it into a diamond for him. But he wouldn't take it. Said he liked his freckles. Couldn't understand it myself. I think they look like piss stains. Say, whatever happened to Ronald . . ."

"Robert," I said.

"Yeah, Robert. Whatever happened to him? Are you still friends? Do you two still write letters together?"

"No, I'm afraid he . . ."

"He didn't get married, did he?"

"Oh no, Superman. He didn't do that."

"Thank God!"

"He died."

"Oh . . . Oh gee, I'm sorry, kid . . . I didn't realize. Choke. The poor kid. Sob. Oh jeez . . . What happened, may I ask?"

"Sure."

"What happened?"

"Well I'll tell you, Superman. One day they said he wasn't a man. So he went away to prove he was. Only he wasn't. So they mortared him."

"Gee, that's too bad."

"For who?"

"For you, kid."

"Yes. Yes it is," I said.

And then he broke another bottle over his head.

Maybe I shouldn't have told him the truth, Robert. About how they laughed at you, then attacked you, then nailed you to a question mark, like Jesus. But I couldn't help it. I felt he wanted to know the TRUTH, Robert.

So I told him:

"Robert was my friend. My BEST friend. The only person I chose to love me back. So he did. Even after the leap. Even after I didn't walk good anymore. Still he loved me and held me and wanted me totally—until his Mom and Dad shot into the room. Until they looked at us like we were the WORST things they had ever seen. I remember his Dad reaching for his belt immediately, instinctively snapping it through the air, and then I saw the shame on Robert's face. And then I saw the tears in Robert's eyes, each one a different color—red and blue and green, like Kryptonite. I tried to protect him but it was too late, Superman. His Dad's horror went flashing through the air quickly, irrevocably—like a bullet it entered him and destroyed him, took him away from me forever.

"And then they tried to kill me, Superman. They tried to kill me the same way they killed Robert—with fear and shame and prayers. And blame. But I fought back. I was TOUGH like you! I told them I'm gonna fly, I'm gonna jump, you can't hurt me, you can't kill me, now I'm Super, now I'm invulnerable, and then I jumped."

And then I hit the ground.

And then I looked him right in the eyes, Robert. Right square in the face, and I said:

"Why didn't you ever write me a letter, Superman? Just ONE letter to let me know? Or why didn't you fly over my house, or give me a sign, or work a miracle? Why must I meet you now, in a bar, when it's too late to save Robert or me or ANYBODY? Why didn't you appear then, when we needed you most—when we were small? When you were big? Why, Superman? WHY?"

And you know what he said, Robert? He said:

"Excuse me a second, will you? I have to go to the toilet."

And he went.

He was in there a pretty long time. About fifteen minutes. I kept watching the door, waiting for him to come out. A whole bunch of other guys kept going in and coming out and going in and coming out. And so I started thinking about Mrs Bacchio because I didn't have nothing else to do except wait, Robert. Wait and remember that day after school when we were in Bacchio's News Stand when Mr Durrelli was late with the comicbooks. And Mrs Bacchio kept looking at us looking worried. And you kept biting your nails, Robert, because it was going on five o'clock and Mr Durrelli still didn't come in with the comicbooks and Mrs Bacchio was still looking at us and she was smiling. And then she said, "My, you boys must sure like comicbooks."

And you said, "We sure do, Mrs Bacchio."

And I said, "You see, Mrs Bacchio, we don't really like comicbooks. We just like Superman and Supergirl and Superdog and Jimmy Olsen. That's all. Except we also like Superhorse and Perry White and Ma and Pa Kent."

And you said, "We sure do" again, Robert.

And I said, "You see, Mrs Bacchio, we don't like Donald Duck and Little Lulu because they're for little kids and not us. And besides, they don't fly or nothing."

And you said, "They sure don't" this time, Robert.

And I said, "We don't mind Batman and Wonder Woman and

Green Lantern and Flash and people like that. But you see, we don't have very much money and so we like Superman the best. That's because he *is* the best."

And that's when Mrs Bacchio laughed and said, "You know, I kinda like Superman myself." And she was the FIRST groan-up we ever met who liked Superman, Robert, and that's why we didn't trust her. And so I said:

"OK, if you like Superman so much then you must know what can kill him, so what is it?"

And she said, "Just one thing. Kryptonite."

And you said, "Hey, she *does* know!"

And I said, "Well, lots of people know that, Robert." And so I turned to Mrs Bacchio and I looked at her for a long time and I looked right in her eyes and then I said, "OK, if you're so smart then tell me what Superman's real name is."

And she said, "You mean Clark Kent?"

And I said, "No, I mean his REAL name on Krypton that his real Mom and Dad gave him before Krypton blew up and he came to Earth in a rocket to become Superbaby and someday Superman?"

And she said, "That's easy."

And I said, "Then what is it?"

And she said, "His real name was Kal-El. And his real father's name was Jor-El. And his real mother's name was Lara."

And you said "GOSH!", Robert.

And I didn't say nothing because I still didn't trust her. So I asked her a bunch of other questions like "How do you get rid of Mr Mxyzptlk!?" And she said, "Mr WHO?" And I said, "Mr Mxyzptlk!" And she said, "Oh, I thought it was pronounced Mxyzptlk!" And I said, "Well me and Robert say Mxyzptlk!" And so she told us.

She knew the answers to EVERYTHING, Robert. And she kept smiling at us. And she smiled real nice, just like all the saints on the Holy Cards smile when a light shines down from Heaven on them. And so we liked her a WHOLE lot. We really did. We liked her more than any other groan-up we met, even the ones we HAD

to like. Like my Aunt Helen who we HATED. And that's why we
felt so bad when my Mom and Veronica next door started
whispering about Mrs Bacchio. And pretty soon your Mom
started whispering about her too, Robert. And before long even
the nuns started whispering about how Lenore Bacchio was
doing something with somebody who she wasn't supposed to be
doing it with. And we didn't know exactly what it was because
we never heard them whispering THAT low before. But we
figured it must be pretty bad because my Mom whispered,
"Does her husband know about it?"

And Veronica next door whispered, "No, but everybody else
does."

And I said, "I don't.'

And BOY did my Mom get mad! She yelled REAL LOUD at me
and told me how I wasn't supposed to listen to groan-ups talk.
Especially when they're whispering. And how I'm not allowed to
go in Bacchio's News Stand EVER AGAIN. And how I better get
outside before she gives me a beating RIGHT THIS INSTANT YOUNG
MAN! And so we went up to your house, Robert, but we still
couldn't figure out who it was she was doing it with.

Whatever it was she was doing.

Whatever it was he was doing, he was sure taking a long time,
Robert. About a half-hour now. I kept watching the door,
waiting for Superman to come out. A whole bunch of other guys
kept going in and coming out and going in and coming out. I
started worrying. Maybe there was a piece of Kryptonite in the
toilet or something? Maybe he was sitting on the toilet dying?
Maybe I should go in and see if he's OK? So I did. I put my beer
down and lit a cigarette and started to walk over and then it
happened. The door opened. He came out. And you'll never
guess who was with him? It was Mr Mxyzptlk!

Honest to God, Robert—it was *Mr Mxyzptlk!*

Right away I tried to think of a way to trick Mr Mxyzptlk! into spelling his name backwards. Because that's the only way to get rid of him and send him back to THE FIFTH DIMENSION where he lives with all the other imps. Because he's MAGICAL and you have to trick him into saying *!kltpzyxM* or else he'll just hang around and make Superman miserable like he always does. Like one time he made all the cars drive up the side of the Daily Planet building and another time he made all the water disappear from everybody's swimming pool. And so Superman had to trick him on the last page of the comicbook by making him read the letters in his alphabet soup which turned out to be his name spelt backwards. Which was pretty clever. But still I was worried, Robert, because I got one good look at Mr Mxyzptlk! and KNEW there was gonna be trouble. Except then I noticed that Superman was smiling REAL BIG. And he was carrying Mr Mxyzptlk! because he's just an imp and he didn't want to get stepped on in that crowded bar. And he carried him right over to where I was standing. And then Superman said, "Mr Mxyzptlk!, I'd like you to meet Jerry Chariot."

And Mr Mxyzptlk! said, "Hi, Jerry!"

And I said, "Hello, Mr Mxyzptlk!"

And Mr Mxyzptlk! said, "Just call me Mr for short."

And I said, "I'm very pleased to meet you at last, Mr."

And Mr said, "The pleasure's all mine, Jerry."

And Superman said, "You can call him kid."

And Mr said, ". . . kid."

And I said, "You can call me Jerry if you want."

And Mr said "Put me down, Superman."

So Superman put him down.

Well, you should have seen him, Robert! His nose came right up to my belly button. Or maybe below it. And it was so hard to hear him down there. And everytime he said something, I wasn't sure if he said something. So I bent down and asked him, "Did you just say something?" And he said, "Will somebody please pick me up!" So Superman did it.

"Thank you, Superman!" said Mr Mxyzptlk!.

"You're welcome, Mr Mxyzptlk!" said Superman.

And then Mr Mxyzptlk! decided it would be a lot easier if he sat on Superman's shoulders so he could see everything. So he grabbed Superman's indestructible cape with one hand, his invulnerable hair with the other, then hoisted himself on to the Man of Steel's massive shoulders. Then he rested both elbows on Superman's head and perched there like a raven.

And then I said:

"I thought you guys didn't like each other too much? I mean, you ALWAYS used to fight and stuff, didn't you? You always tried to get rid of the other person. So what happened? Don't you hate each other like you always used to? Don't you DESPISE each other?"

Quoth the imp, "Not any more."

"You see, Jerry," he explained, "one day as I was flying here from The Fifth Dimension, something strange happened. I was mid-way through The Fourth Dimension when I saw myself going the other way, returning to The Fifth Dimension, and I was flying backwards. And I was crying. And each tear was black, perfectly black, and it scared me. *'What the HELL am I doing?'* I asked myself. *'Why in Heaven's name am I always traveling back and forth from The Fifth? What's so IMPortant about making Superman miserable?'* Suddenly, as I reached the outskirts of The Third, came the answer: *'I don't hate Superman—I LOVE him!'*

"Well let me tell you, Jerry, that's not easy to come to. Not after you've spent your whole life hating somebody as much as I hated Superman. I was REALLY upset. I had wasted so MUCH time trying to make Superman notice me, talk to me, trick me, do ANYTHING to me—as long as he paid SOME kind of attention! And it's no secret, kid, if you want some attention all you've got to do is make somebody miserable. So that's what I did: year in, dimension out.

"Trouble was it wasn't the RIGHT kind of attention. After a while all that misery started bothering me. I started having dreams like you used to have, kid. I started dreaming that I was flying and crying backwards. The tears were falling INTO my eyes instead of out of them. That Mrs Bacchio was watching me, then I was watching her turn on the gas and suffocate. Then I would wake up crying and screaming for Superman to save her. But I KNEW it was too late! I KNEW I had to let her die! I could hear a statue of the Virgin Mary in her pocket, crying . . .

"Yes, kid, it was *I* who intercepted those letters you and Robert wrote to Superman about Lenore Bacchio. That's why Superman never showed up to save her! It was just another of my impish pranks—no real harm intended. HONEST, kid! At the last moment I was going to notify the Man of Steel and watch him rescue her. I had it all planned out. Trouble was she seemed to want to die. Almost NEED to die. There was something about the look on her face as she latched those windows shut. Something about the calm that surrounded her as she turned on that oven.

"I didn't mean to let it happen, Jerry. Please don't look at me like that, kid! It's just . . . well, it's just that I couldn't help myself. She had a spell over me. I explained it all to Superman and he understood. Didn't you, Superman? I told him right here in this bar, as a matter of fact. In that corner over there. I'll never forget how he looked back at me, then leaned forward and kissed me. His hands were still at his sides and his eyes were like bright stars, staring at me as if I were the moon in his sky. As if *I* were the glow that made him so bright.

"He wanted me that night, Jerry. He forgave me and loved me. He knew I would now give him pleasure—not misery. Isn't that right, Superman? Tell Jerry about that first night we spent together. About how happy we were to warm each other's insomnia. To at last be real. Rewarding each other with kisses. Seizing each other's caresses. Correct me if I'm wrong, kid, but isn't that the way you first felt with Robert?

"Well isn't it, Jerry?" he said. Then paused. Then rubbed his fingers through Superman's blue hair and exploded into laughter—high, screechy, ugly, awful laughter that kept rearranging itself. One second it sounded like Sister Mary Justin and the next second it sounded like Veronica nextdoor. And then it was Mrs Bacchio and then it was Lois Lane and then it was my Dad. And then it was a siren, like an ambulance, and a scream. My Mom's scream.

What's going on here, Robert? This dream's becoming too much like reality. That scream sounds too much like a *scream*! I'm afraid, Robert. Everything's out of control.

"C'MON NOW, KID, ADMIT IT!" the imp snapped, and suddenly his words seemed to come from far, far away. From another time or space. Or dimension. One of his eyes turned purple and the other turned orange and his hair seemed to melt as his chin withered as his ear grew long and furious and pointed. Superman just stood there frozen—saying nothing, doing nothing, ignoring this rabid imp who suddenly pointed a long red fingernail at me.

"I *know* how desperately you've always wanted Superman!" he shrieked, his voice full of hate and jealousy—nothing mischievous or impish left in him.

"Always acting so young, so innocent—so *appealing!*" he said. "Well you can't fool me, Jerry! I know your tricks and I'm not giving up without a battle! Superman belongs to ME now and there's no way you can make me say *!kltpzyxM* because it won't work! Do you understand, kid? It CAN'T work because... Oh shit! I said it! GodDAMNit, Superman, I'm disa

p

　p

　　e

　　　a

　　　　r

　　　　　i

　　　　　　n

I couldn't believe it, Robert! One minute he was sitting on Superman's shoulders and talking, and the next minute he was gone! Just like that! He didn't even have time to close the quotation marks. He just vanished. It happened so fast.

!kltpzyxM

"What luck!" said Superman. "I thought we'd never get rid of that Fifth-Dimensional fart!"

"WHAT?" I said. "But I thought you liked him now? I thought you were friends. Doesn't he LOVE you now?"

"Sure he loves me. Doesn't everybody?"

"Except Sister Mary Justin at school."

"Then what do I need his love for? I've got more love than I can handle right now, kid. Just look around this bar. See all those people staring at me, wanting me, desiring me? THAT's the way it is wherever I go. EVERYBODY worships me. They NEVER leave me alone. They want my autograph, or a lock of my indestructible hair, or a kiss. Everybody wants SOMETHING from me, kid—just like you do. Just like Lois Lane did. Just like Mr Mxyzptlk! didn't. That's why I liked him a lot better then—because he was the only person who hated me. Except for criminals and they don't count, not in my book. I mean comicbook. It was kind of nice to find a little hate for a change, but now even that imp loves me. Shit, kid, what can a Superman do?"

"I don't know," I said. "But I know what I'd do."

"What's that, kid?"

"I'd take all that love, from everybody, every ounce of it, I'd take it all and I'd NEVER let it out of my sight. I'd hold on to it, sleep with it, pray to it. I'd buy a gun and protect it. And if anybody tried to take it away, I'd kill them. That's what I'd do. I KNOW that's what I'd do, Superman."

"You know what, kid?"

"What, Superman?"

"You'll never get Super that way."

"You know what, Superman?"

"What, kid?"
"I'll never get Super anyway."

!klptzyxM

"You're growing up, kid."
"No, Superman, I'm groaning up."

!kltpzyxM

"I wish he could have stayed, Superman. I wanted to ask him about The Fifth Dimension, about what it's like there. About how you get there. Say, you don't know where The Fifth Dimension is, do you, Superman?"
"Sure I do."
"Where is it?"
"It's quite a way from here, kid. And it's also very close. It's a pretty hard place to find because you have to make your way through Purgatory, past Metropolis and over the Duck Rock. Then you have to climb back into your mother's stomach and laugh about it all. Believe me, you'll never find it, kid. NEVER!"
"Will you take me there, Superman?"

You should have seen the look he gave me, Robert! He wasn't smiling anymore and he was biting his indestructible lip and his eyes seemed to get bigger, darker, sadder. He looked at me just the way he looked at Ma and Pa Kent when they were dying way back in *GIANT SUPERBOY NO. 165*. And he was crying. And each tear was green. Kryptonite green. And he said:

"Don't do it, kid. Don't try to go to The Fifth Dimension. Not there! It's too dangerous, too painful. There are too many things trying to stop you, to prevent you from making it. Horrible things! Frightening things like Sister Mary Justin, like Veronica nextdoor, like the Holy Ghost! They're hiding behind every rock—waiting for you, waiting to attack you, hit you, kill you! PLEASE, kid! I beg you. DON'T do it. Forget it! We can leave this bar in a while. I'll give you a ride home and we can turn out the lights and touch each other. I love the feeling of another man's body embracing me back. I LOVE the idea of two men together—two buddies, two pals—walking like men, acting like men, loving like men. Stay a while longer, kid. I feel good in this dark corner where there's no one to disapprove. Where there's no one to throw Kryptonite at me. I like the shadows here, and the smoke. They hide me. They protect me. They remind me that I can be honest here, inside, as long as I'm dishonest everywhere else. To find joy in a place where others find contempt, even disgust, makes me feel important. It makes me feel SUPER. Yes, I feel safe here with you. Forget The Fifth Dimension, kid. Have another beer. Touch me. Hold me. I love you."

I couldn't STAND looking at his tears, Robert. Even if they are indestructible, they don't belong there. Not on his face. Not on his PERFECT face! I looked away. I fumbled for a cigarette. He lit it with his x-ray vision. I said, "Thank you, Superman." He said, "You're welcome, kid." We both smiled as I watched the last of his tears roll down his cheek, bounce off his indestructible chest, fall gently to the floor, like rain.

That's when I noticed it, Robert.

I looked down at his red swimming suit and it was flat. PERFECTLY flat. Just like in the comicbooks. Either it was tucked way under, or he didn't have anyThing at all. I *had* to find out.

"By the way, Superman," I said, inching closer. "How's your cousin Supergirl?"

"SUPERGIRL?" he said. "You mean SUPERWOMAN. She's grown up now, you know. Married an airline pilot. He isn't Super, but at least they can fly together. How'd you like that one? HA-HA!"

"I didn't," I said, moving closer.

"Well it's true. That's how they met. One day she was flying along pretty fast, trying to gain enough speed to crash through the Time Barrier. Instead she almost crashed into his cockpit. HA-HA!"

"HA-HA!" I said, moving closer. My hands were getting sweaty.

"So he rolled down the window of his plane. SAY THERE, SUPERWOMAN, he said. YOU BETTER WATCH WHERE YOU'RE FLYING. She looked at him. SORRY ABOUT THAT, she said apologetically. PLEASE FORGIVE ME, she said imploringly. I APOLOGIZE, she said pathetically. And then . . ."

"And then?"

"And then somebody inside the airplane spotted her. I mean, how could they help it? She was just flying along beside the plane and flirting with the pilot. So somebody looked outside and said, HEY, LOOK—OUTSIDE!"

"And somebody else said IT'S A BIRD!"

"And somebody else said IT'S A PLANE!"

"And somebody else said, NO, IT'S SSSSSSUPERWOMAN!"

"And allofasudden everybody ran to one side of the airplane and it flipped over and it started to crash and so Superwoman had to save it on top of page 10. And she also saved him. So he flipped for her. And then they kissed and had a REALLY long engagement. About twenty-five issues. And then they got married. And then it said THE AND I mean END."

I was REALLY close now, Robert. My knee was touching his knee and my arm was also. I was rubbing against him gently— trying to push my body into his Superbody. But still I needed to get a little closer—to touch it, feel it, find out if he had one!

And if it was big.

"And then what happened?" I asked, moving closer.

"The usual," he said, sipping his beer. "They had a nice little house, and then they had a nice little baby, and then they had a nice little another baby, and they needed more room, so they got another house, and so he needed another job to pay for the another house, and then he couldn't sleep at night, and then they lived happily ever after."

"Were they Super, I wonder?" I asked moving closer.

"Were who Super?"

"Her kids," I said. "Were they Super or regular?"

"What's the difference?"

"Oh, about ten cents a gallon."

"Super," he said.

"Both of them?"

"No, just one of them. One was Super and the other was regular. That is to say, ordinary."

"How unfortunate," I said, moving closer.

"Yes," he said. "They NEVER got along. Especially since the Super one was a girl. And the older one was a boy. How would you like it if your little sister kept chasing crooks while you did the dishes all the time?"

"I wouldn't," I said, moving closer.

"Well, neither did he. So he killed himself."

"How TERRIBLE!" I said, moving closer.

"Yes, it was a real mess. He leaped off the roof of his Dad's apartment and splattered all over the headlines."

"Oh no!" I said, moving closer.

"Oh *yes*! And everyone blamed Superwoman. Said she was a domineering mother, that she overpowered him—killed him!"

"Was it true?" I asked. "Did she really kill him?"

"Don't know," said Superman. "But I'll tell you what I think."

"What do you think?" I asked, and I was about as CLOSE as I could get—I was just about to put my hand on it, to find if he had one, when he said:

"I think I'll have another beer."

And he walked away.

And when he came back he handed me a beer that he had bought me, and we clinked bottles, and he said, "Here's looking at you kid!" And he looked at me. He looked me right in my Kryptonite eyes and he said:

"There's two things I've been wanting to ask you, kid. Just two things. I've been wanting to ask you for a LONG time and now I finally have the chance. So please answer, will you, kid. It's REALLY important. Please?"

"Sure, Superman." I said. "Anything. What is it?"

"Well, kid, the second question is a lot easier than the first. So I'll start with the second question first."

"That makes sense."

"OK, kid. Question number one: WHO MADE YOU?"

"Is THAT your question?"

"That's it."

"That's easy."

"That's what you think, kid. You better think about it."

"I don't have to, Superman. I'll tell you right now: God made me. My Mom and Dad made me. My brother Buster made me. Sister Mary Justin and Jimmy Sinceri and Pastor Ponti made me. Even Veronica nextdoor made me. They ALL made me. I didn't really want to. Not really. They made me."

"What did they make you, kid?"

"Is that your second question, Superman?"

"Well it isn't my third."

"Kryptonite," I said. "They made me Kryptonite."

"And what did you do with it, kid?"

"With what, Superman?"

"With the Kryptonite, kid."

"I leaped."

!kltpzyxM

"And why did you leap, kid?"
"For the same reason I wrote you all those letters."
"And what was that?"
"To show them I'm not so little anymore."

!kltpzyxM

Well, you should have seen the look he gave me then, Robert!
You should have seen the way his eyes got dark and slanted. It
was JUST the way Sister Mary Justin used to do it. Honest to God!
I couldn't believe it! He looked at me REAL mean and said:

"Who in the HELL do you think you're kidding, kid? You're
just as little as you've ever been—as you'll ALWAYS be! You'll
never be as big as I am. You'll never be SUPER like me! Sure, you
can write me letters, if you want. Sure, you can put words in my
mouth. You're holding the pencil, kid. But you're forgetting one
thing: *I'm* Superman! I can burst out of these pages, away from
these words. But you're STUCK here, kid! You're no better off
than you were on that roof! Look at your life. Look at it honestly
and you'll see the TRUTH. You'll see yourself standing here, in
this bar, on this page, trying to get as close to me as you can—
trying to reach inside my pants and find love. Well, go ahead,
REACH! C'mon, kid, stick your hand in there and see what you'll
find. Go ahead! DO IT!"

He reached out quickly and grabbed my arm.
"NO!" I shouted. "No, I don't want to! I changed my mind. I
don't want to!"

The room was suddenly quiet. Everybody was looking at us,
staring at us. No one moved. Everyone listened.

"Get away!" I yelled, trying to fight back. But he was holding my arm, squeezing hard, pulling me toward him, hurting me.

"What's wrong, kid? Are you AFRAID? I thought that's what you wanted? C'mon, kid, I saw you looking at it. TAKE IT!"
He burst out laughing, REAL high and screechy, like a girl. Laughing.

He slapped me across the face.
My nose started to bleed. Everyone moved in closer, surrounding us.
Watching us.

I *tried* not to cry, Robert. But he grabbed my shoulders and forced me to my knees and pulled my hair and it hurt, Robert. It REALLY hurt! He looked at me like he HATED me, like he was going to KILL me. My eyes were all watery but I wasn't really crying. "Now reach in there and grab it!" he said.
"Please, Superman. Please don't . . ."
"GRAB IT!" He pounded my head with his Superfist.

I looked around for help, but nobody moved. They all just stood there, like people in church—waiting for a sacrifice.
One man smiled.
Another laughed and sipped his beer.
And I KNEW I had to do it. I had *no* choice!
They were all watching.
I reached out slowly, with trembling hands, and unfastened his Superbelt. I was still on my knees.
Suddenly I felt like a child in a confessional.
Suddenly I felt like a boy on a rooftop, with a cape over his shoulders, about to fly . . .
I looked down at them, at ALL of them—at my Mom and my Dad and Veronica and everybody—at all those faces looking up at me. Then I reached inside his red swimming suit, beneath his blue leotards, and I grabbed it. Honest. I did, Robert! I pulled it out. I held it and touched it and everybody watched. EVERYBODY!

And you know what it was, Robert? You know what Superman had in there?

It was a First Holy Communion wafer.

So I put it in my mouth. Then I jumped off the roof.

Then I woke up.

The Prisoner of Love

The solution came to me in mid-February, as I was sitting on the beach in Puerto Rico, propelled there by a natural laziness and a small income that permitted me to indulge it. Looking at the sea—green jello with meringue topping—it occurred to me that Puerto Rico might be the perfect thing for Martin Chrisman. Why not invite him down, all expenses paid, for a week? I turned to the seawall and checked out the beach boys lounging there. They were looking at the sunbathers hungrily. No doubt about it. Puerto Rico was just the thing for Martin—Martin who had done so much for all of us.

The Movement! Martin lived, breathed, defecated the Movement. Gay oppression, gay pride, gay history, gay love—these brought tears to his eyes, eloquence to his speech. At every march, every zap, Martin was in the front rank, hung with buttons, his fists pumping as he gave the yells. Between times he lived quietly, devoting his time to writing and publishing such pamphlets as *The Warrior Apprentice in Classical Greece, Homophile Themes in Provençal Poetry, Ernst Rohm and the Secret Pact with Hitler*.

Yes, Martin, who lived in poverty for the sake of his principles, needed to be repaid.

I called New York that night. Martin's voice was high and fluty, but underneath I could hear the stubbornness—the very same that had produced *Homoeroticism and the Anarchist Movement, 1848–1914.*

"It's Jackson. I'm in Puerto Rico."

"Oh, Jackson. What is it?"

"I want you to come down here where it's warm."

"I'm busy now."

"Just for a week. As my guest."

A pause at the other end. "Well, I've never been to Puerto Rico. You know we stole it from Spain."

"So I heard. I'll send you the ticket in the morning."

Another pause. "Do you have a typewriter? I'm doing a paper on the berdaches and the Sioux."

"Martin—this is play, not work."

"This is extremely important..." But he didn't get any further because the Puerto Rico Telephone Company, in its infinite wisdom, chose to cut us off.

The plane disgorged 200 passengers before Martin emerged, carrying a straw suitcase. He seemed out of place among those gaudy vacationers—a young-old person with an air of solitude that enveloped him like a caul. He blinked when he saw me and put out a thin hairless paw. I felt momentarily uneasy. I had never been alone with him for a long stretch of time. Perhaps my discomfort communicated itself, because he answered in monosyllables as we drove home, and made no comment at all on the spectacular views.

At the apartment, which was right on the beach, he put down his suitcase and stood in the center of the room. I walked to the terrace doors and threw them back. "Take a look!" I sang out.

He moved forward reluctantly, as if it were a punishment of some kind. On the terrace he removed his glasses—they were hornrims—and squinted against the light.

"How do you like it?" I asked finally.

He looked displeased. It was clear that the Atlantic Ocean had failed him in some way. Then he peered downward. "Who are all those boys?"

"Oh, locals." I paused. "Hoping to make out with a tourist."

He put his glasses back on. "You mean they're hustling?" His voice was full of outrage.

"Well—yeah." I felt suddenly apologetic.

"They've been forced into prostitution by American Imperialist policies," he announced.

Several replies took shape in my mind—defensive, explanatory, aggressive. But I managed to repress them all. We had a long week ahead of us. The best time to avoid an argument is before it starts.

I gave him a cold avocado salad for lunch. While he ate, he told me that a Chinese restaurant in his neighborhood had been caught with a freezer full of dead cats. When I gagged at the news, a bitter pleat formed on his lips—the first expression of pleasure since his arrival.

After lunch we went down to the beach. A shower had just ended and the sky was printed with a rainbow. Martin eyed the arc suspiciously, as if it were a temptation that had to be resisted.

The beach boys had taken refuge under an awning. I knew one of them—Armando—but I didn't wave. He'd soon be over for a cigarette. Martin took out dark glasses and clipped them over his spectacles. The two layers of glass made him look as if he were undergoing an eye examination. He lay back on the blanket, his thin chest gleaming whitely.

Armando spotted us eventually and strolled over, grinning. "You better cover up," he said to Martin, hunkering down, "you gonna fry." He put his hand out to me. "Gotta cigarette?"

I gave him one, watching him cup the match against the trade wind. His face was khaki-colored, with heavy eyebrows. He was wearing jeans and a shirt printed with the signs of the zodiac. It was unbuttoned to his navel. The silky black chest-hairs made a cruciform. As Martin applied oil to his shoulders, he sneaked glances at Armando.

"Are you an *independente*?" he asked at last.

"*Independentista*?" Armando shook his head. "Not me, man. The day the Puerto Ricans take over, I'm getting out."

Martin trained his double glasses on him. "You're in favor of the colonial oppression of Puerto Rico?"

Armando gave him a disgusted look. "You believe that propaganda shit and you ain't never been here before?"

As they talked, it occurred to me that a little time with Armando might be the best medicine for Martin. The only question—how to arrange it? I thought briefly of my own session with Armando the day before. In the nude he was a stunning sight—a chest that curved like a shield, an ass as dazzling as mother-of-pearl. Best of all, Armando had no inhibitions in bed.

I lay back on the blanket, closing my eyes. The sun streamed orange through my eyelids. Yes, a session with Armando was just what Martin needed. But there was a problem of money.

After showering yesterday, Armando had fried himself two eggs in olive oil and washed them down with a Pepsi. As he was leaving, I stuffed a ten-dollar bill in his shirt pocket. My delicacy had been misplaced. He took out the bill, looked at it, then gave me a big Chiclet smile and departed whistling.

I sat up suddenly. "Martin, how about buying us a beer?"

He accepted the coins somewhat peevishly, unfolded his body from the blanket, and trudged to the beach bar. From the rear, his thin neck and peaked shoulders reminded me of a large stork.

I turned to Armando. "Martin likes you, I can tell." I paused, embarrassed. Pimping wasn't exactly my line. "He needs some . . . uh . . . relaxation."

Armando raised his massive eyebrows but said nothing.

"He's a gay liberationist. Gay liberationists don't . . . like to pay. It's sort of . . . against their principles."

"Well, see, I gotta lotta problems right now. My sister, she . . ."

I cut him off. "I'll give you something. See, I want Martin to have a good time."

Armando turned to look at Martin, a white sliver against the blaze of noon. "You sure you know this guy?" he asked.

Martin seemed even more irritated when he came back. "The United States wants Puerto Rico as a captive market for exports," he said, handing Armando a Budweiser. Armando tossed back his head as he drank it. His Adam's apple was strong and corded. "Sit down," he said to Martin, "here." He smoothed a place beside him. As Martin sank down, Armando brushed his hand lightly across his shoulders. Martin seemed to quiver all over, then pushed back his glasses and began to talk about mercantilism.

"I'm gonna take a walk," I announced a few minutes later, but they didn't seem to hear. When I came back, I found the blanket unoccupied. I sat down, trying not to feel exultant. I waited a good hour before going upstairs.

I rang the apartment bell before entering, but I needn't have. Armando, his powerful body draped in a yellow towel, was looking at a pamphlet entitled *The Homophile Rights Movement in Germany*. Martin, in baggy underwear, was frying eggs in olive oil. The smile he gave me seemed to hurt his facial muscles. I had the impression of ice breaking up in spring.

"Well, well," I said, in false heartiness, "look who's here."

"We waited, but you was gone," Armando observed.

"So I was."

Martin served up the eggs with two Pepsi-Colas. I left them eating side by side.

Armando came into the bathroom as I was drying off after a shower. He didn't bother to knock. He stood in front of the toilet and unleashed a thick stream of urine. He hadn't been trained to aim at the porcelain side; it sounded like the Horseshoe Falls. "Your friend," he nodded toward the door, "*buena gente*."

"Martin?" I stifled a slight pang of jealousy. *Buena gente* was a true compliment in Puerto Rico—somewhere between *nice guy* and *solid citizen*. Armando had never applied the term to me.

"I gotta get goin' now," Armando announced. I knew what he was getting at. I gave him a slight nod, full of conspiracy, and told him to wait for me on the terrace. I slipped him the ten dollars a few minutes later. He palmed it while glancing over his shoulder. Martin was washing the dishes.

At the door, Martin held out his hands to Armando. "*Hasta la vista*," he murmured. His face looked younger rather than older—perhaps no more than thirty.

"*Hasta la vista*, friend," Armando's dark eyes glittered. Then he hugged Martin, gave me a pleasant nod, and departed. Martin sat for a long time afterward, still in his underwear, looking at the ocean without speaking.

We were on the terrace that evening, watching the sunset, when Martin brought the subject up. "You see," he said, "they don't want to be prostitutes. The system makes them."

I nodded. The daiquiri was pungent on my lips.

"It's the death culture," he went on.

I nodded again. The sun was half gone. I could almost feel the earth turn.

"Imperialism is dying," he observed, turning his back to the horizon. I watched the last glowing fingernail disappear. "I'm meeting Armando tomorrow," he continued. "He's taking me to La Perla."

I lowered my drink. "La Perla!"

"I told him I read *La Vida*. You know, by Oscar Lewis . . ."

"I know it's by Oscar Lewis," I snapped.

"And I want to see firsthand how the poor people live."

I reached for the daiquiri pitcher, trying to hide my irritation. I didn't really understand it. I had no desire to visit the city's worst slum, yet the thought of Martin and Armando there . . . My irritation thickened, followed by guilt. Wasn't this exactly what I wanted for Martin? Wasn't his visit becoming a success— instantly, and beyond my wildest hopes?

Armando turned up next morning, wearing a purple T-shirt that said *Puerto Rico Me Encanta*. Martin greeted him with a shy smile and a kiss on the cheek. They held hands for a long moment.

"You gonna let me drive the car?" Armando demanded. I had made up my mind the night before—no car for the visit to La Perla. "If you drive *very* carefully," I heard myself say.

"Man, like it was my own." He seemed to know where I kept the keys—in the bureau in the bedroom. As they left—Martin's face pink with sun and excitement—I had to restrain myself from slamming the door behind them.

When I came back from the beach around four, I found them in bed with the door open. It looked as if they had been there for some time.

"How was La Perla?" I asked.

They told me all about it—the tattoo artists, fortune tellers, prostitutes, junkies. "Armando met an old woman who knew his father," Martin giggled. Lying in bed, cradled in Armando's dark arms, he looked even younger than yesterday. It occurred to me that the years were shredding away. "Papa could still get it up when he was seventy-two. Armando says he was a . . . um . . ."

"*Joledor*!" Armando yowled. "Means big fucker. My father was the famous fucker from Manati!"

They both roared at that, turning towards each other. I swiveled quickly and went into the bathroom. As I turned on the water I heard their laughter soften and disappear. I closed the door. I didn't want to hear what came next.

Armando made his pitch while I was fixing myself a rum coco.

"I spent a lot of chabo today," he shook his head.

"Yeah?"

He didn't notice my unsympathetic tone.

"We give a kid something, he was on crutches, like that. I bought these beads from an *espiritista*. She say my Saint Geronimo will take care of me now."

I scowled. "Geronimo wasn't a saint. He was an Indian chief."

"I know that, man." His voice was plaintive. "Now I'm broke. *Pelado*."

The rum coco was ready. I poured it into a ceramic glass shaped like a frog. I could hear Martin singing in the shower.

"You told me you wanted him to have a good time." Armando's voice was accusing.

"Yeah, I did."

"So?"

I couldn't explain it—not to myself, certainly not to Armando. All I knew was that I was trapped in Martin Chrisman's view of things. In his dream world. It was no consolation to know that I was paying the rent on the goddam place myself.

"Here," I thrust ten dollars at him angrily. He looked at me with large sad eyes, then put it away, shaking his head.

As the days went by, Martin changed more and more. He seemed to straighten up, fill more of the space around him. He and Armando spent long hours playing dominoes, howling with glee at every silly move. They traded necklaces of cowrie shells in a little ceremony in which they pledged eternal brotherhood. Martin shopped for and cooked a traditional Puerto Rican *asopao*, using a recipe Armando's mother supplied.

When he was alone with me, however, he trotted out his lectures on Puerto Rican politics. I went along with his theories, holding my tongue, giving place. Armando had been hitting me for ten dollars every day.

But my self-control reached the breaking point on the last evening of Martin's visit. We had had a lovely day at Luquillo, a superb beach an hour's drive from San Juan. Armando had borrowed some spear-fishing gear and snagged a couple of red snappers. We brought them home and got ready for a big evening.

Armando was on the terrace grilling the fish when the argument started in the kitchen.

"There's only one solution to the political situation here," Martin said. His face was tanned now, the seams all smoothed out. He might have been in his early twenties. "We have to start a guerrilla operation in the rain forest. Like in Cuba—the Sierra Maestra." He glanced toward the terrace. Armando was flipping the fish. "Violence is the only solution."

I stared at him in disbelief. "Do you realize that the Puerto Ricans always vote twenty to one *against* cutting their ties to the US?"

He shook his head smugly, maddeningly. "Doesn't matter. They have to be educated. Have their political consciousness raised. Ask Armando. He agrees with me."

"Armando . . ." I started to say, thinking about Armando's reverence for most things American.

"*Now*," Martin read my thoughts. "He agrees with me *now*." The smug look intensified. "I've educated him."

Suddenly I couldn't hold back any more. Everything I had refrained from saying for the past seven days took shape on the tip of my tongue. "How do you know Armando doesn't like being a colonial?" My voice was hoarse, unfamiliar. "Doesn't like being exploited?"

Martin looked at me and I read triumph in his eyes. "Did he ask me for money?" He threw back his head and whinnied. "Did he?"

It was infuriating. I could feel all my good intentions dissolving in a brew of anger. "No," I said slowly, nailing down the words, "but how do you know he didn't ask me?"

That stopped him. His face straightened and his eyes focused into fearful points behind his glasses. "Because . . ." he said at last, "he wouldn't . . . do such . . . a thing." His shoulders hunched and for a moment he seemed terribly young and vulnerable. "He . . . isn't . . . capable of it," He whispered.

I stood up, caught between anger and shame, while Martin stared at the floor. My head was buzzing. Hardly aware of my movements, I headed for the terrace. I knew the sight of the sea would cool me, stop the buzzing in my head, give me a chance to think.

Armando said something but I stepped around him, and went to the rail. The waters stretched away, velvety and black as far as I could see. Why hadn't I told Martin the truth, the whole truth? Why had I allowed the dream, the lie, to stand? The answer came to me on the silken murmur of a palm frond, stirred by the sea wind. I *wanted* Martin to believe the world was full of true love. I *wanted* him to believe it was about to be reformed. His idealism—absurd, misplaced—sustained me. I needed it as much as he did.

The evening ended drunkenly. Martin stripped to his baggy drawers and sang a Spanish song that Armando had taught him.

He seemed to have turned into someone else entirely. When I stumbled out, around midnight, they were sitting on the floor and Martin was stroking Armando's hair gently.

It was the following spring that I ran into Armando in Times Square. He was slumped inside a dirty sweater. He looked like the survivor of a city under siege.

"Hey, man!" I saw a ghost of a Chiclet smile.

"Armando! How are you?"

He told me had arrived in New York a month earlier. He hadn't been able to find work. "I'm broke," he said. "*Pelado*."

The words had a horrible familiarity, and I started to step aside. But I checked myself. "Seen Martin?"

"Yeah, all the time."

A pang of jealousy assailed me. "Why not ask Martin to help you?"

Armando shook his head. "I never ask Martin for nothin'. He don't go for that shit." He paused. "All he got is beautiful ideas."

I snorted. "Ideas about what?"

"About life, man, *life*." He straightened up suddenly and jabbed a left hook into the air. It seemed an absurd bit of bravado on Forty-Second Street. Perhaps he realized it too, because he slumped again. "Can you gimme something?" he asked. "I'll pay you back."

I shook my head sharply, angrily, but then reached for my wallet. He took the bill between fingers that were gray and dirty. He didn't even thank me. Just turned away, avoiding my eyes, while he gave me a peace salute. "Stay cool," he murmured.

I don't know how long I stood there, watching his bowed head disappear through the swarms of people. But I moved on at last, cursing Martin Chrisman under my breath as I realized I would forever be a prisoner of his stupidity, his simplicity, his love.

Phantom Limb Pain

The professor of Russian 101, Evening Section, leapt in front of his demurely fidgeting class that first night like a dissident ballet dancer making his entrance upon the Western stage. Expecting accolades, contemptuous and eager, he stalked towards the casement windows and flung them open, though it was still early spring and seven o'clock in the evening. A shiver ran through his captive audience, but no one protested. In his cheap foreign suit, wearing an oddly spotted tie, he made them feel small, huddled.

He sprang, he paused, he introduced himself. What? His wrists were bone and sinew under frayed cuffs. His hair stood up like a stiff hat of grey fur, brilliantined. His jaw was hacked, his eyes slits of granite shot with mica. He was terrible, frightening, queer.

Although no one besides himself had dared to speak, he announced that tonight was the last time they would use English. Was he speaking English even then? His accent gulped and smeared their language almost beyond recognition. From now on, he said, swinging to a seat on his desk, a giant in momentary repose, it would be Russian, Russian, Russian.

The class of thirteen, now utterly dismayed and hopeless, shivered again, and those who had sweaters pulled them down to cover their wrists.

Up again, bounding among them, he demanded their names.

Six inches of index finger leveled at each in turn, a christening. They would have Russian names now, and not only that, but patronyms. Patronyms, he said, suddenly illuminating the confusions of Tolstoy's novels, were the names of their fathers, with an ending.

Thus Cheryl became Sasha Andreievna. I'd rather have my mother's name, she wanted to say. Or nothing. My own twice. Long ago she had dropped her father's legacy for a newly minted surname. Williamson had become Will. It jolted her to be reminded of her father; she brought out "Andrew" without thinking, then remembered she hadn't written to him in years.

When all were introduced and reintroduced as double-named Russians, their professor repeated his own name. This time she caught it: Ivan Ivanovich. Ivan, son of Ivan. Son of himself. "Ivan the Terrible," he said.

Some of the students didn't get it, were already looking huntedly towards the door, but Sasha couldn't help laughing. Half angry, half amused. He was so conscious of his own power, oh yes, he knew his impression. A typical male. I'll leave at the break, she thought.

He stared at her appreciatively, seeking a bond. He's frightened, she knew suddenly, and looked away. But already he was moving again, to front stage. With nervous contempt Ivan Ivanovich noticed that some of his students had their books already open to the first page. Dramatically he slammed one of them shut.

"Tonight, we begin with memory."

A cool April wind whistled lightly through the brilliant classroom as Ivan Ivanovich began to chant what was obviously the first line of a poem.

He recited it through, paused at the end as if to accept a burst of applause that the students were too timid, too boorish to give, and then turned somber, pedagogic.

"Pushkin," he breathed with stern reverence. "And this is his loveliest poem of all." Ivan Ivanovich did not offer to translate it for them, but instead produced from an expensive but worn briefcase a clutch of badly mimeographed sheets. "You will memorize this by next week."

There was by now a stunned quality to the silence in the room, as each student took a page and saw the rows of compact purple hieroglyphics.

"Excuse me, sir, Ivan, Ivan. . ." a young woman said faintly. "I thought this was a beginning Russian class." She closed her notebook as if prepared to slink away on the spot.

"Da, da, of course it is."

A thirtyish engineering type in the front row exploded. "But we haven't even learned the Russian alphabet. Surely you can't expect us to read this."

There were murmurs of agreement. Sasha Andreievna took heart. They wouldn't just sit there, lumpish and intimidated. "We can't read this," she echoed, pushing the smudges firmly away.

"Read?" he sneered back at them, snatching the challenge up in his enormous fists. "Who says something about 'read?' I say, 'memorize', and you hear 'read'." He paced before them, through vast steppes. "Memory, memory, memory. You Americans know nothing about the memory. Without History, without Culture, you grow up watching your TV. Every eight-year-old child in Russia knows this poem. They know Pushkin and Lermontov, all the greatest poets. By their heart. Da, it is expected." He heated this subject up excitedly, running his fingers through his brisk hair. "Expected, da, expected. But American schools do not teach memory. Recite to me one poem you have learned." Ivan Ivanovich paused a fraction of a second, scanning contemptuously. "Hah! You see? You Americans do not even know your own Declaration of Independence. Now you understand?" He suddenly jumped on to the squat desk behind him, becoming nine feet of messianic zeal. "Repeat after me."

His arms flung north and south, he implored them.

"Weird," muttered Sasha Andreievna, dropping into a chair

across the living room from Edie.

Patient, ready to be enlightened, Edie looked up from her sane British mystery and repeated, "Weird?"

"This teacher . . ." But how to explain him? Sasha hadn't gone home at the break; he hadn't given them a break, had only pushed them on and on through the rigors of the still untranslated poem. At ten, all thirteen students had rushed wildly for the door. Would any of them come back? Sasha would not, oh no. Chalk up a wasted evening to . . . experience?

"Well, Russian . . ." Edie said, marking her book with a finger and dreamily regarding Sasha. "What a thing to study. Ten years out of school and you working all day, too. I'd be exhausted."

Yes, Edie would be exhausted, Sasha thought, regarding her lover pocketed in the chintz like a kangaroo, a plump cat of a woman with soft paws and large vague eyes. Work flattened Edie, movies and plays laid her low, politics enervated her, and friends most of all. She read gothics and mysteries to be soothed, and slept ten hours a night. Weekends she pottered and napped.

It amazed Sasha now that she ever could have been taken in by Edie's lethargy, that she ever found it amusing, endearing. "My sleeper, my dreamer," she called Edie, resting her head on Edie's plentiful breasts, her cushioned stomach, allowing herself to reinvent her mother's caresses.

"Weird," she repeated now. "A madman. All evening he had us memorizing a poem in Russian. By Pushkin. I don't even know what the hell it means. Yah vas lubiel . . . I can't get it out of my head now. But he's crazy, Edie, big and jumpy and something in his eyes like fear. He's punishing us, I'm sure of it. A tyrant, a petty tyrant, just like my father. A stupid Russian man making us take our father's names."

"You should have taken that dance class," Edie murmured, straying back to her mystery. "You like to dance. Maybe it's not too late to change."

"But I've always wanted to learn Russian . . . I need to do something with my brain. . ." Sasha kicked off her shoes. "It's him, he's nuts. Any other teacher . . . oh shit . . . How was work today?"

Edie sighed, a fat morsel of blonde in the mouth of the chair. "Oh, busy. Phone ringing off the hook. Mr J. complaining, I think his stomach was bad today. Some of the secretaries want to organize. How can we? I told them. So few of us. But we could use the money . . ."

Edie sighed on, her blonde hair beading into light under the lamp's glow. I could never ever be a secretary, Sasha thought, irritated, pitying. Lucky that nursing is more organized. We're professionals, at least, though we don't get near enough money compared to the doctors. Still, it's a challenge. Always something to learn, emergencies where you can really help. And no male bosses. The doctors descend and ascend like fake *dei ex machina*. We run the show.

Why then study Russian, or anything? It wasn't that medicine lacked interest. Only that, after ten years, it wasn't quite enough. Every two or three years she'd changed floors: medical, surgical, a stint in intensive care, but that was too hectic. Now she was back where she'd started, on a surgical ward, as assistant head nurse. All the same, mere efficiency had begun to bore her. Hadn't she seen it all by now? Limbs and organs cut away, repaired, reinserted. Sutures and dressings, sterile and disposable, hiding the mystery of healing, the surprise. Then, how like a clock the body was, always hopeful, always eager to get back on schedule, pathetically ready to tick again. Only individuals kept it all fresh, the mind suffering in new ways with the knowledge of mortality. Psychology alone made work interesting, working with people, around people every day. And yet you couldn't afford to get too involved. There was death. And all the complications of loss.

"You're always studying something," Edie said, a little envious, mostly disapproving, and opened her book again. "Last semester it was economics . . ."

Sasha walked over and kissed her lover's smooth forehead, trying not to show, not to feel her frustration. "You look tired.

Want me to make your lunch for you tonight?"

"Oh, would you? Make tuna, we haven't had that for a while."

"You should have seen him, Edie. A complete madman." In spite of herself, Sasha began to smile.

Six students reappeared at the next class session, Sasha Andreievna among them. Embarrassed, complicit, pleased at not being put off so easily, they spoke hesitantly to each other. Students and workers, a retired dentist, a woman who had been around the world. "Did you manage to memorize the poem?" they whispered. "Yes," said Sasha. She hadn't been able to forget it, though she still didn't know what it meant. Yah vas lubiel, she'd sung as she injected pain killers and changed bandages.

Ivan Ivanovich loomed in the doorway like an uninvited guest. Sardonic and sad, his eyes counted them. What did you expect? Sasha wanted to say. You drove them away. Her heart, fickle beast, went out to him. But he wouldn't have sympathy; with a lunge he was among them, keeping his promise: No English.

His hair was gray and gleaming, a rakish tall cap. She noticed his fine eyebrows this time, his angled cheekbones. In the cheap black suit, his shoes glistening like bowling balls, he pranced and strutted. In Russian he pointed and spoke. There was no mention of the grueling poem, though they waited, hopefully, to shine. Instead Ivan started with the basics. Tables and chairs had names, so did pencils and windows. Becoming sentences and questions, the objects in the room danced with Ivan Ivanovich. *Where* is the pencil? It is *here*, it is *there*. He opened his backdrop, the window, and blasted them with spring. They struggled, dutifully, in confusion, to keep up, fitting their tongues around the awkward words, pushing them out louder into the room, ever louder. He had them shouting with his trick of cupping an enormous hand to a small, well-shaped ear.

Then, suddenly, he seemed satisfied and pointed to the clock. In a voice so normal it sounded like a whisper, he announced a break. His students were astounded, disappointed. Knowledge had seemed so near, mastery impending. With reluctance they stretched themselves and followed Ivan Ivanovich into the hall.

There the corridor was swelling with other students, smoking and chattering. Ivan Ivanovich positioned himself near the stairwell and brought out a pack of Camels. In a whispering clump, his students remembered their poem. This, this was how the class should have started last week. The naming of concrete objects, their useful arrangement. But had the memorization been for nothing, then? Sasha, assistant head nurse, used to assuming authority in unclear situations, appointed herself representative and approached the stairwell.

Seeing her coming, Ivan Ivanovich proffered a Camel, courtly, inscrutable. She shook her head, drove straight to the point, ignoring the depth of the mica-flecked eyes.

"What about that poem you had us memorize last week? Don't you want to hear us recite it?"

Ivan Ivanovich affected extreme amazement. "You memorized it?"

"Well, of course." She was indignant. "You *told* us to." He laughed and she faltered slightly. "I don't know what the words mean."

"Tell me", he said, "why you bothered?"

Forty, fifty, Sasha couldn't tell, though she judged age every day at the hospital. His wrinkles were few, his eyes very tired. Close up she felt a stoop in his tall body; his breath was ashy, rasped.

"You said we couldn't memorize. That's not true."

"There were thirteen last week," he stated.

"You wanted to drive them away."

"They were not serious."

"How do you *know*?"

Ivan Ivanovich smiled, showing false and mottled teeth. He bent closer to her, with a thick charm that offended. "Say the poem."

"Here?" Embarrassed, Sasha tossed her head and saw her fellow students peering discreetly.

"Why not?"

The urge to show him was stronger than any restraint. She began, "Yah vas lubiel . . ." only to be interrupted.

"The 'L', the 'L'," he said. "You are missing it entirely. What we have in Russian is the 'dark L', it glides the top of the mouth, from the back to the teeth. Listen."

She listened, missing it, and tried again. She saw him steeling himself, in sadness, in amusement, and tried harder. Faster.

"Very good," he said noncommittally.

She was furious with him, wanted to turn on her heel. What did he expect? Perfect pronunciation? She had memorized it hadn't she?

"What is your job?" he asked abruptly.

"Nurse." She was brief, eying his reaction. If he were impressed or contemptuous, he didn't show it. Politeness fell seamlessly across his expression. He dropped his cigarette and ground it with a shiny shoe.

"Time to get back," he said.

"Any better tonight?" Edie asked.

"Christ," Sasha muttered. She remained standing by the door, emptying the contents of her handbag on to a table, separating stethoscope from car keys, paperback from Russian text. "Who is he, anyway? One of the decayed aristocracy from the way he acts. A White Russian general. You know that poem I killed myself to memorize for tonight? He'd forgotten all about it. We didn't get the chance to say it. He as much as admitted to me that he'd used it to get rid of most of the class." She threw herself the length of the red tweed couch. "The first half of the class was all right," she allowed. "But then, when we went back, we didn't learn anything. Instead, he went on a long diatribe against American teaching methods, the university system, American culture, everything. He's obsessed with the idea of TV, thinks it's our ruin, et cetera."

"Well, you don't like TV," Edie pointed out reasonably.

"I'm not *against* it . . . it just bores me . . . And who is he to criticize us anyway? He came here of his own free will, didn't he? He was probably a cab driver in Russia. I'd like to know what makes him think he can teach this language. I could learn more from just reading the book."

"Careful, your chauvinism is showing."

"It's his chauvinism, damn it. I'm not used to sitting captive, being lectured to by some man. The way he looked at me!"

"Try being a secretary sometime," Edie said without irony.

"I don't know how you can stand it."

"What else can I do?"

Sasha was silent. It came over her suddenly how very tired she was of her own job. She had been tired of it for a long time.

"Why don't we just move to another country, throw everything up and start over?"

"Move . . . you mean pack up and leave?" Edie's soft eyes swept the room fearfully. "But we're so comfortable here."

"*You're* comfortable . . ." Sasha stopped. There was no use in arguing. Edie did not like arguments, they only made her cry.

Edie went back to her only mode of escape, a gothic set in a far land. Sasha knew, if she looked up from the pillow where she had buried her head, that she would see Edie mouthing some of the words. Once it had been very endearing, then irritating, now it no longer mattered. When had love changed, what had it changed into?

Drifting now, Sasha forgot about moving Edie, even Ivan Ivanovich, and remembered a case at the hospital that day. The man in 317 screaming with pain because his leg hurt him. Only his leg was no longer there; it had been amputated the day before. A recognized phenomenon, written up in textbooks, studied for generations. Phantom limb pain, they called it. No pain in the cutting-off point, the wound, but pain further down, where the memory insisted. Not imaginary, but real.

Sasha's cheek scraped the rough red tweed of the couch as she turned to stare at Edie mouthing her book: pencil, window, where is the table, where are you?

"It must be hard to live in a world where no one really knows who you are, not to be able to prove that you have, you had another existence."

"No one ever said it was easy to be a lesbian," Edie looked up briefly from the novel where she was transposing the sex of the hero.

But Sasha had been thinking of Ivan Ivanovich.

Yah vas lubiel, lubov yehsho, bwitz mojet . . . I loved you once, love you still, perhaps . . . Now that Sasha had read the translation of Pushkin's poem it would not leave her alone. It went through her mind constantly at work, interfered with her concentration. She forgot to give a routine medication, had to be called at home, late at night. She let one of her patients go home with his stitches still in. There had to be a way of leaving Edie without hurting her, but how, Sasha didn't know. She found herself dreaming of adventure, travelling to Russia perhaps. She had the money, it would give her a chance to really practice the language. Ivan Ivanovich could tell her what to visit . . . But Edie wouldn't come, and then, Sasha had never much liked travel, the mechanics of it. She liked being in one place, never mind the comfort, but she needed some sense of being useful, responsible. Maybe she could go work in a clinic somewhere, in some underdeveloped country. Edie wouldn't want to go there, either.

Unable to speak, to act, Sasha buried herself in her work, in her Russian class, resolved to master the language better and faster than anyone else. Not for *him*, though think it he might, in his male pride, his foreign arrogance, but for herself.

The class was down to five now. "The Masochists", they called themselves, as if they were a secret society. But Ivan Ivanovich had to be a masochist in his own right. Why else would he subject himself to the torment of trying to teach "this beautiful language to a class of ignorants"?

They had sunk deep into grammar and were foundering badly. Ivan Ivanovich occasionally put out a hand to help, but more often he perched furiously on the island of his desk, like a lighthouse whose beam glares steadily off into the night above a raft of shipwrecked sailors. In some essential way he seemed to be against his students, willing them to fail.

Yet he was perfectly comfortable, it seemed, when haranguing them about the state of their culture. Sometimes, when in a good mood, Ivan Ivanovich would even intersperse his diatribes with stories about his last trip to Moscow, ostensibly to show how American culture had infiltrated the world.

One night he told them about selling blue jeans on the black market. "When I arrived I have my suitcase full of blue jeans, five, six. Every day I put on a pair and go to the streets. The people they come up to me whispering, 'How much you want for those blue jeans?' Then we go to a place and change trousers. When I came back I am richer and I have these many pairs of Russian trousers."

That explained his tacky wardrobe. But what had he done with the money, then? And wasn't there something disturbing about his pandering to the base desires of the Soviets for Western commodities?

Sasha didn't know how to put the question into words, however, feared his flashing eyes. There must be something she was misunderstanding. She saw him looking at her then, with a curious intensity she found so unnerving, and blurted out, "What did you do there, when you lived there, I mean?"

The class held its breath. He had never spoken to them about his early life in Russia. Among themselves they had postulated the wildest, most romantic theories: he was a dissident, a Jew, he had suffered . . . in the Gulag perhaps; he could have been an Orthodox priest, or anything. Sasha continued to suspect that he was a noble of some sort, with that carriage and that head—until she was angry with him, when she returned to the cab driver theory.

"I was a schoolboy, of course," Ivan Ivanovich snapped,

lifting his head high to stare balefully at them all. When he drove
them back to class after their break he used the excuse of their too
friendly curiosity to give them a test on verb endings. He was
especially hard on Sasha, singling her out for the most difficult
forms.

After class he stopped her, the last one out the door.
"Locomotion and conveyance," he said. "I am afraid you do not
understand the difference between the two."

She was putting on her sweater and gathering her books.
Wearily she answered, "I know there's a difference in going
somewhere yourself and going somewhere with a, a book, for
instance, or another person. But I'm damned if I understand
what it is."

Ivan Ivanovich had never looked stiffer, though he tried to
smile. "The difference is that instead of locomoting by myself
now, I would like to convey you to have a cup of coffee."

He had been born in Kiev, in 1935. All his early memories were
of the war. "Although we from the Ukraine hated the Soviets and
first welcomed the Nazis, we soon saw the mistake. Many many
people died. I was taken and put in a camp. Only later do I find
my mother again, but my father was shot for a partisan. One
uncle he went to Turkey and there we went also when I was
thirteen. At night, on a boat. We wanted to come to the United
States but it was at first impossible. That was my mother's hope,
that we would come here for my schooling. She wanted me to be
a doctor. But all the years of my schooling were passed in
Turkey, that useless place. When we finally came I am thirty,
and how could I be a doctor?"

His thick voice had all the embarrassment of confession and
his eyes were so intense that Sasha had to stare very hard at his
enormous hands, laid out flat as corpses on the table. Against her
better judgment they had not gone to a coffee shop, but instead
to "a very special place I know". She doubted now that he had
ever been here before; it was too expensive with its plush booths

and lantern-lit tables, and they were too obviously out of place, he in his ill-fitting black suit and worn cuffs, she in jeans and a sweater.

It wasn't that she was exactly frightened of him, or even that she mistrusted him. Only the faint flush of romance she invested Ivan Ivanovich with had totally dissipated, and instead she was only saddened, immeasurably saddened by the sight of this great broken man beside her drinking vodka.

She had wanted to know the mystery of his life, but had stupidly expected more excitement from it. She wasn't prepared for the paralysing rush of pity she felt hearing him recite the trials of the countryless. It reminded her of a long and sordid illness, leading eventually to amputation. It wasn't a fairytale, not even a gothic; how could she have imagined that he would hide his life if there had been anything marvelous in it?

"Is this supposed to be a student–teacher conference?" she'd cracked nervously as they entered the lounge, and perhaps she really had had some idea that they might discuss her progress in class. She had longed for encouragement like any schoolchild. But if anything were clear now, it was that her earliest intuitions had been correct; he despised teaching, felt it only slightly less humiliating than being a bookkeeper. Yes, he was a bookkeeper during the day, it turned out, not a professor at all. He had only been hired to teach this evening class when the regular professor broke both legs in a skiing accident.

Sympathy did not come easily to Sasha, not towards herself nor towards the hundreds of patients who had passed under her hands. She had steeled herself to cheeriness against the misery of the world; still, in this dim room where the organ hummed like a live beast in the corner, she found herself drifting deep into his failures. After another glass of vodka he told her that he lived with his mother, in a small apartment by the lake, and suddenly she saw it all, saw his exile illuminated as clearly as the small hot lamp on the table.

A refugee, too, she saw herself standing in the snow before a barbed-wire fence that bordered on a heavy white forest of

birches, saw herself taking secret passage in the dank hold of a
cargo ship to Turkey, saw herself in a glaring, smelly bazaar
bartering the samovar from home. She saw herself sharing a
bathroom with a frail and whining old woman, who could only
speak in Russian and refused to have a TV in the house. She saw
herself bound by duty and pain to resurrect each day a life she
had known only by hearsay. For Ivan Ivanovich, to be Russian
was to be perpetually a refugee, to be destined to hate every
country with a hatred so strong it was only surpassed by
ignorance of his own. Even the long-awaited visit to Moscow had
taught him nothing except that even there he was seen as a
foreigner. His mother had taught him everything. She would
read Pushkin's poems aloud to him at night, in the sweltering
towns of inland Turkey, conjuring up his history and
prophesying his future, but powerless, powerless. After the trip
to Moscow, nothing seemed real to him.

Sasha understood now his bravado and desperation in class; he
was afraid of being found out. Russian meant much more to him
than he could ever convey. He could not teach the only thing he
had.

Sasha's own crop of stories seemed suddenly rooted in hard
and stony ground. She pulled at a memory like a weed, but only
the top came off in her hand. When Ivan Ivanovich pressed her
for details, there was little she could say. And yet she too had a
well of sadness inside her. She told him about her mother, who
had run off with another man when Sasha was eight, then died
and been buried in some distant state. She had never gotten over
hating her father for not telling her about her mother's death
until many years later.

"I see now that he made the decision to cut her off to save
himself. He refused to remember her. But to leave me for so
many years thinking her alive, thinking I would find her
someday."

It must have been the vodka, for Sasha was crying a little now,
and Ivan Ivanovich put his big hand over hers. She felt his rough,
ashy breath on her shoulder and pulled away. He must not think

this intimacy was anything more than the chance sharing of sorrow.

She told him about the clear sun of California and the beaches where she swam out to sea. Her lack of friends, her decision to become a nurse and to move away.

It had really been because of a woman she had moved, of course, but Sasha was still sober enough to know not to tell him that. All the same, stronger than anything she had recounted, the memory of her first night with Edie rose up in her. It had been the bed more than anything, the bed as soft as a dream, covered with pieced quilts in worn and fancy patterns. In the morning the sun had slipped in through lacy curtains and Edie had wrapped a quilt around her fullness to make coffee. She hadn't known, when she followed Edie up the coast to make a new home away from both their families, that Edie would never want to move again, that the softness in her would come to be an obstacle instead of a resting place, and that there were other ways of losing people than having them die in a distant state.

"I have a roommate," Sasha said. "We're not getting along so well right now. We're different."

It was far easier to tell him about the hospital, how the work challenged and drew her and was still not enough. "I've had this notion", she said before she knew it, "of working in another country, running a clinic maybe, being more to the patients . . . healing them, I don't know . . ." She stopped, embarrassed.

"My mother", Ivan Ivanovich said into his glass, "says that only God can both give and take away, and that even He will not bring back what is gone. All that men can do is try to heal. . ."

"I'd like to meet her," Sasha said impulsively, leaning towards him slightly.

"She would not . . . no, we cannot go there." He grabbed her hand almost roughly and Sasha was amazed, alarmed even, to see a predatory look come into his gray eyes. "I thought . . . we can go to your house."

Sasha jerked away from him, upsetting her glass, but she couldn't be angry as she mopped at the table with her napkin.

"My roommate . . ."

Ivan Ivanovich tried to take her hand again. Even in his drunkenness he was stiff and courtly. The hunter's look was gone from his eyes; she wondered if she had imagined it. "Please," he said.

"No." But she didn't withdraw this time.

"When I see you in the class first night . . ." He stared at her like a dying man, but she felt the life in him coursing through his rough fingers' grip. She didn't think him ugly now, or even odd. His silvery eyes burned into her like the eyes of someone in a platinum photograph, a relative disappeared, an exile, a mother who had died so far away. And for an instant Sasha wanted to give in to him, to drown her sadness in his, to resuscitate some forlorn hope that life was more than a series of losses and leavetakings.

But only for an instant. "No," she told him firmly, becoming abruptly the assistant head nurse, the independent woman who knew her own heart too deeply to pretend that such distances could be bridged. She loved women, even if her feelings for Edie had changed. She would find someone else, she would find something else.

"American women have no passion," Ivan Ivanovich muttered, jerking to his full height in a burst of masculine pride.

Sasha did not argue. Whatever had been between them, whatever had for a moment seemed possible, was gone forever. Let him think what he liked. She had never understood her father and could not pretend to understand the sexual vanity of any man. It could only reduce her to try. Yet in some obscure way she felt grateful to Ivan Ivanovich, almost as if he had freed her from something. Within this suddenly tawdry and very typical scene she had found the strength to move ahead again.

She left him there drinking, morose and ungainly, his hair stiff as gray bristles, his head between his hands. She left him with his past and with a part of her, and went home to tell Edie what she planned to do.

Edie cried, but some of her tears were necessarily from relief, that Sasha had finally realized what she herself had known for a long time. Having never experienced death, Edie could not fear loss or understand the forced, painful finality of Sasha's decision. Partings had never threatened Edie; she cared only that they remain friends, had only worried that Sasha would take it all too hard. Edie's quiverings of romance were confined to books, and unlike Sasha, she seemed to believe that life never really changed as long as it continued.

Sasha, who had expected to be the one to comfort, had been comforted instead. They decided that, when Sasha found a job in a clinic in Ecuador, Edie would visit her. Edie became almost animated, seeing in this plan no disappearance of affection, only greater comfort for them both, an end to conflict.

"After Russian, Spanish should be a snap for you," she said cheerfully. "I may even try to learn Spanish myself. I could take a class."

Sasha knew that Edie never would. Yet she could picture her with a Spanish book, lying underneath the pieced quilts of her soft bed—this bed where they lay now, touching each other gently—and mouthing the words, *Where is the jungle, where are you?* And for a moment she clung to Edie with all the emotion of a frightened child, knowing suddenly and with a terrible hopelessness that she would always feel abandoned, even if it was she who did the leaving.

"You're such a strong person," Edie soothed her. "You'll do fine. And so will I," she added, almost in surprise.

"I won't forget you," Sasha promised fervently.

"Why, how could you?" Edie laughed, then yawned and closed her eyes, still stroking her friend's hair.

"You will forget your Russian of course," Ivan Ivanovich said stiffly when he learned of her plans. He was awkward with her now in class, self-protective. It was difficult, and Sasha too didn't really want to remember that for one evening, their eyes and

hands had met, that they had, for an instant, been one in sorrow
and loss. They had taken their refuge again in the roles of student
and teacher, with a slight change: sometimes, in the midst of his
withering scorn and bravado, Ivan Ivanovich seemed to recall
that Sasha knew what he was—a bookkeeper, without a TV—
and then a shy, almost quizzical expression would creep into his
flashing eyes and he would go back to the lesson.

Smiling a little tensely, Sasha began to quote him the Pushkin
poem, but broke off abruptly, understanding for the first time
what it was she said, and that they were speaking in a language he
had given her.

"The 'dark L'," he couldn't help snapping, while his old gray
eyes burned into hers with a loneliness he did not try to disguise.
"You still have not got it."

"I can't," she said sadly, then turned so that he couldn't see
her face.

On the night of the last class Ivan Ivanovich solemnly presented
her with a samovar, thirty years old, from a Turkish bazaar. His
mother, he said, holding it tightly for a moment in his huge
hands, had said he might give it to her.

"You won't forget me?" he asked again, his eyes once more
those of a dying man.

She could have told him that the past is never lost as long as
there is someone to remember it, just as a body knows the limb is
there after it is gone. If she could have, she would have placed her
hands on his strong hands and healed him. She would have
healed herself if she could. But she already knew that healing is
not the same as bringing back, and she knew that he knew it, too.

The Book Lover

Under the light of four candles, a naked boy, about sixteen or seventeen years of age, lies on a bed, masturbating himself. Next to him sits an old man, a large book open across his lap. The old man is also naked. He gazes at the book with its worn, leather covers and its pages made of stiff paper, and the boy gazes at his own body, his expression serious, but detached.

I'm standing behind the old man, and looking over his shoulder at the open book. There is no writing in it, but on every page is a hand-coloured print covered with a protective rectangle of tissue paper. Each print, with variations, shows a naked boy, aged sixteen or seventeen, masturbating himself.

The boy is slim and well-proportioned, and the artist has done his very best to bring him alive. He has drawn a canopy over the bed, with a suggestive clutter of shadows underneath, to emphasize the density of the flesh, and he has placed some hard, cold objects in the background—huge, gnarled tables, panels, chairs, a soaring mantelpiece—to throw into relief the warmly glowing skin.

It's a measure of the success of these pictures that each of them creates in me exactly the same sensations as would occur in the presence of a real boy. No doubt this is what one has come to expect of a work of this nature; nevertheless, I still find it strange it should be so. The boy in the book has a kind of reality, but he is not real in the way the boy on the bed is. He is an object; if he exists at all it is only for the benefit of others. His life is dedicated solely to arousing himself in the knowledge that, by so doing, he is arousing us. That is all there is to him. And when we choose, we can always shut the book. Yet, the fact remains, that this boy, made only of ink and paper, does move us. Why should this be?

And why is the old man looking at pictures of naked boys masturbating themselves when next to him is a real boy who is also naked, and who is also masturbating himself?

I can't claim to be entirely certain about this, but I think that a solution to the first question may be obtained by answering the second.

The old man—his name is Julius—is a rich bibliophile. The book he is holding will not be found on any station bookstall. It is a rare antiquarian work published in Paris during the reign of Napoleon III, and Julius's copy is the only one outside the Library of Congress.

What is the nature of this chimerical beast, the bibliophile? A bibliophile does not merely collect books; rather, he collects the same book over and over again. He specializes. He seizes on one small corner of the universe and makes it wholly his own. Julius's library consists almost exclusively of volumes of hand-coloured prints published during the Second Empire, and showing naked boys, aged sixteen or seventeen, masturbating themselves. Other books which may look similar to the untutored eye will be rejected by him if they do not meet his exact requirements. If you were to show him something published in any other country but France, or in any other reign but that of Napoleon III, or which had only monochrome prints, or which pictured boys younger than sixteen or older than seventeen, then you can be sure he would have nothing to do with it. Nothing. The true bibliophile is a perfectionist.

In retrospect, it's possible to see that Julius's obsession with books, an obsession that has consumed the greater part of his life, sprang inevitably out of the peculiar circumstances of his childhood.

His father was a well-known plutocrat, the founder and senior shareholder of a string of companies. From what I've heard, his fortune was built on his tireless energy and his complete disregard for the feelings of everyone he ever encountered. Hating weakness in any form, and unable to forgive his son for being a child, he spent most of his time away from home, in boardrooms and boudoirs, indulging his appetite for self-aggrandizement. With no other relatives to look after him, Julius was brought up first by a nurse, then a tutor. Neither they nor the rest of the household staff cared much for the boy, seeing him as a constant reminder of his father, who, if they had had the courage, they would have happily torn to pieces with their bare teeth.

This was not a very auspicious beginning for any child, and if Julius had not possessed something of his father's will-to-survive he might not have made it at all. As it was, he found some comfort in his solitary life by creating for himself a companion by the name of Joe.

Joe was the same age as Julius, but of a more rebellious disposition. It was Joe who raided the larder at midnight, stealing a slice of angel cake, which Julius then ate; and it was Joe who filled the tutor's folded umbrella with ground chalk, though it was Julius who was caned. Joe's unstinting attention helped reassure Julius that—whatever other reason the grown-ups had to ignore him—the cause did not lie in his own failure to exist. After all, Joe could hardly have talked to someone who was not there.

Merely mentioning Joe to the grown-ups made them angry. At first, he couldn't understand why; gradually, he became aware that, by and large, things were only real to adults when they could be seen or touched, when they barked the shins or fell when dropped; everything else—including Joe—was childish phantasy. It is clear from his actions later in life that Julius was never convinced that the world of the spirit was quite as false as his elders maintained. For him more than most, it has long been the case that we are only what we conceive ourselves to be, that life is not a matter of things so much as of the ideas of things. But as a child he had neither the confidence nor the experience to assert this. The rooted, sharp-edged, adult world soon became far more real to him than his imagination, which swam and changed with every blink of the eye, and was visible to no one but himself. Soon, he too ceased to believe in Joe, who, lacking the faith of his creator, faded away like a ghost in the light of dawn.

Outwardly, Julius's life remained unchanged. His father continued to make his occasional visits home in order to chastize the staff, and the staff vented their frustration on Julius in their usual way, by ignoring him, often for days at a time. He, though, sensed that something was missing from his life, which, by slow deliberation, he decided must be himself. Each time the grown-ups turned their backs on him, he would fade away, till all that remained was a mouth, and a few sensations and impulses that came and went, seemingly without purpose, like bursts of static on a radio. Had this feeling persisted into adulthood, he would, no doubt, have become a perfect replica of his father, and spent the rest of his life swallowing everything in sight. Fortunately, this wasn't to happen.

One day, when he was fourteen, and guided, perhaps, by a residual memory of the spirited Joe, he broke into his tutor's room. Cautiously, he slid open some drawers, and examined their contents. Finding nothing to interest him, he became impatient, and when by chance he knocked over a table lamp, instead of picking it up, he was inspired to give it a hefty kick that sent it rolling to the other side of the room. His fury, having at last shown itself, swiftly grew. He began wildly scattering clothes and books and papers on the floor. As he did so, it seemed to him as though it was not he, but someone else, who was doing these things. He sat behind a wall of flesh, inviolable, and watched his hand empty an ink-well over the carpet; then move into a bedside cupboard, among a turbulent pile of underclothes, and pull out a large, heavy book bound in rust-coloured leather. One glance at its yellowing pages and blazing prints sent him reeling back into himself.

He'd never seen the book before, never before suspected that such a book might exist, yet the feelings produced by it were not new to him. Many times he'd stood in front of the mirror in his bedroom staring at his own reflection, at the one who was both himself and a stranger, and the emotions he'd felt then now came back to him, with an increased intensity, as he looked at the prints. Each print was a mirror, and the boy in it was himself, and the feelings he found expressed in the print were already in him, barely recognized till then, like a stone which time and chance had finally weathered to the surface.

But the prints were not only mirrors; each of them also resembled a lighted room seen through a window. His mind was made up of many such rooms, and going from one to another was like turning over the pages of a book. So long as he had believed that the grown-ups, being taller, could see further than he, he had regarded these inner rooms, these most private of sanctuaries, as part of a dangerous maze, and he had distrusted the feelings of homesickness they had created in him. But now, having found them pictured in a book which, by its ponderous weight in his two small hands, was undeniably real, he could no longer doubt that they were as much a part of this earth as the rooms in his father's house. More so in a way, since what his father had built was but a poor copy of his own desire for omnipotence, while Julius's imaginative world was one of limitless possibilities.

As he examined each print in turn, he noticed that, in spite of the changes in their posture, all the boys in the book held their heads in the same way, their eyes inclined in the same direction, towards a space beyond the picture, a space which—it came to him with the force of a revelation—he alone filled. They were looking at him with the same certainty that he existed, that he was there to be looked at, as Joe had done, but unlike Joe they inhabited a world even the grown-ups could see.

Is it any wonder he stole the book? He couldn't have done otherwise. The book was made for him, and for no one else; only he'd the right to own it. Besides, the tutor would not dare mention the theft.

Julius felt safe knowing he could always turn to the book in moments of self-doubt, and find himself again, but in other respects, his life didn't change, and, after a while, he felt in need of a further reassurance in the form of a second, but otherwise identical book. He was in no position to obtain one at first, but then a fortunate thing happened: his father, while ingesting a whole roast chicken, swallowed a bone and choked to death on the floor of White's.

Julius's first act on becoming a billionaire was to dismiss the tutor, and the rest of the staff—without pensions, of course—and to replace them with a retinue of deaf-mutes. Then he set about enlarging his collection. Every book he bought extended him, made him more real. His library conclusively proved he existed. Even when he was a little older, at an age when he might have been expected to seek out flesh-and-blood companions, he didn't do so, finding in his books a perfection of form life could not possibly emulate. (Or, to put it another way: all the boys in his books were simultaneously in a state of being, and in the process of coming.)

Sometime during his third decade, on a visit to Paris, Julius became acquainted with a bookseller called Bonnard. The name, though it is now familiar to all bibliophiles, was in those days (this was before the last war) known only in Montparnasse, where it was to be found painted in twelve-inch-high letters on the window of a small shop. Inside was an elephants' graveyard of literature, the shelves crammed with the rotting carcases of the deservedly obscure. Someone with a lesser sense of duty than Julius would have escaped from the place after the first coughing fit, but he (as he liked to remind himself) was a prospector, used to shifting mountains of dirt in order to find one speck of gold. He turned the books over with his gloved hands, sustained by the hope that the next book he picked up would be of the kind he was searching for.

Normally, he was disappointed, but on this occasion his luck was in. There, wedged between a textbook on meat processing and a Jesuitical treatise on the doctrine of invincible ignorance, was a book which his experienced eye immediately identified as having been produced during the Second Empire. The short time that elapsed between his seeing the book on the shelf, and taking it down and opening it to reveal its contents, seemed to him to be infinitely long. A whole range of emotions, every sort of pain and pleasure, every variety of hope and despair, gripped him. And when, at last, he observed that each page contained a hand-coloured print of a naked boy aged sixteen et cetera, a long moment of disbelief settled on him, only to be finally swept away by an intense surge of pure joy. Yet reason did not desert him even then, and he slyly glanced from side to side to see if anyone was watching him before returning his gaze to the book.

No sooner had he settled down to relish his new discovery (reliving that first moment of revelation in the tutor's room), than there came from behind him a noise of a man clearing his throat. Caught in the act, he turned to face his accuser, and found himself looking at a bleached and rickety young man with an old cardigan over his shoulders, and a buttered croissant in his hand.

"Monsieur is interested in the book, perhaps?"

"Perhaps."

Bonnard bit into his croissant, and said, "If monsieur cares to step this way I think I can show him some equally charming work." The air was clouded by a shower of hot crumbs.

Bonnard led Julius through a bamboo curtain at the back of the shop, and into a narrow parlour. Books lay stacked ceiling-high against the walls. In the centre of the room was a bare table, and behind it there sat an old woman shelling peas into a basin. She was so wide and squat that it was difficult to tell if she was sitting down or standing up. As there was a chair placed where the edge of her buttocks would have been had they not been fused into the back of her knees, Julius supposed she must be sitting down.

"Mon maman" (or was it mammon?), Bonnard said, indicating with a dismissive flick of the hand the grinning old baggage in her black dress and black stockings. Julius bowed stiffly, and the woman popped a pea into her mouth.

Bonnard was crouching on the floor, building and unbuilding towers of books. "Here, monsieur," he said, and stood up with two fat volumes in his hands. Julius tried to calm his pounding heart. Sometimes, he would go for a year, two years, without finding a single book to his taste; now, three had come to him in as many minutes.

In Bonnard, Julius had discovered a man with an unerring instinct for finding the kinds of books he collected. Henceforward, he was spared the tedium and the disappointment of visiting antiquarian booksellers: Bonnard would do that for him. He knew the book trade, and was ruthless at driving bargains. Julius sometimes put it this way: my books are truffles, and Bonnard is the pig.

Bonnard, in his turn, benefited from the trust placed in him. He was soon able to sell his shop in Montparnasse, and move to a fine new establishment off the boulevard Saint-Michel. Success remoulded him. A new Bonnard emerged, dressed in handmade suits, with a moustache as slim and as dainty as a starlet's eyebrows, and a figure resembling a ripe pear. Maman meanwhile—she whose figure resembled a seed potato—was shuffled off into an apartment of her own, in a different arrondissement from this story. (Julius turns over a page. Same boy, same bed, different posture. The wooden mask that was his face has slipped to reveal a new and more animated mask underneath . . .)

Yet, in spite of what Julius and Bonnard did for each other, it would be inexact to call them friends. Enemies might be more accurate, or possibly lovers, though there was nothing carnal about their relationship. Julius is a deeply secretive person; he does not find it easy to be frank; and up to his meeting with Bonnard has not felt the slightest urge to confess to anyone. Confession of any sort, he feels, endangers his independence. (Of course, this independence is illusory; but being so filthily rich, his employees in all the factories, mines, shops and ships on which his wealth is based are invisible to him, and he feels no more gratitude to them for supporting him than he does to the clouds for bringing rain.)

With Bonnard, it was different. He forced himself to tell him what his needs were because he wanted his help, but he could never forgive him for knowing. And because Bonnard now knew him better than anyone else, Julius was wary of him, fearing that at any moment he might use his knowledge to destroy him. Enemies can always choose to ignore one another, but the bond that linked Julius and Bonnard was less easily broken. That is why I have also spoken of them as lovers; they were helplessly drawn together, and seemed often to act as though controlled by a power that was greater than both of them.

Bonnard, I suspect, felt less deeply about their relationship, probably because he had less to lose, but his feelings too were mixed. Smooth-skinned Ganymedes held no attraction for him; his imagination ran more in the direction of stern and booted ladies of the night. He didn't really understand Julius's tastes, and became less tolerant of them as he grew older. In his more melancholic moods, usually following upon an excessive intake of cognac, the thought that his fortune was based on the servicing of such—what he would have called in private—perverse needs sometimes troubled him. Tears would trickle from his piggy eyes, and he would be heard repeating the word "pimp" in maudlin tones.

I've no doubt, though, that had Julius suddenly died, Bonnard would have wept just as bitterly, and not merely because such a death would have severely curtailed his annual income. By the time we take up our story again, Bonnard was so prosperous that he was no longer dependent on Julius's patronage. He could have managed without him if it were not that he, too, was deeply entangled in the foliage of aversion and gratitude that had sprouted over the years.

This was a state of affairs that lasted until both Julius and Bonnard were old men. At no time did either of them openly admit to needing the other. To have done so would have been to capitulate entirely. Julius certainly, and Bonnard probably, often dreamed of breaking free, and planned to do so on many occasions, without ever actually succeeding.

The passing of the years failed to reconcile Julius to his situation. Convinced that he didn't have much more time left to him, he became determined to create some personal testament, some memorial, that would continue to exist long after both he and Bonnard had perished. It was towards this end that he conceived the idea of compiling the definitive bibliography of Second Empire books containing hand-coloured prints et cetera. No one seemed more fitted than he to perform such a task. It would, he hoped, prove to be the one thing that allowed him to escape from Bonnard.

Until recently he had felt sure that it would not be long before his masterpiece was finished. There were gaps in it, but these seemed unfillable. Certain books, whose existence he knew of by hearsay, had entirely disappeared from all the catalogues. Bonnard had searched for them throughout four continents, apparently without success, and Julius had at last reluctantly concluded that they must have been destroyed—not an unusual fate for works of this nature.

Then, one spring day, he received a letter from Bonnard announcing that he had recently been entrusted with the sale of a large collection of books, many of which—he was sure—would be of interest to Julius. As he read the catalogue Bonnard had enclosed with the letter, Julius realized, to his amazement, that it listed those very books he had been searching for all this time, and which he presumed had been destroyed, as well as others unknown to him.

Now, it must be said that there are at least two interpretations concerning this part of the story, and the reader is entitled to choose between them. According to one interpretation, Bonnard is innocent of any duplicity. The catalogue was sent in good faith, and represented the climax of his career as a sniffer-out of rare books. Alternatively, I've heard it suggested that the books which Bonnard offered to Julius did not, as he claimed, come from a recently acquired collection, but had been secretly accumulated by him over the years, a volume at a time, with the deliberate intention of duping Julius into believing his collection was not unique. His realization that all his life, and unknown to him, there had been someone else working on a collection identical with his own would—so it has been argued—cause him so to doubt himself that he would never again be able to buy a book. In this way, Bonnard is supposed to have planned to free himself from the influence of Julius once and for all.

I must admit that, in view of what subsequently occurred, this second interpretation has its merits, and it would be true to what I know of Bonnard's character so to contrive things that it would be Julius and not himself who would be finally responsible for severing their relationship. And yet, I can't say I'm certain, one way or another. Bonnard might be a cunning little slug—but a heartless one? Would he, after all these years, want to destroy Julius? I'm told that he's recently started going to Mass again. If this is so, it might be seen as evidence of a guilty mind; on the other hand, it could be said that someone who is now living out his last years on this earth, and whose thoughts are turned to the higher issue of eternal life, would be the last person to want to endanger his soul by breaking the Ninth Commandment.

Whatever the actual facts might be, there is no question about the electrifying effect the letter had on Julius. He flew straightaway to Paris. The books in question, several hundred of them, were arranged in neat piles against the walls of Bonnard's office. Seeing them there, Julius was reminded of his first meeting with Bonnard, and of the narrow parlour at the back of his shop. But the kitchen table had now been replaced by a triangular desk reminiscent of the prow of a battleship, and there sat behind it, not an aged maman dropping empty pods into her lap, but a young secretary, her skirt above her knees, and her red-tipped fingers pecking fastidiously at a sheet of carbon paper.

Julius examined the books one by one. Never before in his life had he seen a collection of this size which was so similar to his own. It was almost as though he'd put it together himself. He tried to appear as abstractedly superior as he always did in Bonnard's company, but as on that first day they had met, he could not stop his heart pounding rapidly, and his cheeks flushing with excitement.

"Who was the previous owner?" he asked, making an effort to control his voice.

Bonnard smiled, "I'm afraid, monsieur, I cannot tell you that. All I can reveal is that the previous owner died recently, that he had no relations, and left no will, and that the trustees of his estate have put these books into my hands and asked me to dispose of them discreetly. I wish I could say more, but you know how it is, monsieur—the secrecy of the confessional, professional ethics . . ."

Julius wanted to press Bonnard, but realizing that this made him vulnerable to another refusal, held back. In fact, he held back so long that Bonnard began to wonder whether he was going to buy the books at all; and to goad him, he said, "One or two of my other clients have expressed an interest . . ."

"Nonsense," Julius retorted, "we both know that my collection is unique."

Now, if the second interpretation of events is to be believed, we come to what must have been the sweetest moment in Bonnard's life. Years since, smarting under Julius's patronage, certain words would have occurred to him. He would have carefully polished them into bright perfection, thinking as he did so of the time when they would at last be used, and the effect they would have on Julius. Such a long period of preparation would have caused him to become devoted to the words, so that when the moment finally came in which they were to be spoken aloud—that is to say, the moment in the story we have now reached—he would have felt tempted to hold on to them a little longer and release them at last only slowly, and with reluctance. On the other hand, if Bonnard is innocent of all guile, then we must suppose that it was merely part of the master–servant relationship that made him drool in such a syrupy fashion, saying, "Not quite, monsieur. There has been one other gentleman whose predilection in reading matter has been identical to yours. I refer, of course, to the previous owner of this collection."

Whatever his motives, Bonnard had scored a point. Julius turned away, to hide his face, but would not leave the shop. He wanted these books more than he'd ever wanted anything in his life, and he was prepared to pay almost anything for them. Money was not the problem. It was simply a question of how much humiliation he was willing to take. Even to admit he wanted the books put him deeper in Bonnard's debt, a debt which could not be repaid with anything as worthless as a cheque.

On the flight home, Julius considered his feelings. There was a part of him which rejoiced at having acquired such a superb collection; this was an emotion he had felt many times before, though never to such an exquisite degree. What was lacking was any sense of triumph. No doubt it would have been different if he and the other collector had been old rivals. Then, the fear of defeat and the anticipation of victory would both have been constantly on his mind, and the man's death would have come at last as the culmination of a bitter struggle. But the fact that it was not until Bonnard had written to him that he even knew he had been challenged, took away any of the usual pleasures a conqueror enjoys at the sight of his defeated enemy. Instead, Julius felt annoyed with himself for not having known of this other collector. It was a blow to his pride—was he not, after all, the greatest authority on his subject? Worse still, there seemed no reason why further rivals should not exist. Perhaps even now, in some secret corner of Europe or America or the Far East, there lived a man like Julius whose whole life was dedicated to the study of Second Empire books containing hand-coloured et cetera. Such a man might even be working on a bibliography. Julius's books were to him what the poem is to the poet, and the painting to the painter. To be told that his library was not unique was like accusing an artist of plagiarism.

The two interpretations of Bonnard's motives that I've spoken of had occurred to Julius. He realized that the deal might have been a hoax; but, being of a pragmatic turn of mind, he preferred to work on the assumption that the books he'd just bought had once belonged to a single collector, now dead, as Bonnard had claimed.

Who was this collector? Apart from what Bonnard had told him, Julius possessed only one fact about the man. Inside the front cover of each one of his books was an ex-libris. It showed a snake eating its own tail, and had the letters P.H. underneath. Julius could not recall ever having met or heard of anyone with these initials.

It was the books themselves which offered the best clue as to the identity of their previous owner. Julius's library represented a more enduring version of himself; he assumed, reasonably enough, that it had been the same with this other collector. But if the collector and his library were as one, then it would seem to follow that the presence of two identical libraries was evidence of the existence of two identical collectors. This was absurd, of course; Julius could not be in two places at the same time, nor could he be simultaneously alive and dead. The logic, however, seemed irresistible; and if he did in fact resist it as an affront to common sense, it was only to replace it by a hardly less astounding supposition: that the mysterious P.H., whom he had never met, and never would meet, was his twin, his double.

He wondered how the two of them would have got on together. Surely he would have been able to trust someone so like himself? On the other hand, would not their mutual need for solitude have made them utterly incompatible?

Unfortunately, the one man who would have been able to help him answer these questions was no longer alive. It was too late. No matter how thoroughly he investigated the matter, he would never know for certain. He felt a sudden longing to meet this man who had been so like himself, and the futility of his desire only increased its intensity.

Julius tried to console himself with the thought that a

bibliophile is like a cannibal who enjoys the virtues of those he has eaten. P.H.'s collection was the only part of him to have escaped death. Once this collection was assimilated into Julius's, P.H. would cease to exist, and Julius would no longer be troubled by him. This had always happened in the past; his library was compounded of the smaller libraries of other men that Bonnard had bought for him over the years. True, never before had Julius had to digest as big a collection as P.H.'s, but he could see no reason in principle why this should make any difference.

He waited expectantly for Bonnard to dispatch the books, and to put an end to the speculation about their previous owner that had grown in their absence. Finally, three weeks after he'd first seen them, the books arrived, and he spent a festive day unpacking them from their crates, and arranging them on his shelves. The smaller food is chopped, the easier it is to swallow. Julius broke up the dead man's collection, and redistributed it throughout the length and breadth of his library; no two volumes were allowed to remain together.

To continue with this digestive metaphor a little longer, we might say that what happened next was that these newly acquired books stuck in Julius's throat, producing in due course a sort of gagging noise that could easily be mistaken for the sound of someone weeping in despair. Why was this?

A second metaphor may explain it (this is what is known as changing horses while crossing between two stools). In experiments designed to show how prone human beings are to illusion, scientists sometimes put before their subjects a picture consisting of a dense conglomeration of apparently randomly scattered dots, like a close-up of a pointilliste painting. You can stare at this picture for hours without seeing any order in it, till, all of a sudden—as though somewhere in your brain a switch has been thrown—you notice that some of the dots are arranged to form the shape of a dog, or a face, or some such thing. You wonder why you never noticed this before, it seems so obvious. What is really interesting about this phenomenon is that, once having detected the patterned image, it's then impossible not to be aware of it. The mind can't see a shape as meaningless once it has found meaning in it, no matter how hard it tries.

Now, the dead collector's books together formed an orderly whole. They shared in a common identity which, since it was also the identity of the dead collector, seemed incapable of further development. Having once recognized this, Julius then found he was unable to decompose the collection into its separate parts. Even after he'd destroyed the physical connectedness of the books by redistributing them among all his others, they retained a kind of spiritual affinity with one another that drew them together and made them stand out from the rest of his library.

At first, he couldn't understand why this should be. He hunted round for an explanation, and eventually decided that it must be the presence of the collector's ex-libris that was responsible. This was a visible reminder of the dead man, a last vestige of a once full individuality, stuck there by his own hand. Julius felt quite relieved to discover that the solution to his problem should be so simple. He would visit an engraver and order some ex-libris of his own. The design would be the same as the dead collector's—a snake eating its own tail—but Julius would have his own initials placed underneath. This seemed a fittingly symbolic way of asserting his ownership over the books.

In all practical matters, a man in Julius's position has no difficulty in transforming his wishes into action. The ex-libris were engraved the day they were ordered, and delivered to his house by a special messenger, a nice lad about sixteen or seventeen years old, with a scooter between his legs. Julius paid little attention to him. He retired to his library, and spent the next few hours sticking his new ex-libris over those of P.H. He did not rush. The dead must be respected, otherwise they refuse to go away, and become a nuisance and a danger to the living. Julius licked and dabbed, licked and dabbed with due solemnity. As he did so, it occurred to him how appropriate it was that this attempt to digest the dead man's collection, and to incorporate it into his own, should begin, like all acts of digestion, with the flow of salivary juices.

P.H.'s initials were at last obliterated, and those of Julius stuck over them. Well satisfied with his morning's work, Julius returned the books to his shelves, and waited. But the weeks passed, and the longed-for metamorphosis didn't take place. The books remained as much the dead collector's as they had been on the day Julius had first cast eyes on them. If anything, the presence of the dead collector seemed more real than before. It was only slowly that Julius recognized what had happened. With the removal of the last physical signs of his existence, P.H. had taken up residence in the only place that still guaranteed him a continuation of his life. And where was this? In Julius's imagination.

The personality of P.H. was an emptiness that demanded to be filled with certainties. Yet, every answer Julius proposed, the emptiness swallowed up, so limitless was it. More answers were called for, and more, and each was as ineffective as all the others. The real P.H. remained as elusive as ever, but unceasing reflection on him brought forth a P.H. of sorts in Julius's imagination. Out of the few, threadbare facts that Bonnard had given him, Julius painstakingly crafted a character of his own, someone in all essentials like himself, a scholar, a recluse, a voyeur, and a gentleman. It was this fictional P.H. who day by day grew more substantial.

Though it went against all his instincts, Julius decided that the only sure way of exorcising the ghost was to destroy his books. He willed himself into choosing one from the dead man's collection, and put a match to it; and he watched in disbelief as the lighted pages began to curl. A moment later, he was dashing out the flames with his bare hands, and returning the wounded, but still intact book to its shelf.

The dejection that followed this miserable demonstration of his own powerlessness lasted for some weeks. He became increasingly morose. Clad only in a dressing gown and pyjamas, a pair of shuffling slippers on his feet, he moped around the house. Even the sight of his deaf-mutes failed to cheer him. His bibliography lay on his desk, unfinished.

Then, quite unexpectedly, he received a letter from Bonnard. There was a new book for him to see, and an anxious enquiry: Was Julius well? Why did he not write? In an instant, his gloom had lifted, and besides the firm reality of the coffee pot glinting in the morning sunlight, P.H. suddenly seemed no more real to him than a reflection in a pool of water: a gentle slap of the hand, and he was gone. His old enthusiasm was rekindled. Another book! He laughed aloud, and ordered a second boiled egg.

Yet, this euphoria lasted only as long as it took him to leave the house. The old uncertainties returned as soon as the car set off, and were crowding in on him by the time he reached the environs of the airport.

He realized he wasn't hastening towards Paris in order to buy a new book, but because the trip provided him with an opportunity to question Bonnard about P.H. He intended to make his enquiry casually, almost absent-mindedly, while talking to Bonnard about this and that, thus giving him no indication of how badly he wanted the information. But would Bonnard be so easily taken in? If he was genuinely innocent of any deceit, if the books had been bought by him in good faith, he could—Julius was sure—be persuaded to tell him all he knew: after all, a sensible parasite does not destroy its host. And though Julius expected to have to humiliate himself, he was prepared to do this if it would help rid him of P.H.

Supposing, though, that Bonnard was not innocent, and that he was playing an elaborate and maleficent hoax on Julius. What then? Would he not welcome every enquiry as an opportunity for a further rejection, another chance to wound? His last letter might have been deliberately concocted to lure Julius to his destruction.

And, then, another thought, more terrible in its implications than all the others. If Bonnard stuck to his original story, saying that the trustees of P.H. had sold him the books, Julius would never be able to tell whether he was lying or not. He would be just as likely to disbelieve Bonnard either way. And, in the end, it would not be Bonnard at all, but his own unsatisfied, and unsatisfiable, craving for the truth that would destroy him.

The risk, he decided, was too great. If he stayed, he might possibly delay the moment of defeat. But, if he went...? A hand, which he vaguely identified as being his own, tweaked the chauffeur's left ear, and the chauffeur, understanding the significance of his master's gesture, turned the car round, and returned home.

Knowing that he would never see Bonnard again caused him to feel neither elated nor distressed. He had already, and without realizing it, been preparing himself for the break ever since he first began to question Bonnard's motives. Now, isolated within his own house, and with no one left to confirm, by their attention to him, that he was really present (the servants being merely part of the furniture), he daily grew more incorporeal. Those books which for so long had been a source of comfort to him, now seemed to threaten. A being who was not himself, but who was similar enough to take his place, dwelt among them. It was as though the years had rolled away, and left him stranded again in that period of his childhood, between the disappearance of Joe and the discovery of the book in the tutor's room, when life had seemed at its most pointless. He realized that, if he was not to become enslaved to a chimera, to a shadow, to the invented memory of the dead collector, he must once again find some solid thing through which to express himself, some object that would continue to exist in spite of his momentary lapses of attention and his ultimate dissolution. But what? And where?

A bizarre idea kept forcing itself into his brain. Supposing, he thought, that when I look into a mirror, the image I see in the glass is the real Julius, and I am only his reflection. Who can tell what side of the mirror he is standing on? And he remembered how, when he had discovered the book under the tutor's combinations, it had seemed to him as though the boys in the prints were living in a house full of lighted rooms, and that he was looking at them from the outside. But might not the opposite have been the truth? Perhaps, it was he who was on the inside, and someone who regarded his life as a performance put on purely for his own entertainment, was staring at *him*.

The proposition seemed reasonable, he thought. Or, at least, not disprovable.

Soon, he developed the habit of approaching all mirrors with stealth, in the hope of catching off-guard the one who was observing him, and seeing what he looked like, without the interference of his own reflection. But he was always too quick for him.

Yet what is hoped for often has the nasty habit of coming true. Julius, determined and vigilant, eventually saw what he wished to see when one evening, while crossing in front of the pier-glass that hung at the turn of the stairs, a compulsive glance showed someone who was definitely not himself looking back at him. It was an oddly intimate moment. The two figures remained silent, but not tense. Then, the one who regarded himself as the interloper fled.

The city took him in. There, unaccompanied, he let himself become a part of that mob of idle passers-by which variously resembles a shambling beast, a surging river, and (as it pauses to venerate the treasures in the shop windows) a file of pilgrims. How long he wandered for, he couldn't say. Afterwards, he remembered only waking up with a jolt as something sharp and hard struck him in the chest and thrust him back into himself. The sound of rushing water, of clinking scales, receded down the street. Julius was standing on the pavement's edge, outside the "2001" amusement arcade.

Boys dressed in Levis and T-shirts swam before him in a green light. Smaller lights pulsated beside them, and the air was torn by an hysterical, inhuman screaming. At first he looked without seeing, then he slowly became aware that a boy, standing alone by the door, and in front of a machine from which projected the butt of a rifle, was gazing intently at him. The boy was about sixteen or seventeen. As Julius gazed back, there sprang up inside him an almost forgotten sensation. The blood chugged in his ears, his skin burned, and he was conscious once more of the bone and flesh in which he was clothed.

Then, the boy turned away, towards the machine which was chewing up the rifle, and began to examine the contents of his pockets. An urge quickened inside Julius, and pointed a commanding finger in the direction he should follow. Feeling himself once more, he advanced on the boy, silver coins jiggling in his hands.

What have we here? A happy ending? Has Julius at last found what he's been searching for all these years? Has he come to realize that Joe, his books, his friendship with Bonnard and his creation of P.H. have been merely preliminaries; even, perhaps, wrong turnings?

A stifled sob rises in the boy's throat, and his legs scissor back and forth over the quilt. Julius turns a page of his book, and is confronted by a picture of a naked boy, aged sixteen or seventeen, in the last stages of masturbating himself. The milk of human kindness is flowing between his fingers. The climax has been reached.

Tell me, Julius, do you remember once coining the following aphorism while soaping yourself in the bath? I think, therefore I think I think that I exist—I think. Well, here you are back home, reconciled with your books, and with a fresh realization of those mirrors and lighted rooms, that internal life, next to you on the bed. Do you think you can finally say that you know you are real?

"Go away."

Now, Julius—

"Go away. You seem to forget I know where you came from."

Do you?

"It's all lies, everything you've said about me. Go away, and leave me alone, you damned spook, for God's sake."

Slim

I don't use that word. I've heard it enough. So I've taken it out of circulation, just here, just at home. I say Slim instead, and Buddy understands. I have got Slim.

When Buddy pays a visit, I have to remind myself not to offer him a cushion. Most people don't need cushions, they're just naturally covered. So I keep all the cushions to myself, now that I've lost my upholstery.

Slim is what they call it in Uganda, and it's a perfectly sensible name. You lose more weight than you thought was possible. You lose more weight than you could carry. Not that you feel like carrying anything. So I'll say to Buddy on one of his visits, Did you see the local news? There was an item about newt conservation, and then there was an item about funding Slim research. But newts first. What's it like talking to someone who's outranked by a newt?

Buddy just looks sheepish, which is probably best in the circumstances. Buddy would rather I avoided distressing information. He thinks I shouldn't read the papers, shouldn't upset myself. Even the doctors say that. If there was anything I should know, I'd hear it from them first anyway. Maybe. Yes, very likely. But whenever they try to protect me, I hear the little wheels on the bottom of the screens they put round you in a ward when you're really bad, and I'll do without that while I can.

Buddy's very good. That sounds suitably grudging. He tries to fit in with me. He doesn't flinch if I talk about my chances of making Slimmer of the Year. He's learned to say *blackcurrants*. He said "lesions" just the once, but I told him it wasn't a very vivid use of language, and if he wasn't a doctor he had no business with it. Blackcurrants is much better, that being what they look like, good-sized blackcurrants on the surface of the skin, not sticking out far enough to be picked. So now, if the subject comes up, he asks about my blackcurrants, asks if any more blackcurrants have showed up.

I do my bit of adjusting too. Instinctively I think of him as a social worker, but I know he's not that. He's a volunteer attached to the Trust, and he's got no qualifications, so he can't be all bad. What he does is called *buddying*, and he's a buddy. And apparently in Trustspeak I'm a string of letters, which I don't remember except the first one's P and stands for person. Apparently they have to remind themselves. But I've decided if he can say Slim and blackcurrants to oblige me, I can meet him halfway and call him Buddy. Illness is making me quite the internationalist: an African infection and some dated American slang.

Buddy may not be qualified, but he's had his little bit of training. I remember him telling me, early on, that to understand what was happening to me perhaps I should think of having fifty years added to my age, or suddenly having Third World expectations instead of First. I suppose I've tried thinking that way. But now whenever I see those charity ads in the papers, the ones that tell you how for a few pounds you could adopt someone in India or the Philippines, I think that maybe I've been adopted by an African family, that poor as they are they are sending me what they can spare from their tainted food, their poisoned water, their little lifespans.

Except that I'm not young by African standards. Pushing forty, I'd be an elder of the tribe, pretty much, and the chances of my parents still being alive would be slight. So I should be grateful for their being around. They've followed me step by step, and now I suppose I take that for granted. But I didn't always. Before

I first told them about myself, I pinched the family album, pinched it and had it photocopied. It cost me a fortune, and I don't know what I thought I wanted with a family album and no family, if it came to that. But at the time I thought, no sense in taking chances. Maybe if they'd lived nearer London, if I'd seen them more regularly, it wouldn't have seemed such a big risk. I don't know.

My African family doesn't have the money for photographs. My African family may never even have seen a photograph.

I've been careful not to mention my adoption fantasy to Buddy. No point in worrying him. And touch wood, I haven't cried while he's been around. That's partly because I've learned to set time aside for such an important function. I've learned that there is a yoga of tears. There are the clever tears that release a lot in a little time, and the stupid tears that just shake you and don't let you go. Once your shoulders get in on the act, you're sunk. The trick is to keep them out of it. Otherwise you end up wailing all day. Those kind of tears are very more-ish. Bet you can't cry just one, just ten, just twenty. But if I keep my shoulders still I can reach a much deeper level of tears. It's like a lumbar puncture. I can draw out this fluid which is a fantastic concentrate of misery. And then just stop and be calm.

I used to cry to opera, Puccini mostly. Don't laugh. I thought the best soundtrack was tunes, tunes and more tunes. But now I cry mainly to a record I never used to listen to much, and don't particularly remember buying: *Southern Soul Belles*, on the Charly label. I find records far more trouble to put on than my opera cassettes, but *Southern Soul Belles* is worth it. It has a very garish cover, a graphic of a sixties soul singer with a purple face, for some reason, so that she looks like an aubergine with a beehive hairdo. The trouble with the Puccini was that you could hear the voices, but never the lungs. On *Southern Soul Belles* you hear the lungs. When Doris Allen sings "A Shell of a Woman", you know that she could just open her mouth and blast any man out of the door. Shell she may be, breathless she ain't. There's a picture of her on the back cover. She's fat and sassy. She could spare all the weight I've lost. Just shrug it off. Her lungs must be real bellows of meat, not like the pair of wrinkled socks I seem to get my air through these days.

I treat myself to *Southern Soul Belles* every day or so. I've learned to economize. Illness has no entry qualifications. Did I say that already? But being ill—if you're going to be serious about it—demands a technique. The other day I found I was writing a cheque. I could hardly lift the pen, it wasn't a good day, not like today. But I was writing everything out in full. No numerals, no abbreviations. Twenty-one pounds and thirty-four pence only. Only! I almost laughed when I saw that *only*. I realized that ever since my first cheque book, when I was sixteen, I've always written my cheques out in full, as if all the crooked bank-clerks in the world were waiting for their chance to defraud me. Never again. It's the minimum from now on. If I could have right now all the energy I've wasted writing every word on my cheques, I could have some normal days, normal weeks.

One of the things I'm supposed to be doing these days is creative visualization, you know, where you imagine your white corpuscles strapping on their armour to repel invaders. Buddy doesn't nag, but I can tell he's disappointed. I don't seem to be able to do it. I get as far as imagining my white corpuscles as a sort of cloud of healthiness, like a milkshake in the dark flow of my blood, but if I try to visualize them any more concretely I think of Raquel Welch, in *Fantastic Voyage*. That's the film where they shrink a submarine full of doctors and inject it into a dying man's bloodstream. He's the president or something. And at one point Raquel Welch gets attacked and almost killed by white corpuscles, they're like strips of plastic—when I think of it, they *are* strips of plastic—that stick to her wetsuit until she can't breathe. The others have to snap them off one by one when they get her back to the submarine. It's touch and go. So I don't think creative visualization will work for me. It's not a very promising therapeutic tool, if every time I try to imagine my body's defences I think of their trying to kill Raquel Welch. I still can't persuade myself the corpuscles are the good guys.

One thing I find I can visualize is a ration book. That's how I make sure I don't get overtired. Over-overtired. I suppose my mother had a ration book before I was born. I don't think I've ever seen one. But I imagine a booklet with coupons in it for you to tear out, only instead of an allowance for the week of butter or cheese or sugar, my coupons say One Hour of Social Life, One Shopping Expedition, One Short Walk. I hoard them, and I spend them wisely. I tear them out slowly, separating the perforations one by one.

In a way, though, it's not that I don't have energy, it's just the wrong kind. My head may be muzzy but my body is fizzing. I suppose that's the steroids. But I feel like an electric razor that's been plugged into the wrong socket, I'm buzzing and buzzing but I'm not doing any work. It's so odd having sat at home all day, when your body tells you you've been dancing all night in a nightclub, just drinking enough lager to keep the sweat coming, and you're about to drive home with all the windows down, smelling your own sweat. And sleep.

I can't work. That should be pretty clear. But I've been lucky. I'm on extended sick leave for a while yet, and everybody's been very good. I said I had cancer, which I do and I don't, I mean I do but that isn't the problem, and while I was saying *cancer* I thought, All the time my Gran was ill we never once said *cancer*, but now cancer is a soft word I am hiding behind and I feel almost guilty to be sparing myself. Suddenly *cancer* had the sound of "interesting condition" or "unmentionables". I was curling up in the word's soft shade, soothed gratefully by cancer's lullaby. Cancer. What a relief. Cancer. Oh that's all right. Cancer. That I can live with.

Sometimes I'm asleep when Buddy visits. Sleep is the one thing that keeps its value. He presses the buzzer on the entry-phone, and if I haven't answered in about ten seconds he buzzes again. I know the entry-phone is a bit ramshackle and you can't hear from the doorway whether it's working or not, but when Buddy buzzes twice it drives me frantic. I don't need to be reminded that I'm not living at a very dynamic tempo right now. I'll tick him off one of these days, tear off a coupon and splurge some energy.

Then Buddy comes pounding up the stairs. Sometimes he smells of chlorine and his hair's still damp from swimming, but I suppose it's a bit much to ask him to slow down, to dry off properly and use cologne before he comes to see me, just so I don't feel bruised by his health. I'll bet his white corpuscles don't need a pep talk. Crack troops, no doubt about it. I'll bet he drinks Carling Black Label.

I watch too much television. Television isn't on the ration.

Buddy's breaking in new shoes, which creak. Why would anyone crucify his feet in the name of style—assuming liver-coloured Doc Martens are stylish in some way—when comfortable training shoes are readily available almost everywhere? It's a great mystery.

Buddy likes to hug. I don't. I mean, it's perfectly pleasant, it just doesn't remind me of anything. It was never my style. I'm sure the point is to relieve my flesh of taboo, and the Trust probably gives classes in it. But when Buddy bends over me, I just wait for him to be done, as if he was a cloud and I was waiting for him to pass over the sun. Then we carry on, and I'm sure he feels better for it.

He's still got a bruise above the crook of his elbow, from his Hepatitis B jab. I really surprised myself over that. I wasn't very rational. He wasn't sure whether to have it done or not, and I almost screamed at him *Do it! Get it done!* If I'd had a needle handy I'd have injected him myself, and I don't think getting my own back was my only motive. I remember Hep B. That was when illness came up and asked me what I was doing for the rest of my life. That was before there was even a vaccine.

The back of his neck is something I tend to notice when Buddy visits. It always looks freshly shaved. He must have a haircut every week or so, every couple of weeks anyway. As if he would feel neglected unless he was being groomed at regular intervals. Neglect is what I dream of. I long for the doctors to find me boring, to give me one almighty pill and say Next please. But my case history seems to be unputdownable. A real thriller.

My grooming standards are way below Buddy's, but perhaps they always were. There's not a lot I can do about that now. If the Princess of Wales was coming to pay me a visit, if she was coming to lay her cool hand on my forehead, stifling her natural desire to say Oh Yuk—I'm with you there, Di—I might even trim my fingernails. But not for Buddy. Fingernails are funny. They're the only part of my body that seems to be flourishing under the new regime. They grow like mad. But the Princess of Wales isn't coming any time soon, to me or to anyone like me. I happen to know that now, now as we speak, she's opening a new ward in a newt hospital. A new *wing*.

I think I'm entitled to a home help. I believe that's one of the perks. But I'd rather go on as I am. Buddy told me a story about a man he visited for the Trust—I'm sure he's recovered by now, ha ha—whose mother was jealous of his home help. Just for that, she said, Just for Slim?

I couldn't believe it. I'm still not sure I believe it. But then Buddy explained that the mother was eighty-five, and when her son started saying, Sometimes I feel better but I never feel well, she must have thought, What else have I been saying all these years, fat lot of attention you gave me.

I think Buddy was making again the valuable point that getting Slim only involves being exiled from the young, the well, the real.

Buddy is always offering to wash up, but I'm happier when I don't let him. He doesn't do a great deal to help me, in practical terms, anyway. Tessa next door changes my sheets and does my washing, and Susannah still expects to hear my dreams, even the grim ones. It was Susannah who first suggested Buddy. She felt I was cutting myself off from real kin, that even if I was saying the same unanswerable things, Buddy would return a different echo. I even suppose she's right. I've earned my friends, but Buddy I seem to have inherited, though God knows from who, and whether he served them well.

I sometimes talk to Buddy as if he was the whole Trust gathered in one person. I'll say, My father says you're not reaching him. Why are your collection-boxes massed in London? Why do you insist on appealing to an in-crowd?

But then I let him off the hook and say, Mind you, my mother thinks that anyone collecting for Slim research in Eastbourne or Leamington would get a few swift strokes from a rubber-tipped cane, if nothing worse. And my father chooses to give love and money direct.

Cutting out the middleman, says Buddy. He smiles. He doesn't have a Trust collecting box, of course. I'm not sure I've ever seen one. In fact, on this visit he's brought me a package. It's in a plastic bag, and it seems to be a foil container with a cardboard lid, and foil crimped down around it. I'm very much afraid it's food.

I've fed Buddy once or twice, used a shopping voucher and prepared a simple but exhausting lunch. Those times it has seemed to me that Buddy eats suspiciously little. I mean, he eats more than I do, he couldn't not. And I'm not the best judge of healthy habits. But somehow I expect an earthier appetite. It's certainly true that a little company at table can make me eat more than I usually do, without even noticing, while any sort of greed will inevitably sicken my stomach. So does that mean Buddy is obeying another mysterious Trust directive, and suppressing his true eating self? Perhaps he filled up with food before he came, or perhaps he's going to dive round the corner the moment he leaves, and into a burger bar. Before he leaves I open my mouth to say, Here's some money for your real lunch, but I manage to close it in time.

And now he's returning my hospitality. Go on, he says. Open it. You don't have to eat it now. It'll keep good for a few days. Not that it contains any preservatives.

He has written a few deprecating comments about his cooking on the lid of the container. There's no wishing it away. I edge up the rim of the foil and see inside a startlingly pure green. On the green lies a row of small cigars.

Fresh lamb sausages, he explains, with mint and parsley, on a bed of green pea purée. An old family recipe, that appeared quite by chance in last week's *Radio Times*.

I lower my nose over the container and breathe in the smell, trying to think that it is a bouquet of flowers that I must express thanks for, from someone I like and want nothing to do with, rather than a plateful of food that will stiffen in the fridge unless I am stupid enough to eat it, in which case I will most likely be sick.

Thanks. Can you put it in the fridge for me?

But Buddy has more to say about his choice of recipe. They're skinless, he says. I thought that would be easiest for you.

He's right, of course, with my teeth the way they are now. But I'm sure I haven't complained, I'm sure I haven't moaned to him. Perhaps my habit of dipping biscuits in my tea—not to be looked for in a man of my class—is a dead giveaway to a seasoned Trust volunteer. Next time I feel the need to dunk a digestive I'll be more discreet. I'll do my dunking behind closed doors.

The doctors are trying to save my teeth at the moment, and the last time I went to pick up some prescriptions they were being altogether too merry, it seemed to me, about the dosage that would do the trick. 200 mg, one of them was saying, that sounds about right. And the other one said, Yeeeees, in a kind of drawl, as if it wasn't worth the trouble to look it up.

Buddy is still expecting something from me. Thanks, I say again. That looks very nice. Yum yum.

Kid gloves are better than surgical gloves. Perhaps I should say that to him. That would give him some job satisfaction. I'm sure that's important.

Buddy puts his present in the fridge and heads for the door. He stops with his hand on the handle and asks me if there's anything I want, says if I think of anything I should phone him, any time. He always does this on his way out, and I suppose he's apologizing for being well and for being free to go and for being free to help or not as he chooses. There is nothing I want.

He clatters down the stairs. I remind myself that he clattered up them, so there is no reason to think he is moving as fast as he can and is planning to put a lot of space between me and him, now that his tour of duty is over.

I could check, of course, if I move to the window. I could settle my mind. I could see whether he skips along the road to the Tube, or whether he's too drained to do more than shamble. Maybe a trouble shared is a trouble doubled.

I try to resist the temptation to go to the window, but these days it's not often that I have an impulse that I can satisfy without asking myself whether I can afford what it will cost me. So I give in.

Buddy is moving methodically down the street, not rushing but not dawdling either, planting his feet with care like a man walking into a wind. I know that when I tear out and spend one of my shopping coupons and go out on to that street, I look like a man walking into a wind tunnel. I can see it in the way people look at me.

I look down on Buddy as he walks to the Tube. In the open air the mystique of his health dissipates, as he merges with other ordinarily healthy people. No one in the street seems to be looking at him, but I follow him with my eyes. There is something dogged about him that I resent as well as admire, a dull determination to go on and on, as if he was an ambulance-chaser condemned always to follow on foot, watching as the blue lights fade in the distance.